PURSU

A sudden shriek turned their heads. Owlcurl Dahn was pointing to the doorway where three men stood weaving slightly on their feet. "But they're dead!" she screamed.

Indeed, the huge, gaping holes in the closest torso still leaked blood. But it was the other things, the odd pink growths that trailed in the air behind the men, that set Iehard's reflexes to work. His pistol came up and he fired half the clip. The bodies were chopped down, the nearest cut almost in two. The dead were thoroughly dead once more.

And yet, there was furious activity in that ruined flesh. Suddenly the torso of the farthest one sat up as ruined hands pushed at the floor.

Then the top half of the nearest, eyes vacant, rose on its arms and began to hop toward them...

Also by Christopher B. Rowley
Published by Ballantine Books:

THE BLACK SHIP

THE WAR FOR ETERNITY

STARHAMMER

Christopher B. Rowley

A Del Rey Book
BALLANTINE BOOKS • NEW YORK

A Del Rey Book
Published by Ballantine Books

 Published in the United States of America by Ballantine Books, a division of Random House, Inc., New York, and simultaneously in Canada by Random House of Canada Limited, Toronto.

Library of Congress Catalog Card Number: 85-90836

ISBN 0-345-31490-5

Manufactured in the United States of America

First Edition: February 1986

Cover Art by David Schleinkofer
Map by Shelly Shapiro

To Anitra

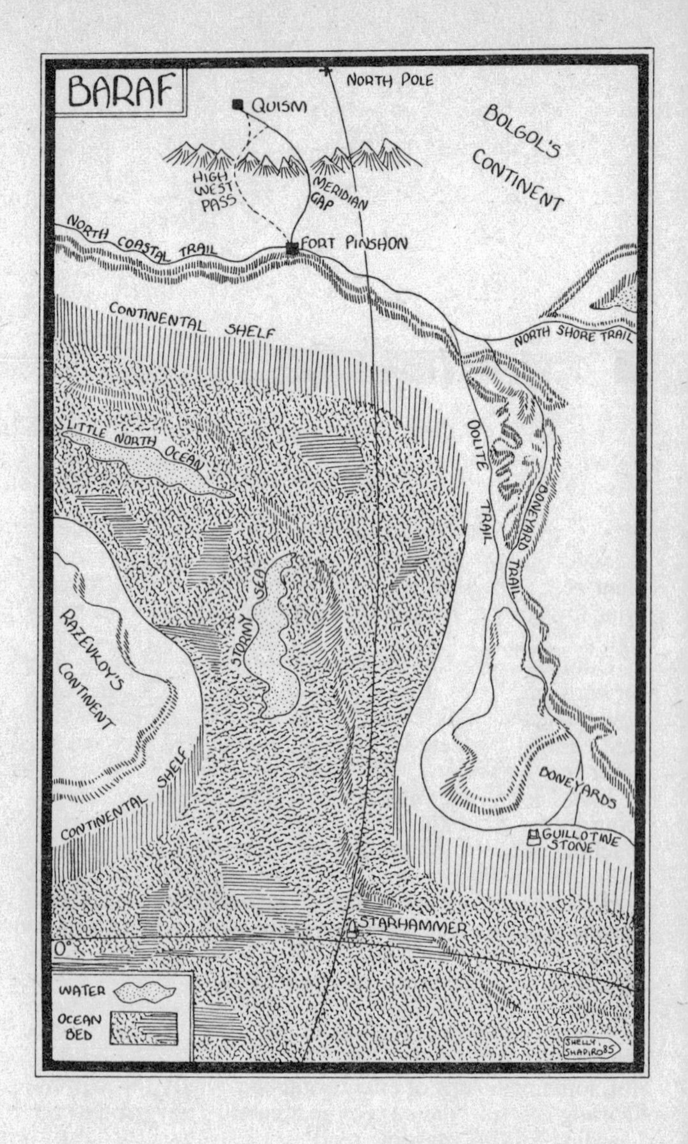
BARAF
NORTH POLE
QUISM
BOLGOL'S CONTINENT
HIGH WEST PASS
MERIDIAN GAP
NORTH COASTAL TRAIL
FORT PINSHON
CONTINENTAL SHELF
NORTH SHORE TRAIL
LITTLE NORTH OCEAN
OOLITE TRAIL
BONEYARD TRAIL
STORMY SEA
RAZEVKOY'S CONTINENT
CONTINENTAL SHELF
BONEYARDS
GUILLOTINE STONE
STARHAMMER
0°
WATER
OCEAN BED
SHELLY SHAPIRO 85

CHAPTER ONE

THE OLD PLANET HAD BEEN A FROZEN WANDERER FOR eons, but now it was dying, baked slowly by the young blue-white tyrant that had snagged it from the void. It turned sluggishly in its far distant orbit while on the ancient seabed the dust howled over the bare basalt, carrying forward the long moan of torment. Electrical energies sparked great lightning bursts against the purple skies.

Out of a wall of dust came the great machine, crawling forward on treads a mile long. Beneath them, the rock powdered and joined the raging dust storm. Above, the vast edifice shuddered, shivered, and shifted forward another ten meters.

Invisible in the dust, the convoy machines called mournfully, great klaxons wailing. In response, the great machine began to build up a refueling field.

In the basalt ocean floor, three hundred kilometers north and east, a cube almost four kilometers on a side began to shake. The vibration increased, built to a crescendo and then with a flash of waste photons, a cubical pit appeared in the crust, four-kilometer-deep walls glowing white hot, incandescent vapor coiling over the bottom.

Energy receptors in the great machine came alive with power. Sparks leaped and sizzled for a moment and then hot, ionizing beams of energy stabbed briefly through the swirling murk to the convoy machines. They ground on, guarding flanks, guarding rear.

No reports came from higher command, no new targets were assigned. In the control center, the Keeper, a batrachianoid robot three meters tall, tried to call the crew once more. There was no reply. There had not been any reply in a billion years. It scanned the terrain ahead and readied the machine for the next lurch westward on the endless march. It knew nothing about the death of planets, it dealt simply with targets.

On terrestrial time scales it was generally regarded as the twenty-fifth century of spaceflight, the fifteenth century of the laowon tyranny and the worst of times for humanity.

From the fertile sector of the Milky Way encompassed by the sweep of the Orion arm, two splendidly similar space-traveling species had arisen. From great golden Lao had come the blue skinned laowon, swift empire builders in Faster Than Light vessels. From humble Earth had come humanity, spreading out in cheerful anarchy on Not As Fast As Light drives.

When they met, the empire was seven kiloparsecs across on the long axis and the sphere of human exploration stretched perhaps one twentieth as far.

The meeting, therefore, produced profoundly contrary emotions in the two sides, while concepts of convergent evolution, pan-life mathematica, and DNA universality, found their ultimate consummation. Indeed, laowon and human were startlingly similar, except that laowon were slightly taller and had skin in shades of blue.

From their pinnacles of advanced industry, both races had burst forth from their home worlds, driven by the indomitable, ancient urge: to be free!

Unfortunately, the laowon were uninterested in human freedoms. Nor were the ancient religious prohibitions against the manipulation of laowon genetic material extended to preclude experimentation on humans. Strange abominations, in vast numbers, began to appear from laowon gene labs. A human slave population that threatened to dwarf that of free humans, grew relentlessly, century by century.

In the Court of the Imperiom Lao, planet-hungry aristocrats, abetted by racist reactionaries in the lao cult, urged laowon colonization of thinly occupied worlds, wherever they might be. Contesting Seygfan groups, the cult, and—the Superior Buro—the Imperial Intelligence organ—were engaged in bitter internecine struggle.

Since the human sphere lay entirely within the palm of the empire, it was only the Imperial Family's iron grip on the space fleets that kept the greediest from tearing up the lao-human treaties and grabbing human worlds at will.

Manipulated by the all powerful Superior Buro and cut off from further exploration by the laowon battle fleets, the human race faced a peculiarly humiliating destiny as the permanent slave race of the laowon.

And then in the year 17082, Lao Record (AD4533) one last, strange hope suddenly gleamed—a scrap of legend borne out of the deep deserts of a distant, dying world and an archaeologist, a man with half his head burned away, were the foundation of a secret that could yet save humanity from the grip of the higher race.

When a small part of this intelligence was given to the decadent ruling elite of Earth, the information was in the hands of the Superior Buro within a few minutes. The Buro was particularly well organized on Earth.

The laowon pressed eagerly. What was the secret? And where did it lie? But the betrayal itself was betrayed, and those who possessed the last hope began a desperate race against the Superior Buro, across the deeps between the stars.

From the beginning, the Superior Buro felt confident of victory. Indeed, the opponents were grotesquely mismatched. And yet, not even the Buro's gigantic computers could calculate every chance, every ricochet of fate.

For example, in the same year that Doctor Ulip Sehngrohn staggered out of the desert with horrifying wounds and his strange story, a boy was born to Hutmother Joana 416, of North West Alley, in the dusty township that served Castle Firgize on the laowon frontier world Glegan. He was part of an experiment by Lord Deshilme of Firgize, a member of the ruling Imperial Family who had chosen exile on the frontier to avoid the fate that had overtaken his brothers at the court.

Fertilization in the laboratory with microsurgically altered genetic material was followed by implantation in the chosen female's womb.

Shortly after birth, however, Jon 6725416 was removed from the experimental batch because he had retained normal human intelligence. His number was printed on his forehead and he was sent to Joana in Hut 416 to raise, outside the laboratory.

From the first days though, Joana also spoke to him his "remembered name"—Iehard, which had been passed on through the females of Hut 416 for generations, kept alive by sheer human determination and cussedness, characteristics that the laowon consistently worked to breed out of the township populations.

Two decades later, Jon Iehard toiled in the great gangs working on the expansion of Castle Firgize that Lord Deshilme had taken up to give himself something to do in exile.

For days Jon's work gang had moved blocks of pink granite, onto the loading elevator beneath the great crane. The elevator took the stones the first hundred meters. The crane lifted them the second hundred, to the top of the new walls of the North tower.

Over them Ushmai, the laowon overseer, was a constant, demanding presence.

Another load was maneuvered into place. The elevator rattled upward. Jon sensed that Ushmai was not watching them so he slipped away to sit by the wall. There in the deep shadows, he was out of Ushmai's sight for once. He relaxed, squatting in the shadows watching the rest of the gang, naked but for the leather aprons and shoulderpads they wore to protect themselves, waiting the next shipment. The men milled around the watertank; they sweated like beasts.

In another minute Ushmai had noticed Jon's absence from the gang. The tall stickfigure of the laowon was moving into range, scanning for the missing worker.

Jon pushed himself to his feet and away from the wall. His hands rested on the blocks behind him for a moment. He felt cracks in the stone. He turned to look more carefully and discerned more cracks. All along the bottom course there were cracks in the big primary stones of the wall. The tower was to be raised another hundred meters, and when completed it would soar three hundred meters above Firgize hill. Since Deshilme preferred to build for posterity, he chose simple building materials—massive blocks of stone, reinforced with steel and concrete. The effect was an architecture of the brutal.

Ushmai was whistling at him. Harsh, piercing whistles. Ushmai was pointing angrily at the watertank.

"Damn the Ushmai," Jon said to Truk and Gus when he returned to his place. More blocks of pink stone were waiting to be lifted onto the elevator.

"The Ushmai is always looking for you," Truk said with a thin smile.

"He knows Hut 416 ate plump wabboo this week," Gus commented.

"Now who might have told you that?" Jon's eyebrow arched.

"A little flopper I know."

"Gus 555 is seeing your sister Wem, that's how," Truk gurgled.

"He never asked me." Jon scowled at Gus.

"Since when does he have to?"

"I'm eldest in my Hut. That's enough reason."

"Eldest *male*, I asked Joana. She agreed all right. Everything square and hutwise."

Arlbi leaned forward. "Look out, here comes Ushmai."

The angular form approached. The white overseer's suit gleamed in the sunlight. "6725416, you have been slacking again. If I have to remind you once more, you'll be for the pain booth, you hear me?"

Wearily Jon groaned his assent in the laowon tongue.

Ushmai turned to go but Jon called after him.

"By the way, there are cracks in those bottom stones. Cracks right through I'd say."

Ushmai purpled. "Cracks? In the Contractor's good stones? Nonsense. What would you know of stone quality anyway? Have you been to the quarry? Have you been among the skilled stone cutters? No, of course not, you are alley stuff, with the wit of a wild wabboo. Stick to what you know, moving stones from pallet to elevator. That's all you have to do. All you're capable of. Cracks! Indeed!" He sniffed loudly and turned on his heel.

The men moved stone. Ushmai oversaw them, the gang on their left who mixed tubs of mortar for their elevator, and the gang on the right who put facing slabs on another elevator.

The men quizzed Jon anxiously about the cracks. He described them as best he could. None were satisfied.

"So Ushmai is taking a cut on these stones, that's for sure."

"Ushmai fancies himself a planet lord. He'll make his pile, buy a jumper, and take his own world. That takes heavy raking from the Contractor. Everyone knows that."

At shift's end they stumbled wearily away. Jon took another look at the cracks. They were definitely wider. He reported it to Ushmai who immediately became ill tempered.

"Get away from me!" he snapped haughtily. "If you repeat these slanders on the good stones of our gracious Contractor, I swear you're for the pain booth."

Jon shrugged and turned away. He was due for the pain booth that week anyway, for wabboo bones in the hut last month. What would it matter if he spent another five minutes in the booth?

But other than Ushmai there was no laowon he could talk to who was likely to listen to his story for more than three seconds. Laowon found human attempts to communicate intrinsically annoying. Humans were meant to be silent, servile, and as nearly invisible as possible.

He turned onto the causeway and followed his workmates back over the hill to the sprawling human township, where restless throngs of workers moved to and fro in the dusty lanes as the shifts changed.

Back at the Hut, a big square room of slatted wood sealed with plastic, Mother Joana and her youngest daughter Troli were waiting with a lunch of tuber soup and dark ration-bread.

The soup was hot and still flavored lightly with the scraps of plump wabboo that Jon had poached the previous week from the Sweetcrystal game preserve.

The door opened and his younger brother Sab came in. Sab was but fourteen, a thin, lithe boy. He worked in the vineyards that radiated southwards from the castle walls.

"So Sab, back for lunch," Jon said in greeting. As the oldest male in the Hut, he took a constant interest in the doings of the others, Joana's four girls and three other boys. All the product of artificial breeding techniques, all as different as they could be.

Sab was a quiet little thing, a docile worker who rarely spoke. He had spent his first years in the laboratory, but had survived to return to Joana. His nights were wracked by dreadful dreams. Once in a while he had fits and tried to bite his own flesh. They had to tie him up on those occasions.

Together Hut 416 ate soup and ration-bread. Joana discussed young Wana's mysterious ills. To Jon, the symptoms sounded like the black-spot virus. He suggested that Joana take Wana to the infirmary, but Joana just pointed at the near-empty money pot. Jon chewed soup and schemed of some way to add to their slender financial reserves. For his own labor he received the ration-bread and water that maintained the hut. The labors of the younger children brought small cash payments, enough so that normally the Hut stayed ahead of the rent and heat bills. Sab and Gelda, who worked in the vineyards, would be due their monthly payment of wine soon. If he sold some of that, there would be money for Wana's visit to the infirmary. If little Wana lived that long, if it really was black-spot disease. It could be awfully quick. And then the Hut would be fumigated. It would stink for months.

There was a sudden noise, a shudder went through the Hut. A few moments later the door banged open, and Little Gita—one year older than Wana—flew in, all pigtails and waving hands. There was an uproar somewhere in the distance.

"What do you think's happened?" Joana asked, peering over the township roofs toward the back of Firgize hill.

"A spaceship must have come!" Sab shouted. "Like the one that brought Lady Magelsa to wed the Lord Innoo. Everyone will take the afternoon off!"

Jon checked the sky, no trace of exhaust fumes was visible against the cloudless blue.

The hill blocked off all but the view of the four towers of Firgize. Except that now Jon saw there were only three! "The cracks!" he shouted. "The cracks in the tower!"

A pall of dust was rising where the great tower had collapsed. Jon slipped out onto the Alley and ran down to the township gate. A mob of human workers was pouring over the causeway. Their faces were a tapestry of rage.

"Hundreds are dead. The whole tower has collapsed."

The men gathered in the township square. Red Urk was hoisted to speak. "The Overseer Ushmai was warned of the cracks!" He bellowed. "We demand the Overseer's expiation in the Agony Booth."

The crowd roared at that and flowed back to the causeway. But at the other end of the causeway the Guards, seven-foot-tall human pinheads, were massed in phalanx. The Guards held their shock batons at the ready. Steel helmets covered their tiny skulls. They were not noted for their compassion; at the whistle they charged the men.

For once the battle was long and furious; the men of the township were enraged by the latest in a long line of disasters brought on by Firgize incompetence. But eventually, the Guards broke through and by late evening had complete control of the main alleys of the townships. All that night huge bounding warriors with diminutive skulls ran through the Huts in an orgy of violence, rape, and slaughter.

In the morning rebel survivors were gathered inside the Keep of the Palace. They were harangued by Deshilme Firgize and then the identified ringleaders were taken for expiation. One by one they were thrust into the Agony Booth. Their chilling screams rang out all day and night, completing the dismal atmosphere that lay over the castle and its surroundings.

Jon waited on line for the Booth, having been marked down by Ushmai himself. Around the captives towered the huge microcephals, who nudged them and tittered at each quavering shriek from a dying man in the booth.

There was a movement on a balcony a few meters above, where a party of blueskins had appeared to witness some of the expiations. Jon noticed the Lord Innoo, heir to Castle Firgize, and his bride, the Princess Magelsa Gnovii among the laowon.

Ahead of him Rad 4623 was thrust into the booth. The clamps closed around his neck leaving only his head visible. The pain began and Rad bellowed mightily.

As the bellows hollowed out into the fluting screams in the "middle passage," so Jon noticed the Princess wince and stop her ears with her fingers. Was she perhaps dismayed at the heavy-handed ways of the frontier worlds?

She looked down and for a long moment his eyes caught hers. Her scrutiny became a very careful one.

An unconscious Rad was removed from the booth and his body tossed onto the pile of those who had already expiated. The big microcephals enjoyed these events immensely, and they were giggling as they thrust Jon into the booth. He glanced back to the blue Princess on the balcony. She had taken her husband's arm and was speaking passionately in his ear.

While the clamps were swung into place around his neck, Jon noticed the booth stank of human excrement, sweat, and pain. He stared back along the line of doomed rebels and those who were drawn up to witness the expiations.

Unexpectedly a command in laowon was bugled down from the balcony. After a moment of shocked hesitation among the steel helmeted pinhead guard, the command was repeated with considerable impatience.

The clamps were lifted, Jon was pulled from the booth and hurried away to one side and around a corner, where a small door opened unexpectedly in the smooth wall of the castle. He was thrust through it.

In total darkness he climbed a winding secret stair. A guard was waiting for him above and he was taken through another secret door, then down a long corridor paneled in pale ochre velvet and wall mural landscapes to a white door. Within, waited the tall, angular Princess Magelsa. In short order she offered him first the velvet suit of a valet to Lord Innoo, and then herself, in her own bed. Not long afterward she conducted his initiation into interspecies sex. She was young and energetic and had acquired a taste for all kinds of unusual pleasures on Ratan, her sophisticated homeworld.

Laowon and human were similar enough physically to find such encounters mutually rewarding, but long afterward Jon lay on the enormous circular bed in Magelsa's bedroom and stared out the window. From far away, almost from another planet it seemed, he could still hear the agonized screams of those who were expiating for the rebellion.

At first his life seemed indeed to have taken a turn for the best. Magelsa arranged for the bar-code on his forehead to be reduced by plastic surgery, but demanded that a slight addition, a small brand with her laowon initial code, be burned into his right buttock.

In the Palace, he worked under the fretful eye of Old Chalmes, the human Head Valet. As Jon worked and learned to avoid Old Chalmes, so he found a wealth of opportunities for enriching the diet of his mother and hut-family. Every week he took them the pickings of the meats, bottles of good wine, slabs of bread and cheese.

After the first few weeks Magelsa's demands upon him began to slacken. He realized that his time as her favorite was coming to its end. He also realized that all was not well within the Firgize household. Magelsa was unhappy. She disliked Lord Innoo, whom she found dull. She hated quiet, rural Glegan with its cool forests and windswept heaths. She longed for the bright lights and excitements of Ratan's great cities. Endlessly, she begged Innoo for permission to travel.

This did not endear her to Lord Deshilme. He had not sought the connection with the Gnovii. They were of Blue Seygfan, he of the Red and thus out of favor at court. Magelsa was a compromise of Seygfan, and while the link did add to the security of Firgize on Glegan, it also represented the leash of control held by the Heir himself.

Indeed, long interstellar voyages were most expensive. The cost of improving Castle Firgize to represent Deshilme's royal lineage was heavy. He would not consider another large outlay of funds. Not while he still awaited a grandson and heir.

Of course, Magelsa applied retroactive contraceptives every day with the hope that eventually she would get her way and be sent home to Ratan. There her disastrous marriage could be dissolved and she could resume the pleasures of her previous life.

Unfortunately for Magelsa, her dissatisfaction had been noted by Lord Firgize's own wife, the Lady Flaam. Flaam believed she had found her last chance to cement her own line to Firgize. Flaam came from the family Castigrii, upstarts on Glegan's south continent. She dreamed of enriching the Castigrii element in Firgize by arranging a match between Innoo and a young female cousin of Castigrii now entering puberty. But to achieve that end Magelsa had to be killed and disgraced. Should there be simply a divorce, once more freeing the princess on Ratan, then Innoo would be forced to wed another female Gnovii. The Gnovii would insist upon it, and they were well placed in Blue Seygfan. Only if there was some provable taint upon Magelsa could their claim be turned aside under cult rule.

One day, therefore, Jon was awakened early in his own bed by a pair of microcephals. Wearing silly little grins, the huge idiots bound him and put him into a sack, then carried him away and released him, much later, in the presence of the Lady Flaam. She was clad entirely in black, seated in a chair carved to represent the snarling skull of an angmot.

Jon realized he was in great danger. The Lady Flaam allowed no visitors and enjoyed a reputation for poisonings in her own family and casually disposing of her human favorites by dropping them into an underground pool swarming with bloodworms.

"You approach the end of your wretched existence, young man, unless you do exactly as I bid you." Her voice was a harsh whisper as she delivered her instructions then ordered him removed.

Back in his own room Jon faced a critical dilemma. According to Flaam, all he had to do was to disarm the security system on Magelsa's suite door and to send a signal when Magelsa and he were next entangled, naked and sweating on her bed.

Flaam and her guards would then burst in with cameras and microphones and catch Magelsa in the act. This would be Jon's pretext for using a hidden weapon, a small energy blade that Flaam had given him, to take Magelsa hostage and to kill her with when the guards went "berserk" and jumped him.

Flaam assured him that should he perform adequately, some other hapless fool would be substituted in the Agony Booth. Jon would instead be released onto the margins of the Polar Continent where a few small human settlements existed.

Was it possible to trust Flaam? He could visualize that last drop into the seething tank only too easily.

Later, alone with Magelsa, he took pity on the young princess and informed her of the plot that was taking shape around her. She had, after all, saved him from the Agony Booth.

Magelsa was instantly terrified. Her mother-in-law was already a figure of grim speculation from all the stories she'd heard. Now she became a source of hysterical fright. Magelsa ran to Innoo, threw herself down before him, and begged him to help.

Innoo was a survivor. He knew his younger brother would cheerfully seize any opportunity to replace him. He also knew that his mother cared little for him and disliked his match with the Gnovii. He made some thoughtful calculations and then called Jon into his presence.

"You must get into my mother's personal quarters one more time. I will see that you are equipped with the weapons for the job. You must kill her. If you succeed, I will reward you with freedom for yourself and your Hut group."

Jon had no choice but to agree. He submitted to the surgeon and one of his canine teeth was replaced with a poison fang. In addition, the end bones of his middle fingers were removed and replaced with artificial bones containing tiny pistols.

Several days later, Jon approached one of Lady Flaam's black-suited microcephalic Guards and gingerly handed the big man a slip of paper, then hurriedly withdrew. Later that same day, two huge guards appeared in the wardrobe where he worked. Solemnly they stripped him, examined him, and thrust him into the sack.

He was dumped out upon the carpet before Lady Flaam's grim throne.

"Why have you not done as I ordered?" She said.

"I cannot gain entry to her bedchamber. She has a new favorite."

Flaam's withered face screwed up in sudden rage. "You lie, I monitor her nightly orgies. She has no new favorite." She pressed a stud on the arm of her throne. A secret hatch opened in the floor, exposing a dark pit. He heard water lapping far below and something else—the excited hiss of bloodworms.

Jon whirled abruptly and caught the nearest guard napping. His hand lanced out, his finger rested momentarily on the man's tiny forehead. Jon pressed down, hard. There was a little *crack*, a flash of pain, as the end of his finger burst, then the guard's head exploded and he fell like some human tree, to land with a heavy thud on the carpet.

The other giant sprang forward, picked Jon up to crush him against the wall, but Jon bit down on the massive biceps. He felt his left canine crumple and spat furiously to eject any remaining poison. The guard fell backward with Jon atop his chest.

The Lady Flaam produced a handgun and fired. The pellet singed Jon's cheek and exploded in the masonry behind him. He dove at her feet and knocked her flying.

For a laowon of more than ninety-six years, Lady Flaam was remarkably agile. She landed well and spun to shoot at him again, but Jon had seized one of the guards' pain wands and hurled it straight into her face. She went down with a shriek and then he was on top of her, his hands around her throat, blood from his finger all over her face, his thumbs pressing deep into her esophagous. A red tide flowed across his vision, a roaring rose in his ears, and when he was finally done, she was dead. He stood up and stared about himself. Blood dripped steadily from his shattered fingertip, and more blood seeped from where her nails had raked his cheek. Quickly, he tilted the bodies into the pit and listened to them hit the water far below. The sound of the worms built to a horrible frenzy. He found the switch on the throne and closed the hatch once more.

Sucking his finger to avoid leaving a trail of blood, he ran to Innoo's apartments with his news. Innoo was not there, an ominous departure from the agreed plan. Nor was there a response at Magelsa's suite. In desperation Jon ran from the palace and hid himself in the woods.

The next day there was a hunt. Microcephals and sniffer grenk worked over the grounds of the estate. Jon ran farther into the hills. He lived wild, but his finger began to rot and after four more days he slipped into the township in search of medical assistance.

Hut 416 on the North West Alley was empty. Its occupants had been taken away to expiate in the Agony Booth.

All day, Jon lay under the floorboards of the Hut and wept. At night he moved silently into the palace and worked his way through the familiar corridors to the entrance of the secret passageway.

In Magelsa's bedchamber the Princess and Lord Innoo quarreled furiously. She demanded to go home to Ratan. He demanded an heir.

"Why do you persist in your refusal?" He bellowed. "My father suspects me of my mother's murder. We must give him an heir lest his favor turn to my brother Lajook."

"Why should it matter?"

"Why do you think House Firgize rots here on this empty world?" Innoo shouted passionately.

She stared back silently.

"Because we are watched! Because my father escaped death only by coming here. Because the Heir will not accept any possible challenge in court. Because Blue Seygfan wishes to fly alone."

"But we're kiloparsecs away from court! We're beyond the back of beyond, we're almost in human space."

"Superior Buro is here. Old Chalmes, the head valet. He is Buro, my father told me ten years ago. 'Watch your words around Old Chalmes,' he said and he was right! I have observed Old Chalmes at work, he is a sly but persistent spy."

"So what?"

Innoo shrugged expansively. "My father escapes death only because they expect a Gnovii link cemented by an heir who will bring Firgize into Blue Seygfan. My father will not give up the Red!"

"Come to Ratan with me. Take one of my younger sisters, she'll give you your precious heir."

"How can I leave Glegan with that slave on the run? If he's found and questioned then both of us will face Expiation!"

Jon slipped into the room quietly and sprang to Innoo's side. He gave them a manic grin and pressed his hand to Innoo's face his middle finger tapping on the lao Lord's forehead.

"Surprise!" he said quietly. "I have to come to collect on your debt to me."

Innoo trembled, his eyeballs rolled up into his head.

"What do you want?" Magelsa's voice cracked with the strain.

"What the hell do you think I want?"

She looked blankly at him. "How should I know what

a human wants? I mean, this is all I really need at this point. A feral human slave interrupting my life."

"How about a feral human slave who's been sleeping in your bed for the last month?"

She sniffed and turned her head.

Innoo groaned miserably, he begged for his life.

"That's funny, that's rich isn't it. You were happy to have me expiate, eh? Blame it all on the *feral* human, right? Think Innoo, one tap on your skull and my fingertip and your head will be joined forever in a little flower of death."

Innoo gulped air. Jon's voice grew cold and hard.

"This is what I demand," he growled and went on to detail his plan, as conceived lying beneath the boards of the empty Hut on North West Alley.

Eventually Magelsa went to the computer console and dialed a large amount of credit out of Innoo's accounts. She purchased two tickets on the next jumper outbound from Glegan, which would leave in two days time. Hers was a long distance ticket, to faraway Ratan. His was for a much shorter hop, to the free human system of Nocanicus, twenty-six light-years away in the direction of the Hyades stars. The cost fully liquidated Innoo's assets.

Then Innoo was made to dictate a full confession of his part in the death of Lady Flaam, which Jon copied and had Magelsa place in Lord Deshilme's personal computer files. It would be summoned up automatically by a simple coded call via telephone. Only Jon and Magelsa would know the code.

During the following forty-eight hours, Jon stayed awake on stimulants right next to Innoo, a handgun in his good hand, trained on Innoo most of the time. Medics came and tended to the rot in his damaged finger. He gave himself doses of local anaesthetic and endured the process while they cut away the tip and cauterized the wound.

Still sweating from that experience, he ordered them to pack a small bag for him. Into it went a bundle of laowon paper bills, some clothes, and a supply of stimulant drugs. In addition, there was a new set of identification papers for himself, describing him as Magelsa's handservant.

On the second day, Innoo, Magelsa and Jon flew to Calb, the small capital city of Glegan, two thousand kilometers west of Firgize. There they boarded the shuttle to the orbiting sat, and after passing through Emigration, passed onto the huge interstellar liner. Jon disposed of his handgun just before the embarkation gate. Now his only defense against Innoo was that coded recording sitting in Lord Deshilme's computer.

He boarded the jumper, keeping close to Magelsa in case she should attempt some treachery. He needn't have bothered. The situation was working out just as Magelsa would have wished. She was on her way back to Ratan, with a horror story to recount to her parents. The Gnovii would sunder their claim on Firgize, and she would be safe. As for Jon, she had come to admire the determination to survive she sensed in him. A determined search had found little rancor toward him in her heart, and even a few embers of her previous passion; he was a lean, muscular young man with narrow face and dark eyes, so unlike the bulky laowon males she had known all her life.

The jumper built up the gravitomagnetic field and departed the Glegan system.

Innoo went back to Castle Firgize with a troubling tale for his father, of an insane Magelsa who had killed his mother and absconded with a human lover. Lord Deshilme never discovered the recording implanted in his computer and never truly understood why the Gnovii consequently cut his connection to them and dissolved the match between Innoo and Magelsa.

Deshilme, truth to tell, felt he'd come out of the affair relatively well considering he was finally free of the Castigrii witch Flaam. He even considered remarrying and was on the point of requesting the Heir for permission to return to court to find someone suitable from the ranks of Blue Seygfan when he was murdered by unknown assassins.

After a week in which suspicion focused on Innoo, a new bride for the Firgize Heir arrived, one Lady Tsinka of the Point of Blue, sent from court. She was three times his age, a near-senile hag with disgusting habits. It was suggested that Innoo would preserve his own future by seeking out permanent vasectomy. Uncertainty concerning the death of Deshilme was, however, laid to rest forever.

Jon Iehard, in the meanwhile, had flown across the deeps of space into the human sphere. The trip took several weeks, subjective, from point to point across the starfields, usually traveling in short hops of one to three light-years. Each time the ship reemerged in normal space, it had to begin rebuilding the gravitomagnetic fields while the navigators aligned it precisely with its destination point, avoiding all gravity nodes along the way. The process could take many hours.

At Ialpitan Space Base, Princess Magelsa said farewell to Jon with even a few tears, and kisses of joy. She was due to board another, larger vessel, a liner that would head out on the truly immense voyage into the far Orion arm, where eventually she would reach Ratan.

Jon watched her go with some misgivings. At the space base, surrounded by laowon military, he felt the most vulnerable to any move by Innoo. He was alone, and without Magelsa to back his story, he might be unable to get Lord Firgize to listen to the tape of Innoo's confession. For all Jon knew Innoo had already seen to the destruction of the computer that contained the damaging file.

But no troopers appeared to arrest him before the jumper unshipped and headed out to the jump point.

Jon shared a small cabin on a crowded deck with an elderly woman who'd been given her freedom and a jumper ticket by her grateful laowon patron after a lifetime of service. She was en route to die in a free human system, and she spent most of her time burning incense and singing Panhumanist hymns in a doleful voice. It didn't take long for Jon to find her company oppressive and he forsook the cabin, spending most of his time idling in the small shipboard library.

Although the vast majority of its works concerned the laowon, a few volumes were devoted to the human race. There he found his introduction to perspectives on humanity that he had never before suspected. He discovered the universal alphabet of human ideografs. He set himself to memorize as much of the seventy most commonly used ones as he could before he reached human space.

As he viewed and read and listened, the enormity of the galaxy, even of human occupied space, crashed home to him. There were thousands of human colony worlds. There were the old settled worlds of the inner core stars and then there were the remarkable High Cultures of the far flung clusters, the Hyades, the Dipper Region, the Aldebaran Group. In all those systems humans ruled themselves. That thought was strange to Jon, almost frightening in its novelty.

When at last the jumper arrived in the Nocanicus star system, they began the wearying period of fusion drive, with aching hours of acceleration and deceleration as the ship nosed into the asteroid belt that was the prime settled part of the system, which had no habitable planets. Finally they reached Hyperion Grandee, the largest single asteroid habitat in the system.

The books and videos he'd studied had described the marvels of a high corporate system in glowing terms—Asteroid colonies! Space habitats! Jon was primed for all the technological wonders, nor was he disappointed. The jumper had to ease its way through crowded space lanes to approach Hyperion Grandee.

On the screen, he'd watched spellbound as spindly ships, all grids and spheres and bright identification lights, slid by. Closer in, past rings of agrihabitats, swarmed smaller craft, only visible by their lights, winking myriads of red and white and blue.

As they curved onto the docking path, enormous shadowy structures passed by on either side of the jumper. Huge, intense lights blazed from a row of hexagonal openings. From the camera view, Jon had the impression they were approaching the hub of a vast wheel. Dimly lit, spokelike things, many times the size of the ship were drifting slowly past them.

The jumper docked with a slight shudder of vibration and shortly afterward Jon Iehard was out on the crowded corridors of Hyperion Grandee, his belongings in a small tote bag slung over his shoulder. He was a free man, standing on human-built floorspace.

The habitat was overwhelming. It pulsed with life, a steady pounding of human surf inside the public ways and open spaces. Rivers of people flowed everywhere, almost twenty-four million of them according to the tourist program. All were connected in some way or other to the centers of finance, trade, entertainment, and light industry that gave Hyperion Grandee its astonishing vigor.

Fortunately he did not arrive penniless, or he would

not have been allowed to disembark. Hyperion Grandee had a severe overcrowding problem. Advertising signs flashed in multicolored frenzy, images poured forth in an overloading fury that he had never imagined before. After gazing openmouthed for a while he found that by contrasting the common ideografs he'd memorized, with Nocanicus Varietals he could comprehend many of the big signs and logos. "SDaba," "Wirl," "Stop No-Joy," "DD," "Alfa Time," there were dozens, hundreds, thousands.

He took the notes of Lao Mercantility he'd packed at Castle Firgize to the first bank he identified, the Baltitude & Oxygen Bank. Inside the bank his notes gave the young woman who ran the small foreign exchange desk quite a thrill; she'd never seen paper money. She found the patterns beautiful, the colors rich and lustrous. However, she had to inform Jon that they were not of particularly high denominations and he wound up with a mere eleven hundred and thirty Nocanicus credit units for them. He only barely qualified for a credit card.

Back out in the city, he wandered in awe through the enormous clefts of the central sector around Octagon Five where structures towered more than a thousand meters above his head. He passed through immense archways, wandered inside broad passageways lined with shops, restaurants, pleasure parlors. Everywhere there were people, millions upon millions, brightly clad in the pastels and primaries that were so fashionable. They surged restlessly through the corridors, their passing giving rise to a susurration that reminded Jon of waves breaking on the shores of the Sweetcrystal in storm.

He ate at snackstands and slept on a park bench his first night. He was duly awakened by the police who let him loose only after a stern lecture about vagrancy and a friendly warning to get the laowon brand removed from his forehead as soon as possible.

Day, night, day, he wandered, finding that the habitat was always awake, always pulsing with life. If anything the night cycle crowds were even greater than those of the day. At some point he paused and booked into the cheapest hotel he could find, a hundred credits a day for the smallest room. He started to investigate the chances of getting a job.

After a day or so he discovered that he'd stepped from

one trap into another. Hyperion Grandee's economy was superservice, high skill. Jon lacked the educational credits required for any jobs outside the realm of service. But one look at the brand on his forehead and the faces of potential service employers shriveled in disgust. He began to hear disparaging words such as "breed," "brand man," and "laoman."

On his fifth evening he got into a fight in a small bar in Octagon One after being turned down for a job as a bartender. Almost the whole bar turned on him and roughed him up. Then he was almost denied entry to a hospital when he produced his new credit card. Eventually he was treated, grudgingly, in a charity clinic.

In desperation, the next morning, he limped to a government job center. But the counselors' recommendations were not encouraging: Jon could, he was told, raise a small sum of capital by selling the rights to his organs to the transplant banks, enough to keep him going until the banks required his heart or liver or lungs. Since he was young and fit and reasonably good looking, he might be able to earn a meager living from the sale of his body for sexual abuse. In the light of the brands on his body and obvious laowon connections, the counselors advised him strongly against this course.

On the other hand, they pointed out, he might easily find a well-paid job on the laowon level of Hyperion Grandee. He even had the accent of the laowon worlds, nasal, clipped. And the laowon population in Nocanicus system was rising steadily as adventurers from all over the vast Imperiom headed toward the human designated zone.

Jon, however, refused to consider that idea. The laowon would not get the leash back on an Iehard. And there might yet be a pursuit by the Firgize.

He had to admit, though, that things looked pretty hopeless, and he began to consider using the microgun still buried in his remaining middle finger. But death seemed terribly permanent, and he faced the prospect with dread.

Then a young woman at the center suggested Jon take the test for psi ability, as there was a strong demand for the psi-able in various jobs. He took the test and was found very sensitive to human fear and rage. He undertook further tests and then received a final recommendation, to the Mass Murder Squad, Hyperion Grandee Police Department; the police department was always looking for recruits who could be trained to track down the thrill killers who plagued Nocanicus. It sounded like grim work, but the money they mentioned was good. Enough for him to get an apartment and be able to live on Hyperion Grandee. But whatever he decided to do, he would have to do soon; his credit was almost gone and he could not afford another night in the hotel. As he had already discovered, homeless people were not allowed to sleep in the parks and corridors. In a few days, therefore, he could expect to be seized by the HGPD Vagrants Squad and hustled aboard a shuttle for one of the grim, older gigahabitats that warehoused millions of poverty-stricken people.

Indeed, he'd discovered that Nocanicus system as a whole was in deep economic trouble. Situated on the edge of laowon space, the Nocanius Corporation had been unable to attract colonist groups for the surrounding yellow stars with habitable worlds. The outrush from the Hyades systems had slowed drastically in recent centuries, since the laowon had taken most of the usable systems that might have attracted human groups. Without the colonists there was no work in building and refueling NAFAL colony ships. Without such work Nocanicus' relatively large population faced slow, remorseless decline.

However, the decline was uneven. On the watermoons and the luxury megahabitats with their small populations, the standards of living were as high as anywhere in the human sphere. On the gigahabs of the asteroid belt, the situation was desperate. Too poor to remodel, some were leaking badly despite the high cost of fresh water and gas from the outer moons.

After thinking it through, Jon agreed to interview for the Mass Murder Squad. They read his psi sense test scores and whistled. They immediately tested him some more. Then they offered him the basic salary and the promise of "liquidation" credits in the future.

He put his thumbprint on the computer pad and explained that he would require some surgery on the middle finger of his good hand. Eyebrows rose when they heard his story, but his new employers agreed to fund the operation. Scores like his were rarely seen. They also enrolled him in speech classes to correct his lao-planet accent, and literacy classes since they found he was a functional illiterate.

A few days later he began basic training as well. He lived in a dormitory with other trainees until he achieved his Competency Badge. He was unpopular with the other trainees for the laowon brand earned him enmity everywhere. He learned to live with the dislike, arranged for plastic surgery, and concentrated on being first in his class. He advanced rapidly to the status of Operative and was quickly fitted with his preferred weapons at the armory. Then he was dispatched to seek out and to kill the pestilential Kill Kultists who tormented the general public.

CHAPTER TWO

TO AVOID DETECTION BY LAOWON AGENTS, THE MESSENger left Quism through the sewers. He rode a caravan south but left it well before the Meridian Gap, where the laowon kept an observation post. He walked through the night to cross the mountain ridge, far to the west of the watchpost.

The following night he wandered through the fringes of the North Machine Belt. In the starlight he observed that tall figures, mutant tribesmen, stalked him through giant, dead machines. He was young and fit; he took evasive action and outran them on the starglitter sands.

By day he dozed on a high ledge, inside a great hulk of corroding eternite. His spot had a good view in most directions, plus protection from the solar glare.

The next night brought him to the dunes of glowing glass. Besides a curve in the swelling crystals stood a towering pylon, connected to a rusting rectangle a hundred meters high.

He ran toward it, a thin man, cutting through the morning breeze.

The young Elchites greeted him warmly, but searched him nonetheless. Their eyes anxiously scanned the distances behind him.

"The man with half a head, I have a message for him."

Their eyes hardened, they bade him wait in a deserted shaft that appeared to have no upper limit. The walls were of some sparkling eternity material. He was still peering upward, trying to locate a ceiling, when a voice beside him startled him.

A gaunt man rode a silent wheelchair. Most of the left side of his face was missing. Instead of bones and flesh, a dark gray medical unit filled the space. It was connected through a tube to a larger unit that rode on the back of the chair.

"They said you have a message for me?" The voice was dry, leathery, with a curious resonance. A faint medicinal smell hung in the air.

"Yes. 'The bird flies, it has reached the system where our hope lies.'" The messenger spoke the words carefully, to make sure each was perfectly understood.

"Thank you," the man said. "Now you may go to the shelter, you have done well." The wheelchair turned and left as quietly as it had come.

The blue sun was coming up on the horizon. Wild purple shadows ricocheted down the dunes of glass, pleiotic flashes of light caught the eyes.

The man with half a head paused beside his secret entranceway. Would they come soon? Would they come in time? He looked into the south and the plumes of the North Temperate Dust Belt. Huge, dead machines marched shoulder to shoulder into the haze as if they were buildings in some deserted city of skyscrapers.

He looked up into the indigo sky. The laowon were up there somewhere, there were always laowon parties abroad on the surface now. One day they would understand the patterns. He prayed that that day would be delayed long enough for the mission to pass safely.

A stray breeze came out of the south, smelling hot, slightly acrid. Dust was coming. He opened the secret door and slipped inside.

It was Crazy Night aboard Hyperion Grandee, the end of the first academic semester and the beginning of Winter Month. There were parties and bands of revelers everywhere. The police department had its hands full, as usual, just keeping the crowds moving in Octagon Five, Six, and Seven.

Down on Octagon Ten the students of Hyperion U. were celebrating in the time-honored manner; the fountains outside Shrad Hall were full of struggling maroon-clad forms. Around them a horde of drunken youths sang bawdy versions of the school song. Inside Shrad the faculty party was going full blast, with toast after toast for Coach Bach, who'd taken the Hyperion team to a 15–3 victory over Nocanicus U. in the annual wintergame.

It was also the night when the top forty students of the senior year were inducted into Orbit, the traditional home to the rulers, movers, and shakers aboard Hyperion Grandee. They were gathered around the clocktower in the darkness, each with an apple in one hand and a whole garlic in the other. At midnight, when the engineers changed the star fields for Winter Month, each would be asked a personal and embarrassing question in front of the others—and all the old members, hidden inside the tower and giggling their drunken selves silly. Depending on how their answer sat with their listeners, the novices would consume either the apple or the garlic. They might also have to take off their trousers or skirts and perform other humiliating exercises.

It was Crazy Night.

But bad craziness was also adrift in the air—blood craziness, murder craziness. The Kill Kults were in action and, tracking them, the Mass Murder Squad.

Theoretically, the forty young about-to-be Orbiters were safe inside the walls of the university grounds; security guards manned the gates to screen guests and visitors. In fact, everyone was so intoxicated that Arnei Oh had had no trouble at all in getting through. He carried a fragmentation device and a short-barrel .44-caliber automatic. Dressed in maroon garb, like the rest of the university boosters, he was undetectable as he passed guards and cops and the throngs of kids and worked his way across Hyades Meadows toward the clocktower.

Arnei was a nine-scalp man. He had taken twenty-three lives in his four assaults on the general public. In the Kill Kults he was one of the top names. His own club, the Dragons of Kali, bet heavily on his success every time he drew the tang.

This tang would likely be his greatest. They'd never forget him after this one!

He crossed through some bushes and paused. A gush of girlish laughter came from somewhere close by, and the grunting of a drunken young man. Arnei sidestepped. Under an ornamental shrub carved into a parasol, a young couple were copulating vigorously. A dreadful little smile broke over Arnei Oh's face. He reached inside his maroon coat for his switchblade. The girl was a magnificent blonde. He could already visualize her scalp hanging in his collection cabinet.

A hundred meters away Melissa Baltitude walked slowly toward the clocktower, the apple and the garlic heavy in her hands. It was important to walk slowly, to look cool and calm. Otherwise the vindictive old men in the tower would make one do all sorts of disgusting things in front of everyone.

Melissa wanted membership of Orbit more than anything in the universe right then. But she dreaded the question—and if Jason Patel had made the top forty, then her spiteful, beautiful former boyfriend would have given them all the ammunition they needed.

She gritted her teeth. Whatever the question she would answer it. And she would eat the garlic and jump around stark naked too if necessary. She would do whatever it took, and then she would be in Orbit and the rest of her life would be assured.

She heard the muffled screams, three of them, from the nearby topiary exhibit, but they didn't seem so extraordinary. A great wall of noise was coming from the fountains where the pigs were splashing and the pig-watchers were getting drunker. So she paid the new sounds no mind. What if some horny little pig female was getting raped in the bushes? It happened every year; she should've known better. Last year there had even been some man-raping out in those shrubberies.

Melissa concentrated on the faces of those around her, gathering around the tower. There was Suzy America; Melissa had always known Suzy would make it. And Simon Weezel, and Garropy Ondine, and others still too far away to make out. Would Suzy America actually marry Bertane Lagode? They were lovers from big families; when the daddies were Megabucks, the kiddies married among themselves. Melissa stilled the excitement she felt and concentrated on walking slowly.

Back beyond the fountain a slim man with staring eyes suddenly turned around and looked into the shrubbery.

With a curse he pulled a short shock rod from his coat pocket and sprinted into the crowd.

Crystal clear on Jon Iehard's psi sense was a mental picture: the knife rising and falling; the beautiful hair; the leather-gloved fist wrapped in the hair; the knife sawing away around the scalp, loosening, ripping, triumph!

He had him! Arnei Oh was in the topiary exhibit. Exulting in grisly triumph as he took scalps.

Jon used the shock rod vigorously to clear students from his way. Curses and screams of pain marked his path. He mashed the rod into the face of some big boy with a bloated belly who got in the way and tried to stop him. The howling face went down and Jon ran right over him and knocked two girls flying as he disengaged from the crowd.

"Stop that bastard!" someone screamed. Footsteps sounded behind him, but Jon ignored them and accelerated across the lawns, his other hand pulling out the Taw Taw automatic .22 that he always wore.

Into the shrubbery he ran. By good fortune he came on the scene of carnage almost immediately. The bodies had been dealt with in Kali Kult manner. Heads removed, torsos slit, and intestines spread far and wide. Jon had seen so much of this sort of thing in nine years working for the Mass Murder Squad that he hardly broke stride. He knew then what Arnie Oh's primary target had to be that night.

The youngsters pursuing him were not so familiar with this sort of thing and pulled up in horrified amazement. Somebody saw that Annie Klein had been scalped as well as beheaded. He was immediately sick in the bushes. The others joined him.

On the green around the clocktower forty-one figures in maroon were gathered in a loose circle. From the clocktower the questions were being put.

"Melissa Baltitude," boomed an electronically distorted voice. "Step forward."

She did so. "Melissa, is it true what they say about you and Suzy America?"

Her heart jumped. How did they know that? They'd been fourteen years old.

And then she became aware that something wrong was

happening on her right. Bad craziness had made an appearance.

A small handgun was firing; there were screams. Everyone was running. A heavyset figure, too old to be a student, was running toward her with a long knife in his right hand. In his left was a small gun. He raised it and she stared into the barrel. She thought she heard her own scream.

But the first bullet missed her by a fraction. And then another figure, slender, legs pumping furiously, came into sight across the lawn. The heavyset man whirled, fired back at the pursuer who yelled at the top of his lungs. He had a gun too, Melissa could see it in his hand.

Then the heavyset man had an arm around her waist, hoisting her off the ground and dragging her toward the clocktower.

"Stop, Arnei!" the pursuer shouted. Arnei covered the gravel in three grotesque bounds and hurled Melissa into the door, driving it open. Arnei smashed through it and rolled into a firing position, his gun roared impossibly loudly in that enclosed space. Hot streaks zinged out the door over her body. Her bowels released as she pressed her face into the tile.

People were screaming and running up the stairs of the tower. Arnei slid in another magazine and pumped bullets up the stairwell. Some of the screams took on a different timbre.

Bullets came through the door, explosive things that dug inch-deep holes in the wall blocks opposite. But Arnei Oh had rolled aside and was in the shadow of the door. His hand stretched out for her arm, She stared horrified, but was unable to move. He had her by the wrist. One strong jerk and she was slammed into him, feeling his hot coffee breath in her face.

He was brutally strong. Still, she swung at him, landing a punch against a leathery cheek. He snarled and then opened his mouth. His teeth were filed to points. He lunged and seized her shoulder and bit down. She screamed, the sound echoing in the small room at the base of the tower.

He crushed her behind him, pressed her against the wall. Shifting position, his gun ready. She watched help-

lessly as he pulled out a black tube about a foot long. He punched a button on it and a dire little red light came on.
He stuffed it back in his coat and seized her by the hair. With a flurry of shots out the door he dragged her across the room to the stairs. In three bounds he was up the first flight, dragging her willy nilly. As she smashed into the wall on the second leap, she felt her forearm break.
Arnei Oh's gun boomed again, and there were more screams from above. But he was trapped, and he knew it, so he would take them all with him. The feat would mark him as the King of Killers in his own time.
He decided on a whim to take the dark-haired girl's scalp as well. He dropped her, knelt on her back to hold her down, and fumbled out his knife. With his gun hand he grabbed her hair and brought the blade up to her forehead, but there were footsteps on the stairs. He cursed. This operative had to be suicidal. He let go and brought the gun up, but the guy kept coming. Their guns boomed, a salvo at ten paces. Arnei's shot took Jon Iehard in the midriff but didn't cut the body shield. Jon's small plastic bullet stroked Arnei's shooting hand and exploded. Arnei saw the man fall, roll, and his own hand fountain blood. The shock turned him and flung him back into the stone wall.
Arnei gasped once and then shrieked his rage. He dropped the knife and reached for the bomb, one flick and it was green. Then Iehard's second shot took Arnei's head off and ended the career of the king of the Kali Dragons. Jon didn't stop, however, reaching Arnei before the body even reached the floor. He picked up the bomb and threw it down the staircase with a scream of warning to any fools who might be down there.
The resulting explosion deafened Melissa, who was lying flat under the operative, and shook dust and stones out of the entire tower. Shrapnel whined around in the downstairs room for a few seconds thereafter.
It was over.
The man got up off her with a groan. She watched open-eyed, breathing in gasps, as he pulled off his coat and fumbled at the straps of a suit of body armor. There was a big dent right in the middle of the chestplate. Melissa could smell herself, and the blood of Arnei Oh, which

was everywhere. She wanted to vomit but before she could, she fainted.

For a few long seconds there was a silence. The peace of the dead once again, thought Jon, who had felt it many times before.

Then from above came footsteps, cautious ones. Outside and some distance away he heard police klaxons. He hoped the medics would be along soon; his chest hurt pretty bad. He felt like he'd been kicked by a horse. He wondered if he had any broken ribs this time.

The first few adventurous souls from upstairs finally stuck their heads into the second-floor room.

Wordlessly they stared at Arnei Oh's headless corpse. Then, hands over their mouths, both men ran for the stairs. The woman following them merely shook her head grimly and picked her way through the carnage and followed them. For a moment her eyes met Jon's, and then she looked away.

He pulled himself to his feet, shed the armor where he was, tucked his gun into his waistband, and bent over the young woman who had fainted. After a gentle shake she awoke. He helped her to her feet.

"My arm," she complained quietly. "It's broken."

"Is that all?" he said.

"No!" She gasped. "My foot." And she would have fallen but he caught her and swung her up into his arms. He carried her down the stairs and outside onto the lawn. The cops were arriving, the klaxons howling off the buildings.

Other people, dozens of them in expensive evening dress, were running across from Shrad House. The anxious parents of the top forty. Jon sat beside the girl and watched several emotional reunions.

But a number of still bodies were scattered around the lawn. Arnei Oh hadn't had long to operate, but in those few seconds he'd taken five lives.

A man fell down sobbing beside the still body of his son. Jon shook his head. This operation had been something of a disaster. He wondered if he would manage to secure the full liquidation fee. Arnei Oh should be worth Triplefull rate, but with so much carnage Jon feared he'd lose a percentage to victims' families. Just then judges were as ill tempered about that kind of business as everybody else.

A tall man in a well-cut gray silk suit appeared, eyes distraught. He caught sight of Melissa.

"Lissa!" He bounded across the lawn.

"Are you all right?"

"My arm is broken, I think my ankle is too."

"What the hell happened here?"

"I don't know, Daddy. Ask this man, he killed him."

The tall, imposing fellow whirled on Jon. "Killed? Who did you kill?"

Jon had it—he faced Jason Pauncritius Baltitude, the gas baron. He'd seen him on TV news.

"The perp's name was probably Arnei Oh. We had a few others for him. Responsible for at least twenty-three dead. Mass killer, the reputed top boy of the Kali Dragons."

Mr. Baltitude gave out a bitter oath. "Why the ordinary citizen cannot have adequate protection against these bloodthirsty swine is beyond my understanding. How did this creature get inside the university grounds?"

"I assure you that wasn't the difficult part," Jon said tersely. He watched the police drive up. An ambulance was with them.

"Medics are here, Miss Baltitude," he said. "They'll give you something to kill that pain, I'm sure."

Another ambulance was approaching. You never knew with mass-murder stuff whether you were going to need one or fifty of the things. Bright lights whirled and flashed around the groves of academe.

"So tell me what happened," Baltitude said. "I want to know how this horror could be allowed."

Jon would have shrugged but it would have cost too much pain. "We were tracking for him. We had pretty good predictions on Arnei Oh. He had enough of a record to give the computer something to get to work on. But these guys are elusive, and it's hard to protect every target. Luckily I guessed right. I thought he'd take a crack here, because of the useless security system. Big crowd, poor security, that's natural meat for a shark like Arnei Oh."

"You were here?" Baltitude seemed shocked.

"Over by the fountains. Bigger crowd there, I was afraid he'd just frag them out of the dark."

"You were over by the fountain, when you suspected this beast was loose in here? You were protecting the pigs when we had the top forty gathered in one place! I think you have some very tough questions to answer, my man. I'll be discussing this with your superiors at the earliest opportunity."

For a moment Jon stared up in disbelief. "I just risked my life to save your daughter, you realize."

"I realize nothing. I realize that your incompetence almost cost her her life. To say nothing of those that lie cold and dead over there. What were you doing while they were being slaughtered?"

"I was running as fast as I could. He started out in the shrubbery, I sensed it then. That's what tipped me off. If he hadn't paused to take some poor fool girl's scalp out there I would have missed him completely. He probably would have killed twenty of your top forty and gotten clean away. Arnei Oh has been at the top of this game for years."

"Game? Are you mad?"

"Game, Mr. Baltitude. I take it that you don't much concern yourself with how these things go on, since they mostly do take place down on the ordinary rent levels. Perhaps you should follow the newscasts more closely. There's a war on out there, these crazies versus the rest of the universe. That's the way they like it."

"Daddy, you're wrong, completely wrong. Now will you please get me a medic, I want some painkillers!" pleaded Melissa Baltitude. "This hurts terribly!"

Slowly Baltitude backed away, and then he turned and strode off toward the ambulances.

Jon got to his feet. "Well, Miss Baltitude, I think I'll be getting along now. I don't think this conversation is going anywhere. So, good night then."

"But I don't even know your name."

"Iehard. Operative Ex-five Double One. Tell your daddy to complain directly to my section head, whose name is Copter Brine." Jon turned and stumbled off to the ambulances.

* * *

In the control chamber of the great machine, the Keeper progressed through a utilities check. Although the crew was unaccountably absent, the machine's routines went on undisturbed.

As it had every so often in the eons of loneliness, the Keeper noticed discrepancies in some sections. Somewhere deep in the bowels of the engineering complex enemy cells still diverted energy, in quite extravagant quantities, from the engineering section power grid. That perennial problem necessitated recharging the energy banks far more frequently than the original maintenance program had ordained. The Keeper had been forced to change programming levels in the effort to find a way around the problem. The Keeper had even grown additions to its own intelligence in the effort. None of the changes had been easy.

The energy drain to engineering was frustrating. The Keeper did not have a real pain-pleasure circuit. In this, its programmable capacities were much less than those of other machines of its own era. It did have a node of dissatisfaction, however, related to failures in execution of prime programs. And over the eons the node of dissatisfaction had grown. The Keeper now had a very great urge to leave the Control Chamber and to go down to the Engineering section and find the annoying enemy cells that diverted so much energy, and render them permanently inoperative.

That idea returned ever more frequently to the forefront of operations in the spherical computational area set inside its massive batrachianoid skull. Unfortunately, the prime program forbade the Keeper's leaving the control chamber before the crew, or its replacement, returned to duty. Eternal vigilance, that was the program's watchword. It was enough to make the Keeper snap its mechanical jaws in sheer frustration.

CHAPTER THREE

JON IEHARD AWOKE FROM THE USUAL SET OF NIGHT-mares: Hut 416 and huge, giggling pinhead guards and silent mass killers who wreaked awful havoc while he fought helplessly to prevent them. It was always the same. Sometimes he thought he might be better off if he didn't bother with sleep.

Around him, his grungy little apartment seemed stale and even messier than usual. An empty booze bottle stood in the middle of a nest of dirty glasses. A pile of movie modules decorated the carpet along with the clothes he'd discarded last night.

He moved, and groaned. His chest hurt like hell. He checked the timepiece. It was six thirty. The engineers would be lifting the filters soon for dawn. Throwing back the covers, he turned the TV on with an audible and examined the instacaf situation.

With a hot mugful, he came back in time to see Blankette Va Vroe, the mayor with the famous cheekbones, speaking passionately about the latest refinancing crisis for gigahabitat Nostramedes. A lot of loans were riding on refinancing, but the wealthy watermoons of William, Ingrid, Shala, and Hideo were balking at the size of their contributions.

He gulped down the instacaf and went in for a shower. The laowon weren't about to disappear, so Nocanicus was in a box and the shipbuilding gigahabitats were doomed.

When he came back he felt much better. The news had shifted to the crime beat. Extra detective Coptor Brine was fielding questions at last night's emergency press conference. Jon listened with half a mind.

". . . suspect was identified as Mood Oh Arnei, or Arnei Oh. Believe me when I tell you this one was one of the worst cases we've ever pursued. The leader of the Kali Dragons, with twenty-three killings to his name prior to this latest outrage."

A newswoman bored in. "There have been charges made about this case, Extra Detective Brine. What do you say to the accusation of, and I quote, 'Gross incompetence on the part of the security forces who could easily have prevented this slaughter'?"

"I guess I would agree. I should add we warned the university as much as three years ago that their security on Wintergame Day had gotten pretty slack. I think you'll have to take it up with them."

"There are also charges against your operative in this case, Extra Detective."

Coptor's big flat face grew hard. "Yes, I've seen those and I would like to state publicly right now that I think they're malicious, unsubstantiated, and stupid. We have precisely seventeen sensing operatives. We can't cover every potential outrage site. Our man on this case performed a near miracle as it was, getting the perpetrator and keeping the loss of life to half a dozen. I think he deserves a medal, not these mean-spirited accusations!"

"Thank you, Coptor!" Jon said as he snapped off the set. He pulled on some clothes and let himself out carefully. Jon was living, temporarily as always, on a very mode-ish ramp. Very pastel, very audio-video-holo; ambisexual singles' parties every weekend. Jon felt like a sore thumb in his grays and blacks, and worked extra hard at keeping his profile very low. He was looking forward to moving on soon. The Mass Murder Squad encouraged its operatives to move constantly. The Kill Kults were well organized, determined, and prepared to do almost anything. Personal security was precious and precarious. In Jon's nine years, five senser operatives had been blown away in their own homes.

Once off the ramp, he headed into the park. The trees and open spaces were lit with the first sunlight of the day, mirrored, filtered, and given an ancient terrestrial tinge by the engineers.

Pretty good crowds were out already. On the paths to the Hyades Monument a cloud of joggers passed him. Two women were flying a kite in the shape of a gigantic female figure, and a small cult group in white robes was burning incense and prostrating itself in worship ceremonies. Dawn brought out a certain kind of crowd. Evening had another. Human variety was infinite on Hyperion Grandee.

He reached the Hyades Monument with its twenty-seven planetary models, each a meter across, with tiny clouds swirling over their miniature oceans. If you stood by the monument long enough, it was said, you would see virtually every form of human weirdness, except the horrors on laowon worlds. You'd see laowons though, plenty of them, especially in late afternoon when the light was closest to that of Laogolden.

Past the monument he turned through a dark grove of terrestrial pine trees. He liked this stretch of the walk the best, and he often jogged down here, too. The smell of the pines was similar to that of the woods around Castle Firgize beside Lake Sweetcrystal in that other life, which some days seemed almost a dream to him now.

He emerged from the pines near the exit to Octagon Five. The ramps there were crowded with morning office workers. Iehard stopped off for a breakfast special. While he ate he checked the news updates. Arnei Oh hadn't been the only bad craziness of Wintergame night. Someone had thrown a fragmentation bomb into an office party on Octagon Two. Nine good citizens had been scraped together afterward for the morticians and another twenty-four were in the hospital. The perpetrator had escaped with barely a witness to the act.

Finishing up his muffin and bacofreef, he passed his card over the table function box and set out for the temporary office.

The Mass Murder Squad was not a big, well-accredited department of the Hyperion Grandee Police Department. Mass Murder, in fact, didn't operate out of police headquarters in Octagon Three. Instead, it moved constantly from one nondescript little office to another. Wherever it went, though, the office was always the same, jammed with computer equipment, screen to screen, wall to wall. Operatives shared desks, assistants crowded the hallways.

In fact, the police department preferred to keep Mass Murder at arm's length. It was messy, nasty stuff, politically dangerous. The whole business of the Kill Kults sent a political contradiction right down the middle of the public mind. Random mass killings, the taking of grisly trophies, the defiant posturing of captured suspects, all these made the public demand harsh, effective measures, essentially "shoot on sight," to stamp out the killers. Unfortunately, that led to the occasional slaughter of the innocent, and that was media poison of the worst kind.

Currently, the squad was working out of a run-down office suite on a ground floor in Octagon Five. It was gray and grim and looked like some elderly gas haulage agency with long-term contracts since the year dot. It was also ringed by invisible security teams.

Jon took the ramp to the main plaza and then moved onto the blue corridor past Zeppo Uniti, who worked the coffeeshop on the corner. Zeppo checked everyone who went by.

Up the corridor was a scuffed gray door marked "Fabulous Bioengineering." Jon rapped three times and then slipped inside.

It was bedlam. The security team nodded him through into the labyrinth of computer screens. Telephone babble filled the air along with fumes of instacaf and syntabac. He shouldered through to the desk he shared with Operative Elvis Kee Hoi Apollo and checked his messages. Most were routine. He paused over one from Melissa Baltitude, in the Downtown Emergency Hospital. It was warm and flip and thankful. He smiled and punched it to phototron oblivion and called up the next.

He frowned. Commander Petrie, Chief Executive of the Nocanicus Military Corporation, wasn't the kind who normally would be in his office at eight in the morning. Nor did he normally call on the services of the killer trackers of the Mass Murder Squad when he had the Military Intelligence Unit already to hand. The message meant trouble. And it had to be laowon business.

With a certain amount of foreboding, he walked over to the Military Intelligence building through the mid-morning crowds. Everywhere he looked people jammed the corridors, flowing over the ramps like waves, a veritable sea of faces, hopes, and dreams. And among them lurked how many random killers? A grim thought, but one that had to be faced: Arnei Oh, king of Kali Dragons, had turned out to be somebody called Danuel Mitshi, who worked as a lighting designer for one of the big ad agencies of Octagon Eight. The kults were pervasive and hard to crack.

The MI offices were in a slim, gray, windowless tower situated close to the octagon station. Security was tight. His weapon was tagged and removed, retina and fingerprint checks were run before he was shown to an elevator protected by steel blast shields.

"Ah, Jon, do come in." In a civilian-cut gray suit, Petrie welcomed him out of the elevator. A slim man of medium height, a scion of a very famous family, the commander was in medium extended age, around eighty-five. Iehard's practiced eye quickly picked out such aging details as the resistant little pot belly.

The outer office was filled with young workers and small trees in ceramic tubs. An air of studious industry filled the place.

Jon saw that Petrie was wearing a little psi field deflector, the metal headband gleamed across his forehead. Must keep the operative from picking up more than he should, thought Jon. Deflectors never worked well with fear sensors. Jon could easily read Petrie's unease.

"Good of you to get down here so fast. We've got a crisis on our hands. An emergency, otherwise I wouldn't dream of interrupting your work. I know how overloaded you poor devils are. Sometimes I think our society's going to the damned, I honestly do. That one yesterday, that? . . ."

"Arnei Oh."

"Yes, that one. Very bad business. Very bad; a *lighting* designer of all things, I read." He sighed. "Well, it's over at last. Do take a seat."

Petrie's private office was bowl shaped, with exotic tropical flowers that grew on mirrored tiers all the way to the mauve ceiling. Iehard sank into a sensual sofchair that started to massage him lightly, almost imperceptibly.

He didn't want to sound ungracious but the thing made his spine crawl. "Is there any way to turn this chair off?"
"Yes, of course, right by your right hand, the stud."
The massage ended.
It was much too early in the day for Petrie to offer Jon a drink, though Iehard had the strange feeling that Petrie rather wished he could, and thus have had one for himself. Perhaps the commander hadn't slept at all well.
"Well, Jon, I won't waste time, we have to hurry as it is. We live in a big system, don't we? So all our problems are pretty big, aren't they?"
Trouble, Jon thought.
"This involves laowon, Jon. It's a dreadful case." Petrie had an electronic wand out and a picture popped up on a TV screen nestled among yellow orchids.
Head and shoulders shot, an old man, face dominated by a large, slightly bent nose; broken and improperly repaired. The eyes were blue and bored into the camera. The gray hair was tied up in a knot at the back of the head. A single earring of red enamel stood out on the heavy tan of someone who had been to hot stars.
"An Elchite?" Iehard voiced a certain amount of wonder. "There aren't any Elchites within a hundred lightyears of here. Not on this side of the Hyades anyway. They're anticorporate."
"He's a fugitive, on the run from laowon justice."
There it was, filthy laowon work.
"What did he do?"
"They say he planted a bomb on a private space habitat, in laowon space, and among those killed were twenty excellencies, including nine Exalted of Blue Seygfan."
Jon sucked in his breath. "Grand Weengams and Twirsteds then?"
Petrie nodded.
"Then the cult is involved, for Bloodrite?"
"Not as yet, not at least as far as we can detect."
"But there is Superior Buro." Jon said it with certainty.
Petrie nodded. Of course there was. Laowon Superior Buro penetrated all known space.
"Noble blood, the most exalted. They must want this old man very badly. Where exactly did it happen?"
"There are quite a few mysteries about this case. All we have is what I told you."

"That's not much to go on." Jon waved his hands.

"I know. I'm sorry, Jon, Superior Buro have a lock on the data. We're not to ask too many questions, it seems. They're very sensitive right now. I don't need to tell you that on the laowon levels they are howling with rage over this. The man is to go to Lao itself and expiate on the chair before the Grand Court. Can you imagine? So we must move quickly but we must move carefully, diplomatically. The last thing they want is a big full-bore investigation. They don't trust the police department whatsoever. That nest of leakers is a very last resort. If this hits the media . . ."

"How long has the man been here?"

"We believe just a few days."

"A few days is enough time for someone to go far. This is a big system."

"We do not think he has even left Hyperion Grandee yet. He was only tracked here by the merest chance. I am assured that the man cannot know he has been followed."

Jon's visions of combing the eight hundred–odd megahabitats, gigahabitats, asteroids, and moons for that face faded. "I suppose that's something."

"Of course, it goes without saying the man is extremely dangerous. However, this is a job calling on your extraordinary tracking skills, rather than your normal, aah, line of work. No gunplay is expected of you. At least that's my fervent hope. But you're the best psi senser we have, Jon. So it has to be you. There was a specific request from the laowon ambassador. You'll be given all the personnel and equipment. I will see to it personally that you have the fullest cooperation of my staff. Any nonsense about your origins and I'll—"

"What's his name?"

Commander Petrie swallowed. There was a short, uncomfortable silence. "Eblis Bey, an Elchite of the Red Crescent. Has been involved in Elchite outrages before this. Extreme Panhumanist, charged in the murder of laowons on at least one other occasion. He's regarded as so dangerous that you are not to make personal contact with him. No communication is permitted, the laowon have stressed this to me several times."

A chime sounded. The elevator was coming up again.

"That will be their excellencies. They wanted to see you in person to impress upon you the importance of the task."

Laowon here? Outside the laowon level, maintained for them free of charge by the Hyperion Grandee taxpayer?

They were anxious indeed.

The doors slid apart to reveal three laowon led by a full Urall in gold and blue. They wore dark glasses, and only removed them when Petrie dimmed the light. Jon's eyes widened at their magnificence.

"His Excellency, Gold and Blue of Chashleesh," Petrie said, bowing low from the waist as dictated in the diplomatic protocols.

Iehard bowed. He felt the compulsion to do so from long ago. These were mighty excellencies, full Weengams of the Blood. The blue-skin superior race were among them! His heart wanted to sing, his feet to dance. He had to fight the disgusting doglike joy in himself.

The Urall was a distinguished-looking specimen, in fighting trim, wide-faced with tawny gold eyes. He wore a black and gold uniform. "Roaring Clusters" glittered on his chest. His skin was a dark mauve.

"The Lady Blasilab of Chashleesh" was a haughty female relative of the Urall, slightly taller than Iehard and with a cadaverously thin face and large teeth. A much paler blue, she wore a green gown, of the high neck, long-sleeve fashion still common in military families on the frontier. Behind her ears she wore triplets of purple spines. She feigned indifference but Jon sensed an intense inspection from under heavy-lidded eyes.

"His Excellency, the Morgooze of Blue Seygfan." Petrie indicated the third laowon, a young male sitll with the heavy uncut mane of adolescence. His chest bristled with family emblems. He wore a dark-blue tunic and met Jon's eyes with a flat, level stare.

Jon tried not to let the shock show on his face. This was the Morgooze of Blue Seygfan itself! Only the hereditary Urall could stand higher.

He knew that each laowon would have noticed the faint scars on his forehead that marked the site of the old brand.

Before anyone had sat down, the Lady Blasilab turned to Petrie and started speaking to him as if she were addressing a gardener or a house servant. "Petrie, have you briefed the operative?"

The commander flushed, forced a smile, and showed the Grand Urall to a seat.

"Yes, Lady Blasilab, he has been briefed. There is not much to tell him in fact. Superior Buro, you see." Petrie was ingratiating, humble. Still, Iehard sensed laowon discomfort. Petrie had been too assertive. They-who-were-innately-glorious might have been offended by human clumsiness. What if the blue ones would leave as a result? Taking away the radiance of their presence! Heaven forfend!

"Damned Superior Buro!" exploded the young male in the lao hunting tongue. "I told you they'd be tampering. There was a clear edict from the court. If they've curtailed information on this case I will lodge a formal complaint. We are to be the primary contact."

The Urall waved a hand, almost indulgently. Iehard heard the overtones, read the intricate pattern of facial expressions that accompanied the words. "Blue Seygfan does not fly alone in its concern in this case. But no Seygfan should raise formal complaints before a proper examination of the details. Otherwise Blue Seygfan will eventually fly alone."

Was inter-Seygfan conflict brewing? Iehard knew that whole planetary systems had been burnt out before by warring fleets dedicated to different Seygfan.

Petrie's knowledge of the face tongue was limited. He had only the formal tongue, the language of the lao court's paper correspondence. However, the Urall had noted that Jon understood their words.

He looked up and spoke to Iehard, in interlingua with remarkable little accent, a sure sign that the Urall had served a long time in human systems. "We have learned that you were born on a lao-ruled world. Why did you choose to leave?"

Iehard knew that deceit would be detectable. "I wanted to be free."

The Urall nodded. "I understand. I would feel the same if our situations were reversed. So you are a man of your race, but now you must cooperate with us. A terrible wrong must be righted. This fugitive, do you think he can be found?" The Urall's great eyes had tightened.

"This evil creature has escaped before!" the Lady Blasilab broke in. The Urall was visibly annoyed at the interruption. Jon, however, had counted the seven marks of lineage Blasilab wore on her taut bosom. In bloodlines she outranked even the young Morgooze. Thus the Urall bit off his remonstrances and continued to eye Jon while she ranted on.

"Once, we had him cornered. But he performed an amazing feat. He escaped our net and we still do not know how he got away. So we must be very certain this time. We must track him very, very carefully. He must suspect nothing. That is why we demanded you. We cannot afford to have dozens of humans blundering about, only the very best."

She stabbed a long, slightly blue finger at him to emphasize her words. Iehard fought the compulsion that made him see sexual attractiveness in her. He found his throat uncomfortably tight as he replied in a quiet voice.

"It is of course very unusual for an Elchite to be found in this sector of the human hegemony." His quietness forced them to concentrate. Laowons often failed really to listen to what humans said. Lady Blasilab, however, interrupted harshly.

"What is this hegemony? You refer to the designated region. Hegemony is a word that is inappropriate to human tongues."

Jon stared into the wrath of the blue-skinned goddess and refused to tremble. He'd been free too long for that.

The Urall chided her lightly in a Tollicki dialect of the hunting tongue. Iehard understood only snatches but the recriminating tone was plain. Then he continued smoothly to Jon.

"This man has traveled a very long way, it is true."

"Just ensure that he is taken this time!" said Blasilab sharply.

Petrie broke in with diplomatic smoothness to describe Iehard in flattering terms.

The young Morgooze laughed suddenly, interrupting. "I know this man. He kills for the Mass Murder Squad, am I correct?"

"Yes," Iehard said in a whisper.

The Urall's eyes widened. "Not in my brief. I will have to speak to my advisers. An odd omission for them."

"But you won't kill the Elchite, will you?" The young Morgooze's eyes were hard and bright. "You see, I must take him to the chair myself and there make him expiate before the cameras. In the name of Blue Seygfan, I demand this!"

As he uttered those words the young lord seemed to expand, to fill the space and speak for all justice, everywhere. His voice resonated in a way that made Jon's eyes blink.

On the psi plane, however, he could detect Lady Blasilab's rage and the Urall's unease. There was a silence in the room.

Iehard took a moment to speak. "I won't kill your Elchite. I only insist on one thing. That when I start the case I work alone, or only with those with whom I choose to work. Later, when I find him, you can come in, but until then I want no interference."

They-who-were-innately-glorious raised their eyebrows in an almost human expression of surprise. But Jon read the nuances of reproach, disgust, anger wisely withheld.

In the end, though, they agreed, most reluctantly, but they admitted that they had no real choice. Lady Blasilab tried to activate the submission/agreement conditioning that she suspected the willful human must have received in his youth. She used the coded allure of her eyes and lips, smiling, stretching, promising. Iehard ignored it all. The Urall even chided her again, which roused her wrath considerably at being thus exposed before a human—he read the face tongue, that was plain.

And for his part Jon knew that no one in the meeting could speak for the Superior Buro anyway. Buro agents would be on his trail. He knew what to expect.

And if he found the fugitive for them? Then an old man would be taken by the laowon and flown at enormous expense at FTL speed all the way to Lao itself and there made to scream and writhe before a crowd of thousands and a battery of cameras under hot bright lights.

A few minutes later the laowon left. Iehard was free to start his search.

CHAPTER FOUR

FROM A PARK BENCH, HE CALLED COPTOR BRINE AND gave him the news. He would be freelancing for the Military Intelligence people until further notice, top priority.

Coptor agreed sourly to what was an unpleasant reduction in his limited force. But if Commander Petrie demanded it, there was no point in raising objections. "Take yourself good care, young Iehard. I want you back."

Then Jon rode the transit tube to Octagon Seven, where Meg Vance had her computer studio. Old Meg Vance was the only person he'd met who truly didn't care about his laobreed origins.

Octagon Seven was the center of the fashion industry. The station exited at the bottom of a wide shaft of reflecting glass walls. On the walls flowed gigantic projected images, models, clothes, faces, colors. Everything shifted constantly and changed frame. Seven was the frantic heart of Hyperion Grandee's nonstop social life.

The crowds on the ramps and on the prime level were heavy. It was a bluecard hour, the card cops were out in force. All bearers of red and green cards had to stay out of the octagon until the hour changed. Since it was just a few days before the Seasonal Festival that would inaugurate the annual thirty-one days of Winter Month, everyone was out shopping for something to wear to the huge corporate parties and the Masque balls that would pound on for days during the ThanksaKrismas weekend.

That's when the habitat mirrors would be tilted to the "winter position," which allowed a fraction less light. The interior would cool about fifteen to twenty degrees and a carefully orchestrated recreation of a terrestrial winter would take place. Right down to the annual snowfall, for an hour or two. It was a mark of Corporate Style, something that Hyperion Grandee and other major corporate megahabs clung to in the face of the slow, remorseless economic decline.

When two card cops in their distinctive brown uniforms demanded his bluecard, he flashed them his squad card instead. Their eyes bulged a little, but one was angry, thinking it a hoax, and wanted to check it in the nearest function box; but the other dissuaded him with urgent gestures and handed the plastic back to Jon. They moved away quickly with anxious glances back over their shoulders. No cop wanted to be involved in *that* kind of business!

He turned off onto a small service ramp and went through a beatup floppy door to a delivery corridor. The glamour soon faded back on the workshop floors. The hideous yellow wall panels were cracked and seamed. There was even some loose garbage, packaging materials and stuff, left in the corners. It could almost have been Main Street in some impoverished gigahab.

But this was just low-rent space with few amenities. Noncorporate workers, who always struggled to survive on Hyperion Grandee, clung on in competitive niches like freelance computer services. This was where Meg Vance lived and worked.

In fact Meg did well enough on the freelance money she earned from the Mass Murder Squad, working as computer backup for Iehard, that she could have had an office on a much nicer level, even with windows. But Meg was too careful with money, and too cantankerous a tenant, ever to move upscale.

In effect, outside the squad, she was Iehard's only true friend. With other people, his laoman identity had always somehow intruded even though his brands were gone. People just hated the laowon so. He remembered a girl who'd been ready to match genes with him once, then she asked him about the triangular notch in his ear. When he told her she went cold. Days later she ended the affair.

He thought sometimes that without old Meg, he would have spaced himself, just gone down to the docking bays and committed a Section Nine crime: "The felonious removal of a human body from the Hyperion Grandee biosphere without approval of the Funerals Board and its Biosphere Fluids Management Committee."

She had always managed to be there when he needed her. It was a debt they were both conscious of but never alluded to. In some ways, he thought, Meg treated him like the son she had never been able to afford. Of course she always laughed their friendship off, said that since she'd come up from the Unders of Nostramedes herself, she never felt right about putting on airs with people from anyplace else.

It wasn't until he fulfilled a contract job on Nostramedes one time that he discovered just how bitter a joke that was.

He turned left onto Corridor 117, which was flanked by dozens of doors, their yellow panels dirty and worn. He reached No. 99 and bopped an entry code into the door computer. It winked its little red light at him as it took his video trace and then the door slid open with a slight squeal of protest.

In the narrow hallway tottered stacks of data modules a meter high. Each was neatly identified by colored tags. White tags were subscription-journal data, to be picked through for selections. Red tags were Mass Murder Squad cases, a whole section was devoted to them. A much larger section, marked with purple, contained Meg's Masque records.

Meg Vance meant nothing to the megahab-oriented social world of corporate Hyperion Grandee. She survived on freelance work. She was also that rarity, an immigrant to Hyperion Grandee from an older gigahab.

But in the world of Masque, the complex computer games in which everyone on Hyperion Grandee indulged, Meg Vance was of the aristocracy. She maintained seventy-three advanced characters in twelve separate games, including a queen in the top game, "Hidden Notebook."

In the main space there was an awful lot of equipment, much of it old. The DAex Ram 44000 that was Meg's primary unit took up only a little room, but its peripheral devices were everywhere. Alongside them were smaller devices that hooked into the DAex Ram's main rival in

Meg's universe, the Bioram Sha3. That device, a flat tank like a tabletop containing forty pounds of human brain cells, grown in thin sheets and laid down in programmable jelly, was actually hidden from view inside a network of support systems that took up a full third of the space.

Meg herself was on the phone, no surprise there. He recognized her friend Ingrid's face on the phoneplate. Meg had her silver-gray hair tied up in an untidy bun, she wore a gray zipsuit and red plastic shoes. She sat on a chair riding an extensor bar, surrounded by five floating flat-screens, with a keyboard array poised to hand. Two other extensor seats hung in the computer pit because on some games—a two-screen combat unit in the Phototronic Gladiation League, for instance—Meg was joined by her friends Ingrid and Sindar.

He went over to the single monitor on a small desk in the corner of the room to review the contents of the mail stop he maintained there. A brochure on datachip gave him a full-color "introductory offer" to an auction of the famous Ugun Huxha ranch on luxury megahabitat Gloaming Splendor. For a mere 250,000 credit units down and 100,000 a year for twenty years he could bid on square-kilometer parcels of habitat forest and lawn.

He blipped the rest of it. His savings account held just 27,000 credit units after nine years' work in the squad. It was hard to get ahead when the price of existence on Hyperion Grandee was so high. Without a corporate rent plan he had to pay half his income for one of the endlessly similar apartments on Medium Rent that the squad found for him.

Of course he'd tried Low Rent, the illegal, sometimes dangerous world of apartments in parts of the habitat structure that were not built for human occupation. Once he'd had a long, narrow room, with a smoothly curved ceiling, situated on an engineering level in the hab-shield. It had been big enough to contain five apartments the size of his present one.

It had seemed a wonderful bargain for 600 credit units a month. He began to make plans for extensive interior decoration. Then Winter Month ended and the air-conditioning heat vent above the ceiling began to work. Through Spring it was like Summer Month, 80 degrees every day. In Summer it became an oven, more than 120 degrees on the day he gave in and moved out.

The rest of the mail was Masque-oriented junk, which he consigned to the wastebasket. Jon had never been more than a Masque viewer.

Meg finished her strategy call and emerged from the pit for an instacaf break. She gave him an affectionate peck.

"Well, I heard the story on Arnei Oh this morning. We were right about the university, just didn't think of the Orbiters. It sounded terrible. Do you feel terrible?" She wrinkled her little round nose at him.

"Today? No. Then? Yes. What else would you expect? He took a goddamn scalp in the bushes, that's what saved us. Otherwise I think he would have fragged the shit out of them and left us with thirty bodies or more."

"Coptor was good afterward." She gave him a cup.

"Coptor is always good. If only the rest of the operation was good as Coptor and you, maybe we'd have a chance."

She chucked him under the chin. "I thank you, wonderboy. What have you got for us next?"

Iehard finished the instacaf in a gulp. "You're going to hate this next case."

She grimaced. "Laowon work again, don't tell me it's that."

His eyebrows rose; Meg was right. She was always right. Sometimes it was uncanny.

"Big stuff. Someone has killed laowons. Lots of them, and there's a big hunt on. We are to track him."

"Why us? Why not Military Intelligence?"

"We are the psi-able. And this fugitive is really sensitive apparently. Look, Petrie himself called me in. I had to listen to three laowon treat him like some servant. They hectored me on the need for quick progress with minimal disturbance. The quarry is exceptionally aware of detection and surveillance. So normal MI procedures are out." He paused, became thoughtful.

"It's worth five thousand credit units apiece too."

"Blue-skin blood money. We're bounty hunters now."

"Yes, that about sums it up. But I don't think we have much choice. They can apply pressure to get what they want."

"What about Superior Buro?"

"Of course. They'll be around."

Old Meg shivered. "That sounds ominous."

"Look, the new Morgooze of Blue Seygfan, for this entire sector of space, was there this morning. He's young. I suspect he has only recently advanced to his full Morgooze. The target has killed excellencies, Grand Weengams and Twirsteds. The laowon are in a state of exalted rage."

"I'll bet they are," she said sourly.

"They'll try to get a bug in here again. You can count on it."

She looked around warily. "Right, I'll put Daisy onto that. Full search program, Daisy!" she called. The DAex Ram 44000 shifted to a program kept resident on a security data module. It began a detailed examination of the room and its contents. Sensor nubs stuck to the walls, floor, and ceiling searched for penetrations.

"Anyway, here's a picture of the target. I've asked for a full dump from MI databank, it should be along soon." Jon fed the datacard into a function box inside the computer pit.

A face blinked into view on the main graphics screen.

"An Elchite!" she exclaimed. "The Red Crescent group from that earring."

"Yes, very fiery group apparently."

"'Man-Must-Rise' and all that." She sipped her instacaf.

"The laowon are beside themselves."

"Serves them filthy right. When I think of all we have to put up with from them. They bleed our system. Every laowon vessel fuels its cavernous tanks with good, easy-access Nocanicus gas. And what do they pay for it? Almost nothing; amounts set by treaty centuries ago. Oh, I know what they say." She looked at him angrily. "We're on the flight schedules of the jumpers and we got some technical help, and we're even allowed a few exploratory missions to some of the least valuable nearby stars. But Nocanicus will run out of easy-access gas within another century at the rate the laowon are pouring in, and we'll be left to slowly wither away in isolation. I mean we don't even have any marginally habitable worlds to go savage on in this system. So we'll either die out or take NAFAL back toward the Hyades and who knows how many will survive the trip in deep freeze."

He shrugged. She was indubitably correct. "There's nothing we can do about it. We have to live by their rules."

"But Jon, Nocanicus was human settled, even before Testament!"

"Meg, we're on the frontier. The laowon could take this system anytime they wanted it. Testament's been dead for a thousand years." His reply sounded too sharp, even to his own ears. But this argument was an old one.

"But it's not forgotten!"

He fought the urge to shrug. This was Meg's dream; let her hang onto it. For quite a while, Jon realized, he'd been avoiding the fact that he had lost his own.

He was just living day by day, had been for years. Sure he saved, but it was pointless. Costs ate everything up when you were just on salary. But saving was only part of it. There was no future, nothing that Jon could feel enthusiastic about. Nothing he wanted to make plans for. No woman who would complete his life.

She saw his mind was drifting. "Jon Iehard!" Her eyes were like green gimlets. "Are you giving up?"

He managed a grin. "No, Meg, we'll never let them rule us. We'll never let them have that victory."

But Iehard knew of the studies predicting that within a decade the population of humans who served the laowon on laowon worlds would likely outgrow the population of humans in human systems.

The High Corporate systems, like Nocanicus, without habitable planets, were just a small lake in these oceans of humanity. Free human expansion had ceased. They were becoming a client race. Human science had stalled. Human-laowon scientific cooperation had been one of the first things the Laowon Imperiom had demanded right after the signing of the treaties. The best human scientists were constantly siphoned off to work on laowon projects.

Time was running out for the human race. Had been since the Testamenters first brushed up against the laowon, far away in the Orion galactic arm.

That meeting had been exactly what Earth had feared, from the moment the headstrong Testamenters succeeded in perfecting their Faster Than Light drives.

For a thousand years humanity had been spreading across the starfields within the realm of the supergiant Canopus. Within the hundred-light-year sphere were hundreds of human colonies. From red dwarf systems with marginal planets, to yellow stars with earthlike worlds. Beyond this sphere were sprinkled High Corporate systems, established on the twin pillars of fast NAFAL colonization and the deep-voice communication system that could plug through the distances between the stars.

In the Hyades stars, the corporations had risen far. They had pushed out to systems like Nocanicus and Testament.

Then the Testamenters had developed their fleet of Faster Than Light ships and gone out to explore the Galaxy. They'd ignored the pleas for caution from older systems.

And then, far away, on a distant star reef, the Testamenters met the laowon.

The shock was something humanity had never recovered from. It was as if Columbus had sailed the Atlantic in 1492 and discovered the United States of 1992 rather than the continent of Amerindians, buffalo, and grizzlies.

The surprise went both ways, however. And the Testamenter ships represented a tremendous breakthrough into a technology that the laowons had never stumbled on. When a misunderstanding escalated into hostilities and the Testamenters destroyed a laowon battlejumper, a spasm of terror shook the entire edifice of the Lao Imperiom, an interstellar social organization that had persisted for nearly twelve thousand years.

The Imperiom reacted with tremendous energy. A full sector fleet, seventy battlejumpers, hunted down the Testamenters and destroyed them in the Testament system itself. Two months later the Imperial Fleet entered the human home system itself and dictated the first laowon-human treaty.

Legend had it that the first humans to enter laowon service left with those same lao battlejumpers. In fact, the laowon found it relatively easy to buy human genetic material, even to buy live humans, who would happily sell themselves to escape the drab life on the Greenhouse Earth of the fourth millennium A.D.

Pretty soon humans became as common a part of laowon life as the laa and pesski, the pets that the blue-skinned lords of the stars had brought with them from their homeworld.

Meg had been reading his thoughts.

"If only the laowon had been horribly ugly. Or reptiles, or anything but so similar to ourselves," she said in a mournful voice.

"Why do you say that? Wouldn't it be worse to service monsters?"

"Silly man, no, they wouldn't have thought us attractive to have around if we were really different. As it is we're physically smaller, neater, and sexier than they are. So they love having us as slaves. If it were the other way around and we had the upper hand, we would never have mixed with them. Would you willingly fill your home up with the big ugly brutes?"

He chuckled. It was true as well that the fashionable look in the Imperiom involved having one's ears trimmed to human size and shape. It was regarded as a point of beauty now, to have gracile ears like the subordinate race.

With a bleep and a red flash, Daisy reported no traceable bugs within the computer room.

"Where to begin?" Meg asked.

"I guess we need to get the MI file dump. Then let's look up the files on Elchites."

"Into the computer pit then," she ordered. He took a seat and dialed up Military Intelligence.

■ CHAPTER FIVE

IN AN AERIE ON THE LAOWON LEVEL, HIGH ABOVE Octagon Six, Commander Petrie attended a most unusual meeting. Despite the fact that he commanded the major security organs of Hyperion Grandee, Petrie had never had contact with the uppermost laowon security controller, a remote personage, beyond diplomacy, not even officially recognized as being aboard the habitat.

Now Padzn Birthamb, Superior Buro chief for Nocanicus system, sat in the twilit shade opposite him. Although the floor was above the surrounding towers, the windows were polarized and the only light came from projectors in the ceiling. Therefore the suite was lit as if it were sunset on ancient Lao.

Padzn Birthamb had a harsh, angular face, even for a laowon. So harsh were his features that he was instantly, recognizably alien. His skin was a dusky blue and he spoke with a strange thick accent that told of an upbringing on a world on the far side of the vast Imperiom.

He wore a plain uniform of black cloth, adorned with a single star, a diamond, on his breast.

Also present was the Urall Gold and Blue.

"So, Commander Petrie, you now understand that this case has political dimensions beyond the immediate surface. That Blue Seygfan itself might collapse in civil conflict. There are certain aspects that must be kept suppressed. Superior Buro has received orders to impact the case."

It was hard to follow Birthamb's strange accent, but after so many years, Petrie had to struggle to suppress a weird sense of elation at actually being privileged to meet his opponent. For so long Padzn Birthamb had been a shadow, a menace without substance.

"In addition there are the military aspects. It is enough for you to know that among the dead on the pleasure habitat was Space Admiral Gufk, commander of the Pleides sector fleet."

Before Petrie could reply, the Urall interrupted.

"The Morgooze of Blue Seygfan carries letters with the Imperial seal. That must take precedence. His initiative is to be the primary one."

"My Urall, there are aspects of this case that are of such extreme importance—" Birthamb began.

But the Gold and Blue cut him off. "Nothing can override the Imperial seal." The Urall knew he faced insuperable odds. Lao was far away, and there were layers of bureaucracy to work through to reach the one who signed those letters for the Morgooze. Nor was the Urall entirely comfortable in his role.

"My Urall, there are perhaps more layers to this than even you are aware of. I have the latest information."

Something in his tone convinced the Urall to proceed cautiously. "What are the conditions you spoke of?"

"There will be a lock of all data connected to the case. Superior Buro will be ultimate arbiter of what information can be released."

"That is tantamount to taking the case away from us!" exclaimed the Urall hotly.

Padzn Birthamb shrugged in the hunter's tongue. His eyebrows rose slightly. "Whatever it means, that is what I must demand. Your pursuit can continue but it is to be a mock-pursuit. The Buro will handle this case."

"Then Blue Seygfan begins to fly alone." The Urall sounded depressed.

"My Urall, this case has implications that go beyond inter-Seygfan conflict."

Petrie was hearing things he didn't want to hear. The death of a lao prince who commanded sixty vessels of war, a fleet with enough power to shatter whole worlds.

The Superior Buro taking control of human information banks, overriding human authority.

"What will I tell the young Morgooze? The fire is hot in him!" the Urall implored.

"Tell him nothing! Let the case continue. The operatives will conduct a search, but their access to data will be severely restricted. Should they come close to anything, we will know about it in time to take action. I doubt they will get very close. In the meantime the Buro has gone on full alert. This operation will receive our undivided attention."

"It will not be easy to keep the Morgooze quiescent. I warn you, Birthamb, you will have to deal with him yourself." The laowon fell silent.

Petrie spoke up. "How is the Superior Buro planning to lock all relevant data away from the operatives?"

A brief silence was broken by Birthamb. "Superior Buro has activated a data control program on all major databanks. No outside access to certain files will be allowed without Buro approval."

"You can do that? Execute such a concept?"

Birthamb did not answer. Petrie flushed angrily but held his tongue.

The Urall changed the subject. "Commander, the man we met today, Operative Iehard is his name. Is he completely reliable? In light of the fact that this case is so gravely important I must ask you this."

"He handles only the toughest assignments for the Mass Murder Squad, a very valued operative. His psi ability is high, especially on the hysterical frequencies. He can sense his targets quite well."

"But there is another aspect. His colleague, a freelance computer operative; she presents problems, doesn't she?"

Petrie shrugged. "Panhumanism is a very human emotion, I'm afraid. We have to live with it."

"This case may not allow for it. Tell Iehard to restrain his colleague."

Padzn Birthamb did not include an "or else" but Petrie was sure it was there.

Not long after that the meeting broke up and with considerable relief, Petrie rode the elevator down, out of the dimly lit laowon level.

* * *

In the computer studio under Octagon Seven the argument had a familiar ring to it.

"No, Jon, you're wrong. There were six Testamenter ships, not five. It was the laowon who opened fire first and the Testamenters then destroyed a third of the sector fleet before they were scattered. They were hunted down one by one after that." Meg threw up her hands at the stubborn look on his face.

"Nevertheless, all their ships were destroyed."

"Not true, not if you believe in the old song."

"Myths, just like the Man-Must-Rise stuff."

"Jon, why do you dismiss it so easily? Just because it's human folklore, it can't have any truth in it?"

"Look, that stuff with Testamenter rhymes in it is great for morale on the gigahabs. I know, you had to really fight to break out of your gigahab heritage; you just can't see history in an impartial light."

"Testamenter stock!" she said sharply. "My parent came from the watermoons of William. He got into a mess in the inner system and could never get back. You know that, Jon, I'm not just gigahab trash."

"All right, I'm sorry." He raised his hands. "You're a Testamenter, Meg, but all the proofs concerning Testament were destroyed fourteen centuries ago."

"There were survivors. They came to the watermoons of William after a long NAFAL voyage. That's one reason why the Williams don't fuel laowon ships."

"In the depths of the ocean where all hope sank . . ." he began half mockingly.

"We laid him down." She finished with a face full of determination. She went on in a hard tight voice.

> Where the gravity's no feather and the light will
>   never reach,
> We laid him down,
> On the breast of the ocean that has no farther beach,
> We laid him down.

She finished the verse and caught his eye.

"Of course it's better when Tier Merier sings it, but you better realize that we Testamenters never give up. I'll convert you yet, once we can break down all that laowon conditioning they gave you."

He smiled, though once that crack about his conditioning would have raised his hackles. Iehard had come a long way in the nine years he'd lived aboard Hyperion Grandee. A long way up, and a long way down.

"All right, Meg, I give in. There is a lost Testamenter ship and we may even find it someday. I bet the laowon find it first though."

"The *Winston Churchill* is out there somewhere, Jon. Perhaps in one of the nearby red-dwarf systems."

"After Testament fell, the laowon scoured all those systems."

"Well, perhaps they went farther away."

"Perhaps they did."

A chime from the DAex Ram 44000 intruded.

"At last, the MI dump." But Jon's eager eyes found only disappointment on the screen.

"Requested files are classified. No access allowed," read Meg.

"Incredible, they won't give us any information."

"Except a photo and the basic ID."

"How are we expected to find anyone without a little background?"

"I'll talk to Petrie."

Jon headed for Petrie's office, not wanting to risk a phone call with the Superior Buro interested in the case.

This time they made him wait. Almost an hour had gone by before he was let out of the anteroom into Petrie's office. The commander had hurriedly donned the psi deflector, it hadn't settled quite evenly around his head.

"Jon, hellishly busy day. Must say I didn't expect to see you again quite so soon. You have news?"

"We've been told we can't get access to information about the suspect and the crime he's committed. How are we supposed to trace him if we don't have any information about him?"

Petrie sighed. This case was becoming more difficult by the hour. He'd just decoded a message on the Deep Access from the Hyades Exploitation Corporation Military Intelligence. The message was already incinerated but the words of warning still burned in his thoughts.

"Jon, there are certain military and political aspects of this case that I'm afraid must remain a secret. Superior Buro is involved. I've been told that if you need any further data you're to submit questions to my office and we'll check them with the Superior Buro and get back to you."

Jon couldn't keep the shock out of his voice. "You mean we can't even access our own databanks here on Grandee? The Superior Buro has control over our own files?"

Petrie pressed his palms together. This could be difficult. He would have to try and explain just a little. "You can't imagine how seriously the laowon are taking this case, Jon." Petrie thought of that message again. His voice took on a conspiratorial tone.

"There has even been a call from the leadership of the cult on Lao for the immediate investiture of Nocanicus by the sector fleet. The whole system to be turned over until they find this man." Petrie shrugged, smiled. "Of course, that is the normal tone that we hear from the cult. They are just as fanatical as our Panhumanists and are allied to some very odd groups on the fringes of the court. Fortunately the Imperial Family favors the Mathematica over the cult and is allied with the Military High Command on this. For which all humans can give grateful thanks, eh?" He gave Jon a bleak smile.

"However, there's a dangerous edge to this situation. The murders have opened Blue Seygfan to possible civil war. As you know, Blue Seygfan is responsible for the entire exploratory thrust by the Imperiom into the Local Star Drift, which of course is considerably larger than the human sphere of exploration. Our sphere lies entirely within the Drift and so our fate is intimately bound up with the success or failure of Blue Seygfan. If Blue Seygfan was to weaken, Red Seygfan would be sure to attack its enemies within Blue. We could have a full-blown interstellar war, all over the Local Drift and right through human space."

And after that . . .

Petrie was nodding. "You see the point, don't you? The extremists in the cult would like nothing more than a civil war and dissolution of Blue Seygfan's control. With sufficient disorder in this sector, the cult could move to establish cult authority, force the Imperial Family's hand, and bring to an end human independence."

"They would do that?"

"If the extremists get their way, that would be but the beginning."

"How shall we find the Elchite without access to information about him and about Elchites in general? This is not a subject with extensive files here in Nocanicus."

"I will press the Superior Buro for some information. More than that I cannot promise you."

Iehard left Petrie's office with a degree of consternation in his heart.

Back at Meg's, he found both computers humming through complex search programs as Meg drove them to find whatever scraps of data the Superior Buro had overlooked.

The big Bioram had completed a full analysis of the photo of Eblis Bey, the Elchite. When Jon read the section on skin and retinal pigments he gave a whoop. "Terrestrial! What are we dealing with here?"

"An Earthman, Jon, just think of that."

"Never met one before, have you?"

"Of course not. This fellow *has* traveled far."

"A terrestrial Elchite, on this side of the Hyades. The skin tones show he has spent time under some pretty hot stars too planetside without much radiation shielding."

Daisy, the DAex Ram, chimed.

"Daisy's been checking the police department's main computer, the entry and exit files."

"If our man came in legally he must be well disguised, otherwise the Superior Buro would already have him."

"You never know what you might turn up. Let's look." Meg gave a little whoop of excitement.

Daisy was piggybacking on another computer search, which was riffling through the files, searching for that same Elchite and some other people.

"Quick, Daisy, dump those images for us." The DAex Ram copied the requested pictures from one screen window while others showed a search through Hyperion Grandee's hotels.

"It's a search from outside Grandee," said Meg suddenly. "In fact, I can tell by those communication codes. See the X designations throughout the openers? That means this is a coded ship-to-ship transmission."

"Which means the *Illustrious*."

"Of course."

Jon felt a twinge of unease. The laowon battlejumper was nearby, crammed with weaponry and Superior Buro shock troops.

Daisy exited the other computer's search program as she detected the first brush of a laowon security program seeking interlopers.

"Close," Iehard said.

"Not really, Daisy's too fast, especially with my alarm code."

Jon shook his head. Meg's confidence in her computers would get her in trouble one day.

"What did we get then?" The DAex Ram put the captured images on screen. They were fuzzy, a pair of pictures of Eblis Bey. Police mug shots from long ago, without earring and long hair. The others were even less well defined, a pair of very pale blond people, male and female, wearing spacer bodysuits with small survival packs on the chest.

Daisy was enhancing the images.

"Who might these people be?" Jon wondered as a very striking female face enlarged on the screen. She had eyes that were peculiarly black in a face that was very pale indeed.

"Deep spacers. Never been out of their ship by the look of that skin, whole lives spent under superior shielding."

The man had a long, straight nose and calm eyes with that same darkness in them. His cheekbones weren't quite as prominent as the female's, however.

"If the *Illustrious* is after these people, they must be connected to our Elchite."

"There's a ship involved!" Meg exclaimed with sudden conviction.

Iehard nodded slowly. "Let's put Daisy onto a search for ships."

"I doubt if we'll find them that easily."

"Nevertheless, it might turn up something. This case gives me bad feelings, Meg. It's like we're going into a dark room and someone's waiting for us in there. You can't touch the sides of the walls when you put your hands out, there's nothing visible in front."

Meg had a grim expression as she switched up some files from another search that Daisy had executed.

"This is from the Jumbo at Nocanicus University library. Look at this stuff and tell me we aren't ruled by the aliens."

The first file up on the screen was headed

ELCHITES: HUMAN RELIGIOPOLITICAL GROUP ASSOCIATED WITH THE STAR TRADERS OF ALDEBARAN SECTOR (232 SYSTEMS WITHIN 30 LIGHT-YEARS OF ALDEBARAN.)
ORIGIN: TEMPORARILY DELETED.
MYTHS: TEMPORARILY DELTED.
RELIGIOUS PRACTICES: TEMPORARILY DELETED.
POLITICAL IMPORT: TEMPORARILY DELETED.

The others were all the same; all had been deleted after the initial descriptive entry.

"They're not subtle," Meg said, "but they are thorough. The same story from both university libraries and seven corporate libraries to which I have current subscriptions. Everything about the Elchites is suddenly unavailable."

"To us but not to the *Illustrious*, I'll bet."

"Jon, what's going on? Why is this case in our laps? Why aren't they handling it themselves? Are we stalking horses for them? Or bait?"

He rubbed his chin. "I don't know, Meg, but we need more information than we've got so far."

A dangerous light had come on in Meg's green eyes. "Maybe we'll have to go after the information in their databanks."

"Laowon data?"

"Right."

"I don't know, Meg, this is weird enough already. Who wants to be caught poking around in classified files?"

"I am not going to let them cut me off from the information we need."

A few moments later Meg's big Bioram was running an unusual piece of software. In the pit, with the progress of the program constantly refreshed in visual images on the main screen, Meg explained it to Jon.

"We know that all laowon ships use the same *X* designations for opening ship-to-ship communications. I just let Sha3 work through all the laowon codes we've accumulated from years of snooping and then we try out the most likely combinations for this time period. Laowon security codes change about every two hours, throughout the system. We think they're beamed in on deep access from the sector fleet high system. Anyway, we've monitored a lot of them over the years and we've been able to predict some of the changes in code as they occurred. You know, laowon are good at complicated things but they're curiously blind to some simpler things. I guess they never thought a mere human would work that hard on their codes." She chuckled, then pointed to the screen. "Anyway looks like Sha3 got through already."

On screen Sha3's emissary probe, represented as a pink worm, was knocking on Superior Buro menus that guarded the big laowon computer memory aboard *Illustrious*.

Sha3 emitted a burst of security code. The first menu wavered, they received an option, and with a keystroke Meg pushed the probe forward into the laowon databank.

"Don't want to stay in here too long, Sha," Meg muttered.

On screen the pink worm danced and split into a number of threads lacing together windows with files on search. Meg started to tap into them and transfer their contents to the Bioram's own storage devices.

A grid formed on the screen suddenly.

"Uh-oh, security program. Quick, Sha, hit the ten zero five evasion mode."

The pink worms writhed through a forest of gray tines that sought to pin them down.

"This is just low level, automatic house-cleaning by the laowon computer."

The first files were being dumped into the Bioram's storage system as Meg drummed her fingers on the keyboard. "Come on, Sha, we can't hang around in here. Auditor program will be moving in soon. Let's go."

Then a thick red line appeared on the screen. A flashing grid of numbers followed and beat Meg's fingers to the disconnect button.

The screen went crazy.

"Oh, no, disruptor program. They've got Sha!"

"What do you mean?"

But already Sha3 was doomed. Its peripheral devices

flickered on- and off-line like strobe lights. On screen a mishmash of image junk flashed as the disruptor program reproduced itself inside Sha3's memory cells until they were completely occupied and the Bioram's complex programming collapsed. In thirty seconds Meg lost six years of careful programming.

She looked up from a quick search of the Bioram's support computers, which monitored its health. "Sha's gone. Whole personality, everything down the tubes."

Jon realized that Meg was ruined in more ways than one. Sha3 was an indispensable part of her Masque characters. With only the DAex Ram 44000 to work with Meg couldn't possibly keep seventy-three characters going night after night.

"Oh, shit! I'm sorry, Meg, I—"

"Damn that Superior Buro," she said ruefully. "They don't mess around now, do they?" Her eyes had a stare of iron to them, they seemed to strike sparks inside him.

He got up and made some instacaf while Meg called a Bioram hospital and booked Sha3 in for a complete restructuring.

Later they went out for a meal. Over dessert Meg had a brainstorm. "I have an idea. It might just turn up something. It's an angle I don't think they can have covered."

"What is that?"

"We'll go talk to my old friend the historian, Clawenton Ravenish. If anyone will know about Elchites in this system, it'll be old Clawenton."

CHAPTER SIX

CLAWENTON RAVENISH WAS ONLY TO BE FOUND IN THE History Institute at Nocanicus University. Meg called and arranged a meeting, then set off with Jon.

First though they went to the Winecellars of Gran Pacifico where Meg carefully selected a bottle of red wine. "Good wine is the only thing old Clawenton lives for, except for his research, of course."

Jon stared at the label. It was nine years old; there were a dozen descriptives; he gulped at the cost.

Meg snorted. "Just charge it to Petrie's gang. If we can't get any information any other way then this is what they'll have to put up with."

After a moment he shrugged. If they got some information then perhaps it would be worth it. But that 10,000 credit units would only be paid if they found this man Eblis Bey. Explaining a bottle of #132 wine might only be practicable in the event of a successful hunt.

Meg paid for the wine, charging it to Jon and ending any further doubts he might entertain.

Nocanicus University was near Octagon Three, in a pair of tasteful towers called the "tuning fork" by disrespectful students, with a green quadrangle set between them.

The History Institute was tucked away behind a library section on the ground floor of the northern tower.

Once inside the unmarked door, Jon gaped in awe at

piles of paper books, many enclosed in plastic bags, that rose to the ceiling in great dusty stacks. They were everywhere, lining the rooms and visible corridors. More real books than Jon had ever seen before.

Clawenton Ravenish appeared out of the back, a wizened gnome of a man in a distinctly unfashionable, fussily cut suit in green gahash. Jon was sure that if he was correct in his surmise that Clawenton was at least one hundred and fifty years old, then the suit might be that old as well.

Clawenton's bald pate bobbed merrily as he recognized his visitor. "Darling Meg, my treasure from Testament. How are you, my dear? Still keeping Queen Alice going in the 'Hidden Notebook'?"

"Actually Queen Alice is having to move into rather new and confined quarters, since the laowon killed my baby Bioram."

Clawenton looked up. Jon thought he detected a surprise in the old man's expression. "Laowon, did you say?"

Meg explained briefly.

Clawenton nodded to himself at the end. "And so what you need is some information about the old Elchite sect." His brow furrowed momentarily. "Odd that you should ask me about them. Somebody else was interested in Elchites a few months back." He tapped his nose with a bony finger. "I can't remember who right now. But, well, it'll probably come to me."

Somewhat portentously he crossed his hands behind his back. "The Elchites, of course, are quite an extreme group. Panhumanists, and indeed I think one could say they were originally Human Supremacist. They used to be classified as one of the so-called ecstatic creeds in the Mingeer catalog. Arose from some blend of Islam, Christianity, and Judaic beliefs. Many authorities now fix the origin of the group right back in the early transsolar period."

He stopped and fixed Jon with a glare. It was like that of some rare, suspicious bird. "But why would the Superior Buro lock away the data?"

John shrugged. "It seems inexplicable on the face of it."

"Obviously there is something they do not want you to know about?"

"Well, Clawenton," said Meg, "that's why we came to you. We thought that perhaps with the historian's perspective you could tell us something."

Clawenton brightened a little. "Well, of course you're perfectly correct. Although the history of gas exploration and storage is my own specialty, I've always maintained a lively interest in the doings of the Panhumanist groups. There are some fascinating cults. Like the Pansperm Sympathoea, an extreme male-supremacist group who have been homosexual with reproductive cloning for forty generations or more. They are said to be radically altered from the human norm in patterns of thought. Their visual arts, for example, have progressed into new, quite bizarre experimentation in the religiosity of sexual depiction." Clawenton's eyes finally alighted on the package in Meg's hands.

"But what is this you carry?"

"For you, Clawenton. I hope you like it."

When he'd pulled off the wrappings his eyes popped quite spectacularly. "Domaine Larose!" he breathed. "Great heavens, a nine-year bottle. How wonderful!" He looked up again with renewed suspicion. "You must want to know an awful lot about the Elchites if you've brought me Domaine Larose."

Jon shrugged. "We have very little information. Whatever you can tell us will be an improvement on that."

"Well, let me think. Here, we'll put this wonderful wine away and I'll go and take a look in the back room."

A few minutes later Clawenton banged a data disc into his old video display.

"Now." His voice slipped back into the didactic mode of the professor. "The Elchite origins date back to the early era of competing nations in space. Several small nations fled to space quite early on. They brought strange, violent creeds with them, like the much-abominated Saudi male cultists."

"Oh, Clawenton! Must we bring such things up? That's just disgusting! Compulsory female circumcision, purdah, and harems! Why, they almost bred themselves into two distinct species, male and female."

"I'm sorry, my dear, but the history of our race is a tragic one, full of dreadful deeds and sad mistakes. One cannot ignore the innumerable crimes committed in the name of religious or ideological frenzy.

"Anyway, the Elchites represent a strange mixture of advanced and atavistic elements in their creeds. There are some very extreme male supremacist practices, for example, but there has also been the growth of the Elchite traders, who first became active about three centuries ago. Most recently a rash of outrages has been perpetrated against the laowon.

"Ah! Now I remember. A few months ago a questionnaire was sent out by the laowon military asking for information concerning the Elchites. It actually emanated from the *Illustrious* itself, I believe. But I didn't respond to it. I'm afraid I'm one of those who rather applauds the outrages committed by groups like the Elchites. The laowon are a greedy, brutal race. They use their advantages to crush us. I wish to resist." He probed Jon with a cold eye. "Does this shock you, young man?"

"No, not at all."

Clawenton looked to Meg. "I suspected as much when I saw you in the company of my lovely young Testamenter here." Clawenton winked at Meg, who smiled sweetly in return.

"Oddly enough, though, when the questionnaire came, I had just come into the possession of some interesting information concerning Elchites, right here on Hyperion Grandee."

"Oh, yes?" Jon said.

"I was researching the recent records of small- and medium-size gas and water companies in the belt. It was in connection with a government project. I found a reference to an Elchite trader, someone called Ulip Sehngrohn. He came here about thirty-five years ago, traded briefly in gases and water, then left Grandee."

"Do you know where he went?"

"That was the curious part. No boarding docket number existed in Hyperion Grandee records. So we don't even know where he came from. He certainly wasn't born here, however, and I became quite interested in the matter when I discovered that, so I researched it more thoroughly. Amongst other things I became convinced that there is an Elchite temple, all packed up in security crates, right here on Hyperion Grandee."

"Really?" breathed Iehard.

"I found that the Elchite trader took a long lease on a small commercial docking bay, on the high dorsal extender. No gravity, a prime launching place."

Jon and Meg exchanged a look. The Domaine Larose had paid for itself.

"Of course you have to wear a space suit up there, but I went out to check anyway." He paused for effect. "You know, that lease is still running and you can't get anywhere near the place. The accessway is secured with a steel gate. The locks are armor plated too. It's a Baltitude Security Company warehouse. They have a good reputation for security."

"Who is listed on the lease?"

"Interesting part that. Lease is held by a wholesale gas company with an address on Sooner."

"Sooner?"

"Small wanderer. Orbits way out past William and then shoots in all the way through the hot stuff."

"Asteroid?"

"Comet. The first settlers made a fortune—cheapest gas and water in the system for a few years. This is way back, in the earliest days of Nocanicus system. Before the laowon."

"That must have been an exciting find," Meg said.

"Well, I never found a departure code for Sehngrohn, but I doubt that he's still in the system. The Elchite traders mostly came from Aldebaran and they were real star hoppers, roving as far as the human hegemony runs. Of course, why he should maintain such secrecy concerning his movement is a matter that perhaps the Superior Buro knows more about than we do, eh?" He gave them a thoughtful glance.

"But I remain convinced that there's a chest full of genuine Elchite ceremonial vestments, objects, maybe even an altar of Earthstone! right here on Grandee. Just think what a sight it would make. Our Panhumanist exhibit in the university museum would finally look like something!"

"Yes, indeed," Jon murmured.

After absorbing as much information on Elchitism as they could, they copied some of Clawenton's disk onto a data module and left the ancient historian gleefully examining his bottle of ninth-year Domaine Larose, Cabernet Sauvignon, from the near-legendary agrihabitat Gloaming Splendor.

They chose to walk together through the park. The day was entering the evening hours. Jon could sense that Meg's mood had lifted considerably. "Because you outwitted them?" He hazarded an easy guess. She fairly skipped along like some gray-haired, fifty-year-old girl of ten.

"Of course, what do you want me to do? Think about poor Sha? No, I prefer to concentrate on our victory. To hell with the blueskins, we found out all we need about Elchitism. In addition we may have a lead of some kind. I say 'hooray, and let's skip to the May.'"

On the park mall they passed licensed stands where magicians, jugglers, and mimes exhibited. Small crowds were gathered around the performances.

They paused beside one quite remarkable display set up beneath a pole with a bright green banner. "Fabulous Fara's Template Show," said the illuminated sign that was set before a small booth beside the stand. A woman in a blue wig and a dress of white sequins stood on the dais.

Her show consisted of the production of exotic bubbles from a strange template, a device resembling a loop braided of several colorful threads. To produce the bubbles Fara simply passed the loop over a customer's head and down to his or her shoulders. When she removed the template and held it still, the bubbles floated from the center, up to a half dozen per person, each a unique size, anywhere from that of a pea to a large orange. All swirled with magically bright color patterns that changed constantly.

The bubbles seemed indestructible too. Fara demonstrated this with a blowtorch and a power tool that she brought out of a chest in the booth. Nothing could even mark them.

No two bubbles were ever the same; some were multicolored, some predominantly of one shade or other. The variety seemed endless as they watched her pass pet animals, a cat and a laowon pesski, and then some houseplants, through the hoop of colored wires.

The cat produced a single, glittering scarlet bubble. The pesski produced small, clear bubbles. Those produced by plants were tiny, opaque globes rather like pearls.

An oddity of the process was that it could be performed

only once on any particular living thing. Subsequent attempts to obtain more bubbles produced nothing.

As she worked, Fara kept up a constant harangue of the crowd, drawing customers forth. For a fee of twenty credit units, anyone could have a set of fabulous Fara's bubbles.

While Jon and Meg watched, a few people came forward, a party of tourists from the watermoons in typical loud mooner shirts. Fara's harangue continued into a brief history of the template, which was clearly not from any known human science. She held it up so everyone could see it clearly.

"This remarkable device is one of the so-called templates that are found on the planet BRF, or 'Baraf' as it's popularly known, a planet covered in the ruins of a long-dead civilization." Jon looked up with renewed interest; the half-believable tales of Baraf had always fascinated him.

"My father, Finius the Bold, was the man who found this template. He spent the family fortune to go to Baraf and mount a prospecting expedition to the Baraf city sites.

"The expedition spent days on the dangerous trails. They fought off marauding mutants. Then two hovercraft fell into a crustal pit and thirty people lost their lives. However, Finius the Bold survived, and in one of those strange ancient places that they call the Boneyards, he found this template."

There was a little spatter of applause.

"He returned from Baraf forty-eight years ago and we have been producing these bubbles ever since. We estimate that it has produced nearly one hundred million bubbles in that time. During the entire period the device has absorbed no known energy or material of any type.

"So where do the bubbles come from?" Fara asked the crowd. She laughed. Fabulous Fara had a great laugh, lots of white teeth. The crowd laughed too, a mite uneasily at first, and then quite happily.

"From out of thin air!" Fara roared. There was more laughter and a little applause. More tourists stepped up to have bubbles made and photos taken.

Moved by curiosity, Jon stepped forward.

"Twenty credits is rather a lot for just a few bubbles, isn't it?" Meg said.

"After one thirty-two for a bottle of wine, it seems like nothing at all, Meg."

Jon's turn came. Fara lifted the template and settled it around his head. As it did so Jon sensed an odd twinge, a palpable pressure on his psi sense, and when the template lifted, a gasp of surprise arose from the onlookers.

Jon looked around. Floating down on the air current was a small, highly unusual bubble—a silvery cube the size of a grape. It shimmered oddly on each face.

Fara reached for it, but Jon was faster and he gathered it into his hands and stared at it. It was light, and cool to the touch. The reflections were buried in a kind of moiré pattern.

"Something has happened. I shall have to investigate it." Fara tried to take it from his hands.

"No, wait, I paid for it, I get to keep it," Jon protested.

And a fierce protective urge suddenly welled up in his heart. It was his cube! No one would touch it. He put it away and refused Fara's entreaties.

"But never before has the template produced anything more than spheres. This is the first cube! You must donate it to science." Her voice had become a wail.

But her complaint only stiffened Jon's determination to retain the cube. It was his, something told him that it was uniquely so and that no one else should have it. "I will consider your request, but for now I will retain possession of the cube."

Meg eyed him strangely as they walked on down the mall and across a wide lawn toward the Hyades Monument.

"It *is* mine. I paid for it!" he said fervently. She laughed then, much amused.

They parted at the monument and Jon headed for the Olde Shrub Bar and Grille, which was set in a dugout in a forested section of the park. It was one of his favorite haunts.

CHAPTER SEVEN

ALTHOUGH IT WAS SUNSET HOUR AND THE LONG GOLDEN beams produced by the engineers were ricocheting through the habitat, the park was barely crowded. Too chill for sunworship so close to Winterfest, and with the shopping frenzy in full fury, all card colors were allowed entry and the card cops weren't even in view.

The cops were struggling instead with the mass of shoppers over in Octagon Seven, all in search of that unique something to enliven their winter outfit.

Being noncorporate and uninvolved in Masque rather left Jon out of the social life of Hyperion Grandee. Sometimes he found this an acute blessing.

Down the avenue of ancient hemlocks he walked with a cheerful stride despite the slight chill in the air. Sunbeams caromed through the trunks. Through some inscrutable foul-up in their own bureaucracy, the laowon had set him a problem, and he and Meg had neatly sidestepped the problem. He already had his next moves mapped out and was wondering if the case might be wrapped up before bedtime.

As soon as he'd eaten, had a chance to shower and put on clean clothes, he was going to the high-dorsal extender to look at the Elchite warehouse and docking bay.

A little breeze stirred a few fallen leaves across the path. He could almost feel 5,000 credit units sitting in his account. Meg, of course, would get her split.

He made a note to check in with Coptor Brine and discuss what might be landing on his plate the next morning, back at the squad.

Eventually the friendly red sign of the Shrub poked into view. A squeaking hinge tape played under the bushes and topiary masterpieces that clustered around the Shrub's low-slung structure, deep-bermed into the park ground. With stone floors, woodlook walls, and low ceilings, the place was modeled on a fourteenth-century English tavern.

Jon passed through the "Jolly Miller" linnet bush, a ten-meter-tall gesture of virtuosity on the part of the park staff, and swung into the Shrub. It was pleasantly empty. He ordered a hot freef sandwich, some salad, and a mug of ale.

The freef was done perfectly, and he always liked the Shrub's style of ale, dark and bitter.

He paid with his card in the table slot function box and tapped out a tip. In some contentment he leaned back in his booth and stared out the window illusion, on a panorama of ancient Earth. That week the Shrub was running a series called "Great Metros of Old Terra." Jon watched in fascination as vistas of romantic ancient cities—Vancouver, Miami, Glasgow—flitted by. He felt again the romance of Old Earth, by which was meant any time previous to the atomic age.

When he turned back to his beer, a very attractive young woman in a tight silk suit was standing close by. Her golden hair tumbled down her shoulders. She smiled, looked away. They were virtually alone.

"Hello," he said. She turned him a friendly glance. Something was decidedly strange: A prostitute of her caliber would not be working the Shrub Bar and Grille. He finished his ale, and she came closer.

"How nice to find someone who isn't out shopping tonight," she said gaily as she sat down opposite him. "What were you drinking?" She wrinkled her pretty little nose at his mug.

"The ale. Alas, I can't have more than one on this occasion, but thanks very much anyway. Do you come down to the old Shrub often?"

"Not much, just now and then."

It was like something out of his favorite sex fantasy.

The lovely girl from nowhere. They were alone—well, virtually—and she was eager to talk to him. Eager to get to know him, and he felt his cheeks harden as he nodded slowly to himself. Superior Buro at work. "Subtle they are not," as Meg always said.

He opened his psi sense out as much as was possible under the influence of a pint of ale. There wasn't much happening. Perhaps she'd had training in psi suppression.

She was so beautiful, he felt a surge of disgust. She'd sold herself to the aliens. How many men had she approached for the blues? She was astonishingly glamorous; most men would find it hard to refuse her.

He stood up and leaned across and quickly kissed her on the lips. She didn't slap him, or protest more than mildly, confirming his suspicions.

"You're lovely. I just had to steal one kiss," he said in a calm voice. "I'd love to stay and get acquainted, but as you probably read in your brief on me, I have good psi sense."

Her face registered a pout of disappointment. "What do you mean?" she said rather plaintively.

"Sorry, but I have to go now." He headed out and back across the park to his home ramp.

When he reached his apartment door his neighbor Onliki popped out of his own door calling Jon's name. Surprised, he looked up to find Onliki wearing an unprecedented smile. Onliki, it seemed, wanted Iehard to come to his next party, to be held on the upcoming festival weekend. A realgoodtime, interesting sex people would attend. Iehard boggled. He and Onliki had barely exchanged words except when Jon complained about Onliki's loud and vulgar audio excesses.

"Onliki!" he said sharply, cutting through the exhaust.

"Whad?"

"Tell the Buro that I don't buy this kind of stuff. I'm not interested, all right?"

Onliki was downcast.

"I sympathize with the loss of this source of easy credit, Onliki, but you will have to explain it to them yourself." But before Jon could escape, the cover had evaporated and the little eyes were narrowed and vicious. "Look, Iehard, I know what you do! So like I intend to get the ramp association together and have you evicted, laoman.

You're not the kind of person we want living on this ramp. You shouldn't be living with normal people, you stink of blood. Killing innocent people..."

Jon shut the door, then leaned against it. Sometimes it was good to see the hatred out in the open; it made him feel perversely better. But now he would have to move; the apartment would be dangerous.

A message was waiting on his computer screen. A call from Coptor. The big man's face was creased with a certain amount of real concern. "Jon, I got a complaint here, full pink docket, come down from the Center Court. Names you as defense in a suit for an awful lot of credit. The Baltitude Gas Company wants your hide, baby. Call me tomorrow about it." Coptor blinked out.

The vindictive oaf Baltitude! Just what he needed, a big lawsuit from a paranoid megabuck.

He slipped off his jacket and took out the silver cube, which he set down on the small sidetable.

The cube shimmered most strangely, moiré patterns disrupting whatever images might be forming on those faces, but the shimmering appeared at odds with the surrounding light patterns as well. He weighed it again in his hand, squeezed it lightly to no effect. Recalling Fara's efforts with blowtorch and drill, he squeezed it harder between two hands. No effect whatsoever could be detected.

What in the heavens was it? Fara claimed the material was inert and had so far resisted all attempts at investigation.

He set it down and went in and showered and shaved. Later, with a clean shirt and a black top coat and a pair of shoes with adjustable magnets in the soles that he'd purchased for a low-grav pursuit years before, he set out.

He headed for the up platform, paused briefly on the platform and then, as a train came in, he turned and jogged lightly back the way he'd come and down onto the other platform. On the way he passed a plump little man whose expression and strong fear signal marked him as a Superior Buro agent. Jon rode the next train to Octagon Seven and took a roundabout route through the dense crowds until he could get to the back service corridor and then down to Meg's.

"Well, look who's so cheerful," Meg remarked when

he walked in. "What did you do, come to your senses and drop this horrible job?" She was working with Daisy.

"No, I think we might see an early conclusion to the case and a check for ten thousand in the morning. Will five thousand credits help?"

"Bah! Sha3 is in the hospital. He will cost five hundred to rebrain, with nothing for all that personality I poured into him." She gestured savagely at the door.

"Since I've been back here the Superior Buro has tried three times to load us with bugs. First it was a fake team from Compubiopsy. *Daisy* wouldn't let them in, that's how bad they were. Then there was a biodisk salesman—a heavenly-looking young man—and then there was a goddamn Newchurcher. 'Let us beseech the Prophet!' he started wailing outside the door. While he was doing it they tried to drill through from the airshaft. Daisy took that out with a voltage surge, burned somebody's blueskin fingers, I hope. We heard stuff falling down the shaft."

"They're on the case all right." He told her of his own brushes with the Buro. "'Subtle they are not!'"

They laughed bitterly.

"Come on, Meg—five thousand in the morning. You'll have Sha3 back eventually, and that's easy money, wouldn't you agree, for what? Twelve hours we've spent on this case."

She grew more serious. "I don't know, Jon, it makes me uneasy. It's blood money. We ought to let him go, leave him be. Why should we catch him and send him to die for the laowon?"

He shrugged. "We have no idea what he may have done. It may have been a senseless slaughter. What difference does it make anyway? If the Superior Buro wants someone they're going to find him in the end. They didn't want us to find Eblis Bey, but we know where he's bound to be hiding. We found out despite them and we found out really easily. So, we have to balance it out."

"It's still blood money. Let the old man go. You don't need the money."

"That's news to me. I have to move again. That means another bribe to another landlord who won't want to have a laoman operative for the Mass Murder Squad in his or her property. I'm afraid I do need the money, besides, he could just as easily have killed them for money himself."

She turned away, a disappointed expression on her face.

After a moment he frowned, put his hands in his pockets. "But I do agree that working around the Superior Buro is getting incredibly tedious. Always the heavy hand with them, always being tailed and bugged. I'm not going to accept any more jobs that involve them."

She smiled then. "Thank you, Jon. I appreciate that." She seemed to brush away a tear. "By the way, here's a little precaution of my own." And she showed him a purple Masque module. "Our Elchite information is now hidden in here. Just in case something breaks in here when I'm not around."

A chime came on and Meg hurriedly set up her Masque entry for a late-evening game, a new challenger for the prime-time entry slot, before "Hidden Notebook." The game was called "Louis Quatorze" and was set in a remote time in Old Earth. All historical details had to be correct for entries to get on the main screen. Meg had entered a serving girl/hunchback duo. Her opening that evening involved an effort by her serving girl, Danielle Lebrun, to entice the elderly Comte D'Aillou into his fourposter bed, where a faction would murder him, thus prompting a change in the keeper of the king's chocolate provision.

Her fingers flew over the keyboard as she picked up a lot of the telling little details that the DAex Ram was just too slow to handle. Fortunately these were group scenes. Meg was responsible only for the image and dialogue of Danielle, a saucy trollop of quite traditional mode. With the Bioram, of course, things would have been much easier.

But with judges and audience watching critically, every nuance had to be perfect if the action was to get much play on people's main screens. A competing scene was set in the winecellar and another in the queen's bedroom. Meg's fingers drummed the keyboard.

She had won control of the scene lighting now. She tightened focus on Danielle's face, noble peasant of French stock. There was an appealing graininess in her lighting. Now came a long steady shot of her cleavage, then her breasts moving inside her fresh white blouse.

Meg had main screen in more than 50 percent of viewer screens now. The Comte D'Aillou was removing his breeches and indicating the fourposter with considerable excitement on his rouged and powdered features.

Danielle's skirts came down and she bent over seductively for the comte's twitching fingers.

"Wow!" Jon said. "Seventy percent now, Meg."

It was true, Meg was pulling the whole audience of "Louis Quatorze" over to her hot little seduction scene. The much more genteel posturing in the queen's bedroom was down to a mere 15 percent while the spanking of a cellarmaid was holding a calculated 15 percent share of mostly male viewers.

Danielle went to work inside the fourposter and the curtains were drawn over the rest, leaving Meg with 72 percent share and a complete triumph over the opposition.

The game switched focus. The king was returning from the hunt with the court in train. A grand tableau scene was coming up in which Meg had no part. She rose for a cup of instacaf.

"What's the prize money like for this one?" Jon asked, watching in fascination as hundreds of perfectly crafted video characters, each operated by a different video artist, was molded into a tremendous "big screen" image. The palace of Versailles, the clouds, the mud of the courtyard, barking dogs, children—everything was in place, including even the hum of the flies.

"Six thousand for the gold, four for the silvers. Pretty good for the timeslot."

Jon knew that Queen Alice in "Hidden Notebook" regularly won the ten thousand prize for top of the top show.

"By the way," Meg said, remembering something, "Clawenton Ravenish called. He found something else for us. Apparently there's a long-held belief on the watermoons of William that the Elchites were founded by the surviving members of the crew of the Testamenter battleship *Winston Churchill*. The crew ditched their ship and came to Nocanicus. They landed on the Ginger Moon and the Mooners helped them to get fast NAFAL back to the Hyades stars."

Jon snorted in disbelief. "Just because there are Testamenters in the Nocanicus system and a lot of them on the watermoons of William, that doesn't mean the *Winston Churchill* still exists."

"I haven't told you everything we've done around here though. I used my probability software to go through the Elchite case."

"And?"

"And I think you should seriously consider dropping the case."

"Not more crazy Testamenter stuff?"

"It's not crazy! There's nothing crazy about it at all. It fits the few facts we have quite perfectly. Assume the *Churchill* fled to one of the nearby dwarf star systems and the crew came here on the lifeboats. From here they went fast NAFAL to the far side of the Hyades and the inner hegemony. A few hundred years later the Elchite cult springs up in the inner human sphere; panhumanist, explicably antilaowon and violent."

"The Elchites were in business before that."

"Yes, but it's clear they were in decline, just one of thousands of small eccentric sects. They got a big boost about the right time."

His expression made her indignant.

"Remember, Jon, the Baada drives weren't like laowon gravitomagnetics. They could have fled a long way from Testament without the laowon being able to track them. Those drives could take you across the Galaxy on one fueling. They used the gravity potential of the stars themselves."

"So why does the Elchite come here then?"

"That's what we were wondering, Daisy and I. Since we didn't have old Sha3 to work it out with I called up the Jumbo at Hyperion U. No lock on Bioram use, there appear to be a few shreds of freedom left to us. Anyway, this is what we came up with."

On screen the king was getting closer. Dozens of grandiose personages in elaborate costumes were riding in and dismounting. In the near distance horns were blowing. A few big, spotted hounds came loping into the courtyard. It was uncannily realistic and Jon had to remind himself that it was all image creation by Masque nuts like Meg.

"There must be another alien race. Out beyond the nearside galactic arm. Perhaps in the opposite side of the Galaxy, but there must be another advanced species, a spacegoing species that the laowon are frightened of. Someone that we can appeal to for help." She grew passionate. "Someone's out there. We don't have to be all alone with the laowon, trapped in their Galaxy, doomed forever to be their slaves."

He wondered a moment. Was it possible? Objections rose immediately to mind.

"The Galaxy is vast. There may be other races but the laowon have been exploring for millennia and have yet to find anything more advanced than us. Nothing else has even had spaceflight."

"Of course, that's what they tell us. But how can we really know? You know perfectly well that very few humans have ever come back from the laowon centers. Our ambassadors, our scientists, the talented psi-able, all those who go to the Golden Court stay there. We don't hear very much from them. We know, therefore, only what the blues tell us."

He hesitated to say anything. She was insistent.

"Look, it fits the patterns we have. The Elchite apparently visited a laowon habitat crammed with noble bloods. What were they there for? Couldn't they have been gathered to meet with these aliens? Perhaps there is an emissary from the other side of the Galaxy. Or perhaps they simply had information about this other race. He killed them all to keep the information secret, and he came here because of the Elchite-Mooner connection that goes right back to the whereabouts of the *Churchill*."

"Here?"

"No, nearby, silly, like the Mooners say."

Then it was time for Roq, Meg's hunchback character, to make a move in the stable setting where he lurked. Meg had planned for Roq to press forward to kiss the royal stirrup and beg for alms. Roq's grotesque face was capable of the most pitiable textures.

On the main screen the king was refusing to dismount in the courtyard because there were too many people and assassins lurked everywhere. Soldiers were pushing forward to block the stable doors. The king rode in. Roq was ready to perform.

Suddenly the screen crackled and an alarm light flashed from Daisy. The word "override" in huge letters was followed by some code in laowon digits, and then the face of the Morgooze of Blue Seygfan appeared on the screen.

Meg cursed and pressed the dump switch, but the override continued. The main screen stayed tuned to the Morgooze's call.

"Damn you!" yelled Meg.

The young Morgooze was unused to being spoken to in such a manner. "Silence!" he bellowed. His mane stood out stiff and his eyes seemed to glow.

Iehard was genuinely afraid at the sight of that anger.

Trembling slightly, he said, "Please switch to another screen, Morgooze. You are committing an act of gross discourtesy, breaking into a Masque scene that my colleague has worked on for weeks." Jon struggled to keep his voice level.

"Get the fuck off my screen!" Meg screamed, desperately hammering an emergency patch code to take her out of phone transmission momentarily and onto another standby line.

"Discipline that female!" the Morgooze shrieked turning visibly purple.

Meg finally got Daisy back under her own control and switched the Morgooze off the main screen and onto a screen that swung up to Jon on an extensor.

The scene in the stable was over. Roq had stood sullenly by while the king passed. The stablemaster had ordered the miserable hunchback to be whipped for presenting such a sad spectacle to his majesty, not to mention a million viewers.

With a cry of disgust, Meg dialed out of the game, then got up from the pit and went in search of instacaf. She lit a syntabac and puffed it angrily.

The room crackled with anger; onscreen the Morgooze was having a tantrum in laowon. "That female must be . . ."

Jon broke in suddenly with the hunting tongue. "She is inconsequential to our great purpose, Morgooze. Perhaps mercy would be the best aspect of radiance to shower upon her?" He employed only a hint of rebuke, exactly as it might have been phrased by a trusted adviser of the same caste. No human had ever addressed the Morgooze thus. He stared, speechless.

"How may I assist you?" Jon asked, trying to be gracious and helpful. Laowon could be so prickly and difficult sometimes.

The Morgooze visibly struggled to control himself. The purple faded. The eyes continued to stare but the harsh orders of command did not leave his lips. He had to remember that this was not Lao the Golden, this was a frontier system in the back of beyond and that it was impossible to get anything done unless one remained on civil terms with the humans.

"What progress have you to report?" he finally snapped.

Jon spread his hands. "Actually, very little so far. The Superior Buro denies access to most of the relevant data. We have barely begun to search as a result. You should ask the Buro why they don't want your mission to succeed. They will listen to you, of course."

The Morgooze snorted, gave Jon an ill-tempered look. "Bah, these are excuses. I want results and I want them quickly. Get out and find this man. Unless you achieve something soon, I shall demand your head when I return to Lao." The Morgooze abruptly cut the contact.

Jon dimly heard Meg give a whistle behind him. "That really ices your cake, now doesn't it?"

Jon rolled out of the computer pit, sat down, and poured some instacaf. "Trouble is he really means it."

"All this for five thousand credits each; is it really worth it?"

Jon wondered how the Nocanicus authorities would handle such a request by the Morgooze. Somehow he doubted he would get that much protection; Blue Seygfan represented a vast power. "We'll find the Elchite, everything will be all right."

Meg threw up her hands in exasperation. "This is incredible. You're saying that unless you jump at this blueskin's command and find something, somehow, with no recent information about the Elchites other than that picture, he'll kill you and take your head back to Lao?"

"Well, he will try, and he can afford to send a lot of killers. I don't know that the Grandee cops would even put up much of a struggle on a laoman's behalf either."

"Now, Jon! You're human. They wouldn't let an alien get away with that."

"Meg, this particular alien is the space-damned Morgooze of Blue Seygfan! Do you understand what that means? He controls a million laowon shock troops, a fleet of three hundred battlejumpers. Blue Seygfan directs the affairs of ten thousand solar systems. Above this young Morgooze are only the Urall and the male offspring of the Urall, if any, beyond the age of seven years. The Urall of Blue Seygfan is third in line to the Imperiom itself!"

Meg shuddered and then began to cry. Somehow this weakness in her was more appalling than anything else. He put his arms around her and she wept on his shoulder.

"Oh, Jon, I can't stand this. I can't stand it that we're not free. That the damned laowon are taking over, snuffing out human freedoms forever."

They sat together for a long time.

■ CHAPTER EIGHT

OUT ON THE DORSAL EXTENSION THE GRAVITY WAS LOW, humans were rather rare, and the warehouse corridors were severely utilitarian.

Before he reached the section he sought, a strip of bonded warehouses sealed behind steel gates, Jon had pulled himself down the handpole set in the center of the cavernous passageway for what seemed like hours.

When he saw the Baltitude Security Company logo, he halted and started counting. At the fifth tier of gates he found the one designated by Clawenton Ravenish, No. 45b. Here was supposed to be a locked gate, a hidden Elchite temple.

Instead Jon found an open gate and an open warehouse that was completely empty. Momentarily stunned, he floated inside the perfectly bare interior. The 10,000 credit units suddenly seemed light-years away again. And poor old Clawenton would have to forget his Elchite ceremonial vestments and altar of Earthstone. Whatever the Elchite trader had left there long ago, the Elchites following had already taken away.

With brows furrowed, Jon hurried back to the gravity zones.

When he finally got home it was only an hour before midnight and he was exhausted. He kicked off his spaceboots and dumped his jacket, yelled at the TV, and poured himself a shot of fuelas incentivos victorios.

He was determined that in the morning he'd tell Petrie he was quitting the job. His chest hurt. The fuelas tasted good but did horrible things to his stomach. He belched.

The phone lit up with a purple flash. Security code. He stared a moment—could he really stand another conversation with the Morgooze? Then he opened the line. To his surprise the features of Melissa Baltitude appeared on the screen.

"Mr. Iehard, I finally caught you in!" she exclaimed a little breathlessly.

On the spot Jon decided she was rather an attractive young lady. "You're out of the hospital."

"Oh, for hours, such a dreary place. My arm's in a sling, my foot's in a big rubber bandage, and I can't go out to the Orbiters' Ball." She sounded quite distressed.

So she was bored and lonely and interested in a little rough trade to keep her occupied? Rich girls had done this to him before. Jon sighed. "I'm sorry about that."

Wait till you see the scars the stupid assistant surgeons left on my ass when they cut out Magelsa's brand. His thoughts rolled down a slightly bitter track.

"So, I had a great idea. I thought I'd call you up and ask you over to dine with me, and you could tell me about yourself and your dangerous life."

"Exactly."

"What did you say, Mr. Iehard?"

"*Very* dangerous life."

"Yes, I'm sure. But now it's so late that I've already had dinner and I'm just sitting here alone, sipping wine and looking out the window."

"You're not a big one for Masque then?"

"I hate computers, Mr. Iehard. I prefer my people real."

Jon had a sudden idea. Galvanized, he got right to the point.

"What would you say if I came over to see you right now? And we sipped some of this wine together and looked out the windows."

She would be delighted, she said.

A few minutes later he hurried away down the corridor, picking up his Superior Buro tail and leading her to the transit stop. There he paused a moment, entered a car ascending to the higher-numbered octagons. A woman in a blue suit had followed him on. He sat down. So did she.

He stood up and jumped out of the car just as its lights flashed to signal the door was closing.

The woman in blue had jumped, too. He entered the car going down to the low numbers and rode two stops. He got off and ran across the platform and into the train going up. He noticed the woman in blue and a man in a tan leisure suit and white shirt.

He rode back two stops and jumped out, ran out of the station, and immediately dived over the retainer wall of the ramp into a huge ornamental pot of ivies.

A few moments later the woman in blue puffed up the stairs and paused. She looked up and down the ramps in bafflement. The man in tan appeared. They conversed together in low tones, then separated, she going up ramp and he going down.

Jon waited, however. After another minute a third figure appeared, a man in a set of maintenance overalls with the logo of the transit line on the back. He stared around him and then spoke into a wrist communicator. A few moments later he turned and went back into the station. Jon continued to wait. A car for uptown finally pulled in. He scrambled from concealment in the ivies and sprang down the stairs and into the car without being seen by the man in the maintenance overalls, who was talking into a phone plate on the platform.

The car whistled away.

At Octagon Fourteen he headed up ramp for the high-rent sector. At the guardhouse below Magenta Mall, he showed them his card and told them to call Miss Baltitude.

The guards' faces shifted from alarm to resentment within seconds. They let him pass with a surly contempt that made him want to laugh. If only they could get invited into the deluxe homes on Magenta Mall by lissome young daughters of the very rich!

At least they hadn't noticed his forehead scars. If they'd known he was laoman he could be sure they'd have tried to hold him. A call to Baltitude Senior, the police, anything to keep him out of their bailiwick.

Magenta Mall was set atop a row of high towers. Grass and bushes dominated the scene. The windows of the manses of the wealthy humped up here and there out of the vegetation like big yellow eyes. Above was the night sky illusion and the curve of the habitat. It seemed a long, long way from the crowds of the corridors below.

He presented himself at the Baltitude mansion. The butler gazed at him with an expression of veiled disgust. He suggested that Jon should go round to the side entrance, where all deliveries could be made.

Jon snorted, half amused. "Tell Melissa that Jon Iehard is here."

Stony faced, the butler did so, after closing the door. Then, with poor grace, he conducted Jon into a room with a wide panoramic view of the habitat spread out below. Melissa Baltitude was propped up in a chair with a phone and a bottle of wine on a table carved into the shape of a man's head. On the floor was an antique carpet of considerable artistry. Pale pink lamps in sconces lined one wall. On another was a complex graphic with lines that shifted, constantly exposing new lines of sight.

"Mr. Iehard, welcome." She turned to the butler. "That will be all, Boomes."

The wine was pleasant, the view marvelous. They discussed the Kill Kults briefly and when she asked him where he'd been born he told her frankly.

"Hut 416, North West Alley, on the estate of Castle Firgize, planet Glegan."

She became a little uncertain. "My goodness, where's that? I've never heard of it."

"Subdirectorate five of Blue Seygfan. It's about thirty light-years away, I think."

"A laowon world, one of those they stole from us!"

"I don't think they would agree with your description, but yes, it is a laowon world."

Her face froze up for a moment. "So you are a laoman."

"That's not quite how I think of myself actually, but in the popular conception—"

"I'm sorry, it's just that—well, you are the first I've ever spoken to. Not that it really matters. I don't see any difference between you and anybody else."

He smiled, bitterly. If she looked closely enough, she would see the marks. "Believe me, I understand," he said.

"Oh, dear, and I so wanted to ask you out to visit our real family home, on Gloaming Splendor."

His eyes widened. The Baltitude manse on the luxury

megahabitat would be an experience indeed. "I'm sorry, I think I'd have liked that."

Her expression became conspiratorial. "Perhaps we'll just keep it a secret between ourselves. If they don't know they can't go getting excited about it. Speaking for myself I don't care one bit whether you were born laoman or not. You saved my life and I feel very grateful for that fact."

He decided he rather liked her. She seemed to mean well anyway. She was perhaps too young to have picked up the near-universal prejudice. "I've been on Grandee for nine years now; I'm acclimatized. Your skin gets thickened after a while." He smiled.

"Have you seen the other habitats of the system?"

"One or two."

"Oh, which ones? Bentley? Versailles? Or Shangri-La? The hanging gardens there are the most beautiful place in the galaxy: it says so in *Albein's Directory*."

"Afraid not. I've only been to Nostramedes and Everton."

Her face registered shock, as if he'd suddenly made a bad smell. "Oh, dear. Well, we never go to those places."

"No, of course not. But they too are afflicted with random killers sometimes, and then they send to Grandee for a team of our operatives."

They sipped wine thoughtfully.

"I just asked because, you see, I have a space-boat, a four-berth Dove."

Jon whistled. A superb luxury machine.

"And I was thinking of skipping Winter Month this year on Grandee and going out to the Splendor and relaxing in the forest."

Forest. The word did strange things to Jon's psyche. It had been so long since he'd seen any trees but those familiar ones that grew in the park. How nice it would be to relax in a forest with Melissa Baltitude!

"A Dove, which model?"

"It's a Classic B. It's an heirloom. Left me by my Aunt Rose. If you like we could take a trip, go over to Shangri-La and then to Gloaming Splendor. I know you'd love it at Baltitude Rancho."

He nodded: he was sure he would too.

"Out by the swim hole, with cold drinks and lots of

sun. We can go riding: my father maintains a stable of a dozen horses there."

Jon boggled at the thought, then remembered that Baltitude Rancho was probably twenty square kilometers in extent. Out on the megahabs life was pretty damn good they said, though of course Jon had never seen it except in movies. "I'd like that," he said. A frown came over his face.

"What's wrong?"

"I'm wondering if I dare ask you something. It might be a big help to me."

"Oh, do ask. I'd love to help."

Briefly Jon explained that he needed to find out when a certain warehouse owned by the Baltitude Security Company had been emptied and the lease given up.

She thought for a moment, then picked up the phone. "Where is the warehouse?"

He gave her the address. A moment later she spoke a series of code syllables into the phone and was rewarded with an access menu to Baltitude Corporate computer files.

In a few more seconds she had it.

"The lease was terminated yesterday and the contents shipped. Funny, there's no destination for the contents although there is for every other listing."

Jon nodded. It fit. And he had been close. But, of course, yesterday he had been hunting Arnei Oh, not this Elchite chimera that constantly receded into the mist.

"You're disappointed. It's not what you were hoping to hear?"

"Well . . ." He grimaced. "It doesn't matter, I've been fooling myself all along on this case. Just one more false lead. Thankfully I didn't spend too much time on it. Thanks very much. You've probably saved me a lot of trouble."

He could see that she was pleased, from the toss of her dark glossy hair. "Some more wine?"

The time went by magically swiftly, and Jon had just got to the point of kissing Melissa Baltitude for the third time, when the door burst open and in stormed her father, Jason Pauncritius Baltitude himself.

"How dare you!" he bawled at the top of his lungs.

"Daddy! Why aren't you at the ball?"

"Because, my dear, I was informed that you and this

laobreed creature were in here together. We can thank Boomes for the fact that I returned in time to prevent anything worse happening."

"Mr. Baltitude, you don't seriously believe that I would harm your daughter."

"Young man, simply by being here you are irreparably damaging my daughter. She is a leader, a member of the Orbiters' club. She can't be going around rutting with the genetic rubbish of the laowon worlds."

Jon's face tightened.

Melissa burst into a wail of rage.

Baltitude Senior called out behind him. "Gosax, Boomes, get in here."

"Mr. Baltitude, I have no intention of damaging even your daughter's reputation. She asked me by to thank me for saving her life. That she has done, most sweetly. I have no claims upon her, nor upon you. And I'll thank you to keep a civil tongue in your head when you address me."

Baltitude sniffed loudly. Boomes and another man, dour faced, big nosed, and heavily built, wearing a black suit, appeared in the door.

"Ah, Gosax, I want you to throw this interloper out onto the ramp. Give him a good drubbing to make sure he gets the message."

"Daddy, don't you dare do this!" Melissa screamed and tried to get to her feet. Jon put out a hand to steady her since she was favoring her bad ankle so heavily. She sat down again with a yelp of anguish.

"Be quiet child, this is for your own good."

"Really, Mr. Baltitude, is that all?" Jon said. "Isn't there some tiny element of personal pleasure in this? Don't you enjoy sending old Gosax here into combat, bashing up the people you don't like? Throwing your weight around like the megabuck you are?"

"Gosax, be quick now." Baltitude was furious.

Jon prepared to defend himself. Gosax noted the positioning of one trained in martial arts. The bigger man lunged, confident of his own powers. Jon evaded, they whirled together, legs snapping high, punches and blocks slipping off with explosive smacking sounds. Gosax missed a swing, Jon went inside and kneed him in the crotch.

Gosax, however, wore protective garments and the blow did no more than push him away.

"A tricky one, eh?" he snarled and produced a small shock rod from inside his suit. It was the illegal kind. They could all hear it sizzle in the still air.

Jon also sensed a burst of explosive rage directly behind him. Rage and fear. The combination often produced mental images for him and this time it gave him the "sight" of the back of his own head. The cane was rising, Baltitude's fury along with it.

Jon lashed out with a back kick and drove Mr. Baltitude to the floor. Boomes went to assist his fallen master. Gosax leapt at him with the high-energy shock rod, Jon barely escaped a smack with it and was forced to defend himself against a furious onslaught. He rolled with it into a wall, and then ducked one blow but took another in the shoulder. That stung him and he was moved to grab Gosax's lapels and butt the man, very hard, his forehead mashing the big meaty nose.

Gosax stumbled back bubbling blood and Jon kicked him in the belly. The nasty little shock rod spilled to the floor and burnt the expensive carpet. Jon retrieved it and swatted Gosax across the face with it, knocking the big man head over heels in a shower of bright blue sparks.

Gosax didn't get up. Jon prayed he hadn't killed the fool. Boomes alone stood between him and the door.

"Well, Boomes, how much do they pay you around here?" Jon motioned with the shock rod. "Enough to make you want to get in my way?"

Boomes darted aside. Jon blew Melissa a kiss.

"My apologies, Melissa. Thank you for a delightful interlude and for your assistance. Good-bye." Jon made his way to the front door, smashing the shock rod on the marble pate of a statue of Pauncritius Baltitude III, founder of the Baltitude Gas Company.

■ CHAPTER NINE

CLIMBING DOWN FROM THE HEIGHTS OF MAGENTA MALL, Jon rode transit round the habitat curve to Octagon One. He exited onto the Blue Moon Plaza. He needed to think and he wanted somewhere nice that wasn't his sleazy little home. He slipped into the Bird o' Paradise. The Bird was a quiet spot known for a clientele that was mostly spacecrew.

Of course spacers were desperately gregarious, hard-drinking fools who attracted a thick crowd of hustlers, whores, and smugglers, but in the Bird, they drank quietly. That was the trademark of the place—it was somewhere to go when your hangover was too bad for Vio's or The Tubs or the other spacer bars. Still, like the rest of the Blue Moon bars it had a lot of anxious, sometimes plain terrified people, playing bad games with the Hyperion Grandee Export Import Police.

Jon accepted a beer from the robot and paid with his card in the function box. He wondered whether to call Petrie, resign from the case, and maybe look to emigrate to another big habitat with a need for psi-able people who were good with guns. It was clear that he faced some problems just ahead.

Gloomily, he watched a pair of spacers in Baltitude Gas Company suits, silver and yellow, on their way to the doors.

For all he knew in the very near future he was going

to be fighting for his economic existence against a horde of Baltitude legal sharks. Unless Coptor could swing some leverage on the board of the gas trustees.

Of course that wouldn't help much when it came to dealing with the Morgooze of Blue Seygfan.

Jon decided that at the least, it would be wise if he moved apartments again in the very near future. He wondered about trying Low Rent again, somewhere that didn't even have an address!

He sipped the beer and tried to relax. Almost immediately he began picking up a very strong fear signal.

Someone quite close by was absolutely terrified. But what rocked him was that instead of the image of paraheroin or prisonhab that he expected, there was an image of sly laowon faces, the Superior Buro!

It was from close behind him, in the next booth. A woman, on the verge of hysteria. He got up and examined her briefly as he slipped past.

Her eyes flicked up and down the room, constantly checking for "Buro."

He recalled her face. A blond woman, slightly built, fragile in appearance with wide cheekbones and eyes that were peculiarly large and haunting. She was one of those identified by the DAex Ram from the *Illustrious*'s file search. She even had on the same gray spaceline-style jumpsuit, with a small device marking the collar.

Two Pan-Nocan pilots got up from the bar, Jon took one of their seats. Kept the woman under observation.

His psi sense could feel her fear, very strong. That constant image of "Buro," and others, more fleeting, such as one of a bird that flew against a background of stars.

He sat very still, trying to absorb as much as possible from the woman's thought vistas. For a while there was nothing, than came a dreadful image. A great man, a hero to his race, being torn to pieces on a rack by cruel machine pincers that lanced down upon him from a battery of bright lights.

It was the Elchite, he had no doubt. And she was terrified that something awful was going to happen and that it was somehow her fault. Abruptly she panicked and got to her feet, paid clumsily for her unfinished drink, and rushed past Iehard to the door.

Jon followed, slipping through the crowds with all the

tricks in the tracker's book, which turned out to be essential since she was as nervous as any mass killer he'd ever followed. She kept stopping and looking behind her, then running on. She left Blue Moon Plaza and went down the connector to the ramps.

She turned onto a down ramp and he followed but found her waiting at the first bend, scanning the crowd coming down. He passed her and saw her heading up and crossing to the entrance to the departures terminal.

He ran after her, although now she was sure to notice him if she turned and looked back.

He realized he had to call in Petrie, get some Military Intelligence people to help.

But the woman was already through the doors of the docking terminal and there was nothing to be done but to sprint after her and try to keep her in sight.

He burst through the doors, quickly scanned the lines of people around the spacelines' counters. There was no sign of her. Then he felt a nova of fear go off somewhere above him. He looked up. She was on the departures platform, checking the crowd below. Their eyes met. She turned and ran through the departures gate.

With an oath he struggled up the escalator, pushing through crowds of late-night revelers.

Inside the gate there was no sign of her. He checked the departures monitor.

At Gate Three an indicator was blinking, that for the Nostramedes shuttle. He cursed again and ran for the gate.

A trio of security goons in black uniforms and helmets were shutting the gate on a cargo of convicted felons. The other shuttle doors were already closed. Jon waved his ID in the face of the squad leader, a squat young woman with red hair. She waved him away at first but then she caught sight of those initials, saw the Mass Murder Squad emblem, and swallowed heavily. For a moment he thought she was going to bolt. He could feel her terror—a Kill Kult outrage on her beat was her worst nightmare.

"Open a gate for me!" he yelled, breaking her out of the trance. She whacked a stud on her box. One of the passenger doors opened and the trio of guards ran away as quickly as they could manage.

Jon boarded without delay. The door hissed shut behind him and he found himself in a small compartment with a dozen old people, their suitcases strapped to their seats. There were a few empty seats to choose from. He picked one by the aisle.

The gray-and-blue wallpanels were grimy and cracked. The old people bore an air of forlorn resignation. They were service workers for the most part, without corporate rent plans. The retirement bus was taking them out to Nostramedes habitat. Their faces were gray, taut with apprehension.

The shuttle lifted clear of the blast shields and cut in its motors on a primary burn that immediately made the worn seating exceedingly uncomfortable.

Somebody's luggage broke loose, a bag burst, and tapes and underwear skittered around the compartment. A woman sobbed piteously.

The trip took hours, and there was no way of checking to see if the woman in the gray tunic was aboard. The shuttle's internal phototronics were all broken except for the main screen in the cabin ceiling.

Since Nostramedes trailed Hyperion Grandee by a million kilometers and the bus was no luxury liner, the engines boosted for a long, long time. Everyone was aching from acceleration effects when the engines finally cut out. A long period of weightlessness went by as videos flickered on the main screen. Jon probed around him with his psi sense but could detect no trace of the terrified blond woman. He prayed she hadn't somehow given him the slip and stayed behind on Hyperion Grandee while he went off on a million-klom goose chase. This job was becoming a source of nothing but exasperation: One minute those 5,000 credits were virtually in his hands and the next they were snatched away again! Besides which, he now had a roundtrip to Nostramedes at 640 credits to add to the tab for the nine-year Domaine Larose!

Hours later, as the shuttle approached Nostramedes, they were shaken by the long period of deceleration. On screen the gigahabitat slowly swelled into an enormous torus circling a boxy hub with immense openings above and below.

The shuttle floated down the vast central well of Nostramedes' docking bay, which had been built to accommodate NAFAL colony ships. They connected with a slight shudder then they were kedged inside, into a medium-gravity section. The steel bulkheads opened one by one to disgorge the passengers in small, easily handled groups.

There was a cursory ID and customs check, then passengers filed to the elevators. Most were destined to ride to retirement levels and small one-room apartments with reasonable air quality; others, like the convicts, were heading to the Unders and stinking oblivion.

Aboard Nostramedes there were few rules, but chief among them was that you received only that which you paid for. In advance.

A row of elevator doors opened, closed, but Jon glimpsed a dome of blond hair atop a slim figure in gray. He struggled over to the elevator and slammed his security override card into the function box to halt the car, but the box spit his card out and flashed a "Credit Only" sign on the antique monitor. With a tiny snarl he inserted his credit card and was then allowed to use the security card, having paid four credits for the privilege.

It was too late to halt the elevator, the car was already on its way back. People behind him were getting impatient. He punched up the computer memory and got a display menu. Visual quality was poor and the display shuddered a lot, but the credit software had tracked the recent transactions.

Seconds later he had the data. She was using an expensive All System Card, drawn on the William and Oxygen Bank on Hyperion Grandee. No address, no Nostramedes background. And she had gone all the way to the Unders.

Angrily he banged his credit in again and paid for a ride. The doors opened on an interior daubed with bizarre graffiti.

The ride was a gut-wrencher, zipping through hundreds of retirement levels. Jon couldn't help thinking of the place as a gigantic sausage of human beings.

The doors banged open and the cloying reek was quite staggering, like the stench of rotten teeth bubbling through excrement. Jon tried not to breathe too much. The Unders of Nostramedes hadn't changed since the last time he'd been there, on an active contract pursuit five years previously. It was still the closest thing to the medieval concept of hell.

Scattered glow lamps provided a somber twilight that

tinted the moist air brown. Dimly visible were huge concrete ribs arching over spaces originally intended to accommodate the assembly of huge sections of colony spacecraft.

The air was bitter, it made the lungs ache and the eyes water. It was an atmosphere for ghosts. The glow lamps were lost in nimbus.

Around the elevators stood small groups of black-suited guards, with goggles, breathing apparatus, and air tanks. They waved shock rods at the new arrivals, urging them away from the cleared space in front of the elevators.

To one side was a line of rectangular cabins where air tanks could be rented. Beyond those the grids began. Crouched on the grids, hunched into the distance, were the millions of the most wretched of all, the "breathers" of the Unders. From this vast crowd of the destitute came a low murmuring noise. A faint groan from an economic grave. No one wasted much energy on the Unders, it was simply too precious.

The air-tank supply firms were guarded by a clump of ragged Undersmen wearing only airmasks, tanks, and genital pouches. In their hands they bore short billies. They parted magically in front of a credit card, though.

It was the matter of a few moments to obtain a pair of tanks, a breathing mask, and some goggles. In addition Iehard rented a small headlamp, since there was no public illumination on the outer corridors.

He headed into the Unders.

The crowds in the vast chambers stupefied the imagination. Stark naked, they squatted on the grids, breathing the air before it was sucked at last down into the sludge tanks and renewed.

In theory at least, all those people were maintained on a single, daily seven-ounce serving of nutritional paste donated by the Nocanicus Charity Authority. However, on the grids, the weak had to give up something to the strong if they wished to spend an hour or two up on the inner vent, by the roof, breathing air a little less putrid than that nearer the floor. Most breathers gave up enough of their ration to look semistarved. The grid bosses and their platoons of goons herded them up and down rickety staircases that rose to the ceilings, where platforms hung from the upper vents and people could sit for a suck of fresher air.

Jon moved along the edge of the grid chamber. At the walls the ranks of breathers were jammed back by the pathway bosses who kept the routes open with shock rods and portable function boxes, which walkers were forced to feed credit if they wished to progress anywhere.

At last he came to the end of the first great chamber. A series of dark holes showed in the murk, corridors leading to the next.

There was so much woe in this place that the psi sense was hard to use. When he did it brought on strange emotional reactions. He felt moved to tears, his hair rose on the nape of his neck. Several times he felt a strange choking sensation.

He stumbled into one long dark tunnel after another, with stinking wretches sleeping the length of the floor, and finally emerged, exhausted, one air tank gone, and gloom settling over his hopes. The 10,000 credit units had floated away again. He had to call in, tell Petrie what had happened, and hope for the best. Let the MI people rip the Unders apart. It was probably time they got their hands dirty anyway.

He climbed some worn stairs into the Unders high-rent sector. Along the higher walls were jerry-rigged platforms with buildings of puff wall erected like so many human bat nests. Outside one or two little phototron signs identified bars.

Burly guards with clubs stopped him and extended a function box. Wearily he paid another credit to continue.

Outside the first bar he paused to tuck the Taw Taw into his boot top then rolled up his holster and stuffed that into his other boot. Then he headed in. It was a Chinese-style place, the Shai Chee Woop, and it served the aristocracy of the Unders, the grid bosses, the air magnates, and their flunkies. At the door he was frisked, carelessly, and after another credit deduction he gained access. The guards were fat and lax and never considered his boot tops. He decided to keep his air tanks, and just pulled the mask away and let it hang from the chin strap.

He bought a soft drink and headed back into the darkened interior looking for a booth with a phone plate that was unoccupied. He found one at the back. He sat down and ruminated for a few sips. There was no help for it, he had to call in and admit defeat. He started dialing out of Nostramedes. It took time and cost credits at several steps along the way.

Because he was concentrating on the forty-digit code for a call to Military Intelligence, he failed to react instantaneously when two figures slipped into the booth.

They held knives to his throat and kidney. "Don't move a muscle, friend. You've got some questions to answer," a voice whispered harshly in his ear.

"There must be some mistake," Iehard said.

"You better stop thinking about resisting and concentrate on staying alive, sunboy!" a second voice growled.

The first man was searching him for weapons but he, too, failed to think about boots. He did pull out Jon's wallet, though.

They were no professionals, that was clear.

They urged him out of the booth. "Walk between us and walk real carefully, or you get shivved. Understand, sunboy."

"Look, if it's credit you want just point me to a function box. There's no need to give me a blood test to see if my credit's any good." He winced as the knives dug into his skin.

"Shut your face. We're not trying to rob you."

He got fleeting glimpses of the men. Both were pale, blond, tall, and thin. They wore gray one-piece spacecrew issue.

Then they'd pushed out of a maintenance door into the alley. Without his mask on, the stink returned full force. They hurried through a littered back alley and then a door opened to their knock and he was forced into a pool of light in a storage chamber of some kind. Rows of pallets stacked with containers occupied one end. A foldup table and chairs were set up beneath a naked lightbar to one side.

More of the blond people in gray space tunics stood around. And the woman he'd been pursuing. They all had air tanks, goggles, and breathing masks, dangling from the chin straps.

The woman was older than he'd first believed. In her middle years, he decided, and obviously under a great deal of strain. She was staring at him with a mix of fright and rage.

Jon noticed that nobody was wearing obvious handweapons. Then a man, a little taller than the others, and older, with a slight stoop to his shoulders and a gaunt face, came closer. On the lapels of his tunic was a spaceline device. He had several black enamel badges beside it. He, too, exhibited signs of extreme anxiety. "This is the one?"

"That is him. I sensed him when I was waiting for Porox. Who never came."

"Be quiet! Stop talking or we will have to kill him—do you want blood on your hands?" To Jon he said, "Why do you follow us? Are you an agent for Superior Buro?"

Jon didn't reply. These people were on edge. He needed to choose his words carefully. The pair that had brought him in were younger, with very short haircuts, and had expressions of furious intensity on their pallid faces. They looked capable of using the knives.

"I work for the Nocanican Export Import Police. You're suspected of illegal entry with a false credit ID."

The tall man held up Jon's own ID. "This says 'Mass Murder Squad.' What does that mean?"

"He's a senser, a filthy senser," the woman said in a harsh voice. "He must work for Superior Buro!"

"Officer Dahn has Superior Buro on the brain," said one of the intense young men. They had relaxed their hold slightly.

"Shut up, M'Nee, you little bastard," the woman spat back.

"Silence, both of you. In the authority vested in me—" the tall one began.

"Will you space that stuff?" M'Nee snapped. "If I hear about the damned taxpayers one more time I'll scream. Let's kill this creep and get out of here—we're in danger, we must get on!"

The tall one reacted with a vigorous shake of the head. "There'll be no killing. I gave my oath to the board and that's final, do you understand?"

M'Nee rolled his eyes in disgust but refrained from a further retort. The tall man swung back to Jon.

"You probably are a spy for the laowon, but we don't have time to make a proper investigation. You will live and I will even give you a message for your master: Tell them that they missed the Bey; he has already flown to the stars. Tell them they will never find us now, that we are too far ahead."

"We must kill him, Captain," the woman said desperately.

"No. We will incapacitate him and leave him here. But we will not kill him. He has not harmed us and I promised no bloodshed."

"What if he has already called in his masters?"

"We will be gone. They have missed us."

"If I might be allowed to say something," Jon began.

"Do not speak, servant of the laowon. We allow you to live because we are merciful men. We know what you are."

The door opened, another blond woman came in. "Everything is ready, Captain."

The others started to leave. The captain nodded to the young minders with the knives. They shifted position a little more.

"Break his ankles, tie him up, and leave him here. Lock the door."

He turned to go and Iehard felt his guards move again as they prepared to do him violence. Jon acted as taught in the squad combat school.

Summoning energy into his arms and shoulders, he abruptly slammed both elbows out, pushing both men away. Their knives missed him and he somersaulted forward. But his landing was poor and he fell sideways. The men were on him, a boot caught him in the side, but then he had the Taw Taw in his hands.

The sound was deafening in the small room. The first slug took the kicker in his leg. Blood sprayed from the ruined limb. The second man tried to grab the gun but he was too slow and too far away. The Taw Taw boomed again and the unfortunate M'Nee's forearm shattered as he was spun away by the impact.

Iehard sprang out into the dark corridor after the leader. He saw running figures and called out an order to halt. The gun came up. A hiss sounded in his ear and something slammed between his shoulders very hard. He was flung forward, went down in an untidy roll, but came up with his gun in both hands, pointing back toward his assailant.

But he saw nothing to shoot at except something like a dark-green billiard ball with two red dots glowing like malevolent eyes. Then a hammer blow in the chest knocked the air out of his body.

Before he could get his breath back, a man had straddled him and was punching him in the face while screaming, "You filthy bastard!" over and over. Jon managed to get an arm up to ward off the blows, and then struck back, wielding the Taw Taw like a club. On the second try he made contact and the man was gone, but before Jon could climb back to his feet, something hard struck the back of his head. The whole scene turned off with a *click*.

CHAPTER TEN

PADZN BIRTHAMB WAS THE LAST TO ARRIVE. THE BURO men stiffened to attention at the sight of the laowon chief. The room was a shambles, the computer equipment had been torn loose and pushed against one wall. File modules were scattered over the floor.

"Everything of interest has already been entered on the files aboard *Illustrious*, my lord." The speaker was the section leader, Benks, tall, overbearing, brutal.

"There was nothing in my orders about destroying the suspect's equipment and files."

The section leader's jaw dropped. Wasn't this just another smash-and-liquidate operation? Pull another of these rebels out and deliver her to the Brutality Room. Anyone traced inside laowon military computer files was a legitimate target for liquidation.

"I thought, my lord."

"I know you did, Benks. A bad mistake. Someone in your position should know better. Did you never ask yourself, 'Well, what if we release the suspect?' Did you not imagine the kind of legal trouble she could present us? Did you not even pause to think that the woman might have colleagues who would be extremely upset, who might initiate legal problems for us in Nocanicus courts?"

Of course, Benks had never concerned himself with such thoughts.

"My apologies, Lord," the man stammered. "I will make amends."

"Indeed you will, Benks. You will begin by restoring this disgusting little human pit to exactly the condition it was in when we removed the woman. Do you understand? And you will do it quickly. The deity alone knows what trouble you may have caused us already."

"The woman, Lord?"

Padzn Birthamb turned a freezing glare on the man. "What is it, Benks?"

"Is she coming back here?"

"I don't know, Benks. At the moment I'd say that was rather up to her, if you see what I mean?"

When Jon Iehard returned to wakefulness it was with more than just a splitting headache, and also with a lot less.

He was sore just about everywhere and he was stark naked. He'd been picked clean by the scavengers—everything was gone, air tanks, clothes, boots, the lot.

He coughed, his throat and lungs were sore from breathing the stinking atmosphere of the Unders. The back of his head sported a goose egg and there were painful bruises on his chest.

He'd been hauled into a narrow side alley by the scavengers, and it was almost pitch black.

From far below, beneath the grids, there came a titanic suction sound. The sludge tanks were being refreshed. A few seconds later a stench of stunning strength rose through the Unders adding fresh excremental odors to the reek.

As he contemplated the loss of his credit card, his ID, his gun, and everything else, he realized how serious his problems had suddenly become. Getting out of the Unders might prove pretty damn difficult.

And after he did that, he'd have to explain this mess. The case was blown now. No doubt about that, and the blame was all his. He should've called in the MI right at the start.

Then he remembered! He had a clue. It was pretty slim, but it was all he had to go on. He'd have to hope that if he moved quickly enough he could catch up. It was time to move.

The air at the top of the corridor was unbreathable, it

burned the lungs, so he progressed in a crouch. The stink was overpowering. The roaring in the sludge tanks echoed like the cries of some gigantic animal through hot damp air.

The walk through the corridors was a nightmare. He kept stumbling over people, who would rise and assault him furiously for the trespass. Without a light or clothes or shock rod, he was just a breather like the rest.

When he finally found his way back to the main elevator banks it was feedtime in the ventilation chamber. The naked multitudes were lined up in an endless chain to receive their seven-ounce helping of a squishy, yellow-green feed, served in an edible paper cone that contained essential minerals and bran.

The feed was pumped from long nozzles that depended from the ceiling and were controlled by a squad of black-suited guards. The shock rods sparked again and again off the backs of the greediest, keeping them in line, although every time there was a spill a dozen or so wretches would hurl themselves at the precious goop on the floor.

Jon decided to try the guards at the elevators, although he dreaded their likely reaction.

As expected, they looked up with truculence writ large on their faces. They were intent on an erovideo and did not care to be interrupted.

He tried to hold himself upright, to accentuate the difference between himself and the wretched breathers all round. His explanations fell on deaf ears.

"Get off with you, you scrawny breather, go get your feed," said one fellow, lazily waving a shock rod.

There was one young officer, however, who did respond. Not as hardbitten as the others perhaps.

"You say you have an active credit number. Do you know the number? I can check that quite easily."

"Yes, of course I can remember. It's—" But he was not allowed to finish.

"Oh, give it up, Tunx. Can't you see it's just some old gibberer from the grates. Give him a couple of strokes with the rod and send him back to the feed. You're missing the really hot bits."

Another man rose and laid about Iehard with his shock rod, which imparted hefty stings each time it came in contact with his skin.

Smarting and burning, he was driven toward the vents.

In gloomy despair he watched the elevators coming and going every half hour as they brought new arrivals and, much less frequently, took someone away.

He had to get to those elevators, he had to get off Nostramedes.

The guards watched the erotic video for a while longer, laughing uproariously from time to time. Then, with much cheerful banter, the group broke up, and Jon pressed forward again, catching up with the officer named Tunx.

The shock rod came up. Iehard stood his ground.

"You're making a mistake. If you don't believe me, just let me punch in my alarm code. I have gray code for emergency contact with my superior. I assure you, you'll be remembered."

Tunx seemed dubious behind his face mask. "You scutbellies are all the same, always trying stuff out on us. I tell you I'm tired of it."

"Look, I work for the Hyperion Grandee police. For the sake of your own career, let me get to a function box. I'm not asking that much of you, am I?"

The guard swung his shock rod menacingly. "All right, but if this is a game of some kind then I'm going to give you a few licks of the rod to remember me by."

They approached the elevator banks. A battered switchboard and multifunction box module was controlled by a bored Nostramedes Communication Company woman, who looked up from the novella she was watching with considerable annoyance.

She would have sent them away if she could but Officer Tunx was a rising star in the Guard and she didn't want to upset him. "All right, use line seven. But be quick, I haven't all day to be pandering to foolish breathers."

Jon's fingers were fairly shaking as he stabbed out his code. He got it wrong once, and the unit flashed a terminate sign, but he recovered swiftly enough to get the call reaccepted. Of course it took the communications company's computer a full minute to get around to accepting an emergency call from the Unders. Finally it beamed it to Hyperion Grandee.

Tunx was getting impatient. "Look, breather, I told you you were going to get it." The shock rod crackled with energy as he turned it up to the maximum.

The NocanCo woman was grinning. "I hope you're going to give it to him good and solid, Officer Tunx."

"Thanks, you're a big help," Jon told her. She scowled.

The guard started to order him away from the phone, when at long last the little monitor lit up and Coptor Brine's great ugly face filled the screen. "Jon. What the hell are you doing on Nostramedes? And if this call isn't from Jon Iehard, then what the hell are you doing using his code signal?"

"Coptor! It is me, and I am on Nostramedes and I'm in the shit all right, but I'll explain all that later. Just get me out of here, man. I need a credit line. I'm trapped on the Unders."

Officer Tunx pressed forward and yelled into the microphone, "Does this character really have a credit line?"

"Who is that?" snapped Coptor.

"That's one of the elevator guards here on the Unders, Coptor," Iehard said quickly. "It's all right, he just wants to be sure he hasn't made a mistake in letting me make this call."

Coptor took a moment to digest this. "Well, listen to me, Guard Whoever-you-are. Standing next to you you have the best damned operative the Hyperion Grandee Mass Murder Squad has ever had, so you better be damn careful with his behind and get him back to me in perfect shape just as soon as you damn well can, or I will personally see to it that your career will be short and unpleasant. You got that?"

A few minutes later Iehard had a credit line, a new card from Nostramedes Centrobanc, and a one-piece suit he bought with the card at the elevator side stall.

The elevator opened to his card. Inside it smelled fresh and tasted cool. He spent the whole ride just breathing, noticing how wonderful it could be.

CHAPTER ELEVEN

BEFORE HE COULD EVEN TAKE A SHOWER, THE LAOWON had him arrested and brought before them. They began a merciless debriefing, with frequent threats of Hypnogen should he not cooperate fully. From the beginning the Lady Blasilab screamed invective.

Iehard did his best to reply calmly, to keep his voice even and polite. His success enraged Blasilab and she was soon purpling at his "impertinence."

Jon also kept back a single name, a crucial name, that for some reason he felt compelled to retain. He wondered at this behavior, felt both guilt and a weird sense of triumph.

"Imbecile! Incompetent!"

The Morgooze behaved as if in laowon "frozen rage." Any movement might become a lethal stroke aimed at an incompetent underling. "Fool, you have let the monster go free!"

They raged on at him and finally left, bodyguards all around them and storm clouds above. The Morgooze threatened most dreadful dooms.

At last Jon was allowed to limp into a shower, get clean, and visit the medical section.

He had black bruises on one side of his face and massive, circular bruises between the shoulder blades and on the left side of the chest. He was pronounced fortunate not to have fractured ribs or skull. When they'd finished he wore medipacks on his biggest bruises and bandages on the rest. Slowly he limped home in an MI exercise suit. It was early evening. He found it hard to believe that less than thirty-six hours before he had started out on his fool's errand.

The 10,000 credits had evaporated, and he had a battle ahead with MI over the Domaine Larose, the flight to Nostramedes, and sundry other expenses. Someone had written LAOMAN OUT! in large blue letters across his door. He looked across to Onliki's place. The corridor was silent, but he had the feeling that attentive ears listened for his reaction.

He let himself in, made some instacaf and lay down on the bed. He was utterly weary. He tried to call Meg but received no reply except the answering file on Daisy. He left a message then put his head down with a great sigh and prepared to sleep.

He was just sinking into a pleasant oblivion when a brutally loud knock sounded on the door. It was repeated, along with a megaphone voice calling his name. Groggily he got up and went to the door. He looked at the screen. A pair of men in yellow-and-silver uniforms were outside, along with a woman in the red and blue of the Police Commission Political Section. He opened the door.

"Jon Iehard?" He nodded.

"Apparently you failed to make a court appearance this morning. The Baltitude Gas Company presented a suit against you and won judgment for two million credits. Immediate payment was demanded and all your accounts, credit, and possessions are to be impounded at once. These gentlemen are from Baltitude and they have come to seize any possessions that may be deemed valuable enough to sell. Please stand aside, do not hinder them in their work."

She attached a long pink-and-blue docket to his door, just above the word "Laoman" that already decorated it.

He stared as the movers entered his apartment and took away his antique rug, his ornately carved side table from the watermoons of Ingrid, his pair of pleasant watercolors by M'Aicey of Camleopard Al Kuds. At the last moment he went to the side table and grabbed up his clothes and plucked the silver cube from Fabulous Fara out of a little antique Earthbowl, just before it, too, went out in their arms and was loaded onto a hand cart.

When they'd finished, he was stripped of everything

but one suit of clothes, his boots, and the little cube. The last thing taken had been the TV, which had wowed plaintively as it vanished out the door.

They left and he sat down on his bare mattress. All the materials of nine years of life had been taken away. He would appeal the suit, he might even win it and eventually he'd get it all back, but for now it was gone and it made him feel frighteningly hollow. Everything hurt. Life seemed to have reached an astonishing low point.

He slept for eight hours, then he pulled himself out of bed with enormous effort. He was a mess, it even hurt to open his mouth. His face was swollen and puffy.

Under the medipads his ribs were purple and yellow. He whistled to himself. This kind of treatment was almost enough to turn Jon Iehard, reasonable human being, into a religious fanatic, a Panhumanist Elchite even.

He showered, put on his remaining clothes, and looked forlornly around his stripped apartment. He now owed that wealthy oaf Baltitude. He wondered how he was ever going to get even.

He went down to the Mass Murder Squad. The place was alive with activity; a "bad one" was in progress. Coptor and both wing squads were out hunting around Octagon Six for a frag bomber who'd terrorized the early-morning office rush.

The computer operatives were hard at it. Monitor screens flickered throughout the warren. No one paid Jon much notice. He limped into his own desk and removed his spare Taw Taw .22 and a box of ammo clips from their hiding place under the desk top. Next he took an ankle holster and strapped it on inside his boot. He knew better than even to try on a shoulder holster.

As he left the office, a Buro tail fell into place behind him. The security litany ran through his mind—"Number One, he's the obvious one. Number Two will be somewhere behind him, he or she will not be obvious." But that day he didn't mind if they saw where he went.

He rode transit to Octagon Seven and went straight to Meg's. The door opened to his card, as normal, but once inside all his worst suspicions were confirmed.

The computer pit had been rearranged. The office was too clean, it even looked as if it had been dusted. Most unusual of all, the DAex Ram 44000 was doing nothing but answering telephone calls. Normally it would have been working on Masque routines, building up character programming.

Nor did the computer know where Meg was. "No data" was all it would put on the screen in response to his questions. That spoke volumes.

He examined other pieces of equipment. The data transfer printer had worn its inkers down to nubs. When he scanned the piles of data storage modules, he noticed they were not in Meg's precise patterns.

Superior Buro had taken Meg and they had dumped and printed out everything they could use. Unless—

He called Ingrid Kopelin.

Her anxiety was immediately obvious. "She's been gone for twenty-four hours at least. It must have been the Buro. Oh, Jon, I'm so afraid for her."

"If Meg was hiding, where might she go?"

Ingrid shrugged. "Where indeed? I don't think Meg thought much about hiding. If she was in trouble with the Buro she'd have stayed by the computer, in communication with a lawyer to the very last minute. But I checked and she never called. They must have come very suddenly."

Then he looked at his own desk. Everything had been put back more neatly than before. He presumed it had all been filmed.

On his notepad he found a small scrawled note. Meg's handwriting. Dated the day before.

"Jon—Roq left a message for you."

What did that mean? He looked at Daisy dubiously. The Buro would have loaded the computer with bugs. Meg meant him to check this on another system. He went to the stack of file modules and took down the one marked "Louis Quatorze" and pocketed it.

His jaw set grimly, Iehard headed back to Octagon Five and Petrie's section. Everything hurt like hell, but he persisted in moving his arms and gradually his muscles loosened up somewhat. His left side was finally the only place he really had to favor.

The reception officer returned after a moment with word that the commander was in a meeting. Perhaps an appointment could be made for another time, or day? Iehard said he'd wait, and wait he did, until, after a little more than an hour, Petrie suddenly emerged from his office and escorted Jon inside. A guard frisked him, removing the Taw Taw.

"Jon, I have bad news for you."

Iehard sat down heavily. So they had given Petrie the unpleasant little task of telling him.

"Where is she?" he breathed. He could smell Petrie's discomfort despite the little suppressor band.

"You know how they are, Jon. They wanted to teach her a lesson, a short sharp shock. After all, they caught her inside military files aboard *Illustrious*."

"What do you mean, 'short sharp shock'?"

"You were raised on a laowon world, Jon—you know their methods. Your friend has gone to the Brutality Room."

"They did *that*! Just for trying to find me some information on this filthy fugitive of theirs! And *you* let them!"

Petrie flinched.

"Who rules in this system?" Jon screamed. "And tell me, why is this case such a goddamn secret anyway? They either want me to find the man or they don't, which is it? I mean, I'm sorry, Commander, please accept my apologies, since we are being awfully nice about all this, but what are they trying to do? Yesterday I almost got killed tracking someone who I'm sure is related to the case, and now they've put my computer op in the Brutality Room!"

Petrie spread his hands wide, summoned his best empathic tone. "Jon, I'm sorry. But why do you think the Buro would tell me? Believe me, between MI and the Buro there exists an, aah, 'adversarial' relationship, only we have to be the gracious loser most of the time. You can imagine what that means to all of us, to our morale. But I want you also to understand that I win a few, here and there, and those wins sometimes involve getting someone back. If she keeps her tongue in check, your Meg may be back with us tomorrow, chastened but alive."

"If they kill her I swear I'll—"

Petrie waved his hands anxiously. His voice hardened. "Don't say it, Jon. No threats. Now calm down, quickly now."

Jon saw fear in old Petrie's face and he realized he was going too far. They would have to take him out of service after this; the laowon wouldn't want him running around armed, making threats against blueskins.

And that would ruin everything. Suddenly an enormous realization sank home. He had his own agenda now. All the rules had changed without his even realizing it.

Without paying attention, he listened to Petrie's smoothing of the roiled waters. As soon as possible he retrieved his gun and headed out again. He chose to walk through the park, thinking things through. They'd given him back his gun! He imagined that Petrie had already given someone hell for that.

By the time he'd reached the Hyades Monument he'd made up his mind. He turned on his heel and sprinted suddenly through the crowds, down into the Brambles, a wild section of woodland with many paths. He knew it well from his regular jogging run. He left the path precisely where he could vanish most easily in dense shrubbery. He watched from concealment.

A woman panted down the path. He could sense her disquiet; she'd lost him and she knew her masters would be upset. She was running hard, a handbag flying out behind her.

He waited until she was gone and then doubled back, cutting diagonally across the park to Octagon Nine where he caught a red-line car all the way to Octagon One. There he headed for the Gas Exchange. Inside that enormous tower he took the elevator to the reference library. Once in a computer booth it was a matter of moments to log on and find the entry he sought.

POROX, NATHAN, INDEPENDENT GAS DEALER. ADDRESS FOR COMMUNICATIONS: INDIAN TREND, SOONER. COMM. NO. 7234588–9P.

The entry on Sooner arrived a few seconds later.

SOONER: COMETARY REMNANT, APPROX. MASS 20M KILOTONS. HIGHLY ECCENTRIC ORBIT, 22 DEGREES ABOVE NOCAN EQUATORIAL PLANE AT PERIGEE IN REGION OF ORBIT OF WILLIAM. COLONIZED IN YEAR 12 OF NOCANICUS SYSTEM EXPLORATION. POPULATION IN CENSUS OF AD 4420, 436,288.

He ordered a geographical printout on Sooner, plus a printout of gas delivery schedules between Sooner and Hyperion Grandee.

He read through the schedules while gobbling some lunch in a small restaurant that served the office crowd from Gas Alley; the sector included the dozen towers of the giant gas and chemical companies. There were lots of Mooners too. The embassies of the watermoons of William and Shala were next door. The Mooners kept their embassies close to the docking structures, thus showing a certain degree of disdain for "official" Hyperion Grandee, which was grouped around Octagon Five, several kloms away.

It was immediately apparent. Sooner was very close by, a matter of a few million kloms. This was the busy period for the Sooners, marketing gas and water to the nearest habitats as they fell through the belt. Sooner was sure to be crowded with ships, mostly tankers of course, all trying to get in to the loading docks and out again before being carried too far into the inner system.

He noticed a construction contract listing as well. The Sooner sunshield was being refurbished before they passed into the torrid zone around Nocanicus.

His next stop was a little mercantile bank, Banco Gasto, on Element Walk. He stopped by the safe deposit counter. A few minutes later a clerk brought up the box. He removed a special credit card blank, one that Meg had made for just such a situation as that which faced him now.

The card had nothing visible printed on it, but its surface was primed with Meg's deadly supercode. It was the result of years of Meg's work with her baby Bioram.

If the card worked, then for a while—a few hours, perhaps even a day, until the habitat mainframes caught on and switched access codes in all the function boxes—Meg's supercard would override credit and ID requirements as effectively as a Nocanicus Authority Executive Security Card.

With it he would be very hard to trace, which was going to be very important for a while.

But first he entered an executive function box booth. He used the card to create a temporary RAM buffer in the booth, big enough to unload the file concerning the hunchback character Roq, from the Louis Quatorze module.

There was a file he didn't recognize, a random number. He looked it up. Roq sprang to life.

"Jonno! Didn't Roq do well in the king's return to the stable?"

Roq faded off the screen. The file ended. Iehard punched up the file containing Roq's big scene. Hell, Roq hadn't done anything in that scene except get horsewhipped for being sullen in front of the king. What was the message about?

There was now a shortened version of the king's return from hunting, surrounded by courtiers on horseback and wornout hounds. The servants cheered, trumpeters sounded off. There was nothing unusual about it. Iehard was on the verge of flicking forward when it suddenly cut to a stable interior, rushed, background was full of dropout. Roq awaited the entrance of the king.

This is where they had been before the Morgooze so rudely interrupted. But now Roq turned full face to the screen. In the character's gruff, almost unintelligible speech he said, "Jon, warn them, the *Illustrious* is not alone. Another battlejumper is on station at William. They are not discovered yet, but the laowon suspect they will head for William. They must be warned."

Roq winked. "Now you'd better erase this section," he growled.

Hurriedly Jon did just that, then collapsed the temporary RAM buffer and retrieved his supercard. He hurried down Element Walk and went downramp to the Arterial. He chose another phone booth.

He called Melissa Baltitude at the Baltitude home number. When the phone answered he gave it the private code she'd given him but kept his face plate off. When she picked up the phone, he told her that since her father had completely bankrupted him that morning, there was nothing keeping him from accepting her wonderful offer of a little boat ride out to the fabulous megahabitats.

She was overjoyed. They could leave as soon as he was ready. Perhaps she could finally teach Daddy a lesson. He suggested they meet at the Dove model B's parking slot. She gave him the address and promised to have the boat ready to go when he got there. He emphasized that last point. She blew him a kiss as they cut the link.

He headed for Kugs, the big department store. He needed a lot of stuff, starting with spacesuits and an invalid chair.

It was hard to concentrate. Old Meg had been ahead of him all along, as usual. Thinking of her brought a lump to his throat, tears to his eyes.

Now he had to get through; he must not fail her.

In fact, he had a responsibility to the whole human race.

CHAPTER TWELVE

BEFORE ENTERING THE ELEVATOR RUNNING TO THE LAO-won level, Jon Iehard donned a new, crisp white uniform, a size too large. He carried a folding wheelchair and a small backpack. Beneath the whites he wore full body armor, more plates than usual. For the Taw Taw, he carried three twenty-shot clips.

When he emerged in laowon space, into the pseudo-light of evening on ancient Laogolden, he blended perfectly into the crowd. White was the attire for servants there. The blues themselves wore military uniforms—harsh, simple, stark lines—or the more elaborate regalia of Seygfan.

Like most employees of the Hyperion Grandee police forces, Jon knew the legendary address he was heading toward, only too well.

He steered a path through the curving Massgiers Boulevard. The ceiling was fifty meters high; elegant white facades in the neoclassical laowon mode—flat planes, heavy bevels—occupied the walls. Discreet entrances, shrouded by potted shrubs, gave access to the apartments beyond. Massgiers Boulevard eventually opened onto Lanushka Avenue where one entrance was masked by six fat polpun trees, all in green flower and exuding the usual heavy, musky odor. The door itself was a modest real-wood affair, seven feet by five, an antique from some ancient fort on Laogolden or Ratan, inlaid with an intricate pattern of Early-Archaic lao hexagrams.

At the door stood two Superior Buro guards in black uniforms, handweapons strapped into holsters. Jon approached, set down the wheelchair and turned to them as if to offer his ID card. Instead he flicked an electric blade into the leading officer and produced the Taw Taw with the other.

"Open the door!" he hissed.

The stricken guard was already choking on a terrible amount of blood; the blade had chopped right through his neck and buried itself in the door behind him with a thunk. He quickly coughed up his life and lay still, but the blade was digging into the door, its charger whining shrilly.

He retrieved the blade, prodded the stunned guard through the Buro's front door, and then coldly shot him through the head. The big body tumbled heavily to the dark green rug in the Buro's outer lobby. A startled receptionist jumped up and opened her mouth, but his bullet took her the next moment, along with the officer in a black tunic who was leaping for the relative safety of the space behind her desk.

He emptied the clip into the rest of the laowon standing, bunched, in the doorway. Only one managed to get his own weapon out. The shot whanged off Jon's chest plate uselessly, staggering him for a moment, but too late. Then Jon was alone with a pile of laowon dead. Trembling fingers slid a new clip into the Taw Taw and then quickly unfolded the wheelchair and locked the legs in place. Parking it beside the door, he slipped into the next suite of offices.

He ran down a darkened spiral corridor, lined with doorless cubby holes, and as he ran, he shot laowon, wearing earphones, intent on tasks or monitor screens. None made effective resistance. The corridor curved back on itself past an empty conference room. No security provisions had been made against direct assault. Over the millennium, it had become unthinkable.

There was a guard at the door to the inner section. The fellow knew that something was up, he had his gun out when Jon came round the corner but his first shot was wild. He had no opportunity for a second. He still had no clear idea what was happening when he hit the wall behind him in death.

Inside that door he surprised a trio of laowon operatives. They responded with the lightning reflexes of their training. But Jon had the initiative. The Taw Taw took one in the face. Jon's foot hammered the second in the groin and he ducked to avoid the neck-breaker kick thrown by the third.

He spun, another kick rocked him into the wall, but the Taw Taw beat the third laowon's follow-up blow. Jon shot the knee, preventing the leg from rising, flipped the electric blade into the second officer's back, dropping him to the floor for good.

He was breathing hard by then, and the gunfire had produced a degree of alarm in the inner section. He heard someone shout. An overweight laowon appeared in a doorway, then ducked back with a fearful shriek. Jon caught him pulling a handweapon from a drawer in a lao-baroque desk. The Taw Taw finished its second clip.

Someone had killed the lights, but Jon sensed laowon fear and he set the electric blade to boomerang, then flipped it around a wall partition to gut the wily section leader who waited there with a loaded handweapon.

He ran on, but found himself running out of opponents. One senior officer got off a shot from his office door but the slug glanced off Jon's chest armor and barely broke his stride.

In the laowon view the only thing human beings understood was force. This view was a natural outgrowth of the imperial system that had evolved on Laogolden. In addition there was a natural tendency to see humans as dangerous, irresponsible inferiors who were only kept from wholesale murder of their blue-skin betters by fear of a painful death.

Most human systems that supported laowon populations also had Superior Buro stations. Where there were such stations, there was always the dreaded "Brutality Room." There, the Superior Buro brought human criminals seized on charges laid against them by laowon victims. The Buro screened complaints; only a few were actually proceeded upon, and the Buro was careful not to overuse the Room. In fact, they usually did not kill the people brought in. This increased the legendary stature of the place among the subject human peoples, since it produced still voluble, if often permanently inarticulate, survivors.

Based on laowon punishment principles, as encoded in the *Imperiomix Lao*, the Room was actually a small hospital. There were white walled interrogation clinics and padded cells. Even rooms for surgery, but the main room was given over to the practices of physical punishment.

On the occasion of the tri-mode punishment of Docket No. 813, the gallery above the punishment room itself was graced by the aristocratic presence of the Lady Blasilab of Chashleesh and the young Morgooze of Blue Seygfan. Behind them sat a pair of officers from *Illustrious*, wearing the black and gold tunics of the space navy. The four laowon watched impassively as the Superior Buro operatives applied their instruments to the naked woman strapped on the frame.

Again and again the instruments sparked and crackled and Meg Vance's body jumped and wobbled. She had long since ceased screaming. There was no point. It was better to be far beyond speech, in a trance state, somewhere approaching death. Meg had reached the tertiary punishment mode.

The first mode, applied to humans of either sex, involved a horribly humiliating hour of sexual abuse by two or three special bred brutalitors; pinhead males who became sexually uncontrollable in the presence of almost anything mammalian. Of low intelligence and ferocious drives, they quickly reduced prisoners to the necessary state of low self-esteem that was prized by the operatives in the secondary and tertiary modes.

Only after the brutalitors had exhausted themselves did the Buro's skilled operatives begin their work. Electrodes were attached for induced pseudosmothering, followed by pseudodrowning and then an extreme claustrophobic anxiety.

As Meg's personality profile had revealed, those deaths were the worst imaginable to her. While in a state of complete disorientation she'd received injections of tenderniche to sensitize her nervous system, and then the operatives in shining white tunics had begun their work with the pain wands—the tertiary mode.

The nerve fire had wrung every tear from her body, her throat was a dried husk, she could protest no longer.

Still the punishment continued.

Lady Blasilab affected a yawn. The Morgooze ignored it, intent on the chastisement of the willful human. The Morgooze was determined to exact revenge from the humans at every opportunity. He had made a request to the Central Fleet Command for the blood rights to Jon Iehard, the incompetent operative who had lost their one trace on the Elchite murderer. *"The Bey was gone, flown to the stars . . ."* Somehow those mocking words refused to leave his mind. Already he dreaded his return to Laogolden. What would the Heir say? What would the old Widow Maker say?

Of course, he would blame it on the Superior Buro. The fool Petrie could be taken for evidence. The Morgooze decided to take the initiative. Instant, furious assault, that was the way of Blue Seygfan! And just possibly, if he could steamroller the court, they would throw him Padzn Birthamb, for an expiation. The Morgooze would have Birthamb up on the rack right after Jon Iehard's extravagant expiation beneath the camera lights.

The laowon became aware of a disturbance in the outer corridor. The Morgooze looked up in annoyance. There should be no interruptions. This was an expiation before a full Morgooze!

The door to the Brutality Room opened and a figure in a white uniform slipped in. The Morgooze watched in surprise as a human, unescorted by laowon operatives approached the rack.

Aghast, the Morgooze heard the solid "thuck" sounds of Jon Iehard's Taw Taw as the human shot the three laowon who were torturing Meg Vance. Shocking red blood spattered the white tunics.

With yowls of rage the Morgooze and Lady Blasilab called for guards to slay the impious human intruder. An invasion of the Brutality Room! Such a thing had never been dared! It was unthinkable!

Jon looked up, saw them, and fired in a single fluid movement. The Morgooze spilled over the rail and landed on the matted floor with a thud. Lady Blasilab's head burst the next instant and pieces flew back over the seats of the gallery.

The two officers from *Illustrious* were standing in their seats, stunned. Where were the Guards? How did the impious human dare to do this? Then the exploding slugs hit them, and they toppled into the row behind them.

Jon broke Meg free from the rack and drew a black coat around her body, then buttoned it up to the neck.

Her soft, middle aged body was slick with sweat and mucus. The pain wands left no visible marks, but there were many bruises, scratches, and cuts from her battle with the pinhead rapists.

She moaned. He whispered fiercely in her ear. She shut up. Somehow he managed to convince her to hang onto him, piggyback style, as he went back out through the offices of the Buro. He had to step over a number of dead laowon before he reached the door.

Outside he got her into the wheelchair he had waiting. It was equipped with straps, which he fastened with fingers that were barely shaking. Something that he noticed with considerable surprise. Here he'd surely provided his own sentence of death yet his deeds seemed remote, impossible. He couldn't fail now!

Then Jon was pushing Meg briskly down the laowon corridor to the elevator bank. In the artificial eternal sunset of Laogolden, laowon he passed in the corridor assumed he was a servant taking an elderly patron for a stroll above the park. The elevator bore them to the transit station far below, and a car was along within moments. His luck held good.

In fact, his crazed audacity had worked far better than he had ever imagined. The Superior Buro had been struck a hammer blow. So devastating an attack, that, until the surviving Buro operatives on the off shift woke up and came into the office, nobody would know it had taken place. For the moment there was no Superior Buro on Hyperion Grandee.

Jon and Meg rode the transit cars to Octagon One. Then Jon loaded her onto a low gravity manhandler pod, and they climbed on the escalator to the docking parks for small craft, on the outermost dorsal extension.

Melissa Baltitude was waiting inside the Dove model B, a high expression of the boat builder's art. An aerodynamically smooth exterior gave onto a luxurious interior of inlaid stone panels and sleek white acceleration couches for four people. Polished brass accoutrements decorated the purple glass control screens. A smaller cabin at the rear concealed a tiny galley and bathroom facilities.

He pushed Meg on board, and loaded her into an acceleration couch, thankful for low gravity. The piggyback ride had been a nightmare experience for his bruised back and chest.

Melissa was staring at him openmouthed. "Jon, what's happened." She noticed the green medipack on the back of his head, plus the purpling bruises.

"There's been some trouble." He took a look at the clock. "Let's go, time is short."

"Who?" She began.

But he cut her off. "I'll explain when we're out of Hyperion Grandee."

Twenty-eight minutes had passed since he'd left the Superior Buro. He strapped in and Melissa gave the computer the go-ahead. The Dove rose and flew away down the exit funnel.

Outside Grandee a moderate amount of traffic was moving in the inner lanes, but they soon emptied out, permitting the Traxon engines to cut in full for a primary burn that pressed the Dove's passengers deep into their seats. When the burn ended, forty-five minutes after the slaughter, the first screams of public outrage were hitting the airwaves. Jon first detected heavy bursts of activity on the laowon channels. Then it suddenly erupted on the human news channels. Jon covered all the major ones, and found interesting nuances in the coverage. Channel 99, the biggest news net, was very noncomittal. Someone, it didn't mention who, had committed a mass murder upon laowon. The big rival, 109, insisted that the identity of the chief suspect in the case was an operative of the Hyperion Grandee Mass Murder Squad.

While he was listening to the first rounds of instant analysis, Meg came awake. Jon was ready with painkillers and a cup of nutrisoup. She groaned, opened her eyes, and blinked in astonishment. Then she screamed, again and again, and writhed, cowering in the acceleration couch. It was unnerving, the sounds were so animal, so desperate. Mucus streamed from her eyes, her mouth, her nose. Her sobs had a deep, tearing quality that made them hard to listen to.

When Jon tried to comfort her she shrank away from him with fluting little cries of terror, so he grimly injected a sedative into her, watching until it took effect. Then he left her and floated over to concentrate on the news programs he had windowed around the screen.

Melissa Baltitude was staring at the coverage with horrified eyes. The noises coming from that woman were awful, disgusting; they made Melissa's skin crawl.

Jon said nothing, but flicked around on minor channels for additional scraps on the story.

"Jon what is it? Who is this woman? What's happened to her?"

He took a breath.

"Her name's Meg, she's an old buddy of mine. We were on this case for the laowon. Tracking a fugitive Panhumanist from out-system. She broke some of the laowon rules; they took her to the Room for it."

Melissa's eyes widened. Meg's gargling sobs were terribly loud and close by. "What happened?" she breathed.

"I went in and broke her out. Killed a lot of laowon—every one of them that I found in there."

Her eyes popped in alarm. "Killed?" It sounded as if she was in trouble. Daddy had warned her! She felt an instant pang of guilt.

Jon continued monitoring the radio spectrum with feverish intentness.

They'd been in flight for another twenty-five minutes before there was a definite identification of "Jon Iehard" as the wanted fugitive. But by then the Dove B was in secondary burn, a remote speck from Hyperion Grandee and fast receding from it. Just one in a galaxy of similar small craft.

An embargo on all departures from Hyperion Grandee finally went into effect. Even a few commuter ships that had put out for nearby megahabs were ordered back.

"How long do you think it will be before your father discovers you're missing, Melissa?"

"He won't, I already told him I was going to take a winter break on the Splendor. He hasn't even called me; he can't be worried. Perhaps he just hasn't connected the two things in his mind yet."

Jon mulled it over. Would they have enough time before the laowon set out to track the Dove? It was impossible to say. He imagined they were turning Hyperion Grandee upside down for him. When that proved futile they would consider less likely possibilities, like Jon and Meg's escaping in a space yacht.

"Meg and I would love to come with you all the way to the Splendor. But we've got business at a little way station, not too far out of your way. I have the new course coordinates here. If you'll signature them, I'll feed them into the computer now."

"Where are you taking us, Jon?"

"Meg and I have a date with some very important people. We have a message for them and humanity's last hope is riding on their mission."

Something in his voice choked off her urge to reply. She initialized the new course coordinates.

CHAPTER THIRTEEN

THE TRIP TO SOONER WAS UNEVENTFUL BUT RATHER long, taking two days to complete after a long burn that severely depleted the Dove's fuel stocks. Jon told Melissa what he could of the events in which he was caught up. After a while she grew quiet and withdrawn and they didn't converse much. Then, at last, a bright speck in the forward sky began to fatten and bulge and the Dove began to decelerate hard.

Jon's chief concern was Meg's continuing disorientation. At times she crooned softly to herself, then slept deeply but awoke screaming with pain and fear. She sucked on the straw when he offered her nutrisoup and when she was awake he'd attempted to explain what had happened, but she remained generally unresponsive.

"Shock, that's all it is, Melissa. Happens to most people in the Brutality Room. Only about eight percent fail to recover, but this sort of appearance spreads the fear. That's all the blues want."

As the comet's big ablation shield resolved on their screen into a ring and then a disk, Jon had the computer tuck the Dove into the long lines of robot tanker ships lined up for access to Sooner's refinery.

Behind the ablation shield they could see the seven-kilometer torus that was the Sooner habitat.

By trading both sides of their long orbital pathway, belt

manufactures for watermoon gas and water, the inhabitants had done very well for themselves.

Soon the Dove floated into the immense tanker docking bay. Lines of tankers were connected to the nozzles on the habitat bulkhead at one end. With computer assistance Jon guided the Dove to a gentle halt beside the bulkhead. The space was vacuum and barely illuminated, but with the Dove's headlights they could see a small airlock, presumably for the occasional maintenance worker who had to enter this domain of robots.

"If you just line up around the other side of this refinery, you can refuel the Dove. We've taken you about three hours out of your way, if you intend to go on to the Splendor. There's a good chance they'll never even connect you to us. If they do—well, you'll be protected, your father is Jason Baltitude."

She struggled for her reply for a moment. "And you seriously believe that you're going to escape this system and go to the stars? The laowon are sure to catch you."

He shrugged. "I guess we don't have any other choice. If I'm wrong and if Meg was wrong, then we're probably dead. I know they'll want me to expiate at the least. But I don't think we're wrong, so don't worry too much about us. Just make the best time you can to the Splendor. When I get back I'll send you a message. Maybe we can get together somewhere."

She stared at him, speechless. He was crazy! The laowon would take him and he would die, screaming his lungs out, somewhere far away.

He started fitting Meg into a spacesuit. Then he put on one of his own, inflated the Dove's little airlock, and piled into it with Meg and the wheelchair. As the door closed he blew Melissa a kiss. She stared back, wondering why she felt such a strong impulse to cry.

Most people, of course, came onboard Sooner through the arrivals terminal, two docking bays above Jon and Meg. But the function box at the refinery airlock was the normal type and Meg's supercode had an easy time of it, fooling the immigration and bank auditor programming. In a moment they received a green flash and the hatch opened.

Just inside the small airlock was an elevator, with another function box beside it. Jon took a minute to run a swift address check and then to book a hotel room under an assumed name.

When they emerged into gravity again, it was to a wide plaza space inside the light well of an enormous building. Around the plaza were restaurants, shops, and office entrances. Towering above were the four corner prongs of the building, a tower that rose halfway to the roof of the habitat.

In the far distance, glimpsed through the space between the corner towers, was another tower of similar shape. Above and beyond were a blue sky illusion and a vista to an impossibly distant horizon. The land was flat, patched with dark-green splotches of forest. Rivers glinted silver in the sunlight. It was virtually impossible to tell where the reality ended and the illusion took over.

They checked into a modest hotel suite and showered and ate a fast hot meal. Jon wolfed down eggs, freefburgers, and fries. The food smells finally broke Meg's spell for a while. She consumed soy nuggets and eggs and fries. They drank copious amounts of fruit juice.

He checked the TV and radio channels. Sooner was far from excited about the case, it seemed. The hot pursuit he'd been expecting had simply not materialized, which surprised Jon. A system-wide hunt had been announced and the *Illustrious* had moved over to Nostramedes on the second day. But that seemed the limit of the laowon activity, at least so far.

Meg's code would have left very little trace in all the computers it had violated, but Jon reasoned that full auditing programs might eventually open the Superior Buro's eyes. However, he had underestimated the degree to which his massacre of the Buro had disrupted their operations and the search.

But he knew it couldn't be long before the Buro caught up. There was no time for sleep, on a bed with sheets and gravity. Instead he fortified himself with hot coffee. Meg had lapsed into sleep following the food. Jon gave her a swift inspection. The medipacks were working on the worst scrapes, no bones were broken that he could find. If her mind came back into focus, she would recover.

As soon as he was ready, they slipped out of the hotel and rode an elevator to a high suite on the southeast corner.

On the door was a sign that read POROX GAS CO. in small black letters. Jon knocked, entered, pushing Meg ahead of him.

Inside was a small reception room with walls covered in brown natufibers. A young man in a dark-blue suit sat behind the desk; behind him was another door.

Jon wasted no time. He leveled the Taw Taw at the young man's head. "Up, and go ahead of me, through the door. No tricks or you won't even have time to be sorry."

The young man left his seat hurriedly, almost fell down in his eagerness to comply.

There were several rooms, all decorated in natural earthtones. In the biggest room, behind a glossy realwood desk, a fleshy brown-skinned man wearing a white silk suit was engaged in furious argument with several blond people in gray spacecrew wear.

They looked up in horror.

"Nobody move!" said Jon sharply. The gun swung back and forth to cover them.

"It's the Buro!" screamed the woman he'd pursued to Nostramedes.

Hurriedly Jon contradicted her. "No, it's not the Buro. You're wrong, I'm here to help you. I have a message for you."

An atmosphere of hysterical tension rose in the room.

"What do you mean?" the tall, stooped captain said. "You are the one who almost destroyed us."

"Nevertheless I'm not the Buro. I have a message and in return for delivering it, I want to book passage with you, for both of us. We cannot stay in this system, the laowon will kill us."

There was an explosion of rage from a man wearing a heavy cast on his right arm. It was the one named M'Nee.

"You murderous swine, I'll kill you." He twisted to his feet, eyes flashing in fury and a small gun trembling in his good hand.

Jon didn't hesitate. His foot lashed out and the gun flew across the office and bounced off the window. His own weapon continued to cover them.

The woman was beside herself. "I told you we should have killed him, you wouldn't listen to me, oh no, not you!"

"There's no need for anyone to get killed. If you'll listen to my story I think you'll agree. It won't take long."

He sensed vast unhappiness in them.

Nathan Porox spoke up from behind his desk. "Before anybody books passage for anybody, somebody's got to settle for the cost of the fuel. I'm sitting here looking at a docket that will impound your ship unless I receive payment. All this gunplay won't mean exhaust to a robot without that!"

Jon chuckled. "And how much is required?"

"Twenty-six thousand credit units." Jon produced a card, snapped it into the function box on Porox's phone computer, and dialed the credit through from Hyperion Grandee Centabank. Meg's code supplied the bank computer with perfectly tailored analogs in place of true account number codes. The bank computer stuttered over them for a few moments but then accepted them. Meg's code had passed its stiffest test. But a major bank's auditing programs would soon pick up an error of this magnitude.

Porox watched expressionless.

"Fuel the ship, you've been paid."

The captain was plainly stunned. "What do you want?" he said weakly.

"We want to come with you, to the stars. I can't stay here—I killed laowon to get to you, you see. So we must hurry, we can't afford to wait."

Porox's face was several shades darker. "Did I hear you correctly? You killed laowon to get here?"

"You did. And I'll kill you, too, if you don't get that fuel moving soon."

Porox made urgent motions to his assistant, who dialed the docks.

"You want to come with us?" said the woman named Dahn.

"Right."

"Why?"

"Because I understand, I know why you're going."

"You do?"

"Look, I'll explain the details later. Just tell me whether you'll deal. My message for two births on the Bird." He ventured a little hunch of his own.

Once again their faces were stricken with horror and he knew he'd been correct.

"How can you know these things and not be Superior Buro?" the captain said indignantly. Jon detected a faint whine in the man's voice. It was a sign of strain, of worry. Around the captain was a blanket of psychic panic. He was clearly terrified for his life. Jon wondered briefly why such a man was dicing with the Superior Buro for the fate of the human race. He didn't seem the type for that sort of thing.

"This is my friend Meg. She worked it all out, you see. While I was chasing you for them. She went to the Brutality Room as a result." They stared, unnerved, at Meg's slack face which peered at them from her blanket.

"Look, it's complicated. I know. But all you really have to understand is that I've changed sides."

It took them a long moment to digest this. They conversed furiously among themselves, finally looked up.

"All right, what is this message?"

"With Porox in the room?"

"It's all right, Porox is with us."

Jon took a breath. "The laowon expect you to head for the William system. They have stationed a ship there to intercept you."

"How did you come by this message?" Captain Hawkstone asked.

"My colleague penetrated the computer aboard *Illustrious*, the battlejumper." They nodded, they knew the ship. "She must have found the information there."

"Interesting."

"Interesting to the Superior Buro. They took her to the Brutality Room for it."

Hawkstone blanched. "And?"

"I broke her out. I killed a lot of them to do so."

Porox groaned. "You killed the Superior Buro?"

"As many as I could. Should slow them up a bit."

"Good god, man, that will stir them up."

"It already has, I should think. This was two days ago now."

"We will have to use the direct route approach." Hawkstone spoke in an ominous tone. "If this message is correct, we can't wait for an exploratory orbit. We'll have to emerge on the dark side and initiate atmospheric descent immediately."

Jon could see they were bewildered and rather frightened.

"I don't know what to do," the captain confessed.

"No significant change there, then!" Dahn snapped.

M'Nee was holding his cast, his face tight and gray. That kick had cost him something. "*He* can't come with us!" he rasped. "I refuse."

"Look, I just bought the fuel for the trip, so forget leaving me behind—It's a death sentence. Same for the lady."

"I don't care, I won't have it."

"And who are you to make the decision? Shouldn't that be up to the captain here?"

M'Nee looked sullenly at Hawkstone, who wavered. "For all we know you are laowon spies. I can't allow it."

Jon laughed. "Look, if we were working for the Buro do you think you'd be sitting around here? I think they'd be putting you under with the Hypnogen about now."

There was a sudden knock on the door. Everyone froze.

Jon looked warily at the door. *Were* the Buro here so soon?

"Cut the lights," he hissed to Porox. In the dark, Jon flattened himself against the wall. The door opened slowly and silhouetted in the opening a small sphere floated at head height.

There was a collective release of breath. The lights came back on. Jon stared, speechless, as a glossy green ball with tiny red dots like eyes floated in with a slight humming sound.

"Emergency!" it blared like a demented audio chip.

Jon jumped.

"Emergency! Cold, no energy! Emergency!"

"It's hysterical, someone get a heater," the woman said.

"What is it?" Jon asked in awe.

"That is Rhapsodical Stardimple," Captain Hawkstone said wearily. "A mote, one of the great motes of Baraf."

Jon stared at the glossy little beast/machine. Porox's assistant had brought out an ornate cigar lighter, which he lit. Immediately the ball flew to hover over the flame.

"What is the emergency?" the woman asked. "Rhap Dimp? Why are you here?"

The ball had been murmuring to itself in a squeaky little sing-song. It squawked, "Emergency!" once more.

"We heard that, but why?"

"Yes! Yes! The Bey, there are the aliens. Superior Buro. They are at the spaceship. The Bey is there, I escaped."

"How far is it?" Jon said urgently.

"Not far," Hawkstone replied. "They'll no doubt be down here in a few minutes to arrest us too. Might as well just sit still and wait. This is the end to this whole mad quest." He seemed resigned.

"Oh, no!" sobbed the woman. "We'll all go to the Brutality Room."

Jon decided to act rather than await his doom. "If it's not far, perhaps we can get there in time to rescue matters. Laowon are flesh and blood, they can be killed."

They stared at him, but the mote sped forward and hung in front of his eyes. "You are the one called Iehard!" it piped. The glossy little eyes were like drips of brilliant gel.

"That is my name."

"Yes! You are the one that killed the aliens. On all channels, system-wide search!"

The others looked at him with renewed questions.

"No time for this, where is the Bey? We have to get there before they can take him away."

"Yes! Follow me." The mote brayed and charged from the room with Jon close behind. He found the mote was capable of a steady thirteen kilometers an hour in the corridors. He jogged to keep up.

They rode an empty elevator to the light-gravity passenger terminal. Jon sprang after the mote and into a corridor leading to the docking station. Black-uniformed figures were ahead, blue faces, eyes opening wide in shock and alarm.

Jon brought up the Taw Taw, his first shot spun the leading Buro agent into the wall. His second beheaded the laowon behind him.

Two other laowon held up an elderly man in bloodstained white robes. They raised handweapons, but it was a fraction of a second too late, because Iehard slammed into the one on the left and the mote struck the one on the right and they were hurled backward in a heap. Jon clubbed one, was struck in return and thrown against the wall, but the mote swung and fired itself at the laowon's head and rendered him senseless. Jon's gun sparked twice more. There could be no mercy when dealing with Superior Buro.

Jon looked around. Officer Dahn was the only one who had kept up with him. Then the captain emerged from an elevator.

"Quickly, grab the old man. Get him into the ship."

Dahn looked at Jon. Looked at the dead laowon. She seemed stunned by this turn of events.

"Look," Jon shouted, his voice breaking. "We are all dead if we don't get out of here. The ship is fueled, let's go."

"There was not supposed to be any killing," she whispered. "Nothing like this." She gestured helplessly at the dead laowon.

"They were Superior Buro. What else was there to do?" Jon surprised himself, his conditioning lay in shards. He had killed laowon again, would do so again if he had to. He felt no shame, no disgust. It had been a necessary act of war.

"Look, let's get moving, why don't we?" He seethed with impatience.

Jon ran back, found Porox's office and Meg. They had left her there, alone. Quickly he pushed her along the corridors and into the elevators. He half ran the distance to the docking tube. An airlock was still open. He plunged in.

The ship interior was unexpectedly plain and utilitarian, with hundreds of blue seats laid out in concentric rows in a central circular space. Above that, through a "Crew Only" access tube, was the bridge, also laid out in a circular pattern beneath a radial array of screens and instruments.

They had arranged the man in white robes in a seat. Jon looked down on his quarry. There he was at last, Eblis Bey. Then he lifted Meg out of the wheelchair and put her in a seat in the row behind the Bey. He strapped her in and then folded up the chair and slung it underneath the seats.

The mote appeared suddenly, floating along one and a

half meters from the floor until it hovered next to the Elchite. Jon came over and gave the man a quick inspection. A shock-rod rash was plain on the side of his neck, and his nose had bled heavily for a while. He had been struck a blow or two, but there appeared to be no fractured bones. The man seemed much older than in Commander Petrie's photo.

A voice on the PA announced immediate takeoff. Jon strapped in next to the Bey. Only a handful of other crew members were in the main cabin, most were on the bridge.

A ceiling screen came on giving them the view inside the bridge. The screen subdivided; one view showed the exterior of the Sooner docking bay, where lines of tankers patiently waited.

Hawkstone's voice came over the PA, sounding stronger, more confident. "This is Captain Hawkstone speaking. Welcome to the Luft Line flagship *Orn*. I suggest that everyone strap in completely, use the full webbing provided in the sides of your seats. The computer informs me this may be rather a rough ride."

Indeed there was already a strong vibration in the floor. A deep groan came from somewhere.

"Engine room," Hawkstone said, "get me full field in two minutes. We are entering emergency drill now!" Red lights began to flash all around the passenger cabin.

Two minutes! Jon recalled the hours he'd spent between jumps on the laowon jumper from Glegan.

There was a new tone in Hawkstone's voice. A liner captain with two decades of service behind him, he felt stronger at the helm of his ship, surrounded by the mass he'd grown so familiar with.

Jon decided the *Orn* was a short-hop liner, jumping business people around inside a single system. No wonder the people were acting strangely. They were just ordinary space crew caught up in a mission that was getting more dangerous by the moment. Jon had a lot of questions for the Bey, but they'd have to wait until the old man had recovered consciousness, at least.

Then the *Orn* broke away from the docking arm and rose rapidly through the flight paths, pressing them all into their seats.

"Officer Dahn, please get me position of *Illustrious* at this time," Hawkstone said quietly.

The acceleration went on and on, a great weight on their bodies, squeezing them down.

"*Illustrious* currently in docking mode at gigahabitat Nostramedes," Dahn reported. "Distance four million kloms."

"Thank you, Officer Dahn. Engine room, how's my field?"

"Coming right up, sir. Inside two minutes."

Everyone's voice was now measured, steady, as if in the habits of spaceflight they found security, unlike the alien risks of habitat or planet.

"Sooner Central Control is screaming blue murder!" another woman commented quietly on the bridge.

"Here comes an override!"

A face burst onto the main screens.

"Unidentified ship! What the hell are you doing? You're way too close to us to be using gravitomagnetics!"

"Sorry, Sooner. We don't have time to explain," Hawkstone said. "Get him off the screen, Bergen."

"Yes, sir."

"What the hell do you mean, you 'don't have time'?"

"Exactly that," Hawkstone said quietly. The override vanished.

"Where's my field, engine room?"

"Coming up fast, but do you think it's safe, sir? This close to Sooner's mass?"

"We have no choice, I'm afraid. We're all cashiered by now anyway."

"Cashiered?" Someone snorted impatiently. "We're all *dead* because of that crazy gunman you picked up. The laowon will take us for public Expiation. Red-hot pincers, everything, all in front of the television screens."

"Shut up, M'Nee. We don't need to hear any more of that," Officer Bergen said.

Jon held back his own angry retort.

Seconds ticked by.

"*Illustrious* is moving now, sir. We have definite double image there, she's unshipping fast."

"They know where we are now. I'll bet they're in a hurry. How long before they can bracket us?"

"They'll have to turn the ship, we have thirty seconds perhaps," Officer Dahn said bitterly.

"Where's my field?" Hawkstone was now audibly anxious.

"We're all dead because of you, damn it!" someone screamed. Jon wondered who it was she was blaming.

"It's that damned Elchite. He came to Ornholme for payment of the debt. He could not be refused. We had to do as he asked," Hawkstone replied hotly.

Jon imagined the great battlejumper slowly turning to bring its weaponry to bear.

Then the *Orn* jumped. There was a strange, wrenching moment as the gravitomagnetic bubble formed and the ship surged through the wormholes of space-time.

Then it was over and the screen showed nothing but stars, faraway brilliant points.

"Ship will rotate to provide point five gees in passenger section," the computer announced.

Everyone was breathing hard, the PA reverberated to it.

"On my trip to Nocanicus from Glegan, where I was born, it took the ship hours to achieve each jump," Jon exclaimed in wonder, and heard his voice echo excitedly over the PA.

Hawkstone's voice was measured, slightly sardonic. "Spaceliners normally do everything they can to protect themselves and their passengers, Mr. Iehard. Our chances of reaching this point from that jump were no better than three to one, according to the computer. But if *Illustrious* had completed that turn we would've had no chance at all. Four million kloms is short range for a laowon battlewagon."

"You think they could have destroyed us, just like that?"

"Disabled us more likely. At that range they could shave your mustache off with the primary laser."

"But where are we now?"

"On the far side of Nocanicus, opposite where we were. We performed a simple, random-gravity flip-flop. Our jump spin was absorbed by the star. We traveled around its gravity center along the lines of the magnetic field. It increased our chances of survival by twenty percent."

"So *Illustrious* can't detect us yet."

"Precisely, nor can the ship at the Ginger Moon. We're on the far side of Nocanicus from William too."

Jon noticed that Eblis Bey was coming round. He unstrapped himself and went to get some water. When he returned he went to sit beside the old man. The mote emitted a warning buzz and swung in front of him.

"No! Contact is not permitted!" it screamed in its bizarre, mechanoid garble.

"I won't touch him, he's coming round, look."

Eblis Bey sat up with a groan and put a hand to his head. "Am I dreaming or simply dead? I never thought there'd be a ship to take you to heaven."

Jon laughed. "Neither dead nor dreaming. You're back aboard the *Orn*, and we've given them the slip."

The Bey now focused on Jon. He groped for the water and drank it in a gulp. "You!" he exclaimed. "I should have known at once."

"What do you mean?" said Jon.

"You're the one on all the broadcasts, a system-wide search is on. Seventeen laowon, they say."

Seventeen! If he was taken alive the laowon would have him expiate for a long, long time.

"And aren't you the Eblis Bey I was told is a fugitive for killing two dozen laowon, with Grand Weengams and Twirsteds among them!"

The Bey gripped his shoulder. His eyes glittered. "Well done, young man. Let me welcome you to our expedition. We are in need of a fellow like you. We have some dangerous work ahead of us."

The mote suddenly brayed, "Welcome!" Jon smiled. A welcome had been a rarity so far in his life, he was happy to accept one anywhere, even from a talking billiard ball.

CHAPTER FOURTEEN

COMMANDER PETRIE STARED DOWN AT THE FIGURE wrapped in bandages with a mixture of personal fear and considerable perplexity.

Padzn Birthamb struggled to speak. He had absorbed two shots from Jon Iehard's Taw Taw. The first had blown out through his abdomen. His survival was a small medical miracle. The second had blasted off the left side of his lower jaw, as he'd dropped behind the front desk of the Brutality Room, when the madman burst in, his gun spraying bullets.

The medics had patched him together and fitted an emergency speaking tube directly to this laryngial region. It made flat, metallic sounds.

Birthamb's mood was bleak. He lived because he was tubed into several medical peripherals built into the bed. He might never leave it again. But he also realized, with a cold clarity that made him feel infuriatingly helpless, that he would still go to the Chair of Expiation in front of the Imperial Court. He had failed so totally and abysmally that the Imperiom could only respond by rending him to pieces for the TV cameras.

The Morgooze of Blue Seygfan was not dead. The Lady Blasilab was. Which was the worst thing to happen was entirely unclear to Padzn Birthamb, but the net result was plain. Further humiliations abounded. The man Iehard had virtually wiped out the central Superior Buro post.

Of the twenty-three operatives only four had escaped injury, because they were off shift and asleep. Only three others had survived. The antipersonnel weaponry of the Mass Murder Squad had advanced the science of ammunition to a dreadful point of efficiency. In most cases operatives hit just once with those exploding bullets had died instantly. Padzn Birthamb was unique, a survivor of two shots.

Birthamb's throat caused him considerable pain as he explained all this to Petrie.

"So, I will go to the Chair of Expiation, Petrie. You know what that means?"

Petrie nodded.

"They will tear me apart, shred by shred."

"So I have heard." Petrie seemed to take the news calmly enough.

"A new section of the Buro will be arriving within hours to take over here at Hyperion Grandee. You will be expected to give them your complete cooperation."

"Of course."

Birthamb seethed with hate for humans. The subrace had destroyed him after a career that had been so promising. It was with pleasure that he pronounced Petrie's death sentence.

"I want you to know that I have seconded your name to the Fleet Sector Command for immediate termination, preferably in public with the full application of lao military law. Your incompetence in selecting that maniac has allowed the Elchite fugitive to escape."

"Incompetence?" Petrie barked hotly. "I was asked to get the best sensing, psi-able operative on the Mass Murder Squad. I did that. He even got a contact with the people you seek. An incredible feat considering how you worked to undercut him from the first!

"In addition, has it occurred to you that had I been told that the Superior Buro intended to seize his colleague, the woman, and put her through the Brutality Room, I might have counseled you to forego the use of someone like Jon Iehard, who already has his own reasons for disliking the laowon!"

Birthamb almost choked in rage. "Out! Get out of here, out of my sight. Soon you will receive your orders, very soon. Did you know the whole sector fleet is in motion?

Admiral Booeej himself is coming here. Blue Seygfan is in utter turmoil. The cult is howling for revenge on this entire system. Now get out!"

Birthamb's body convulsed on the pad.

Petrie stumbled out, afraid now for all Nocanicus. Admiral Booeej himself was coming!

The outer system of Nocanicus contained five gas giant planets—Abdul, William, Ingrid, Shala, Hideo. Of them, the last four were relatively small and cool. In addition, they had an abundance of perfect watermoons, like William's half-dozen jewels, rich in hydrocarbons, water ice, ammonia, nitrogen, everything that was required for a high cultural civilization, except metal.

The existence of those moons, as much as the major asteroid belt, had been the prime reason for the colonization of Nocanicus. It had no habitable planets, only two airless rocks the size of Mercury orbited inside the enormous asteroid belt.

Between the moons and the asteroid belt were the natural strings of trade, metals for gases, skills developed in different settings, essences, entertainments. Their populations swelled, with a billion or more in the belt and about half as many on the moons.

Hyperion Grandee rode near the center of the main belt. Currently it was in conjunction with William and in opposition to Abdul.

The *Orn* now floated on the fringe of the opposite side of the main belt. Abdul rode a few degrees behind, brightest star even at one hundred fifty million kilometers distance. The nearest known habitat was the Camleopard-Al Kuds and that was twenty million kilometers away. Drones were released at once to scour the neighborhood. An astronomical probe was fired out of the equatorial solar plane to search for laowon battlejumpers.

The roids close by were all small rocks of interest only to prospectors. The *Orn* detected no spacecraft in the vicinity.

Aboard the *Orn*, Jon Iehard faced his questioners across the aisle of the main passenger compartment. On the big screen above their heads was a computer-enhanced image of the system.

Meg had been placed in a bunk in sickbay, under sedation.

"How can you expect us to believe this?" Finn M'Nee snarled. "You are a laowon spy. You have been sent to betray our ultimate destination. Nothing you say can change this."

Jon shrugged. It was clear to all that he was never going to be accepted by M'Nee, an intense young man with harsh, elitist views.

Owlcurl Dahn however was another story. She was the coordinator of the group, someone from Luft Line's administration, not regular spacecrew. It was clear that she was the Bey's chief supporter. Others were less enthusiastic. Jon detected several currents at work. M'Nee, Flynn, Chacks—all young men with intense expressions who were contemptuous of the captain and the woman Dahn. The rest of the crew—Bergen, Hargen, Wauk, and Kolod—seemed to ignore those three and were ignored in turn.

Toward the Bey, the three young men were formalistically obedient, like soldiers of lesser rank with an officer. But there seemed little real friendliness in their relations.

Jon had to admit his own confusion, but he suspected they were Elchites. Around their minds he found a roar of anger and sharp stabs of fear. He hesitated to press deeper.

The other crew members treated the Bey with either exaggerated deference or a paradoxical anger.

Officer Dahn now gave Jon another appraising look, "On Ornholme we were warned that laowon spies would be everywhere on this side of the Hyades. I think they were right, but I cannot believe the laowon would truly sacrifice so many of their own for one spy."

"Foolish woman!" M'Nee said witheringly. "The laowon are completely unconcerned about such things. If it suited the High Command's purposes they would overlook many more casualties."

"You Elchites are of that mind, but I doubt that even the laowon could be so heartless with their own personnel," she retorted.

Jon looked at M'Nee more carefully. So he'd been correct. There seemed a world of difference between M'Nee and the Bey. Perhaps they were in different sects.

He noticed Captain Hawkstone, eyes vacant, lost in gloomy introspection. A husk of a man, caught up by accident in terrible events beyond his control. He was desperately treading water, trying not to let his fear become cowardice. He was only there because he had had the misfortune to be the only active space captain aboard Ornholme when Eblis Bey came to the habitat to demand payment of the old, old debt.

"Nonsense, nonsense," the Bey broke in. "It is entirely possible that the laowon would sacrifice numbers of lower-echelon personnel in advance of their interests. However, young M'Nee is in error in thinking that the Superior Buro, in active pursuit of us, would allow itself to be destroyed. But for Iehard's massacre of their operatives, they would have seized us long before you'd finished bargaining with Porox. So, in my mind it is settled—Jon is with us. The unfortunate Ms. Vance is perhaps more of a paradox, except that I believe she has just been swept up in the tide of history that accompanies our passage. Can you not feel it? We bring the blade of salvation toward the neck of the tyrant race."

M'Nee snorted disgustedly. "Put them to the Hypnogen. Then we'll know for certain."

"There isn't time for that—we must get to the connection soon. Do you think the laowon won't reinforce the fleet here?"

"Tell me one thing," Jon interrupted.

"What?" Dahn said.

"Why do you need to go to William?"

"Because . . ." She trailed off.

"But the aliens are out in the distant starfields. How can we get to them if we go to William, where the laowon are waiting?"

Hawkstone intervened. "We have to go to William first, in order to go on to the stars. The *Orn* doesn't have the fuel to reach our ultimate destination. We'd have to refuel at laowon systems several times. They'd be waiting for us eventually."

"Then how will we reach the aliens, to get help?"

Eblis Bey laughed. "I fear you have been laboring under a misunderstanding. We shall have to explain things more fully."

He paused. Something was happening on the astronav

holo. A group of red blips had sprung into existence in the watermoon system around William.

Officer Bergen on the bridge reported, "Captain, we have an arrival trace in William system—ten, no, eleven battlejumpers. More coming in all the time. Looks like the whole sector fleet is on its way to Nocanicus."

"I have arrivals in the belt," another voice said. "They must be on combat footing; they're just popping out in midbelt and damn the consequences. Hyperion Grandee is center of activity but smaller ships are turning up in other sectors."

The Bey noticed the proliferating red dots scattered about William and the main belt. "Admiral Booeej is on the move then. The game is set, Captain. I would imagine that Booeej has been given some inkling of the true nature of our mission."

Captain Hawkstone struggled with it. Finally he gave in. "All right, we'll continue the mission."

Jon read the shiver on Eblis Bey's face. He'd feared that Hawkstone might crack.

"We will continue as planned," Hawkstone said quite calmly. "However, I would like it logged, which record I shall request be ejected before connection, that I protest the wanton misuse of this Luft Lines' vessel. I think we are all going to our deaths."

"The *Orn* is your ship, Captain. I thank you for your most heroic offer," the Bey replied with a gracious smile.

"This is a mad business..."

"We have no choice, Captain, despite the cost of the ship. We must go to William." Administrator Dahn tried vainly to bolster the captain.

"Besides, the ship will be controlled by the software developed by the Elchite brethren. They have worked on it for a long time, haven't you, M'Nee?"

"The software will do the job. If the connection can be made, we will make it."

Jon's forehead furrowed. "I don't understand. *Why* are we still in Nocanicus system? Why is the fleet concentrating around the watermoons of William?"

"Because we must go to the very heart of the William system, and this name is one that the laowon have managed to pry from the musings of a traitor far behind us, on Earth. We have been keeping a few jumps ahead of them until now, but they have caught up again."

"The laowon told me that they captured you but you escaped."

The Elchite turned angry eyes on him. "As always, the laowon exaggerate in these matters. They came close, but we knew of their approach." He sighed.

Officer Wauk on the bridge cut in on the PA.

"We have a laowon vessel, cruiser-class jumper, in vicinity of El Zanzahab." A winking red dot had sprung into existence on the outer fringe of the belt, in the same quadrant that hid the *Orn*.

Eblis Bey eyed the dot with obvious distaste. "They're getting closer, but since we're sitting still at low energy levels and they're arriving at high ones we can see them and they can't see us. Yet. Of course, eventually a probe will find us, so we will move soon, on the *Orn*'s final journey."

"On our own final journey, more likely," Hawkstone muttered.

"Where are we going?" Jon said.

"Mr. Iehard, have you ever heard a little piece of doggerel called the 'Testamenter Lament'?"

"You mean, 'In the depths of the ocean where all hope sank . . .'?"

"Yes, 'We laid him down, Where the gravity's no feather and the light will never reach.'"

"Well, I've heard it all right."

"But have you heard the third verse, the hidden verse?"

Jon looked up with a puzzled frown.

"It's the verse that begins, 'In the depths of the ocean where our hope sank, we laid him down,' just like the popular verse, but it goes thus:

> In stormy midlatitudes we secured him, and laid him down,
> Tucked close to Nemo's Piston a million fathoms round, where we laid him down,
> So don't look for us in sun's light lest the laowon hunt us down,
> To Hope and Nemo's Piston, a million fathoms round.

"Nemo's Piston?" Jon repeated.

"What would you say if I told you we're taking the *Orn* directly to the resting place of the Testamenter Battleship *Winston Churchill*?"

Jon was rocked. Then he exploded. "Meg was right, she was right again, damn it!"

Admiral Booeej was coming. The Nocanicus System Governing Authority had assembled hurriedly to greet him. Members from the outer systems had been ferried, without warning, to Hyperion Grandee aboard swift jumpships.

Laowon were everywhere. Petrie's section, the entire Military Intelligence building, was swarming with Superior Buro laowon in black tunics. For convenience, the meeting was to be held there, in Commander Petrie's very own office.

Among them were still a few of the other things, the cyborgs, with human faces and power-graphite bones. Petrie had never felt such a chill in his heart as when the three shock troopers had burst into the section. They moved impossibly quickly, like the flickering of insects. Things that married human genetic material, like cloth, to machines. The eyes were so obviously artificial. The plate armor so convincing. It was hard to even see them unless they stood still or moved unusually slowly.

Now Admiral Booeej himself was coming. His huge jumper, the *Conqueror*, had docked. Security teams lined the route.

The admiral was tall, threatening, his purple face filled with fury. The door closed behind him with a cyborg guard on either side of it. The admiral moved across the room and sat at Petrie's desk, almost pushing the commander out of his way.

"There is a new rule here. Imperial military conditions have been imposed." His voice was harsh, his accent that of the distant Orion arm.

CHAPTER FIFTEEN

HALF A MILLION KLOMS OUT, THE *ILLUSTRIOUS* RAN DOWN the Dove model B and took it on board via suction tube. In minutes Melissa Baltitude was marched into the presence of Captain Ilefeit.

"We have traced a departure trail. You have visited the habitat Sooner."

Melissa tried to bluff her way out. "My name is Melissa Baltitude. I don't know the meaning of this outrage but I can tell you that my father, who happens to own one of the largest gas supply corporations in this system, will be just as angry as I am as soon as I can tell him about it."

Captain Ilefeit regarded the human girl with amusement. She was not unattractive, if rather too thin for laowon tastes in human girls. Ilefeit himself preferred laowon females, something that he admitted was slightly old fashioned for the space service these days. Perhaps he would let the junior officers play with her first.

"I think I should inform you that you aren't the only member of your family under arrest. Your father was taken by the Superior Buro about three hours ago. I believe he is in the Brutality Room."

He enjoyed the look that came over her face.

"We know that you visited Sooner; I conclude that you carried the fugitives Jon Iehard and Meg Vance. Any court of laowon justice would give us the blood rights to you on that basis alone."

Melissa was lost. She stared helplessly at the laowon officer, so cold and blue and cruel. It was impossible to read his alien gold eyes; his face was inhuman. Yet she could tell he was enjoying himself.

Her life seemed to have disintegrated violently. She began to think that it would have been better if that bullet from Arnei Oh hadn't missed her outside the Clocktower a couple of nights before.

Aboard the *Orn* last minute checks remained to be made. The crew went about the list with grim faces, convinced they were going to their deaths. The young Elchites sat in the bridge, openly armed to prevent any thought of mutiny. Eblis Bey sat with Jon Iehard in the main cabin, and they drank a dilution of a fiery distillate the Elchite carried in a sleek little flask inside his robes.

The Bey seemed in good spirits; he toasted their mission.

The mote lay on the Bey's thigh, inactive, its tiny eyes retracted. It looked exactly like a glossy green billiard ball.

The Bey caught Jon's expression. "A fascinating little monster, no? Strangely enough, from what I can deduce from my little friend, motes were a kind of pet. They had to be grown, but they remain, in a fundamental way, machines."

Jon recounted his experience with Fabulous Fara and searched in his pockets for a moment before finding the little silvery cube. He brought it out.

The Bey's eyes lit up.

"Marvelous, this is another of their eternity substances. Some of their machines are built of similar materials. High albedo, thin, even transparent, but *indestructible*! Yet other machines have completely rusted away. We infer their presence in the long-ago from concentrations of iron oxides in the surrounding rocks."

He turned the cube over in his hands, "The saddest thing, perhaps, is that most likely we will never find out what this is or what it is made of. From Rhap Dimple's descriptions of the ancient sciences, the flowering of the arts employed biological principles and techniques to crystals and even machines. Things were constantly being grown. How, or why, or even what was grown we have much less conception of."

He was about to hand the cube back when Rhap Dimple became active with a squawk.

"Trace! Yes! Unit to report!"

"What is the matter?" the Bey asked. The mote hovered over the cube and a blue spark passed between them.

"Hey, that's my cube!" Jon said, reaching for it. But when he took it, it was hot and, it seemed, slightly smaller than before. "What happened?"

In response, he felt something strange impinge slightly on his consciousness, a shiver, a wind, a premonition.

"Traced! It is you!" The mote hovered in front of him.

"Me?"

"Where were you traced?" squawked the mote.

"I'm afraid I don't understand. What do you mean, Rhap Dimple?"

"You carry tracer! Made recently, strong signal! Where were you traced? Where is the ancient master! Yes! Only they can trace!"

Jon looked to Elbis Bey. "Do you know what it's talking about?"

"I would hazard a guess. The so-called template must produce a solidified mental trace of living organisms. Your cube is such a trace. The mote can sense it somehow."

"It was warm when I took it back from you. Fara said that all the bubbles were inert."

"But yours was the first cube. Perhaps the others all lacked something in their creation."

As Jon tried to explain how he'd come to receive the cube, the mote hovered.

"I'm sorry, Rhap Dimple," Elbis Bey said. "There are no ancient masters left."

The tiny sphere emitted a curious little groan, then it suddenly brayed, "Lack energy! Emergency!" and it sped off to the galley microwave ovens.

They stared after it.

"An amazing device, if that is what it is. You must tell me how you came to possess it."

Eblis Bey sighed. "One day I will. It's a long story, that one, but one day I will give you an account of my adventure as a young man. It has a bearing on our mission."

Jon returned to the question that loomed uppermost in his thoughts as the ship prepared for the next and last jump.

"What if the *Churchill* isn't there?"

"It will be," the Bey said imperturbably.

"What if it isn't in working order?"

"Then we will have an hour or so to fix it. If we cannot, then we are doomed and so is our mission. I am assured, however, by the head of our Testamenter Research Division, that the ship is most likely in perfect condition. The drives will be operating, idling, keeping it floating in William's hydrosphere. The technical people tell me that the Testamenter Drives use a variant on the technology of the deep link, which gives us instant communications access across the deeps. Such drives are easier to leave running than to turn on and off, apparently."

"What is Nemo's Piston?"

The Bey chuckled. "Questions, questions! Can I never satisfy you? Nemo was the nickname of Captain William Shrad, of the Hyades exploration vessel *Jules Verne*. It was the first ship here, the big planets are named after the crew."

Jon shook his head in surprise. He'd never heard that scrap of history before.

"The Piston is a storm vortex in William's northern hemisphere. It rises above a volcanic outbreak in the deep mantle. The *Churchill* is moored in the lee of the Piston, a relatively peaceful region. At that point, the hydrosphere flows east to west past the Piston at about one hundred kilometers an hour, but in the eddies directly behind the storm vortex is a dead zone with hardly any current flow."

The Bey's eyes twinkled. "The *Orn* has been specifically reinforced for the mission. It will be flown by the software developed for us by young M'Nee and our technical group. Everything has been calculated quite finely. *Orn* will enter the upper atmosphere some distance from the Piston but will angle toward it through the gas clouds and then we will descend inside the vortex to the level of the hydrosphere. The real moment of danger will be in moving from one ship to the other. We replaced one of *Orn*'s airlocks with a special elevator. A pressure-proof car will ferry us across. Then *Orn* will be sent aloft on its last journey. And the Orners will have paid their debts to Elchis."

Jon's brows furrowed. "What do you mean?"

"Since we took in the crew of the *Churchill*, nine hundred years ago, the children of Testament have been indebted to us. They had left the ship via a gas-company booster to escape William's gravity and they went to the Ginger Moon where they took fast NAFAL to the Hyades. Of course by the time they reached their destination, the Superior Buro had its spies everywhere. They came to us for help; we hid them well. You see some of their descendants around you today."

"The Orners?"

"Of course, the cult of Elchis is very old, young man. Even then there were Elchites spread across the clusters. The temples were beautiful, if perhaps a little sleepy at that time. But in taking this action against the laowon we were revitalized. We conceived our great project. Gradually, our heroic energies were increased until at last we were ready, whenever the call came."

The PA crackled into life. Captain Hawkstone announced that they were preparing to jump. Jon quickly made sure Meg was strapped into her bunk, then returned to strap in himself. A heavy vibration began, lasted for a few seconds, and ceased as the ship jumped.

The *Orn* pitched itself into the William system like a big fly fallen into a pool of starving trout. Before the ripples had passed the outer moons, lumpy battlejumpers were rocketing inward on intercepts.

But the *Orn* had emerged only a few thousand kilometers above the cloud tops of vast blue William. One aspect of such a risky maneuver was the tendency for a jumper to acquire enormous spin momentum, from the conflict between the gravitomagnetic drive fields and the big planetary gravity node. The acceleration effects would convert everyone aboard to gruel if not compensated.

For the first half second or so the ship wobbled, violently unstable, but the computer programs assumed control, the crew took correctives as prescribed by the software, and the chemfuel rockets blazed into life, holding the ship stable, fighting the spin tendency.

Held fast against the spin, the *Orn* pitched forward, sliding straight down into the outer layers of the atmosphere. A fireball enveloped the hull as William's gravity sucked the ship down, shuddering vibrations rocking the crew members in their acceleration couches.

On the screen, William bulked enormous. The horizon was flat, and huge storm systems coiled one after another, endlessly, through the gas belts.

The *Orn* rattled on, heavy thuds coming from somewhere up front as the ship blazed downward through the clouds of methane ice crystals and into the deeper atmosphere.

Although the exterior view screens had lost almost all light, the computer enhanced what it could get. The *Orn* was angling through clouds toward a vast gray rampart of darker clouds that swirled up and across the flat horizon.

The first big chutes opened, slowing the ship and jerking everyone up against the seat belts. The chutes vanished, crisped in seconds. The secondary and tertiary chutes opened and again, everyone was hurled hard against the crash straps.

High above them, the first laowon battlejumpers were swinging around William in tight orbits, powerless to interfere.

The laowon commanders flinched before the outraged countenance of Admiral Booeej which stared out at them from their command screen.

One finally broke the embarrassing silence. "They have realized their failure. They commit suicide like honorable soldiers facing overwhelming odds."

Booeej shook his head violently. "Dispatch probes. Monitor the vessel. They did not come here to die unnecessarily."

With furrowed brows, the ship commanders fired probes into the dark atmospheric depths below. There they picked up the *Orn*'s smoke trail, even though it was blurring rapidly in the five-hundred-kilometer-an-hour winds of the upper helium layers.

Aboard the *Orn* the tension was broken by Captain Hawkstone's matter of fact announcement. "We have first definite radar trace. We are locking on now. I have initial arrival calculation of fifteen minutes."

Explosive cheers sounded all over the ship. They had contact! A window opened on screen to show the radar trace: a fat blip, it hardly wavered. The *Churchill* was still there!

Then there was a hard white flash from above and a hundred kilometers behind. A nuclear explosion roiled William's atmosphere. Eblis Bey spoke before anyone could panic.

"No cause for concern, just a little surprise for the laowon. We have to keep them off balance at this vital juncture. So I have arranged for several salvoes of mines to be left in our trail."

"The laowon will be blinded," Jon said with renewed respect. The Elchite showed himself to be a dangerous prey once again.

"For a little while. Now, Mr. Iehard, you must study these screens. When we are aboard the *Churchill* your posting will be in the engine room. The men you so unfortunately shot, M'Nee and Riley, are our engineers for the next lap. They have spent years studying the layouts of the engine room, but now they are incapacitated, so you must help them in their tasks."

Panels with hundreds—thousands—of colored switches appeared on the small screens built into their seats. There were banks of buttons and arrays of indicators. Iehard was appalled at such antiquated looking stuff. "They must have been crazy. Why didn't they let the computers handle it?"

"They were religious, Panhumanists. Did without computers wherever possible," Eblis Bey said.

"An odd extreme."

"Testament was a proud system. They believed solely in the exalted human spirit, in particular their own. They forsook advanced computers in favor of intense mental preparation of their own children. They were a headstrong folk, and refused to heed the calls of other systems. They took their ships out to the galactic arm, and brought the laowon down upon us."

"The laowon would have found us anyway," Jon objected.

"Most likely, but if all human systems had had the Baada drive, with hundreds of ships, we could have fought them off. Their empire is precarious, torn by huge warring factions. It might have split into warring Seygfan and chaos. We could have drawn a line, written very different treaties! Instead we are a defeated people, a race edging into perpetual slavery. There is much to curse the Testamenters for."

The *Orn* plunged on toward the hydrosphere of William, where the North Hemisphere Vortex caused a ten-thousand-kilometer hurricane in the dense clouds of green ammonia ice hurtling on helium winds. At the rear of the vortex a small region of stability lay between the circulating walls of blue clouds, warm from the volcano that was still churning lava and ice thousands of kilometers below, and the eddying wind storms howling around the oval vortex.

Like a dark tear, an upwelling of liquid water dripped from the great blue eye of the Piston, and at the crest of the hundred-kilometer-high wave form the Bey expected to find a twenty-kilometer-wide sphere of pressure-ice and steel, enclosing a pair of giant Baada drives.

Strapped into his acceleration couch Iehard tried to concentrate on the displays of switches and lights that he would soon have to operate, and fought the urge to look at that enormous storm, the walls thousands of kilometers high, whirling past at seven hundred kilometers an hour.

The darkness grew quickly, and yet they could still see dimly that the ramparts of cloud ahead were moving very fast, whirling around the hot material upthrust from the lower depths.

"Computer Approach program now running sir," someone said.

They tensed. Absolutely nothing was to be seen on the screens but whirling darkness and the computer's simulation graphic, which showed the *Orn* as a small red dot, and the *Churchill* as another, with cross hairs on its center.

The ship had slowed to a crawl, falling now through a thickening mist of icy ammonia and water vapor, tossed out of the inferno far below.

Steadily, the two dots grew closer and with perfect precision the software delivered the *Orn* to a docking position with the Testamenter battleship, nuzzling up to the bigger ship's north pole.

Outside the *Orn*, temperatures had risen fast as they ploughed into the heatsink of this near fluid layer in the atmosphere. The pressure on the hull was fast approaching a ton per square inch and would only increase. Then Jon noticed that the ship's motion had slowed greatly but he still felt a heavy drag as if under deceleration.

"You feel the planetary gravity now, Mr. Iehard." Eblis Bey said with a grim little chuckle.

"Of course," Jon said. He noticed the mote was resting in the Bey's hand. He wondered idly if it was warming itself too.

Voices continued passing information to and from the bridge.

"Computer says approach read out is as expected, sir. No obstruction of the docking channel visible."

"All right, prepare the docking tube. Officer Bergen, are you ready to make the tube secure?"

"All ready, sir."

The *Orn* shuddered and there was an audible bump.

"Outer lock is opening sir," someone said, and then they all heard it, a demonic howl, echoing through the structure of the ship, the roar of vast planetary rage from the enormous storm.

Jon shivered involuntarily. A habitat dweller for nine years, he'd forgotten bad weather, and this was the worst wind storm he had ever heard.

The moan it made was uncanny; the vibration cut right through the huge mass of the *Orn* as if it simply wasn't there. It set everyone's teeth on edge. It was terrifying.

"Coupling is complete," Officer Bergen said in a surprisingly calm tone. The sound of engines whining down could be heard faintly and the wind roar was suddenly diminished.

"*Churchill*'s airlock is opening now, sir. I have readings showing a breathable atmosphere, but temperature is low—things will be pretty damn cold in there for a while."

"Thank you, Officer Bergen. Well done, everyone. May I suggest that we disembark? The Computer says the *Orn*'s hull is breached now, and that unless we get out within eight minutes we'll be operating in an atmosphere of ten percent methane at a temperature of less than three hundred degrees below zero."

They all unstrapped and began making their way to the airlock, moving carefully because of the one point five gee gravity. The temperature inside the *Orn* was dropping fast, and there was a strange smell in the air.

Jon went to the sick bay and took charge of Meg once more, easing her into the wheelchair. He trundled her sleeping form down to the airlock and into the elevator. Around him were Dahn, Bergen, M'Nee and Chacks. The elevator shifted into gear with a whine and moved out of the protective security of the *Orn*'s airlock.

Frost icicles dangled down the walls. It was very cold in the connector tube and they could hear the wind outside, louder than ever, a roaring demon that tugged at the massive spaceships and shifted them, perceptibly, every so often. It was a long ten-second ride before they reached the open airlock of the *Winston Churchill* and stood inside an immense metal cup. They waited, shivering; the temperature was sliding rapidly downward. The air in the tube was painful to breathe.

The inner lock opened at last and they pushed through to an immense empty space, where a few dim lights pointed out the size of the place but did little more to penetrate the dimness. It was very cold, but still a little warmer than the tube. They could breathe more easily.

Then lights came on with a blaze, dozens of bar lamps that were set in the vaulted ceiling. They were in a large room with a domed roof. Heavy machinery humped ungainly out of walls and floor. The walls were of raw-looking puff-concrete.

Clearly the Testamenters didn't waste energy on design beyond a sense of strict utilitarian purpose.

Pumps were whining into life. Captain Hawkstone and Eblis Bey came through with the last of the crew and the airlocks closed behind them.

Officer Bergen had floor plans of the ancient warship. She directed Jon to an elevator that deposited him on a floor with medical ideographics on the wall. He manhandled Meg into a bunk and strapped her in. She remained quiet, in deep sedation. Then he went to find the engineering section where he'd been posted. To get there he rode a hand-operated elevator to the center of the sphere.

He emerged in a vast space, a kilometer across perhaps. He stood on a platform that cut the space into hemispheres. Great shapes were snugged around one another beneath the platforms. Staircases lead down into the depths. On the main floor was set up a V-shaped bank of screens and panels. The equipment had a weird, lumpy look about it. The metal surrounds were raw cut, with no attempt to polish them up. Cables and wires in thick profusion trailed out of the back of the cabinets and ran to three wide access ports cut in the wall.

Finn M'Nee and Officer Chacks, another young Elchite, joined him. M'Nee hid his dislike of Jon long enough to brief him on what they would have to do.

Jon already knew that the four major sections on the left side of the display were controls for one drive and the four on the right were for the other. The pair of central panels were the computer crew interfaces, plus diagnostics and emergency systems. In addition, there were controls for the ship's immense chemical rockets, used for docking maneuvers and short distance trips within planetary systems.

Jon took up station on the left. M'Nee went to the right. Chacks stood in the center. Under M'Nee's instruction they began flicking red toggles up and green ones down. The toggles had to be moved in groups of seven, set out in arrays of twenty lines apiece.

By the time they'd completed one bank there was something different about the ship: A deep vibration had begun.

"The drives!" yelled Jon.

"Yes, Mister Iehard, we have the drives on full power. Now do you believe?" Eblis Bey spoke over the intercom PA.

He was interrupted by a coughing growl from four banks of heavy chemfuel boosters set into the ship's underside. They roared for a few seconds on the first test firing.

"Seems we have full power on the boosters," M'Nee said.

Jon flipped switches. He believed; he had the fervor of the newly converted. As they finished another bank, the ship gave a jolt.

A red light flashed.

"Vector performance in left Baada drive is compromised," said Chacks.

"What is the degree?" M'Nee snapped.

"Possibly one, one point five percent."

"Is that statistically significant?"

"Hard to say. This ship is a thousand years old. Who knows what that might mean? Perhaps nothing, perhaps everything."

"Ask the diagnostic program. One slip and we'll all be subspace microparticles." Chacks continued his check.

Captain Hawkstone suddenly broke in over the newly activated PA system. "Officer Dahn says the computer is operable and quite sane. Bergen says we'll have warmer air in about an hour."

"Chemfuel engines are fully operational," contributed M'Nee. "We can ignite any time. The ship has refuelled itself from the exterior atmosphere, it seems, just as was predicted. The tanks are full."

"What about the laowon though?" Jon voiced a nagging fear.

"The laowon are in for a surprise," replied Hawkstone on the PA. "Everyone strap into the acceleration couches. *Orn* has begun final ascent. We will follow."

In a few moments, the huge engines belched into life once more and began developing the billions of pounds of thrust they had been designed to generate. With a sudden jerk the ancient battleship shifted from her moorings and rose on four columns of white hot fury into the murky atmosphere. On board, they gripped the sides of their acceleration couches and stared grimly at the view-screens.

CHAPTER SIXTEEN

"WE CANNOT REGAIN THAT RADAR TRACE, ADMIRAL."

Admiral Booeej hunched grimfaced over the screen. The bright flashes that lit up his face were more of the damnable nuclear bursts used by the Elchites to hide their ship. The flashes sparked for a few seconds more, deep inside William's gray-green gas mantle.

Booeej looked at a side monitor where a blip was frozen in the screen memory. Too big to be just a jumper. Booeej turned the problem over in his mind.

The small jumper had plummeted into the atmosphere, under power, yet heading most certainly to total destruction. Jumpers just didn't have the powerful engines needed to escape the gravity of a gas giant. *Orn* would sink until it was crushed.

Was this suicide then? Had the Elchites been thwarted in their mission by the presence of the fleet? And then chosen to die rather than be taken? Or...

By the scales on the blue balls of Horg! Was it possible! Could he, Booeej of Red Seygfan, be wrong along with the rest of the Fleet High Command? Was Blue Seygfan correct, then, in maintaining that some truth lay behind the romantic human myths? Even in this legendary mare's nest? Yet, if they were just going to die in the depths, why were they placing so many probe-destroyers in their wake?

His blood seemed to cool as the logic carried him into most unwelcome areas.

If this was the hidden resting place of the last Testamenter ship then Booeej would have to proceed very carefully. His orders were straightforward: He was to capture any such ship that he might find.

The loss of the Testamenter ships with their unique drives was still seen as the single greatest error in all history on the part of the laowon military. And those same revolutionary drives gave the Testamenter ships a big advantage. They were not affected by gravity spin the way laowon jumpers were. They could jump much closer to William than any laowon ship.

Thus Booeej would have to disable any such ship the instant it appeared. And then, somehow, rescue it from the consuming gravity of William. Maneuvering so close to a gas giant, even a small one like William, was highly problematic. The battlejumpers were running through their fuel reserves at a prodigious rate.

Booeej inquired again about the fleet of heavy tugs he had ordered from Ginger Moon. They were still minutes away.

A Testamenter ship would be huge. That big blip on the probe radar had been at extreme range. Booeej grimaced. How was he going to keep the behemoth from falling back into the atmosphere?

It could be lost forever, and Red Seygfan would fly alone at court. He would be accursed, the Imperial Family might even demand that he expiate before them on the chair.

On the other hand, if he let it get away without an accurate fix on its destination, then his staff would join him in Expiation, probably on global television.

"We have a radar trace, rising fast, vector three-oh-four."

Booeej's heart leapt. They came!

A solid blip, large mass, moving rapidly upward on chemical boosters through the atmosphere of William. No jumper could carry enough fuel to reach escape velocity.

"Lasers lock on this target," Booeej said in an urgent voice. By the Seygfan, this was it! Incredible!

But the radar trace was merely the *Orn*, on her last voyage, boosting upward against William's gravity, consuming all the remaining fuel in a decoy run.

The laowon were taken, though.

And then the *Orn*'s ship computer turned on the ship's

gravitomagnetics and tried to jump. The laowon engines strained at the gravity potential around them and then they failed. The *Orn* shuddered out of the *now* of present space-time and then returned a moment later, but minus the protective bubble of the gravitomagnetic field—the mass of the ship intersected with a considerable volume of William's atmosphere; billions of atoms were directly converted into energy.

The flash was vast, hundreds of kilometers across, a bright bubble of incandescent gas and vaporized metals that opened through William's cloud mantle.

Aboard the battlejumpers, the laowons turned aside from their instruments in disgust. Booeej let out an aggrieved expletive.

The ancient ship had blown up. Fourteen centuries resting in high pressure had been too much.

When they turned their eyes back to the screens, the boiling vapors were rising into a pale chartreuse tornado amid the ice clouds. and then they saw the black speck that had suddenly risen through the margin of the boiling clouds.

On the big screen it opened toward them, twenty kilometers or more across, and ominous, a flattened black sphere, slowly rotating, featureless, the sure sign of a force field.

"By the souls of dead Seygfan!" someone whispered.

"Fire! It must not complete the turn! Fire, you fools!" Booeej called.

Hands snapped to the laser controls but already the heavy spheroid was gone, twitched out of William's upper atmosphere on the force of the planet's own gravity potential.

The purple drained from the admiral's face. In a strangled voice he snarled. "Get me a fix on that departure's singularity! Where the hell did they go?"

It was apparent that the ship had traveled outward from William. Because of the gravity problem, it couldn't have reversed through the planetary mass. In fact, a quadrant of most probable destination was soon discernible, a sector covering only ten degrees on a side.

"How many systems within thirty light-years in that sector?" Booeej barked after a swift perusal of the secret Superior Buro data running on his own monitor.

"One hundred seventy-four" was the reply.

In moments, lumpy battlejumpers had scrambled to jump points and hurtled out of the Nocanicus system.

Ulip Sehngrohn stared out the slit window high in the cliff of Bolgol. The raging blue-white fury was dimming, its tiny disk, which could only be observed through thick lead glass, cut the horizon, and a wild, purple dusk fell over the landscape.

Tiny lights began to flicker on in the slit windows on the opposing cliffs of Razevkoy and Fernica. Above the cliffs, where the canyons met, the sky had become a lambent tapestry. Startling mauve clarity was threaded with golden shreds of cloud.

The city of Quism was coming to life. Engines coughed into life in the garages by the Meridian Gate. Dozens of treasure expeditions were setting out on the trail to the south, heading for the dangers and potential wealth of the Oolite trail and the North Shore and the Boneyards.

All through the long polar night, expeditions would continue to leave the city for the south. Caravans of armored hovercraft carrying eager-eyed prospectors and scientific groups.

During the strange glories of dusk, the wealthy expedition patrons would traditionally throw banquets in those high cliff rooms that were left empty in the daylight. The Sunset Clubs would sip imported wine instead of the native bean distillate and watch the hovercraft wending southward. They would speculate happily on the likelihood of success, although all knew that one out of four expeditions would not return. Then the spectacular auroral displays would begin, the signal of the long polar night's true beginnings.

Sehngrohn, however, had already been there for hours, and he watched more than just the sunset and the dust clouds above the departing convoys. For beyond the gap between Razevkoy and Fernica was the spacefield. Private shuttle companies ferried passengers and cargo up and down from orbital space once or twice every day. Their multicolor elevation balloons lined the field, like a set of enormous spansules in a giant's drug cabinet.

A sound behind him heralded the coming of his assistant. "We take delivery of the hovercraft in five hours,

Ulip. Everything will be ready within an hour or so after that."

"Good, Nike. We will want to move quickly, the lao-won are restless. Two military shuttles have landed in the last hour. I can feel their unease. Something has slipped badly. The Imperiom shakes."

A dwarf star gave off a dim red glow on the main screen. "Where are we now?" Jon Iehard said.

"A hiding place," Eblis Bey replied. "This dwarf isn't on anybody's charts. It's about eight light-years to the next system. Nobody's made it out here yet. We left one of the *Orn*'s spaceboats here, because we knew the *Churchill* wouldn't have any left."

Even as he spoke, the radar screen showed a small trace; the boat computer had recorded the arrival of the *Churchill* and was on its way to intercept.

"How far have we come?"

"Nocanicus is about twenty-five light-years back of us. We've the big jumps yet to make."

Owlcurl Dahn put her head in the door. "Come on, Iehard, we've been drawn for torsion magneto inspection. There's a lot to be done."

The huge battleship stretched silent and eerie around them as they rode the lateral elevator line. Most of the side sections were empty—rows of dormitories, store-rooms, endless dark corridors.

"I wonder what they planned to do with all this?" Jon said.

"They intended to send colonizing parties out in their ships. That's why they built on the same sort of scale as the old NAFAL liners."

Eventually they were deposited in one of the ring conduits that surrounded the torsion magneto cables. They began to move along the cables, their lights seeking breaks or cracks caused by the strain of that wild escape from almost inside the atomic blast of the *Orn*, with only the gravito-magnetic fields protecting the ship from severe damage.

It was hot work in the narrow cable conduits. There were miles of connections to check. And there was just enough room for two humans to stand up in, in long stretches.

At every kilometer was a major junction box to be

checked, each set directly facing a radial elevator shaft that connected to the central section. The box plate was held by a countersunk starbolt. Jon used a star wrench to remove the bolts. Owlcurl Dahn examined the interiors for damage.

As they worked they talked about Ornholme in the distant Asdali system and about the ancient debt to Elchis.

"Nine hundred years, Mr. Iehard! Not all the Orners today remember the importance of the Elchites to our ancestors. That is why some of the crew seem so unwilling. They do not realize that without the Elchites our forebears would have been taken by the Superior Buro. And this ship and their heroic efforts to preserve it would have been lost, and the laowon would have the Baada drives. Which they have never discovered on their own."

Jon snorted. "Laowon science is static. Their empire is a corrupt monster teetering on disintegration. Only the constant draining of human science has kept them moving forward these thousand years."

"Exactly, Mr. Iehard. Which is another reason why our mission is so vital."

"But do you know what exactly it is that we search for?"

"Mr. Iehard, I may not tell you about that. Only the Bey can tell you. Nobody else in the crew knows the secret, not even the young Elchites."

He shrugged. Such secrecy was understandable in light of the effectiveness of the Superior Buro.

"Another point. I think I need to know who are Elchites and who not. The young ones are fiery fellows, aren't they?"

"Incendiary, Mr. Iehard. And Finn M'Nee will surely bear malice toward you. I have found him most difficult to work with."

"Why is that do you think?"

"The Elchites hate women—M'Nee and Chacks are lovers. They are mostly samesexers. Their cult is anti-female."

"The Bey?"

"No!" She laughed. "Not Eblis Bey, but he is special, and from Earth. Can you imagine, he comes from the homeworld. Even on Ornholme we think of Earth as far, far away. Which is true—it is seventy light-years from the Asdali system to Sol. But now that seems almost neighborly! We are making jumps of that distance itself!"

"Are the Elchites of Earth different then from the rest of the creed?"

"If the Bey is a true example then it must be so. He certainly has an appetite for women. Since he's been aboard I believe he's been to bed with all three females in the crew—myself, Dahlia Bergen, and Rewa Kolod."

Jon laughed, the sound ringing inside the conduits.

They worked on, eventually reaching the conduits that ran through the south pole of the ship. Occasionally lamps shone down the long shafts above their heads to form pools of light on the junction boxes.

Another box, this time in darkness, another plate, another countersunk starbolt. They were nearly three quarters of the way around. Dahn kept her lights trained on the bolt while Jon braced himself to get good leverage. The muscles in his chest groaned in complaint. This one was stiff.

He shifted position, got a good grip, strained.

Then he caught a fleeting image, a ghostly shriek of hatred from somewhere above him and a torsion wrench spinning in darkness.

Jon cannoned into Owlcurl Dahn. They sprawled and with a terrific *whunk* a heavy wrench bounced on the steel junction box and shot into the wall with enormous force.

The reverberations echoed in the narrow conduit.

Jon let out a bitter curse.

Owlcurl Dahn was pale. "That could have killed you! That was criminally careless."

"No, Owlcurl, not careless at all."

Admiral Booeej was a pale shade of puce as he listened to the young Morgooze of Blue Seygfan.

"For such incompetence I personally shall tear apart your sex organs with the electrified tongs. Your expiation will be accompanied by that of your senior officers, family, and relatives."

"Lord, I was given an impossible task."

"Impossible! You shall have the hot coals, the frozen

skewers, your children will be mutilitated before your eyes . . ."

From his hospital bed the Morgooze continued to rage. Booeej swallowed heavily, tried to compose his thoughts to acceptance of fate. It was hard, damnably hard.

CHAPTER SEVENTEEN

When the ship had been completely checked and a number of small repairs made, they gathered in the cavernous refectory for a final meeting before the last jump.

The Elchites studiously ignored Jon, but he was sure from the rage on the psi plane that they were the ones that had tried to kill him.

At Jon's request Dahn had said nothing about the incident, but Jon was aware that he would have to be especially careful from then on. They had meant to kill. If they tried again he would have to strike back.

Eblis Bey stood. "My friends, saviors, acolytes, we have come to the last, most momentous part of our journey. And soon you will learn just where it is we have been heading all this time." Groans were heard from some of the Orners.

"When we get to the new system we will disembark and the *Churchill* will be put out on a long solar orbit to keep it hidden. We shall not need it again unless we are successful with our main mission."

"Then I take it, Bey, that you at least know where we are going." Hawkstone sounded bitter.

"Captain, we all regret the loss of the *Orn*. But I urge you, think instead of the future in Asdali system, building ships with Baada drives."

This drove Hawkstone to snort angrily. "We have one

more jump to make, a long one. Who knows anything about these drives? We may just as easily become merged with the subuniversal flux. Once more, we have to risk our lives for this crazed scheme of yours."

"I'm sorry you feel that way, Captain. But we have no choice. And my scheme, crazed or not, was approved by the highest councils of Elchis."

"Of course we have a choice," Hawkstone blustered. "We could take the lifeboat and strike out for the nearest civilized system."

"That's eight light-years away, Captain. The trip would take many years."

"We would live."

"Just possibly your chances would be higher than ours, but who here would really like to spend twenty years in the spaceboat?"

No hands rose. Hawkstone lapsed into sullen silence.

"We are settled then. We will jump and then land together. Then we will part at last and only volunteers will go on, with me, to the end."

"If I were asked," Bergen muttered, "which I am not, you understand, but if I were, I would say forget this nonsense of the Elchites and take this ship home to Ornholme as soon as possible. I would never venture away again."

Dahn let a momentary flicker of annoyance cross her features. "We had to come to pay off the debt. It was just your misfortune to be on crew schedule when the time came. Ornholme has lived with knowledge of the debt for nine hundred years. When the call came we had to respond. I have found this project an exceptionally difficult and dangerous one, but we are acting for the good of all Ornholme."

Officer Bergen made no further comment.

The meeting broke up. Jon headed to the galley counter. The food preparation systems had survived the long hiatus, as had the freeze-dried rations of fried bananas, eggpowder scramble, and mashed-potato slurry. It was awful, but it was food. Owlcurl Dahn joined him.

"What will you do when we reach planetside, Jon?"

"I'm not quite sure what I'll do. I must find some medical assistance for Meg. She will need a long rest wherever we go. As for myself, I will go with Bey if I can."

"Then we will travel on together. I am pledged to go all the way too."

He had almost finished the mess on his plate when Eblis Bey appeared and sat down with them. The mote floated down to rest on the table between them. Its brilliant eyes dimmed then seemed to go out.

Eblis Bey noticed Jon's wondering gaze. "Yes, it's resting, conserving energy. You are curious about my little friend here."

"Indeed I am. How many have ever seen one of the great motes? It is a remarkable creature. Already it has provided me with a service by describing my silvery cube from Fara's template."

"If it is a creature. It maintains that it is not, but it cannot explain its own processes very well. In truth, we hardly understand anything about the things."

The Bey produced his flask and poured Jon a sip of a fiery terrestrial distillate called Cobra.

"Tell me about Earth," Jon said.

Eblis Bey paused a moment, gathered himself. "You have to understand that Earth can live again. We will bring the planet back to life, you see. That is our ultimate goal."

"I don't understand. Earth is dead?"

"Largely, as a consequence of the greenhouse effect. The biosphere has been degraded to the point of collapse." His voice hardened. "But we shall bring her back. Earth will be green and lovely once again. We can save her with mass migration and enforcement of the sterility code."

And Jon saw the Elchite fires burning in the man's eyes.

An idea occurred to him. "Where were you born?"

Eblis Bey blinked. "Born? Why do you want to know?"

"Put it down to professional curiosity. Military Intelligence wouldn't tell me much about you. Now's my chance to get some answers."

Eblis Bey smiled slowly. "You were good, they say."

"At tracking?"

"And the rest."

"They trained me until that kind of violence became second nature to me. I do not enjoy it."

"Yes, of course. I understand." Eblis Bey nodded.

"But you didn't tell me where you were born."

"All right!" The Bey threw up his hands. "I shall satisfy

your curiosity then. I was born in the city of Sector Three. It's on the continent of South America. But I spent most of my life in the So Cal Dome in North America. These are places that are hard to describe. Enormous beyond anything you can imagine—forty billion TV screens and the oceans are dead! The diet is poor except for the elite and the elite live in dread of the masses. The masses would happily devour the elite, because they blame them for what has happened to our world. That is Earth. It is not a pleasant place."

"My ancestor Jenjamin Iehard, he was from a city called Airstrip Five. Do you know it?"

"A South Pole colony, I believe, one of the older domes. No, I've never been to the polar continent. It was once completely covered in ice, did you know that? A beautiful shining sheet of ice without a single city! The littoral was home to a multitude of wild creatures, and in the surrounding oceans lived the whales, who foraged in the rich waters. But the whales were eaten by the barbaric Japanese long ago, and later all the other animals died out when the ice melted and the clouds filled the sky. It is the same as the other continents now, just wind, desert, and domes."

"How would the Elchites renew the Earth then?"

"First there would have to be mass emigration, which at the moment the laowon will not allow. Then we would turn to all the terrestrial species that have been exported to other systems. As the pollution rates were lowered terraforming bacteria could take a grip. We would cool the planet with solar deflectors and cause more of the water vapor to fall out as rain. In time, that would wash out the carbon dioxide again, and that would allow the planting of adapted trees and sea kelp to renew the ancient cycles."

"But why won't the laowon allow emigration?"

"Because a weak, decadent Earth suits them. A renewed Earth would only give humanity something to unite around and that would pose a problem."

He saw Jon's eyebrows knit.

"Yes, you are correct. It will take a long time, but we will do it. We are determined. Once we have shaken the laowon from our backs."

Jon nodded vigorously. "I wanted to ask you about that. Where are the aliens that can help us?"

Eblis Bey smiled. "You and your friend Meg made

some astute deductions, young man—quite frightening really, considering how little evidence you had." He looked about Jon for a second as if afraid of eavesdroppers.

In a hushed voice he said, "Did you know that there is an alien species that the laowon fear? Twice in the past thousand years they have been forced to burn entire worlds. They used nuclear weapons, until no life of any kind survived."

"What is this? What are you talking about?"

"On both occasions they burned small laowon colony populations. On the most recent occasion they burned a small human population as well, which is how we in the brotherhood came to hear of it."

"But why?"

The Bey seemed to calculate something in Jon's eyes. "Because apparently this is a more dangerous universe than human thinkers have allowed themselves to believe. The laowon are afraid of an alien lifeform that they refer to only as the 'advanced parasitic form.' On both occasions that they burned worlds they did so to exterminate this lifeform."

Jon's brows furrowed. "Are we going to find this lifeform?"

Eblis Bey gave a bitter laugh. "By the gods, no! Let us pray that we be spared that!" Jon saw that actual tears were running from the old man's eyes. He dabbed at them, unembarrassed.

"I'm sorry." Jon felt awkward. Why did he weep so?

Eblis Bey recovered himself. "No, we're not going to seek out that lifeform. And I hope that none of it will find us. But it is connected with our destination. You see, young Jon Iehard, you are correct to a degree. We are searching for something alien, something that will break us free of the laowon tyranny. We seek a remnant of an ancient world, a talisman of hope from so long ago that when it was built there was not so much as a clam on the Earth to feed on the algae."

"When?"

"A billion years ago, I mean. We were saved, before we were even born, by the heroism of an early race, a tragic race of high attainment."

"Who were they?"

"Sadly we cannot even pronounce their name in their

own tongue. We can't speak much of it at all; we lack the rattle pods and throat drums that were so important to them. Their gift of vocalization was as much beyond ours as ours is beyond that of lower mammals. Their languages were like terrestrial chinese, dense in phonetic nuances.

"They were batrachian, soft-skinned amphibians that evolved considerable intelligence. Theirs was a rich emotional and cultural life, built around the mating dances with songs of great length and metrical complexity. Yet there was also the inherent tragedy of their breeding rate. They were forced to devour their own young as a method of population control. They called themselves the Wisdom Wishing, and they were a gentle people. They fled from our universe long ago, their world shattered and dying. Before that, however, they had rendered a great service to the rest of our Galaxy."

"Why, what did they do?"

"They stopped the Vang."

"The what?"

"It is one of the very small number of words in the batrachians' languages that we can pronounce easily. To the best of my knowledge, it translates as 'omniparasitic vermin.' I think it was the same lifeform that has so frightened the laowon."

"But if they stopped it—"

"Oh, they did, they smashed the Vang power, but they could not completely annihilate all of it, or them. The Vang appears to be a complex species with many physical forms and aspects. It seems that small particles were somehow left and dispersed into the Galaxy like a bacterial infection. Twice now the laowon have encountered this infection. Both times they have responded by burning an entire world."

"How horrible."

"Yes, indeed, though it is interesting nonetheless to know that the laowon are not invulnerable."

"And your ancient race, what happened to them?"

"Ah, the poor batrachians—they were a slow, profound folk. Matured by aeons of slow evolution in the swamps and coastal littoral. Their sciences of biology and conservation were their highest, but when they had to, they developed tremendous technologies in mere decades and left ruins of such size and complexity that we still stand before them in awe and amazement.

"What happened?" The Bey shrugged. "The details are few and far between but I have researched them diligently all my working life. Unfortunately the archeological records are scattered, and much of the best information is today in laowon hands. However, we do know that they were advanced in sciences like astronomy, but not in ballistics. Eventually, though, they sent out astronomical probes beyond their own solar system. It was then that they discovered vast fleets of colony ships heading toward their system. The ships were slow NAFAL so they had a century or more to prepare. The batrachians built enormous astronomical instruments utilizing the complete spectrum. The great telescope was apparently constructed in outer space and had a distance of many millions of kilometers between the giant lenses. With such instruments they observed that beyond the advancing fleet were worlds upon worlds inhabited by a single lifeform. In addition, colony fleets were crawling across space to many other systems surrounding the Vang homeworlds. They clearly faced a terrible peril."

Eblis Bey sipped coffee, considered his words. "The batrachians had been a slow people. Their cities were low and quite unremarkable, built in harmony with the estuaries and tidal mud flats that they preferred, none of the glories of human or laowon architecture. But then they rose up and welded the entire resources of their planet together in a crash program of defense."

"Did they manage it?"

"Not quite, they were unversed in war. The Vang advance forces arrived and swept aside their defenses with contemptuous ease. The batrachians had completely underestimated the ferocity of combat. Their losses were dreadful, but certain methods of Vang warfare helped them to rethink. They swung to the opposite extreme, the ruthlessness of the weak. During their great program they had discovered a physics of supergravity that is still far beyond us. They turned to it to forge a weapon with which to destroy the Vang fleets and Vang homeworlds. But even as they did so, Vang lifeforms were dropping onto their planet. The batrachians realized they were doomed. They had wasted most of the useful mass in their solar system as gravity potential for their weapons. All they could turn to then was their own sun, which they used to transport what was left of them into the flow of time and, I believe, to the remote future."

"But what happened to their planet?"

"Its sun gone, it was flung into the interstellar void at orbital speed and drifted there for a billion years or more."

"How do we know of it then?"

"It was captured by a young blue-giant star, some time in the last few thousand years. More recently it has been colonized by human beings." The Bey stood up. "Come with me and I will show you."

A few floors above they came to a small room that Eblis Bey had appropriated as an office. They entered after he had carefully checked the corridor.

"No one we cannot trust completely may know this until we get there. Not even the young acolytes of Elchis."

Eblis Bey took a small holocaster from his sleeve and set it on the table. A sharp little hologram sprang into place, a star system.

"The primary is Pleione, one of the seven sisters of the Pleides. She is hot and she is young."

The star was tinged blue-white. The representation made it seem tiny and far away, a hot speck of fury.

"Of course she is much too young to have planets of her own. In fact, it is doubtful that she will burn stably long enough for planets even to form from what is left of the nebula that surrounds her."

Nevertheless, outside the ring of gas and dust particles a small brown planet rolled past in the projection.

"But, you see, she has a planet, a captured wanderer, a most interesting little world that we humans call BRF, or colloquially Baraf."

Jon stared at him. "Baraf," he sputtered, and pointed at the resting mote. "Where the mote was found!"

"Indeed. And it is there that we will find the Hammer."

"The Hammer?"

"That smashes stars, the ancient weapon of the batrachians. With it, we can free humanity of the laowon yoke."

CHAPTER EIGHTEEN

THE BAADA DRIVES FUNCTIONED PERFECTLY FOR THE last two enormous jumps across the stars, but when at last the great battleship hung on the fringes of the Pleione system the left drive broke down with an appalling howl of tortured metal. A few moments later the computer shut everything down except the auxiliary power supply and left them shaking in their seats with their fingers stuffed in their ears.

They crowded around the astronomical screen on the bridge. Not far away a small dark planet orbited. A pall of dust hung over most of the northern hemisphere, but here and there narrow strips of blue water laced the surface.

A conference was held. No one was prepared to stay aboard the crippled *Churchill*, and thus the spaceboat would be heavily crowded on the short hop to the planetary surface.

The great Testamenter battleship would be left to float on in solar orbit, a near hulk.

Eblis Bey pointed to the small planet on the screen. "Behold the planet called Baraf, wherein resides our last hope for human freedom.

"As you can see, the oceans are greatly reduced. Most of the ancient seabeds are now exposed. The dust belts are one result, since the primordial oozes have dried and been taken into the upper atmosphere."

"What happened to make the oceans shrink so much?" Jon asked.

"A sad side effect of the little planet's salvation from eternal freezing. Baraf was plucked from the interstellar void about twenty thousand yeas ago. For most of that time the planet was safe. It warmed up, the ice melted, the oceans circulated once again, and in time life might have returned. But the orbit is eccentric. About two thousand years ago Baraf passed close to Pleione and was scorched. The oceans largely boiled away."

"How did anyone ever come to discover this planet?" Officer Bergen said. "Who would want to colonize here, surrounded by these giant white stars? There's too much radiation."

"True, and indeed it was only by the remotest chance that Baraf was discovered at all. Just another aspect of the case that gives encouragement to the view that there really is a God of the humans, or at the very least a merciful God that looks upon our struggle for freedom with favor."

He smiled at them. "But the fact remains that it was discovered by three survivors of a shipwreck long ago."

"Way out here?" exclaimed Jon. "We're far beyond the outer limits of human exploration."

"Their ship was the *Stapledon*, one of the earliest High Corporate exploration vessels. Very fast NAFAL, the crew were kept in hibernation. But the computer malfunctioned, accelerated to maximum speed, and kept it up for centuries."

"I wonder why?"

"Apparently it had formulated the 'Two God' problem for itself, a noted hazard with some early generations of advanced computers, especially the so-called tenth generation. It was a mathematical black hole from which they hardly ever recovered, becoming obsessed with the need to prove that they were, or were not, God incarnate.

"However, after several centuries it decided the problem was just an irrelevancy and made a rare recovery. It began to decelerate and to wake the crew, but already the ship was on the verge of a dense interstellar dust cloud. They abandoned the ship just before it blew up in the cloud.

"As a result there were only three survivors: Anatol

Bolgol, the expedition's biologist; Levia Razevkoy, the astronav; and Lotte Fernica, the medic. Theirs was the only lifeboat that escaped the wreck. They also survived the subsequent seven-year voyage to reach this habitable little planet.

"Their radio broadcasts were identified a century later and a rescue mission was sent by laowon jumper, but there were already thousands of their descendants here and they had discovered amazing artifacts of their lost world."

They all looked at Rhapsodical Stardimple, where it was floating, optics glued to the planet in the skyplate.

"The vast machines, the boneyard cities where the ancient Barafi populations died en masse, and the odd remnants of their culture, the motes, the templates, the pops and snaps. Of course once these things became known, there was a constant stream of people from all over the known Galaxy. Even a few laowon adventurers come here, overcoming their pathological fear of radiation."

"But you say 'thousands' of their descendants were here?" Jon voiced his puzzlement. "How could there have been thousands of them in such a short time?"

"It was remarkably simple. Old Bolgol was a biologist and a medical doctor, Lotte Fernica was a geneticist and although Lotte was far beyond childbearing years they did have Levia Razevkoy. They decided to produce a large family with her eggs and Bolgol's sperm. It was a natural response to their situation. They were alone on a strange and hostile world. They knew that Pleione's radiation was dangerous and so they colonized the extensive caves at Quism on the North Pole. In a remarkably brief time they overcame the difficulties and produced a crop of one hundred and twelve viable fetuses, mostly female. They also produced the mutated beans and rice that grow on the north polar patch, which, like the South Pole, is the only part of the planet that has anything like reasonable climate."

Jon stared in wonder at the planet below.

"The next generation was much easier, of course, and after that it got out of hand. At the last count there were four distinctly different mutant species running wild in the northern deserts, robbing archeologists and prospectors.

They've become quite a menace. Most are cannibals. They maintain herds of meat people. The tales that are told of them are quite horrible."

"How can they survive Pleione's radiation?"

"The mutants live underground in the day, they infest the surface at night. Especially in the northern machine belts and the ancient city sites. It is said they have made genetics their religion and Anatol Bolgol their god. There are rumors that clones of Bolgol and Razevkoy continue to live out there, among the wildest tribes like the Blue-grain Hardscabbies."

"It sounds like a savage place," Officer Bergen commented.

"It is. And the city of Quism is just as savage as the desolate wastes. It is a city ruled by force, not law, and that is something you must all remember while we are here. At any moment violence may strike. You must all be on your guard for the duration of your stay."

After course corrections for the chemfuel boosters were fed into the *Churchill*'s computer to ensure the great ship maintained a stable, distant, orbit about Pleione, they crowded into the spaceboat, but the journey to the planetary surface was uneventful and, with the main parachutes deployed, they floated down onto the spaceport at Quism.

Dimly visible around the port were long rectangular fields, dark with vegetation.

Hundreds of kilometers away, a wall of mountains was made visible by a line of white snow that dappled its peaks.

Eblis Bey had briefed them but still the reality of Quism was rather intimidating.

The boat was met by a convoy of small armored vehicles. Tense-looking young men appeared from within. They made the sign of Elchis, a cross in the air with the left hand.

Eblis Bey went out to meet them in a thin, warm wind, with the mote floating at his shoulders. The leaders kissed his hand, the rest waved weapons and saluted the Bey with a roar.

Watching at the edge of the spaceboat's airlock, Jon noticed an odd expression on Finn M'Nee's face; eyes narrowed, lips pinched in disapproval. M'Nee caught him looking at him and flashed him a glance of unrelieved hatred, then turned back into the cabin.

They quickly disembarked while an armed group from the spaceport docking authority rode out an electric trolley to tow the spaceboat into the cliffcut hangars.

With the four armored cars as escort, they would ride a bus into the city itself and take lodgings in a centrally located hotel. Meg and the injured Riley would be taken from there to the Elchite shelter where a small hospital was maintained.

Quism was an old, underground city. In its warren of limestone caves seethed a population that survived principally by supplying, protecting, and robbing treasure hunters and archeologists.

At the side of the concrete spaceport apron was a line of barkers for the rival bus owners. They set up a raging din at the sight of six travelers with luggage.

"My bus is the most comfortable in this system!" screamed one garlic-scented driver with a belly that protruded well over his trouser tops.

"His bus stinks of the Scurmachers he just carried in. All that boilweed fume!"

"My bus is best bus!"

"You will boil in hell alongside your ancestor's liver!"

"Your ancestor was my ancestor so who the hell cares!"

"You will be defiled by my dog!"

While they argued, swift-fingered accomplices attempted to pick the travelers' pockets and steal anything remotely valuable that might present itself.

Jon Iehard noticed the technique at once. He positioned himself close to Captain Hawkstone as two young, olive-skinned men lurched into him. Hands went for the small pack on Hawkstone's back and the loose pockets of his overall rain slicker.

Jon rapped the hand in the pack with the butt of his Taw Taw and caught the hand lifting Hawkstone's Ornholme ID card from his pocket.

The owners of the hands cursed furiously, but at the sight of the gun they moved away sharply.

Officer Dahn shook her head gloomily, then gave a small scream. Jon looked up to see two boys were pushing Meg Vance away in her wheelchair. Jon sprinted after them and recovered her.

"Cannibalism is a constant threat here. Women sell their own newborns to the butcher, the dead seldom need be buried or cremated. Be alert at all times," Eblis Bey chided.

They chose a yellow-and-black bus that belched black smoke and rode on oversize tires down a corrugated roadbed into the city and, finally, to the forecourt of a hotel. The Travel Aires was dug into the solid rock. A wall of reinforced concrete blocks rose in front, and armed guards patrolled the blue-and-white forecourt. The guards wore stiff maroon-and-blue tunics and carried two-handed automatic pistols that looked to Jon like imitation Taw Taw .45s. He noticed the signs of body armor under the tunics.

The guards on the forecourt and the young Elchites in the armored vehicles eyed each other with a mixture of disdain and contempt, but neither side spoke. One surly guard spat eloquently after sharing a comment with a colleague. The Elchites looked up along the barrels of their machine guns. The surly guards fell silent.

After paying the bus drivers, Eblis Bey was forced to tip all the forecourt guards, who would accept only intersystem value vouchers or notes of Lao Mercantility.

Hawkstone was quick to complain. "So again we must pay out credit! There is no end to it!"

"It's essential if we don't want to lose people—have them stolen right off this forecourt. As I said, cannibalism, slavery, robbery, all are highly common here."

The Orners groaned.

Eblis Bey smiled. "I will personally explain the necessity behind it all to the Ornholme Financial Council."

"You think that will be easy, don't you?" Hawkstone said derisively. "You'll be telling them after they've learned of the loss of the *Orn*."

After considerable, ill-tempered haggling, Dahn finally agreed to book them all into the hotel under the special rate for ongoing expeditions, a hundred credit units per person per day, plus a percentage of eventual profits. Dahn paid over more intersystem value vouchers with ill grace.

The interior of the Travel Aires was a startling blend of fortress and hotel. Whorled concrete ceilings, blast shields about all the main doors, a large, quiet interior courtyard with a fountain, and small trees populated by exotic songbirds.

Outside the windows of Jon's room, the blue-and-white striped concrete forecourt opened onto the Grand Levee, a babbling thoroughfare jammed with traffic from the Meridian Gate to the Spaceport Gate right through the heart of the city.

The rooms were of all sizes and shapes, cut from the native rock at intervals over four hundred years. The interiors offered comfortable enough beds, baths, and light that was filtered from overhead shafts.

Jon dropped his small tote bag on the bed after extracting his gun and the small silver cube. Then he rejoined the Elchites and accompanied them to their shelter with Meg and Riley.

The shelter was hidden beneath a tenement block in a densely crowded slum section of Razevkoy Precinct. To get in they entered a small basement doorway, crossed the cellar, and went down another narrow hole into a warren of underground rooms.

Young men and women in blue robes came and took Meg and Riley into a small hospital ward.

Jon explained what had happened to Meg and to Riley. The chief medic stared at him, emotions mixed, but sedated Meg. "She has served Elchis well. We shall care for her and when she wakes we will explain where she is and how she came to be here."

Jon shook hands with Riley, promised to come back and see him as soon as the mission was completed.

"All right, young sunboy, you do that. I'll not bear a grudge, but I warn you, be on your lookout for Finn M'Nee. Sharp as a sandsnake, worse than a spiny pfister is that one."

Jon rode an armored vehicle to the hotel. The streets were thronged, and he saw innumerable mutations from the human norm. One of the most common forms was often seven feet tall, the skin thick and coarse and mottled with blue patches.

Once back in the hotel he had barely time to grab a meal and use the bathroom facilities in his room before being called to a meeting in Eblis Bey's suite.

When he got there, Owlcurl Dahn was arguing vehemently with several thin-faced young men with sun-bleached hair and heavily tanned skins. The young men shared that intensity, that "fire of Elchis" he'd observed before.

"I tell you, I am coming, all the way to the south. I was appointed to this mission by the Ornholme Executive Council without whom none of this could have happened. Furthermore, I resent your attitudes. Since I'm paying for all this, I don't think it's unfair for me to be included in the planning!"

The Elchites muttered among themselves, while the Bey conferred briefly with Jon. Then he drew him across the room to the Elchites.

"Jon Iehard, meet some of my young brethren here. This is Aul, Karak, Yondon, and Gesme."

"Well, Master Iehard, were you satisfied with our hospital in the shelter?" Aul was a hatchet-faced youth with a shaved head and unhealthy complexion. "The medics will take good care of her. It seems that she has given much to Elchis."

"The facilities seem extremely well equipped, especially considering their surroundings."

"The dedicated sons of Elchis on this cursed world have sought to hide themselves rather than construct a showy temple. We have secrets that the laowon must never find out."

Jon nodded understandingly. "Of course, and what kind of presence do they keep here? The Superior Buro has a station, I take it."

"A small one, three operatives only. They are easily kept befuddled. Our greatest problem is keeping human treachery in check. There are always those who would sell us all out to the blues given the chance. Anything for money, that is their creed."

"How do you achieve security then?"

"By the strength of our reputation. Betray Elchis and the retribution will be long, hot, and bloody. Everyone in Quism knows this."

"I see." And indeed the young Elchites seemed a tough breed, tight, sinewy. Undoubtedly good with their weapons.

"Gesme is to go with you and Officer Dahn, to the street of armorers," Eblis Bey said. "We will need weapons in the southlands, and you are probably the most knowledgeable among us concerning guns. Officer Dahn will accompany you to prevent overspending. She is concerned to keep down our costs, which are largely being borne by the Ornhole Council."

They then discussed the schedule ahead. They would spend a single sleep shift in the hotel before gathering at the Meridian Gate where the expedition vehicles were being readied.

After discussing with the local Sons of Elchis the kinds of predatory activities expected from the locals, Jon concluded that everyone should carry a handweapon and that half a dozen rifles and one or two heavier items might do for above-average attempts. This to provide security in what he imagined would be the conditions out on the barren southland wastes. The Elchites agreed with his estimates but also advised him to include some grenade launchers.

"Very useful against cannibal tribesmen, who fear mutilation greatly; it normally dooms a warrior to the stew-pot."

The weapons-purchasing party left the hotel with one of the maroon-and-blue-clad guards walking behind them, his automatic openly displayed. Around them, the levee throbbed with chart sellers, merchandizers of survival equipment, and mutant guides to the interior.

Through the crowded tunnels endless conspiracy swirled. Bandit troops kept thousands of spies in business, seeking expedition routes and times. Equipment merchants were often double dealers, reporting on their sales to the chiefs of mutant tribes beyond the Meridian. Then dealers would reclaim their equipment, patch up the bullet holes and sell it again. A dozen independent "police" authorities existed, any of which could swoop on an expedition in search of "illegal" equipment, which in practice could mean anything. Normally such searches were prevented by the payment of a security fee beforehand.

In the city center, in the Fernica cavern, were the alleys of the equipment dealers. Around the city perimeter, clustered at the gates, were the garages that leased transport. Between them and the various banking and investing sectors traveled a constant stream of rickshaw traffic, pedaled by the lean, pale urban people who called themselves the Quiz.

However, to reach the street of gun sellers they simply strolled a few blocks down the Grand Levee, which bisected the huge Fernica cavern. It was aswirl with a throng of great diversity.

Long-neck mutants with blue eyes and black skins, from the interior, mingled with pale urban hustlers and peddlers. Pureblood Japanese dwarfs ran hither and thither through the crowds carrying packages on their heads.

There was a constant roar of exclamations, imprecations and bawled curses. In the central strip a constant jam of bicycles, rickshaws, and motor drays added a mechanical hum to it all.

Jon soon noticed that nobody got anywhere very quickly in ancient Quism.

The levee split into two and swept round a gigantic rock that sat in the middle of the cavern. Cut into the rock were tunnels and dozens of windows with balconies.

From the windows hung the faces of children and eldsters. The sounds of amplified music, with a curious skittering rhythm, echoed from the stone walls. Pungent smells of cooking and sewage filled the air. At the Alley Salteem they turned inside and entered a world of dim illumination and countless small shops.

A few meters farther in brought them to a section where dozens of weapons dealers kept shops and warehouses. They proceeded down several alleys, each narrower than the last with a lower ceiling of rock, and after consultations they selected the House of Blaas and pushed open its natural wood door.

It was a small space, with a counter of polished wood under a pair of fiber optic lights that gave everything a brown and aged tone. Antique handweapons were arrayed on the walls in glass cases. Behind the counter stood a tubby, hairless man who introduced himself as Blaas. On hearing their request he brought out well-worn catalogs. Jon asked to see certain items to check them for weight and feel. Blaas ordered them up from a cellar below.

Eventually Jon selected six high-powered rifles, a pair of long-range grenade launchers, a dozen bomb packs, and a set of locally made handguns that fired shotgun charges rather than bullets and were designed for non-expert users.

For himself he bought a Taw Taw longbarrel, a monstrous .35 recoilless that fired a variety of ammunitions. Jon had always been good with handguns, but with Taw Taw longbarrels he'd been the best in the Mass Murder Squad, achieving an accuracy close to that of good rifle marksmen.

But when Owlcurl Dahn saw the price tag she nearly fainted. "Sixteen *thousand* units!"

"I doubt that you will regret them once we are under the eyes of the cannibal tribes."

She paid over the notes without further comment.

They packed the weapons and the salesman hailed a pair of burly mutants with ridged skin thick and wattled, to haul the packs for them. Jon observed the dullness in the mutants' eyes. Blaas noted his interest.

"Those are just glass, I don't like the sight of empty sockets. I always have these mutants blinded as well as gelded, it's a big help in keeping them docile. These are Hardscabbies, deep-desert mutants of an intractable nature normally. But I've been very successful with this pair. I feed them by hand sometimes."

With many cautious glances around them they returned to the fortresslike hotel without incident.

Other groups had not been so fortunate. Officer Bergen and Captain Hawkstone had been robbed at knifepoint in the clothiers' bazaar. Bergen had almost been dragged off herself by the robbers, but her screams had drawn just slightly too much attention and the robbers had finally desisted.

Hawkstone was priming himself with distillate at the bar, Bergen was semihysterical in the lounge. Eblis Bey had disappeared on a mysterious errand but was expected back soon.

Jon called everyone else together and demonstrated the weapons and then distributed them.

They ate together and then retired to sleep. Eblis Bey had still not returned when Jon finally drifted off after taking apart the Taw Taw longbarrel, cleaning it, and putting it back together.

CHAPTER NINETEEN

WHEN HE FINALLY GOT TO HIS BED, JON FELL INTO THE sleep of true exhaustion, too deep for dreams. He never heard his door creak open. The first warning came from a sudden weight that shook the bed as something huge knelt on it. He came awake, still groggy, to find enormous hands around his throat. While he tried to claw them away, someone stuck a syrette into his arm and not long after that he went back to sleep.

When he was brought round he found himself in a dark room, naked and trussed firmly at wrist and ankle. A gag had been stuffed in his mouth. A heavyset figure leaned over him in a reek of smelling salts. Someone else stood in the background. A conversation about him was in progress.

"Leave him whole, why don't you? I can get a good buyer, laowon Mercantile notes. The female blues are always looking for good human slaves." The speaker had a strange singsong accent.

Then he heard Finn M'Nee reply in a voice that chilled him. "Before he is sold he is to be castrated, blinded, and his tongue cut out. In addition he must only be sold to a human owner. Remember, I speak as a brother of the lodge. Vengeance will be visited upon you if you transgress."

"Sell him to some bandit group from the interior. Get

him out of the city," another voice said. It was Gelgo Chacks.

"Little use he'll be to them. What would they want with such a useless slave?"

"We do not care. Sell him as I say or you will hear from us again!"

The menace in Chacks' tone was unmistakable.

"Remember, handle him with care. He's dangerous as a spiny pfister."

"What the hell's that?"

"Don't ask questions. Castrate and blind him and then sell him."

"Cut out his tongue. Remember, we will be watching."

They were gone, Jon was left alone. After what seemed an hour or more had passed, the door opened and the heavyset owner of the singsong accent returned. He was accompanied by a dimly visible figure. A sickly sweet perfume entered the room.

The fat man held an electric torch that he kept in Jon's eyes while he pulled him around. "See, he's perfectly good for anyone's bed. He has his parts."

"So I see," said a nasal female voice.

"Good proportions in most features. He's not bad-looking."

"I doubt, Bompipi, that you are the best judge of these things."

"Why, madam, I am partial to either sex."

She laughed throatily, then asked, "Why do you think they wanted castration?"

"Elchites! Who knows what the reasons are for Elchite outrages? Perhaps he crossed their path in the street on a holy day, perhaps betrayed them to the laowon. Who can tell? Whatever the cause, he must be blinded and his tongue cut out. As to his organs, I must say it makes an old slaver's heart quiver to waste anything so useful as good parts on a slave."

"Yes, excellent parts. In truth, there's no understanding Elchitism. Weren't they responsible for bombing the Church of St. Anarch?"

"Yes, madam, I believe they were."

"Hundreds killed and for what? There was never an explanation."

"None that I recall, madam."

"Well. Take his eyes and tongue if you must, but leave the parts, and deliver him to my apartment."

"Certainly, madam. And may I assure you that the House of Haal will employ a reputable surgeon for the operations. Would you prefer natural-looking artificial eyes or plain glass balls?"

"Why don't you send round a catalog? I'll review your range."

"Of course, madam."

They left and Jon tested his bonds. There was no likelihood of his breaking them. As far as he could tell his fate was assured. He would be blinded and sold to the old woman.

The expedition would go on without him; they would not be able to afford the luxury of time to find him. Finn M'Nee would doubtless claim that Iehard had betrayed them anyway, and in a while they would believe him.

He returned his attention to his bonds.

The homeworld of the laowon was Lao the Golden, in a system almost two kiloparsecs distant from Nocanicus and Pleione. On Laogolden there had been climate control and strict population regulations for seven thousand years. Only one hundred million privileged laowon were allowed to reside there in the fabulously restored cities of the mythic past, Rashtria, Klummersk, Golg of Gold, Shubbui.

The seat of the Imperial Family was in Rashtria as it had been in the mythic era of the First Emperors and the beginnings of the space age.

In the fabled tower called Egon's Finger, a conference racked by anxiety was in progress.

Magnawl Ahx, Chief Executive Officer of the Superior Buro, placed a data module in the computer slot.

Watching him with uneasy eyes were the ruling group of the aristocracy. The Urall of Blue Seygfan, the Urall of Silver Seygfan, Grand Admiral Sneem, and both the Prime Minister of the Mathematica, Walwan Gao, and the High Minker of the Cult.

Viewing the proceedings with suspicious eyes were the opposition, the Morgooze of Red Seygfan, the Morgooze of Green Seygfan, and the Shgalon of the Cult.

The doors opened and the Heir Apparent entered.

Red and Green Seygfan exchanged glances. Both had heard of the discomfit of Blue Seygfan and the subsequent Imperial rage, and rage was clearly apparent on the Heir's features.

The Heir Apparent strode to the table, a space opened for him instantly.

Magnawl Ahx swallowed. "Your Highness, all the Elchites we captured on Earth have now been brainstripped. From three of them we extracted the same tale. They speak of a weapon, a hidden weapon that will be powerful enough to upset the natural order of sentient life and end the empire."

"What kind of weapon is this?"

"I have some projections here, your Highness. The truth is we do not know enough, but the Elchites were proved correct on the matter of the pirate battleship. The hidden weapon and the Testamenter ship were also linked together in the memories of these Elchites."

The Heir was young and fiery. His eyes blazed at Grand Admiral Sneem.

"The ship which the fleet allowed to escape!" he hissed.

"We will recapture them. They cannot evade our fleets for long." Sneem's anxiety was plain.

The Heir held up a receiver and ostentatiously placed it to his ear. "I have listened to my Imperial wavelength for thirty hours now and I have yet to hear anything from that miserable wretch Booeej. How you could have entrusted something as important as this to a blundering fool like that, I cannot imagine!"

"Your Highness—"

"Silence! Booeej will expiate as soon as he can be brought here. My fraternal blood brother, the Morgooze of Blue Seygfan, has requested both the hot pincers and the freezing skewers. They shall be applied."

Sneem sighed. There was no help for it. Booeej was doomed.

"Now." The Heir whirled upon Magnawl Ahx. "Show me your projections and tell me what you propose to do about finding these accursed Elchite terrorists!"

Jon didn't have time to do much more than reflect on how hard it was going to be to get out of his shackles when the fat man with the singsong accent returned, this time accompanied by a giant, a mutant of gross and unattractive feature that stood seven feet tall and was built like a bear.

The smaller man, Bompipi, had on a richly embroidered robe and carried a light shock rod, which he slapped smartly on Jon's cheek. The power was low, the shock mild.

"Awake, my friend, your life is about to take a great change of direction. There is no help for it, surrender to the process. I am Bompipi, the best slaver in Quism. I take good care of my property, so you may rest assured that your mutilations will take place in a properly equipped medical facility. They will even use anesthetics! So you see how well we treat you!"

Bompipi's fat face curled into a weirdly affable smile.

"Og Uk here will carry you to your fate like a baby, resting in his arms. Think of it as one last chance to use your eyes. Isn't that a thought to focus your attention! Concentrate on the colors and shapes, the shades and textures. Store away these impressions so you will have them to console you in your later years."

Jon looked around desperately. There was no escape. Bompipi read the horror in his face.

"Come," he exclaimed. "You have a comfortable enough future ahead of you. Selected for the bed chamber by a most wealthy lady! Indeed, blindess should prove a positively blessed aspect of the life ahead of you since the lady is very old, although still possessed of strong, ah, appetites."

He motioned to Og Uk, who picked Iehard up and cradled him in his arms like a child.

Through the crowded thoroughfare Og Uk strode with Bompipi the slaver behind. Around them hundreds of people went about their business without paying the slightest interest to his plight. The sight was common enough, some poor fool taken by the slavers.

Jon looked about in desperation. Was he to be blinded, silenced, and sold into a numbing slavery, while fellow human beings stood by and ignored this evil? He tried to shift his legs about, to disturb Og Uk in any way, but was unable to. Og Uk simply clamped him more firmly. The gag was tight in the back of his mouth, there was no way even to call for help. They entered a white-tiled hallway where bright mirrors mocked him with images of his own helplessness.

Og Uk held him down on a hospital couch while a pasty-faced youth in a white suit strapped him to it.

Then Og Uk left the room. Jon dimly heard a conversation in progress down the hallway.

A tray of probes, scalpels, and other tools was placed over his chest. Anesthesia equipment was pushed into place.

The attendant in white removed his gag and helped him rinse out his mouth with a little water.

"Thanks," said Jon at last.

"I hear you're to be blinded," the attendant said in a cheerful high-pitched voice.

"And have my tongue cut out."

"Bompipi must have a very particular customer in mind for you. Frequently we take off the parts as well." The youth moved in mincing little steps as he cleaned and polished the operating equipment.

Jon realized they'd taken off this youth's parts long ago.

"Look, you really ought not to go through with this."

The attendant gave him an amused look. "Well, everyone knows that, silly. Of course they ought not to. But"—he sighed—"they are going to go through with it. This is a cruel universe most of the time. Console yourself with the thought that they are spending good money on you. This is no gouge-and-chop butchery, you know. Doctor Dawl does good work. As to your new life, look at it this way: Whatever it is that you're going to, it'll be better than death."

Jon fought the desperation he felt. "You may be right, but listen to me anyway. I can take you to a great treasure."

"Oh, can you now?" The attendant gave him a sly smile. "And what might this treasure be? The lost radium template? A great sustainer? Twenty pops and snaps?" He flapped his hands in Jon's face.

"Huh! And how often do you think I've heard this line from some poor fellow about to lose his stones? You can't imagine the things I've been offered in this job."

"I mean it, I know where there's a mote!" Jon could feel the chords standing out in his neck.

The youth gurgled in mirth. "Now I know you're lying. The motes were all found centuries ago, all were sold offworld. Be quiet, be thankful you're to keep your stones!"

"One has returned."

"Oh, really!"

"Yes. Really."

Perhaps the certainty in his voice did it, but the attendant finally gave him a long, hard look. "If I tell her that you said this and it turns out you lie, it will go badly with me. She's extremely vindictive."

"Who is?"

"Doctor Dawl, of course, who is due to blind you in a few minutes."

"Tell her to put me under with Hypnogen. If I lie she can go ahead and take my eyes. If not she'll see that I don't lie."

The youth flapped his hands. "She will also see where this treasure of yours is located, so she will simply blind you for Bompipi and go and collect it herself. Believe me, she has little sympathy for her fellow human beings. She will make sure to collect what she can on you."

"She will never get close to the treasure without me. Go, tell her, but make sure Bompipi is gone first."

Another long look followed.

"You are from offworld, aren't you? And you sound like you arrived pretty recently." He sighed. "Well, maybe you do know something."

The attendant left the room. He returned shortly in the wake of a woman with dark hair pulled back under a medical cap. She had a thin, bloodless face, large protruding eyes, and plump, well-fed lips. Jon could easily imagine her sucking the blood from her victims.

She examined Jon carefully. "Why are you lying?"

"I'm not, use the Hypnogen. Find out for yourself."

"Hypnogen, eh? I suppose even that might seem preferable to blindness and the loss of one's tongue. You are going into a new world, my friend." She chuckled. "Bompipi told me of your amusing future. Perhaps you should be thankful both for the loss of your eyes and your tongue. Eh?" She gurgled maliciously.

"No one can lie under the effects of Hypnogen, you know that."

"It might kill you, though, and then what would I be? Several thousand credits out with Bompipi, who gives me so much work. No, why should I take that risk on some harebrained dream?"

"Should you succeed in possessing the mote, Rhapsodical Stardimple, you would become one of the wealthiest persons in the Galaxy. You could have a whole world in exchange."

Doctor Dawl's eyes were like telescopes zeroing in on that extravagant possibility.

"Just a moment," she said, and turned to consult a computer console on a cabinet by the door. A moment later: "That is not a known mote, but the computer says it is a predicted mote. One of a group thought to inhabit the Equatorial Machine Belt. You might have easily invented this."

She studied him briefly, made a quick decision. "Most men in your position come up with absurd offers, quite understandable, of course. Well, you look healthy enough; you can probably stand a dose of Hypnogen. And if you speak the truth, there will be wealth indeed. And if not then nobody will miss the extra hour."

She turned to the attendant and snapped, "Prepare me a syringe of Hypnogen!"

They brought him round about an hour later. He was still suffering the side effects of the Hypnogen. Everything blanked occasionally to gray. Sound became mud, he could barely understand human speech. Walking was not going to be easy either. Waves of nausea passed through him without warning, mucus streamed from his mouth and nose.

But he could see! His eyes were still whole. Gratefully he felt them and had another shock. His hands and feet were free! He had barely reacted to that thought when he discovered something strapped to his ankle. He reached down and discovered a stout leather strap with something round embedded in the leather opposite a locked clasp.

Doctor Dawl spoke from behind him. "A charge of explosive is attached to your foot. On a strap on my wrist, I carry the transmitter to the detonator. Should you attempt to escape you will lose your foot. I do not believe your new owner will be overly concerned about whether you still have both feet."

The attendant called from the door. "Bompipi is on the line. He wants to know what the holdup is."

"Tell him I had another case, a priority—emergency surgery, anything—and that he will get his slave back soon enough."

She turned to Iehard and injected a stimulant to override the effects of the Hypnogen.

"Dress in these clothes." She handed him some robes. When he had complied she said, "Come, lead me to the hotel. I want to see this mote at closer hand."

He watched her put an automatic handgun and a refrigerated specimen jar into a small bag that she slung over her shoulder. They rode in a rickshaw down the Grand Levee and climbed out on the forecourt of the Hotel Travel Aires.

The hotel was as before. Guards marched about noisily, guests moved timidly between them. At the desk Jon asked for the keycard to his room. Doctor Dawl was to wait there while he tried to decoy the mote into her trap. She carried a special stunner, charged to paralyze motes, and the refrigerated specimen jar would serve to keep the captive mote dormant at low temperature.

But to his consternation Jon learned that the expedition had checked out and that the Superior Buro had visited the hotel within the hour. Everyone was still abuzz from the spectacle of laowon operatives abroad in the dangerous human quarters of the city.

Doctor Dawl cursed disgustedly behind him. "Enough," she snapped. "We will return to surgery. Come." She gestured imperiously to the door. Jon looked around wildly, then punched the doctor in the face with every ounce he could put into it. She fell head over heels into a big potted cactus and he ran on into the hotel down some stairs and into a maintenance corridor as guard boots pounded in pursuit.

He blundered into a kitchen filled with young people in white smocks and hats. They gazed at him in wonder for a moment. He ran through and on down another corridor. He tried another door, found another corridor. Guard whistles spread the alarm somewhere behind him.

He needed a knife, a file, something sharp. There had to be a workshop or tool room beneath the hotel.

There were sudden loud voices coming from ahead.

He opened a door at random and ducked into a dark storeroom.

The voices went past and dwindled. He was about to open the door again when a tiny voice went off about a foot from his ear and he jumped and whirled around.

"Yes! We must hide, Emergency! Hide together!" It was the mote, Rhapsodical Stardimple.

"Hello, Rhapsodical Stardimple. What's happened?"

"Greetings, Mr. Iehard. Finn M'Nee said you were a traitor."

"Finn M'Nee arranged for my disappearance. It's no wonder he called me traitor. But come, what are you doing here? Where is the Bey?"

"I do not know! Emergency, an acute lack of energy. I had to recharge on a heat duct and when I returned to the rooms they were empty. I waited but then others came. Laowon. Superior Buro, I think. Yes! I hide. You hide. We hide."

Jon couldn't suppress a smile at this motish interlingua. "That's right, Rhap, we hide.

"But I've got to find something with which to cut this strap off my ankle." Iehard opened the door a crack. "It carries an explosive charge which will be detonated by the slavers."

He tried other doors, finally found a butchery. Knives, some of them exceedingly sharp, hung in racks. He selected a boning blade, thin and extremely sharp, that he could force under the strap and turn.

The little knife was horribly sharp, the blood began to run almost immediately. He continued sawing. The strap was damnably tough, and he was sweating in streams. In his mind's eye the guards were using a stimulant aerosol to bring Doctor Dawl around. Her first action would be to reach for the stud on her wrist.

Blood was flowing copiously by the time he finally sawed through the thing and hurled it away the length of the room.

Then he sat down and tried to staunch the bleeding.

Rhap Dimple appeared. "If require medical supplies, look in other room where I hide. I floated beside containers of supplies. You are spilling necessary functional fluids."

Jon followed the mote into the corridor, looking cautiously up and down for guards. Just as he closed the butchery door there was a sharp detonation and objects struck the inside of the door with considerable force. He imagined Doctor Dawl's vindictive features as she triumphantly stabbed the button.

Jon was still trembling a little as he applied the bandage and sprayed antiseptic on the cuts.

When he finished he turned to the mote. "I think we must go on the offensive at once. Certainly we don't want to stay here any longer. Presumably the slavers will continue to hunt me. Even worse, the Superior Buro is awake and that is very dangerous."

"What do you suggest?"

"First I would like to repossess my gun and, perhaps, to settle a score. Once I can find some different clothes."

"Yes! I am ready!" The mote sounded ready indeed. But Jon knew that he couldn't let Rhap Dimple fly in the open in Quism without garnering extremely unwanted attentions.

The mote hovering at his shoulder, he searched the basement rooms, until he found one packed with hotel uniforms including ceremonial capes in plastic sacks hanging on long rails. He found pairs of black boots on a rack. After trying several pairs he finally found some that went over the bandage and still fit reasonably well. He clothed himself in trousers of twill and matching shirt and ceremonial cape. Then he grabbed the mote in one hand—the mote was warm to the touch, smooth and hard in his palm—slipped it under the cape, and quietly walked up a back passage to the ground floor. People were yelling in loud voices somewhere at the front of the hotel. All the windows were barred and the doors were locked. He continued on down the hotel's corridors until he found a group of elevators.

Jon waited, anxiously looking up and down the corridor. If the guards saw him from a distance they might take him for one of their own. But if they came close they must penetrate his slim disguise.

An elevator opened. A leathery-skinned, mutant Japanese pushed out a pair of laundry hampers. Jon slipped aboard and descended to a subbasement marked DELIVERY. He came out into a wide space filled with drays and delivery carts. Gang bosses and laborers were busy moving goods onto freight elevators. The guards in a booth farther down the wall noted his uniform and looked past him. He headed up the exit ramp and out onto an alley that fed into the Grand Levee.

He stopped a couple of native Quiz to ask directions and soon found the slavers' alley, near the junction of Razevkoy Prospect and the Grand Levee.

Bompipi's establishment lay behind a front of marble bas reliefs depicting lurid sexual acts. The door was of imitation wood and brass. The narrow windows were of thick purplish glass. As he pushed it open and entered the shopfront, a bell rang in the backroom. Jon released the mote, which flew up close to the ceiling and hovered.

Then with a jaunty smile he greeted Bompipi. At the sight of him Bompipi's eyes almost popped out of his head.

"What! Well, well, well, how wonderful. Your foot was undamaged after all. I knew that woman was lying; she'll get no more business from Bompipi, that's for sure. So, you're back, excellent. Madam Proopune will be so relieved. I'll just call Og Uk to carry you in."

"I wouldn't trouble yourself," Jon said.

"It's no trouble, no trouble at all. Be calm, compose yourself, Og Uk will be with us in a moment." Bompipi pressed the alarm bell.

Heavy feet stamped up stairs and the huge form of Og Uk thrust through the doorway.

"Seize him!" Bompipi said.

Jon backed away. Og Uk came on, a silly grin on his huge, bland face.

"You're making a mistake," Jon said.

Bompipi chuckled indulgently. "Am I? Making a mistake? What do you know about mistakes? She gave you Hypnogen, she said. It seems to have addled your brains. I'll give her Hypnogen! Hah ha, that will be some fun. She's played Bompipi for the fool once too often."

And then the mote hurtled down on Og Uk's head, striking such a heavy blow that the giant sank, stunned, to its knees. Jon coolly kicked Og Uk in the throat with as much force as he could muster and then advanced on Bompipi.

The slaver's eyes were stretched wide as he stared at

the glossy green mote hovering in the room. "Great Sand-gods of the Mighty, it is a—" Iehard leveled him.

A quick search of Bompipi's premises revealed the longbarreled Taw Taw and a lot else besides. Bompipi had mounds of human clothes and possessions stacked in his storerooms. Jon found his space jacket and he also pocketed a beautiful hunting knife with a monofilament edge so sharp it cut easily through wooden doors, even pieces of metal. The blade retracted within the handle at the press of a button.

With the knife he cut into a strongbox that disgorged wads of Laowon Mercantile notes. Jon pocketed them and, after tying up Bompipi and Og Uk with their own cuffs, he set off for the caravan garages that surrounded the Meridian Gate. It was time to get out of Quism.

■ CHAPTER TWENTY

AFTER STOPPING AT AN EXPEDITIONEER'S OUTFITTING yard, Jon moved on down the Grand Levee toward the Meridian Gate. He now wore stout desert boots and a suit of wind-resistant polyfiber. His headgear was a tight-fitting windcap with sun- and wind-goggles and blast flaps.

In addition to the Taw Taw longbarrel that he'd recovered at Bompipi's, he wore a Bahnkouv .330 assault rifle on his shoulder. For it he carried four clips of explosive shell and eight of antipersonnel soft jackets. On the back of his belt he had two satchel charges, two antipersonnel grenades, and his binoculars. On his wrist he wore a sophisticated computer radar/radio that strapped on next to the chrononavigator.

With the mote hidden inside his desert-rate topcoat and the monofil knife in his boot, Jon felt like a walking armory as he moved through the crowds and dust.

Hydrogen-powered IC engines roared steadily from the garages clustered along the last stretch of the levee. As he got closer, the smell of the night air outside the city, cold and laced with oil fumes, filled his nostrils. A hive of activity surrounded the gate portal.

Expeditions were gathered on the forecourts of commercial garages. Groups of vehicles were loaded, then moved down the levee on their rubber skirts, engines whistling, and out through the relatively narrow portal about four hundred meters away. Above the portal the roof rock of Quism was blackened back to the lightbars. Metal inspection walks climbed the walls.

On the first walk, three meters above the roadbed, Jon noticed a tall figure in a laowon-cut military uniform. Instinctively he ducked aside into the shadows cast by advertising panels surrounding the forecourt of the Desert Beater garage. A pair of squat four-seater mantids were being loaded on the concrete apron. A dozen figures in buff-color desert wear were gathered about another, much larger craft with heavily ablated front windows and nose cone.

Iehard checked the portal through his binoculars. A tall blue figure in Superior Buro uniform was filming the departing caravans. Jon made out a pair of human-sized figures standing behind, guarding him in the shadows.

Clearly Superior Buro were in action, but with only their local forces. Jon however could easily imagine the frantic activity in the sector fleet if the local Buro had indeed picked up a trace of Eblis Bey. He had to move fast before reinforcements appeared.

However, the laowon's equipment would most certainly be primed with his likeness. He doubted he could pass by the camera without its alerting the Superior Buro.

Jon replaced the binoculars and considered the antipersonnel grenades.

A few minutes later a figure in desert khaki slid along the rock wall beneath the catwalk on which stood the laowon. Suddenly something small and dark was lobbed onto the walk. The man in desert garb ran back into the shadows.

A deafening crack resounded in the portal space, and where the laowon and his camera had been, there bloomed a white-and-pink fog of vapor and hot smoke. Pieces of the three figures rained down inside the portal for several seconds.

Jon secreted himself in the shadows of a side alley between two garages. A few moments of near silence pervaded the levee. The explosion had been shockingly loud and unexpected. All had noticed the laowon officer and discussed his presence and unusual activities. Now they stared.

After a full half minute a few crept cautiously forward to examine the remains. They poked about, but in truth there was little to be found in the mess. They returned to the garages. A babble of conversation followed that lasted less than a minute before engines roared and expeditions headed out the gate, in their haste to get away before the inquiries began they passed directly over the bloody fragments.

Reassured that the ancient manners of Quism had prevailed once more, Jon entered the forecourt of the Chequered Mutant garage and quickly arranged to hire a stout four-seat mantid and driver, a grim, taciturn fellow named Braunt. After a brief bout of haggling, Jon paid with Bompipi's cash, torn between his desire to conserve the cash and the powerful urge to get out of Quism before the Buro arrived in force.

A few minutes later Braunt eased the mantid off the forecourt and, with lights blazing, they whistled out through the portal, heading south directly for Fort Pinshon, which sat astride the junction of the two major treasure trails, the North Coastal and the old Oolite. There Jon hoped to catch up with Eblis Bey. If he missed the Bey there, Jon knew only to do what Rhap Dimple knew, which was to head south into the equatorial dust belts. Of course Braunt would not go farther than Fort Pinshon, but Jon could hire another driver there, one of the deeper desert specialists. However, when he asked Braunt if such drivers would be willing to go as far as the equator, the gaunt man gave him a startled look.

"Nobody goes that far, there's nothing down there but the worst mutants and dust."

"Where does the Oolite trail go then?"

"All the way down to the Tropical Boneyards, at the southern tip of Bolgol's Continent. But that's all north of the worst dust. Only idiots and archeologists go down off the continental shelf. You look it up on the computer, it'll show you. The chances of dying out there go up dramatically once you move off the trails either inland or down onto the seabeds."

"Why should that be?"

"Both ways you get into dust, and mutants. Plus on the seabed there's always groundquakes. Even the Oolite trail has been shifted twice these last ten years because quakes keep chopping bits off the Boneyard Headland."

Jon examined all the locations on the maps projected by the computer. It was more important than ever to get to Fort Pinshun in time to catch up with the Bey and the Orners.

Outside the portal it was full polar night. The skies blazed with stars. Red taillights trailed south toward the distant Meridian Gap. Dozens of expeditions, large and small, roved ahead of them leaving clouds of thin white dust behind them that blew away slowly into the dark bean fields.

The seats in the mantid were comfortable, if a little worn. The front windshield was split by a central divider. The passenger's side was cracked and pitted with the unmistakable trace of a bullet impact.

He concentrated on the map. Most expeditions headed south for Meridian Gap, a deep cleft in the mountain barrier lying between Quism and the rest of the Bolgol Continent. On the far side, the major trail doglegged back to the west and on down to the ancient coastlines where the city sites and Boneyards were. There, on a promontory overlooking the edge of the continental shelf, was Fort Pinshun.

"What if we avoided Meridian Gap?" said Jon.

"Sheer madness. On the other side of the West Mountains is the range of the Hardgrains Bluescabbies. They are led these days by Blood Head, a terrible warrior indeed. Only the most heavily armed caravans dare the direct western route to Fort Pinshon. Which is why Bengo's has done such a good business over the last few years."

"But it would be much quicker to go over the West Mountains, wouldn't it?"

"The trails are steep, it's bad on the engines. You know, the High West Pass is two thousand meters high. Gets damn cold up there too."

But Jon was sure the laowon would be watching the caravans coming into the Meridian Gap. "Nevertheless, I wish to go that way."

"Did you not listen? Are your ears defective? On the far side is Blood Head. Why do you wish to end your days in the Bluescabby meat herds?"

"We will defend ourselves. Perhaps if we drive quickly enough they won't even catch up with us."

Braunt began easing off the accelerator; the mantid slowed.

"What are you doing?" Jon said.

"I'm stopping to let you get out. If you want to go over the High West Pass I suggest you get yourself another car and driver."

Jon brought the Taw Taw longbarrel out and aimed it at Braunt's head. "If you don't get your foot back on that accelerator and keep it there I'll simply leave your body here at the roadside and drive there myself. I'm sure I could master the details as I went along."

Braunt paled. Jon gestured to the road ahead. The mantid surged forward again, Braunt angrily hunched over the steering wheel. A few colored lights appeared in the distance and slowly grew into a cluster of illuminated signs erected above a buried waystation called Last Water & Hydro.

Jon insisted that Braunt turn right and head southwest toward the mountains on a trail that was visibly underused. As Braunt drove, Jon ostentatiously took notes. Soon he felt reasonably confident of being able to keep the hovercraft in forward motion. There didn't seem to be much to it in fact since the controls were largely computerized.

They had left the bean fields behind. Oddly shaped trees and other mutant terrestrial plants grew in dark clumps beside the road. After an hour they had seen only three other vehicles, all coming from the opposite direction.

Very occasionally they would see a speck of light from some distant farm or mutant's shack. It was inherently peaceful. Jon allowed himself to relax a trifle, with the gun still ready should Braunt get any ideas. The tension of the last few hours began to fade. He realized he was really exhausted.

On reflection he decided that Quism was not a city he would in any way miss. He hoped Doctor Dawl was forced to undergo prolonged restorative dental surgery and that she would find Bompipi sharing the same hospital ward.

The dark prairies gave way to rocks, clumped with mutant forests.

"We approach the mountains. Now is the time to reconsider. Let us turn back. I could take a side road and rejoin the Meridian Highway in less than three hours. Don't sacrifice our lives for nothing."

"Drive on," Jon muttered.

Braunt, with increasingly gloomy looks to either side, began to take the hovercraft up a long sloping path, scarcely fit to be called a road so cut up with gulleys and loose stones was it. Eventually, as they curved around the side of a small mountain, Jon saw the first glimmers of dawn-light in the east. The long polar night of Baraf was ending.

"We'll be going across the foreland in daylight. The mutants won't bother with us. One vehicle, two bodies, and their supplies, it would hardly be worth it. They prefer to stay below ground in the daylight. Which is a sensible thing to do, I believe."

"And you don't have the brains of a mutant!" Braunt snapped.

"Exactly so," Jon agreed.

Braunt made no reply. They wound on higher into the bare flanks of the mountains, which were heavily scored by erosion. The light got progressively brighter. Jon could see the western ridge of peaks quite clearly. They were covered in frost and a dusting of snow. He looked eastward with his binoculars but could only identify the nearer of the mountains overlooking the Meridian Gap.

As they climbed farther the hovercraft engines protested.

"Of course, if we break down on the Hardscabbies' range then nothing we do will save us from joining the meat herds."

"Don't worry, Braunt, I'll save a bullet for each of us."

Braunt stared at him for a long moment then turned back to the track.

Slowly now they wound up the last, highest stretch and came into the Western High Pass. The light was getting strong, as bright as normal daylight on Hyperion Grandee.

Passing around a curve they were greeted by a vast vista of the plains of Bolgol, which ended in a dimness, a cloudiness that stretched from one end to the other of the horizon.

"What is that?" Jon asked, gesturing to the cloud.

"Any fool knows that's the Northern Dust Belt. Looks pretty quiet to me from here. I've seen it when storms twenty kilometers high come rolling right up to and even through the Meridian Gap. Winds can top two hundred kilometers an hour. Not as fierce as the equatorial belts, of course, but very hard to keep a hovercraft moving forward in."

Jon looked again at the distant line of haze. "Then our luck is definitely in today! Forward!"

They moved to the end of the pass and descended toward the arid plains below.

Jon wondered how anything, mutant or not, could survive on that terrain; it seemed absolutely barren.

The hovercraft swooped around the curves now, the computer fighting the craft's tendency to go out of control by angling the fans and tilting the bow up to get a braking action from the hoverflow.

Jon looked down into the grim gulleys. Jagged boulders filled the stream beds on their flanks. If they went over the edge he doubted that either of them would survive the impact below.

They came around a large rock that had been sundered in two by whoever had built the road.

On the top of the stone stood a tall figure wrapped in brown cloth. A heavy rifle boomed, the bullet smashed the already cracked window plate of the mantid. Glass flew inward.

Braunt gave a cry, almost lost control. Another bullet whined off the mantid's roof. Jon fired back through the window, holding the Taw Taw in both hands. The bullets whined off the rocks but succeeded in driving the marksman into cover.

Then they were past him and turning into another corner. A bullet smacked against the rear window, but the glass held, merely cracking radially around a small impact pit.

Another ricocheted off the boulders to their right and then they were out of the line of fire, sweeping down a long, gentle incline.

"We're dead if we get caught in a dust storm now," Braunt said with an angry gesture at the smashed window.

Jon examined the map carefully. Several hours' driving lay ahead of them, across the foreland to Fort Pinshon. The sun was rising fast, and the dust would soon begin to kick up off the ancient seabeds as the first storm of the day began. He thought they would be lucky to make Fort Pinshon.

It was already painful to look out at the desert. Jon pulled down the polarizing goggles, noted that Braunt had done the same. Made a mental note to watch the driver.

CHAPTER TWENTY-ONE

DESPITE THE FACT THAT THE LIGHT QUICKLY BUILT UP to a fantastic brightness, the desert remained surprisingly cool for the first hour or so. Braunt and Jon were both forced to slip the big glare goggles down over their polarizers so they looked like huge insects rather than men. But to look outside with naked eyes now was to risk eye damage, possibly blindness. For a certainty, one would not see much in the tremendous glare generated by Pleione, now a blazing white fury well above the horizon.

The heat began late in the second hour. They were making good time traveling over endless dust flats. In the far distance heat devils were whirling the gritty dust into the air. Jon began to feel it, a breath of dry warmth from an inferno. A mind-sapping heat that flowed in through the broken front window like some alien force, permeating everything with its terrible power. Soon they were sweating heavily. Jon tried to shrug it off.

"If we continue like this, I calculate we'll reach the fort in another four hours."

Braunt gave him a withering look. "If the mutants haven't taken us under the ground. Besides, it hardly matters, we're soaking up radiation now. You weren't under any illusions about the roof of this vehicle were you? If so I must inform that it is not radiation proof."

"An uncomfortable thought I agree, but I have no

choice. We serve a higher purpose than our mere personal wishes in the matter."

"Oh, do we now? And what the hell might that be other than the pockets of the tumor surgeons?"

Jon realized he couldn't tell the man, or trust him not to reveal what he might hear to others, including the Superior Buro.

"I'm afraid I'm not at liberty to tell you."

"Oh, wonderful. How did I get this crazy in my cab anyway? What did I do?"

"Save it, you'll understand soon enough. I just can't tell you now."

"Isn't that what religious fanatics always say?"

Jon shrugged, stared out at the sunbaked dust.

"Will you at least tell me what cult you represent? If I'm being sacrificed, it seems only fair that I know for which madness it is."

Jon realized that he, himself, barely knew what the tenets of Elchitism were beyond a veneration of things human and terrestrial, including the plan to regreen the Earth.

"I don't belong to any cult and this is not a cult affair." But as he said it, he felt a sudden loss of confidence in the whole enterprise. What if he had come all the way for nothing? If, for instance, Eblis Bey was wrong, was just some charming madman from Earth? Jon decided that the existence of the mote, which remained dormant, conserving energy next to his chest, was proof against his fear. The Bey spoke the truth; somewhere down there on the equator in the great dust belt lay their hope, the Hammer of Stars. They had to get to it before the laowon found it.

In the distance he saw a dark mass, and beyond it another. Soon he had made out several of the squat shapes many kilometers away to the south. They looked almost like office buildings or giant abstract sculptures.

Braunt gestured toward them. "The first big machines. We're on the fringe of the North Polar Machine Belt. Means we're on the lower foreland right in the Hardscabby country now, and naturally we've been under observation for the last hundred kilometers or so."

Jon peered around uneasily but kept one eye always on Braunt and the Taw Taw at the ready. Braunt sensed Jon's readiness. He stifled his own plans for revenge on the mad offworlder, concentrated instead on the dust flats ahead of him. It was much too late even to consider going back.

Jon continued to doubt that the mutants would be interested; the single mantid was too small a target.

They whistled east and south, across the dust.

Ahead of them an astonishing glow had begun. Bright beams began to shine into the cab of the hovercraft, some so bright they produced rainbows on Jon's goggles.

"What the hell is that?"

"Glass dunes, a feature of the north machine belt. Crystals that reproduce themselves when they receive sufficient solar energy. Some claim the crystals are the final evolutionary product of the ancient ones who built the machines."

"An interesting theory."

"As relevant as any of them—the truth is we have no idea what any of these remains are. Anyway, the dunes are pleochroic, they throw brilliant colors, different on each axis, constantly changing, flickering. They say it drives men mad in no time."

Beams green, orange, pink, blue, magenta, all flashed over them for a moment before falling behind. They were maddening, thrilling, stroboscopic. Jon had never experienced such intense sense of color. Braunt advised against looking out the broken passenger window too long.

Jon turned his head and glanced northward. He let out a gasp. Braunt whipped around. A black vehicle on huge balloon tires had suddenly caught up with them. At the windows loomed menacing shapes. A pennon fluttered from a long antenna above the cab, its device a scarlet skull on a black background.

"It is Blood Head! As I feared. They will run us down for meat."

"Accelerate!" Jon yelled. "How do I open this rear window?"

In response Braunt merely cursed. "Insanity, from the very beginning. I hope you are fattened for some special feast so that I can see your despair grow with the days. They always bake feast meat alive."

Jon fumbled the window bolt; finally it dropped open. Brilliant light flooded in but the Taw Taw longbarrel came up and Jon squeezed off a clip of explosive bullets that pocked the black cab's windscreens and tore big holes in the tires, without noticeably slowing it down.

He reached behind for a satchel charge and primed it, waited, and then tossed it into the path of the black cab.

The explosion fountained dust into the air. The cab rolled straight through it, but then it slowed, turned aside, and came to a shuddering halt.

Jon turned back to Braunt, who continued to drive at top speed into the pleochroic dunes.

"They've given up."

"Because we're going into their ambush. Look!"

Jon looked forward. Another black-cabbed machine on big wheels had rolled down the shining face of a giant dune to block their path. Light caromed madly in twinkling, dazzling arrays all around them. Jon pulled out the assault rifle and sprayed a burst of fire into the black cab. Explosive bullets made a halo of smoke and dust around it, while Braunt took evasive action, swinging the hovercraft up the side of a dune and passing behind the balloon tires.

Bullets whined off the hovercraft as Jon hurriedly fired back before closing the rear window.

They raced on through the gulleys between the dunes of glass, heading south and east whenever possible, eyes open for further black cabs.

After a while they realized that the pursuit had ended. Braunt climbed a long slope to the top of a dune and looked back. In the distance, through a riot of sparkling color like some desert composed of gemstones, they could see a pair of black dots, grouped together on a green glass dune.

"Onward to Fort Pinshon," Jon said with a grin.

Braunt stared at him for a moment, then returned to the controls.

The mantid continued to whistle down the dunes, through cascades of light so brightly colored that it penetrated even the heavy goggles and polarizers and produced rings and whorls of color in their vision.

Above them the sky had gone white as Pleione crept slowly toward the zenith.

The sweat ran freely inside their suits, and Jon felt his feet squelching in his desert boots. He rummaged about for a waterbottle. The wind coming in the window carried more and more grit. It was hot air, perhaps 110 degrees Fahrenheit. It was hard to breathe.

Occasionally they passed the ruins of enormous machines. Only the parts made of eternite materials still stood, like the inexplicable shells of gargantuan molluscs. They formed spires, boxes, complex walls, folded columns, many were half buried in the drifting pleochroic crystal. Others reached two hundred meters into the air.

Gazing at the strange shapes, sometimes upright, sometimes piled loosely together, where the disintegration of less resistant materials had dumped them, Jon recalled Eblis Bey's saying that the ancients had grown their technological artifacts. Their strange organic quality was totally unlike the large-scale constructions of human and laowon.

Up ahead he spotted a wall of green eternite that had been cast in a spiral curve. On top of it fluttered a blue banner. A crude concrete box had been cemented to the top of the eternite wall.

"Fort Pinshon up ahead," announced Braunt.

"We made it, Braunt, we're going to make it."

Braunt grinned dourly and shook his head. "Damnedest, craziest thing I ever did."

Behind the green wall they found what appeared to be a heap of enormous plates, piled on each other in loose chaos. Each was fifty meters or more across.

Within and underneath this pile was Fort Pinshon. In front were several crude structures in concrete, with sandbag walls and embankments arrayed in a semicircle around them. The mantid growled down to the main gate and after a swift perusal by guards crouched behind a 20-mm cannon with nine rotating barrels, they were allowed into the outer compound.

Jon pulled out some laowon Mercantile notes. He gave them to Braunt, who pocketed them eagerly and then watched stonefaced as Jon climbed out of the mantid. There were no farewells.

Fort Pinshon was an exotic outpost of civilization, built where a unique coincidence of a spring and the sheltering pile of giant plates made possible a sizable human habitation.

Crops were grown on irrigated patches of dust in the rear. In the upper parts of the pile dwelled a tribe of settled mutants, many of them of the dwarf Japanese type so prevalent as slaves in the city of Quism.

On the ground floor were several large spaces, almost rooms, with an oval configuration, that served as combination hotel lobby, dining room, marketplace, and campsite. He passed several groups of desert nomads wearing white or gray robes, sitting around horribly smoky campfires in front of their black tents.

At one end, next to a crescent-shaped opening, a long counter had been erected. It was of marble, pockmarked here and there by bullets. Over it a tangle of barbed wire was supported on steel struts. At one end a machine-gun emplacement kept a pair of barrels directed out at the rest of the room. A big sign in several languages warned against the open use of guns.

Jon found that by paying over more laowon notes he could rent a space inside the security zone of the fort, but he had to check his weapons first and the checkers were thorough, removing even the monofil blade from his boot.

He went on through the crescent-shaped passage formed by the accidental resting together of two massive plates. Inside he found rooms that might easily have been in a hotel lobby on another world, or even Hyperion Grandee. Elegantly decorated with rugs and wall hangings, they were lit by fiber optics to a pleasant dimness.

First he found his space, a coffin-shaped cubicle large enough for a bed and a sleeper. He visited a communal shower and hosed off the sweat and grime of the journey. Then he returned to the main rooms and found a bar.

Slaking his thirst with a cold beer and marveling at finding such a luxury in that harsh environment, he listened to the conversation around him.

Several trail guides, identifiable by name badges on their desert shirts, were discussing some incident at the bar.

"It just goes to show that you simply cannot expect deep-desert mutants to deal honestly. They don't understand the logic of a repeat customer. All they want is your money and then they want your flesh," said one with a round badge of scarlet and gold that proclaimed "Umpuk's Trailways, the best for ten years."

"Look, Angle," said another in a black suit with "Bayu Nashe" stenciled on his back in white, "there are some deep-desert mutes you can use. You just have to be careful. It's the same with everything in the deep—you have to use the mutes, you have to talk to them if you want to know what happens down there. Nobody else goes there, you understand. Nobody else knows."

"Bah, they're totally untrustworthy and they'd soon as kill you for the larder as look at you," Angle Umpuk replied.

"Well, this group was unusually foolish if you ask me. It was plain to see. Imagine hiring Hardscabbies!" a third man said.

"With women, including attractive ones in the group. Incredible!" agreed Umpuk.

"They deserved what happened. Such foolishness had to be punished most intensely. It is the law of the desert."

Jon felt a tremor at these words. Officers Bergen, Dahn, and Rena Kolod had been with the Orner group. Were they the women under discussion?

He was about to investigate when a movement caught his eye. A tall figure in red was coming through the tables at the far end of the bar. A laowon, bodyguards behind him, striding unconcerned through the treasure hunters, looters, slavers, and guides at the tables around him.

Jon looked for marks of nobility on the lao's tunic and found none. A rogue then, an adventurer, some lordling who had been thrust out of his family. Or possibly an upstart, some laowon commoner or criminal, with the mass of wealth required to travel the far spacelanes.

The laowon had leather accoutrements, shiny from use, including a holster at his hip. Jon looked after the retreating back and then slipped across to the bar.

The guide named Angle Umpuk met his gaze.

"You're wondering what a blue lord of the universe is doing out here in this forsaken waste?"

"Precisely."

"That's Romsini. He's lived out in the forelands for thirty years, they say. Big treasure hunter—found forty pops and snaps in one cache." Umpuk extended a hand, they shook.

"I'm Angle Umpuk, treasure guide for the North Shore and the lesser Boneyards."

"Glad to make your acquaintance, Mr. Umpuk. I

couldn't help overhearing your conversation about a group, with women, that was in trouble."

"Trouble? I'll say. They came through late last night. Let some mutants talk them into hiring them as trail guides for a trip off the continent, down the Oolite trail somewhere. It sounded like archeological foolishness to me. They wanted to reach the equatorial machines."

The man named Bayu Nashe turned around at those words. He had black hair slicked back along the sides of his head and a small earring in either lobe. "Don't tell me you've got another suicide case there, Angle. Or is he just an archeologist?"

"Suicide?" Jon said.

"Going down the Oolite is bad enough right now because of the groundquakes, but the only remaining fort down there is Harib Zar's at the Guillotine Stone. The Hardscabbies have been cleaning out all the littler places. Last week they busted in the Krib and added another twenty to their meat herds."

Jon's bafflement must have shown.

"It means there's nowhere to seek safety if the mutants try and run you down," Angle said.

"Besides all that," Bayu Nashe continued, "once you get off the continent and down on the ocean floor you're getting into the equatorial dust, and then there's the crustal pits. Walls go straight down for four kilometers. There's thousands of them, scattered throughout the equatorial dust."

Angle Umpuk intervened. "Very few people choose to go that far. Life on the Oolite and the North Shore is dangerous enough, especially now that the Hardscabbies are taking anyone they can find."

"What happend to the group of people?"

Umpuk grimaced. "Poor fools wouldn't listen or wait. I wasn't going to take them down the Oolite, not until sunset anyway. If you put on speed, you can reach the Boneyards in one night that way. And you can shelter down there pretty safely in the day. But as I said they wouldn't wait, took off like they had the Superior Buro after them." Umpuk chuckled at the absurdity of such an idea.

"Of course as soon as they were ten kloms south the Hardscabbies took them, or rather they took half of them.

It seems some of them were a bit quicker on the uptake and had taken steps to watch for treachery. They escaped, but most of them, including the females, went down some Hardscabby hole in the wastes. I imagine they'll go for feast meat."

"What happened to the others?"

"They came back here, regrouped, and then set off again. They claimed they were going to rescue their fellows. But they left one behind. You'll find him out on the courtyard. He was just standing there looking stupid so some mutant grabbed him and dragged him into a tent. I should think he'll end up back in the larder."

"How long ago did all this happen?"

"Well, let's see, I think the survivors got back here about dawn. I guess they stayed just long enough to refuel and buy ammunition. Their mantids looked pretty shot up—it must've been a battle down there."

"How many were there?"

"Four of them, one old fellow with long gray hair and three strange young ones. Cultists of some kind, I'd say."

So the Bey had survived with some of the younger Elchites.

Jon thanked Umpuk and headed back to the outer cavern where the mutants were camped. Jon retrieved his Taw Taw and knife and kept a wary eye on the heavy figures slouched outside the tents and balloon-tire trucks.

After a few minutes' search he found Hawkstone, leashed to a peg in the ground with his wrists bound behind his back.

"Captain Hawkstone, we meet again," said Jon, squatting down beside him.

Hawkstone stared at him dully. The events of the past twenty-four hours had been too much for him. His tongue lolled in his open mouth. Jon feared the captain had been reduced to idiocy. "Captain, we've got to get you free now. Do you think you'll be able to walk away beside me if I cut you free?"

The captain's adam's apple wobbled. He gasped. "Yes. What are you doing here you, traitor? Did you come back to finish us off?"

"I'm no traitor. M'Nee arranged for my disappearance.

I'll explain more fully later since I see your present employer has put in an appearance."

From within the tent appeared a heavyset mutant. His skin was knobbled and warted and a deep brown. His head was shaved and yellow tusks curled from his mouth. He was a head taller than Jon and considerably wider. His genital pouch had been made from a human skull and he wore little else but shaggy desert boots. In one hand he held a heavy whip made from braided human leather. "What do you do talking to my meat?"

"Who are you?" said Jon, rising to his feet.

"I am Gnush Two Tusks. That is my meat. You will be my meat too unless you go away."

"How much money do you want to free this man?"

"Money? Laowon notes?" the mutant said with a leer. Jon nodded.

"One fifty." Gnush lurched a step closer. "Do you have money on your person now?"

"One fifty is too much, take seventy."

"Seventy! This is fine meat, we will eat for a week on it."

"Seventy is my best offer."

"Mr. Iehard, surely you're not going to let financial considerations enter into this?" Hawkstone said plaintively.

"Seventy, Gnush. That's my offer. It can only go down."

Gnush came closer. On his hip a knife handle projected from a scabbard carved into his own tough hide.

"Why shouldn't I simply take you as meat too? And your money?"

"Because I'll kill you, that's why." Jon's Taw Taw longbarrel appeared in his hand. The mutant blanched slightly. Then he regained composure. He waved toward the nearby machine-gun nest.

"If you fire at me, the guards at the desk will kill you. That is the rule in the cavern. Will you die to save this meat?"

Jon whipped out his own knife and the little monofil blade sparkled between them.

"Then we will duel with knives. It's all the same to me."

"You will be my feast meat. I will force-feed you for six weeks and then we will bake you in your own juices.

I can almost taste it now, hot, bubbling with fat. It will be good."

Gnush pulled out his blade. It was astonishingly long, more than half a meter, Jon estimated. In contrast the little monofil seemed like a toy. He wondered if he had miscalculated. Perhaps there was a limit to Gnush's greed. Perhaps he should have offered more. But it was already too late for bargaining.

Gnush moved forward with startling rapidity for one so large. Jon evaded the rush but felt the big knife blade slice along his left cheek. Blood dripped from the cut.

Gnush came again. Jon ducked, weaved, swung a foot into Gnush's midriff. It felt like he'd dropkicked a medicine ball. He moved away, again only just missing a lethal sweep of the big knife.

Gnush lurched after him and surprised him with a sudden punch from the free hand. It caught Jon's shoulder and sent him sprawling.

Gnush chortled and prepared to jump on him knees first. Jon rolled, twisted, felt a big hand catch him by the shoulder. Gnush swung with the flat of the knife. Jon thrust out the monofil and it sliced cleanly through the mutant's blade.

Gnush groaned to immense discontent. Jon slashed at him, the little blade neatly opening up the huge man's arm from wrist to elbow. Blood gushed from the wound, and Gnush roared and tumbled back. Quickly Jon moved after the stricken mutant, who swung a mighty fist that the blade separated into halves. Blood, bones, fragments sprayed Jon and Hawkstone. Gnush let out a vast complaint and staggered back holding his ruined hand.

"You have damaged me!" he exclaimed in agony.

"Get in my way again and I will kill you."

Jon bent and slashed the leash that restrained Hawkstone. He helped the captain to his feet and cut the wrist shackles.

Gnush had been joined by two females of the same mutant tribe. They wore similar skulls over their genitals and their breasts. They tended their fallen giant's wounds with vicious glances at Jon, who lead the slightly stunned Hawkstone away by the elbow.

Later, in the bar, Jon got the rest of the tale out of the captain after plying him with several drams of distillate. He left the captain after a while and went out to find Braunt and the mantid.

CHAPTER TWENTY-TWO

MELISSA BALTITUDE STARED IN HORRIFIED DISGUST AT the images on the screen where her father was shown being brutally raped by the muscular pinheads of the laowon Brutality Room. Drool was slipping from his lips, his eyes were vacant, staring.

The Superior Buro officer beside her switched it off. "That is the Brutality Room."

"And you call yourselves the higher race." Her voice cracked. "You disgust me, all of you."

The flat golden eyes stared coolly at her. The blue skin was tinged gold in the warm lamplight of the room. It was hard to believe she was on a mighty battlejumper in deep space.

"Nevertheless, you will do exactly as we tell you or you too will undergo that experience, and worse."

Melissa tried to say no; she dug deep for some angry retort to fling in his face. But nothing remained. If they could actually do that to her father, who ruled the Baltitude Gas Company itself, what could they do to her? The realization left a cold pit of fear, a seed of vacuum in her stomach. It ate her strength, she felt her knees tremble.

She knew now how the laowon ruled humanity so easily. If they were prepared to use such vile methods, to do anything in pursuit of their goals, they were unstoppable. No civilized society could stand against them.

"How you can call yourselves a civilization defeats

me. You are nothing but barbarians with superior technology. We are the civilized race, and you fear us because of this. Your culture must be thoroughly rotten to allow such disgusting methods."

The laowon in his black tunic with a small blue star merely shrugged. "In truth, there are those who would agree with you. These things are the custom of thousands of years. Many regard them as atavistic, even foolish. But others point to the longevity of our system and its evident success. They say that the Imperiom merely reflects the natural order of evolution. The highest forms are those that control all others and use them as they see fit. Those aspects of first-level civilizations that we have dispensed with include the emotional concept of pity for the weak. The Imperiom allows for no pity. Thus were the Seygfan first developed, thus did they win the Last Laowon War, and thus they remain today, eleven thousand years later."

He paused, fingertips pressed together. "So, your bubble of human civilization, what does it represent? Barely two thousand years of high technology. A competing morass of unconnected powers. Do you mean to say humanity works no cruelties, no injustice, no misuse of power? I can cite examples of human behavior to make you tremble with horror. Your societies too are riddled with the ugliness of the passage to evolutionary glory. Unfortunately for you we came first and we shall rise far above you. The human is not destined to share that glory, but to live as a valued servant of it."

"We would not have oppressed you." Melissa was shaking, but whether from fear or anger she wasn't entirely sure. It was almost like alternating current, one second the rage, the next the fear.

"Would you not? Yet your own history is filled with blatant and horrible examples of oppression between your own nations and tribes! Would you have treated us any better!"

She stared at him, tried to find the words, but realized he was probably correct. The universe was of dark, uncertain purpose. One blundered around in it until one was seized and destroyed. If Arnei Oh's bullet had hit her, perhaps it would have been Suzy America's lot to be there, to have witnessed such a scene.

"What do you want me to do?" she croaked at last. Her throat was dry, horribly so.

The laowon snapped his fingers. The doors opened and a young laowon orderly in space-navy green appeared with a tray and a glass of water.

They had been waiting for her to say that! She wondered if her emotional swings had been chemically orchestrated. She realized she was outfoxed from the start, cornered by giants, a mouse among intelligent lions.

An image sprang into view on the screen. Jon Iehard's narrow face, the deep-set dark eyes, the thin lips, cleft chin.

"You know this man?"

"Yes. Slightly."

"You are part of a very privileged group. Very few do know him and of those we have lost two."

"Oh?"

"A woman, that traveled with him. You met her yourself."

"Yes, a compopper. You destroyed her in the Brutality Room."

"There was also a detective. He died."

"How?"

"The details are unimportant. We are processing the rest of his department for any scraps of information we can find. You, however, have been spared the brainwiping. We have a mission for you instead. It involves this man."

Neither Braunt nor Hawkstone were at all pleased with Jon's decision to include them on the rescue mission to the larders of the Bluegrain Hardscabbies.

Their complaints had gradually worn down from sheer repetition as the mantid headed down the south trail into the machine belt. With the broken window replaced, the air conditioning was working and they drove through the midday brightness in passable comfort. Hawkstone stared out at the ruins in awe.

"It's like driving through an endless city where all the buildings were spaced exactly the same distance apart."

"The Bey told me that the ancients grew these things."

"Grew? How does anyone grow something like that?"

Braunt pointed to a structure composed of curving tubes of black eternite.

Jon shrugged.

The machines passed slowly, each five hundred meters from those to the north and south and half that distance from those to the east and west.

Around their bases pleochroic sands drifted, sparkling furiously in the afternoon sun. Gradually the shadows behind them grew longer and darker as the day wore on.

It was like a landscape from a dream, Jon thought. Abruptly he noticed something that stood out against the dreamscape. A human figure, in sand-color desert garb, flitting behind a machine.

"Slow down," he shouted. "Ambush!"

Braunt looked wildly around and prepared to accelerate, but no bullets whined their way. Instead, just ahead a pair of mantids could be seen in the pool of shadow cast by the bulky machine.

"Pull up over there. This must be the Elchites."

"For all you know the mutants have taken these Elchites and are waiting for us to do just what you're proposing."

Jon scanned the cabs of the mantids. No one was in sight. Could Braunt be correct? He hardly wanted to find out by getting shot or captured.

"Stop," he commanded. Braunt kept going. Jon prodded him with the assault rifle. The hovercraft slowed, idled.

"Back up."

Very gradually they approached the silent mantids.

Jon opened the door on his side, ordered Braunt out on his side.

A figure stepped around the edge of the nearby machine hulk and aimed his rifle at them.

Jon recognized the Elchite Acolyte Gesme.

"Gesme," he called, raising his hands in the air.

The rifle didn't waver. Jon thought Gesme was about to fire. "M'Nee lied! He was responsible for my disappearance—had me kidnapped by slavers."

The rifle stayed high. "That's a serious allegation. Do you have any proof?"

"Nothing except myself. If I'd betrayed you I wouldn't have come all this way to find you."

Gesme thought that over; there was an inescapable logic to the reply.

He saw Hawkstone in the cab and the lean figure of Braunt. "Who's that?" The gun gestured.

"Braunt, my driver, brought me down the fast way, over the High West Pass."

"Why did you bring the captain back? He told us he wanted to go to Quism and find a way home. He is a coward."

Jon fluttered his hands. "Not too loud, Gesme, he'll hear you. Things are really delicate right now with the captain. He starts hearing voices and things."

Gesme wavered. Then a whistle sounded, faint but audible. He looked off into the distance. "All right, stay where you are. We'll let the Bey decide. They're coming back now."

A couple of minutes later four figures in full desert uniform with goggles and breathing apparatus came out of the blazing heat.

They stepped into the shadow and lifted the bugeye glare shields, retaining just their polarizers against the blinding brightness.

At the sight of Jon, Eblis Bey broke into a broad smile. "I knew you'd be back," he said.

The young Elchites paused, swallowed, stared at the Bey.

"It's all right," he bellowed. "This is Jon Iehard. He's no traitor, are you, Jon?"

He put his arms around Jon and clapped him on the back. "I see you brought the captain back too. However did you manage to inspire him to return with you?"

"I had to bring him; I pulled him out of some mutant's meat herd just a day away from the stewpot. He's lost control, I'm afraid. But I brought you someone else too." And Jon gave the Bey the mote, which awoke at the first touch of the old man's hands.

It immediately squawked and yowled in a strange, complex tongue that meant nothing to Jon. To his amazement, the Bey replied in a passable imitation of the same noises.

Eblis Bey looked up at him. "Mr. Stardimple is greatly in your debt, Mr. Iehard, and he confirms, at least, that you wore a slaver's band on your ankle."

The other Elchites came forward to shake his hand.

The Bey then produced something from a pocket on the inside of his suit.

It was the silver cube!

Jon smiled. The little cube felt cool and pleasant to the touch.

"I found it in your hotel room. When I saw it I knew you could not have disappeared voluntarily."

"I'd missed it. I wondered what had happened to it."

"Come over to the mantid and I'll brief you on our plan. Time is short, as usual."

Jon left Gesme to guard Braunt, Hawkstone, and the mantid.

The Bey switched on a screen and ordered up a map of this sector of the machine belt.

"When the winds pick up again and the dust gets thicker we'll head on down the trail another few kilometers. We captured a mutant and made him lead us to the Hard-scabby larders."

"I heard that you hired them as trail guides."

"A terrible mistake. If I hadn't been so worried that you'd been taken by Superior Buro I never would have considered it. As it was, they only succeeded in their ambush because the Ornholme people refused to take sufficient precautions."

"The trail guides seemed to think it was a mistake too."

"We will teach the mutants a lesson," the Bey said grimly. "But we must move quickly. We have missed our first appointment with the man with half a head. We shall have to try and catch up with him in the south where he awaits us. With the Buro so close on our trail I did not dare approach him directly in Quism."

While he explained the plan and showed Jon the layout of the larder, a space enclosed beneath a great fallen disk, the wind outside began to moan. In the middistance the dust thickened.

By the time the Bey had finished the dust was howling past them and was so thick it was hard to see more than fifty meters in any direction.

Jon returned to Braunt's mantid. He urged the sullen driver to follow the other two hovercraft into the wind.

Keeping the others in view, they pushed forward into billowing white clouds. Together they left the southbound trail and headed across a bumpy dunefield toward a distant tower. When they reached it they stopped.

The Bey and the Elchites clambered out. Jon turned to Braunt and Hawkstone. "Well, my friends, here's the moment of truth. I'm getting out here to try to rescue the others from Ornholme. Obviously I can't prevent you from turning back to Fort Pinshon. So you'll have to make your own decisions."

Hawkstone wore a look of acute distress.

Jon slipped out into the wind, ran to join the Elchites. The wind was a physical force. He had to lean into it to make progress. Around his boots the pleochroic crystals were shifting, flowing, running over the dunes.

He sensed Braunt starting up his engines and driving away but he didn't look back. He hadn't expected them to stay.

The Bey pointed ahead. Dimly through the clouds he could see a smooth mound shape. A dark hole at its mouth. "The front entrance of the larder."

Wisps of black smoke rose from a pipe that jutted from the dark entrance, but the wind quickly dissipated it. The cannibals prepared for their next feast.

"We'd better hurry," Jon said. "You keep up the pressure at the front, while I creep in the back hole."

"Gesme, go with him," the Bey said.

They separated. Jon and Gesme moved clockwise around the huge circular plate that roofed in the Hardscabbies' hole, creeping carefully through the dunes toward a pipe stem that jutted from the sand a short distance from the plate. No one guarded it; the Hardscabbies had never thought that outsiders would actually want to visit their larders.

A crudely knotted ladder of human hide and femurs led down into the dark. An odor like that of roasting pork assailed their nostrils. To his disgust, Jon found himself salivating.

"I'll go first," he whispered, then climbed over the edge and began to descend. Gesme attached a small radio transmitter to the edge of the pipe, which would rebroadcast their signal when they were ready.

Jon listened hard for movement below but discerned nothing. With any luck the mutants would be too busy feasting to keep a good look out. Cautiously he worked his way down the pipe, trying to keep the ladder's movements to a minimum.

When he reached the end of the ladder, however, he found a problem of a quite unexpected sort.

The ladder simply terminated in midair, yet he judged the floor was about seven meters below. He was hanging in midair in a big room with circular walls. Boxes and sacks were stacked around the sides.

He sat on the lowest femur and began swinging the ladder back and forth. When it was moving as far as the storage boxes he swung down to hang by his hands and then dropped the last three meters onto the boxes.

It was a harder landing than he'd expected. A box collapsed under him, he teetered for a moment on the verge of a fall, then the pile of crates stabilized. Heart pounding, he crouched still for a few moments and listened.

The sound of festivities came from somewhere nearby—some coarse singing or chanting accompanied by drums and a piercing flute.

Jon climbed carefully down the boxes to the floor and crept to the doorway, an aperture as high as the room but only a meter wide.

He looked out into a very large space, cut up into room-sized sections by walls and equipment. Several of the black-cabbed vehicles with balloon tires that he and Braunt had fought off were parked in the center. Beyond them was the primary light source, a big glow bar sticking straight up for five meters.

Here and there in the farther parts of the space, other lights were visible in what he presumed were private quarters.

Close by was a stack of coffin-shaped boards, hanging on thongs from a large frame. His eyes passed over these at first, seeing nothing to interest him, then they returned to a flash of white and orange, a medical cast in the shape of a fist and forearm! There were other human outlines on those boards. He observed several men and women strapped down on them, connected together by a black hosepipe.

There was no one in sight. Jon glided over.

Bound down on the boards, the men and women were attached to a force-feeding machine. Above the machine was a small hopper filled with an oily-looking feed mix.

The tubes ran into their throats. When the machine was turned on, the feed would be pumped into them.

Among those tied to the boards were Finn M'Nee and Gelgo Chacks. They saw him, faces alight in astonishment. Next to M'Nee was a small woman now swollen to a grotesque volume. Jon estimated she weighed at least three hundred pounds.

This then was mutant feast meat. He gave M'Nee a long cool stare then left them behind and moved on into the big room. A chamber formed by walls of puffcrete opened to one side. He glanced in. Two mutant females, with small human skulls on thongs covering their genitals and breasts, were working on a pile of tubers, peeling and cutting and mashing them. They had the same, thick, lumpy skin as Gnush Two Tusks. Their long black hair was tied up with finger bones on top of their heads.

Jon returned to the storeroom, pushed several crates into a pile underneath the thong-and-bone ladder, and whistled softly to Gesme.

When they were both on the ground, Jon pressed the comstud on his wrist and the code signal flashed to the main rescue party.

He waited a few seconds, then he and Gesme shifted into the main room and took positions.

Half a minute went by. Jon could feel M'Nee and Chacks' eyes pressing on him from the shadows where they waited helplessly.

He was half inclined to leave them to the mutants.

Abruptly there was a blast of sound and bright flashes of light in the front entrance. More explosions followed and the lightbar disintegrated. A chorus of screams and roars of rage came from the mutants.

Mutant males leaped to the entrance to fire long bursts out into the daylight with hand weapons. Jon and Gesme rose and began shooting them down from behind.

More screams. The two women he'd seen before ran out. Each carried a long knife and ran straight for him. His assault rifle cracked twice and the bullets exploded in their heads, sending fountains of gore and brain matter over the puffcrete walls. A bullet whined off the puffcrete behind him, showering him with dust and splinters. He dove for better cover and worked his way into the room.

Bullets, tracer and explosive fragments were richocheting everywhere and figures were struggling in the main doorway as more explosions rocked the interior.

Jon ducked behind a bale of human hides with heads and limbs attached. A movement caught his eye: A huge mutant male, with fighting tusks agape, suddenly emerged from behind the bale.

Jon had barely rolled aside when a long knife struck where he'd been crouched, then the mutant was upon him. It stank of oil and blood and possessed terrible strength. In a moment it had bent him back and was bringing those tusks to bear on his shoulder. Jon screamed from the stabbing pain and drove his fist into the creature's heavy belly. It bore down harder and a fist the size of a plate slammed him in the face. He felt another big hand groping for his throat, when Gesme appeared above them and brought his rifle butt down on the mutant's head, once, twice, three times, before it finally went limp.

Jon pushed it away, got to his feet, found his rifle. Blood was trickling down his arm from the tusk wounds.

"Thanks," he managed before a trio of mutants charged across the floor. Jon and Gesme fired, the guns shuddering in their hands, until all were dead. Jon dropped the rifle and drew his Taw Taw longbarrel. He stalked through the ruined rooms. But the battle was over. The remaining mutants were lying facedown under the guns of the Elchites. A pile of half a dozen bodies filled the front entrance.

The Elchites had about them the fire of righteousness, their eyes seemed to blaze under the lifted goggles and polarizers. Jon observed that one of them, Yondon, lay among the dead mutants. Another, Dekter, was having a shoulder wound bandaged.

"Where are the Orners?" asked Jon.

"Over here," said the young Elchite named Aul. He led Jon around a partition of skin stretched over a metal frame. In a pit seven meters long and five wide were dozens of people, including the surviving Orners, Dahn, Bergen, Hargen, and Wauk.

"Where is Rewa Kolod?" Jon asked Officer Wauk, who had tears running down his face, though whether from relief or sorrow was unguessable.

There was a pressure on his arm. Jon turned to Aul. "Kolod is over there."

Jon looked where he indicated and saw Rewa Kolod's

head on a pole. On a grill were arrayed her limbs and pieces of her torso, dripping fat into the coals below. Jon felt a long moment of nausea, then turned away.

The Elchites put a ladder made of human bones down into the pit and the contents of the Bluescabbies' larder climbed out.

"I think we should hurry and get away from here," Eblis Bey said. "There are bound to be visitors from the main shelters of the tribe. We don't want to be trapped in here."

Jon could not have agreed more. Ignoring the cuts in his shoulder, he moved to the back of the shelter and cut the people free from the force-feeding machine. The grotesquely overfed woman fell down weeping hysterically, trying to kiss his boots. Finn M'Nee and Gelgo Chacks got up from the fattening boards with long, level stares. They said nothing, and when they were able to walk again, they went quickly to the main entrance and left.

Jon turned to Gesme. "No thanks from them, eh?"

"They are a strange pair. Truly they are not popular with the rest of us."

While the Elchites tended the wounded and guarded the entrance, Jon and then Gesme siphoned fuel from the mutants' vehicles and loaded it onto a captured hovercraft, an older vehicle called a turtle, with seats for six people and storage trunks at front and rear.

With reserves of fuel and ammunition taken from the Hardscabbies, the expedition regrouped around the pair of surviving mantids and the turtle.

There was a long moment as Eblis Bey inspected Finn M'Nee and Chacks. They stared back impassively.

"For some reason you have lied to me and committed a most dangerous crime." Neither moved to protest. They stared straight ahead, unseeing.

"Unfortunately, we haven't the time to hold a hearing to investigate the matter now; it will have to wait. However, should there be any repetition of these problems we will have to resort to summary methods. All personal dislikes and feuds will be forgotten as of now! Is that understood?"

M'Nee's head bobbed in a barely perceptible nod.

"All right. M'Nee and Chacks will ride in the turtle with the Orners. Jon Iehard will take Yondon's place in the lead mantid. Everybody to your places, we must hurry."

The Bey turned to the other survivors of the Hardscabby larder. "We have no spare equipment for you. I suggest, however, that you ransack this place for supplies and try and make your way to Fort Pinshon. You are about thirty kilometers south and west of the fort. I would suggest these vehicles here as your best method of transport to safety."

A gaunt man in the tatters of a surface suit pointed to the few surviving mutants lying facedown by the entrance. "What about them? Will you kill them or leave them to us?"

The Bey looked at the shuddering mutants with revulsion. "Cannibalism is a disgusting atavism. Perhaps it would be better to kill these creatures. On the other hand, mercy is one of the greatest of human characteristics. We will leave them to you, and I would suggest that time is more valuable to you than the joy of revenge." The Bey turned away and strode toward the entrance.

The escapees from the larder searched for weapons with chilling little cries.

Jon found Owlcurl Dahn staring at him. "You came back for us," she whispered. "M'Nee lied."

"Yes," he said simply. She noticed the blood on his shoulder, the cut on his cheek.

"You are wounded!" She reached out to examine the damage. Officer Bergen joined them then went to the turtle and returned with a first aid kit. Owlcurl Dahn applied antiseptic and a medipack to the gouges.

"The question that gnaws at me," Jon confessed, "is why does M'Nee risk our mission for such personal hatreds?"

She shrugged. "I do not know, but I am glad to see you again and to have those charges against you disproved." The dressing was completed. She gave him a little kiss on the cheek as he pulled his desert suit back over his shoulder. They parted and she climbed into the turtle, which started up with a roar of engines and moved out through the front entrance of the larder. Jon followed, trotting to catch up with Eblis Bey.

CHAPTER TWENTY-THREE

THE PARTY OF FOUR HOVERCRAFT, THREE CROUCHED, black mantids, and the lumbering turtle regained the Oolite trail without further molestation by the Hardscabbies.

They headed for Fort Pinshon, to renew supplies and to obtain a new guide before heading south. The winds had died down somewhat, the dust had thinned. They drove across a flat plain of shimmering sequins, the hulks of ancient machines on either side in perfectly spaced multitudes stretching into the smoking distance. Light dust whipped from the dunes into the heatscatter of the sun.

Eblis Bey was consumed with anxiety. The decades-old plan for contact was in ruins. He had panicked in Quism and run too soon. Ulip Sehngrohn had been unable to arrange a firm meeting site. All the Bey knew was that Sehngrohn would be in the south. If not at Fort Pinshon then at Bengo's in the Boneyards, or at Guillotine Rock. He had not been at Fort Pinshon and now the Bey had lost half a day or more in freeing the Ornholme people.

He trembled at the cost in time, the deadly delay. The Buro had been very close. He could not fail now! Not when success was so near.

But he knew well that a surface guide was a necessity for their journey. They were unversed in the myriad perils of the vast, dried-up ocean beds. Out there, in the winds of the equatorial dusts, the land changed shape frequently. Groundquakes and volcanism were just one aspect; others were the crustal pits, a unique geological aspect of Baraf, where the land gave way abruptly to holes several kilometers deep and wide, with sheer cliff walls.

Then there were the far-desert mutants. The Zun people and the Outer Hardscabbies. In the Boneyard sections of the trail there were a thousand other perils to beware of. There was no getting away from it, they had to have a guide.

They were about ten kilometers outside the fort when they became aware of a heavy, repetitive drumming sound coming from the west. It grew louder.

The Elchite driver, Aul, said, "Hardscabby wardrums, I think. They have found our handiwork."

The drum sounds were enormous, triumphing over the wind, electronically amplified, distorted noise, broadcast via groups of enormous speakerhorns that brayed into the wind.

"What will they do?" Jon asked.

"They will probably attack Fort Pinshon. It happens every so often. The mutants swarm in and sometimes they even capture one. They take everybody for meat, burn what's left, and depart."

"And within days new proprietors are installed on the sites, rebuilding furiously," Gesme added. "The forts are very profitable to operate."

"Why do they not take over the forts more permanently?" Jon wondered aloud.

"Few travelers would willingly risk the mutant forms of hospitality," said Aul with a grin. Gesme guffawed. Jon noticed the Bey's worried frown, however.

"If the fort is besieged, though, we will be trapped there. We have to go south immediately. Is there any other trail?"

"We need water, we're low on food as well," Aul said. "Superior Buro has most certainly divined our presence here by now."

"I found them filming departing expeditions," John said. "They had been to the hotel. They may have established a presence in the fort."

"We can't go there, then," Aul said.

"Look," Jon cried, "up ahead."

Down the trail from Fort Pinshon came another pair of mantids, at full speed, heading south. From the nu-

merous nicks and pockmarks on roof and side panels, Jc
recognized the leading machine as Braunt's.

As they came closer they slowed down. Figures climbe
out and waved. Aul brought the mantid to a stop.

Braunt approached, braving the blinding light and wind

Aul opened a window. The cab filled with dust and th
sound of the wind moaning across the dunes.

Braunt brought bad news. "You won't want to get int
Fort Pinshon. The laowon military are there. They'r
landing equipment directly from space. Whole place is i
an uproar. We barely got out."

Braunt was joined by the trail guide Angle Umpuk
They clambered into the mantid, bringing more cryst
grains that winked in polychromatic glory whenever th
sunlight caught them.

"This is unprecedented. Laowon military, droppin
straight from orbit! They came in by the hundred. Kille
dozens in the outer yard. You've never seen anything lik
these cyborg shock troops of theirs." Umpuk recognize
Jon. They shook hands.

"Braunt and I happened to be on the apron, exchangin
engine components, when it started. That's how we go
away."

"Hawkstone?" the Bey said, gripping Braunt's han
suddenly.

"He's with me. I was going to take him to Quism—h
said he had money. Seemed a better idea than leaving hi
there for the mutants."

There was a short silence. Then the Bey said, "We ar
faced with a dilemma."

"Indeed we are," Angle Umpuk said. "I heard the drum
start up. The Hardscabbies have gone on the trail of blood."

"They are coming up the trail from the south. To th
north lies the fort and the laowon military. What lies o
the east and west?"

"West of here is all Hardscabby territory. They'd trac
you easily. East their control fades out as you get into th
continental interior. It's pretty empty, but it's also out o
your way. Braunt said you were going south, deep south."

"Mr. Umpuk, are you offering your services as a guide?"
the Bey inquired silkily.

"Looks like I don't have that much choice."

The Bey paused a moment. It seemed a heaven-sen

opportunity. In the Book of Elchis, the Great Prophet was quoted frequently on the subject of seizing opportunities, on taking care so the deity would take care of one, and so on. If ever a time had come for marrying Elchis to the moment, this had to be it.

And yet he strained to perceive the webs of the Superior Buro. That feeling which had never left him that he worked within their machinations and was anticipated and guided all the way. It was impossible to believe in this fantasy. He, a mere schoolteacher, in late middle years, to defeat the laowon Imperiom! How had he gone so far? Escaped their nets so often? He had never believed it possible, not at the beginning, especially not after the events on Earth. In his heart the Bey had felt that their efforts were doomed. But somehow his people had overcome each trial in their path. This suggested to him that his passage had been prepared most carefully all the way by the Buro, which simply sought to find the man with half a head. If they could put Eblis Bey and Sehngrohn together, they would have both latitude and longtitude for the position of the machine thirty years ago.

Yet if they knew of the machine, knew that it was there, why hadn't they scoured the planet months before, when they first got word through the treachery of the diktats on Earth?

Once again he came to that question mark that had lain over his mission since the beginning. The laowon had most certainly brainwiped the Diktat of Sumatra. Yet they had not discovered the secret. Did that mean the diktat committed suicide? Or had they killed him? A sudden heart attack? A stroke during the interrogation? It would be typical of Superior Buro arrogance. To put that weak old man through a harsh interrogation that killed him before they wrested the vital aspects of the secret from him.

If the diktat had died before giving up all he knew, then the laowon knew no more than the Diktats of Los Angeles could have given them—and *they* had only a few scraps. Nothing substantial, just what they had squeezed from the poor men and women who were at the disastrous meeting where the secret was first brought to Earth. Thus the laowon were still following *him* and, somehow, this quixotic adventure by a frail old teacher retained a chance of succeeding.

Now here was a guide. Could he be Superior Buro? The possibility existed, yet there was no choice. Swallowing his misgivings, he turned to Umpuk. "What would you suggest we do right now, then?"

"Go to the ziggurat machines, climb the farthest, and wait for the Hardscabbies to go by. They will attack the fort. While they do that we will run south and hope they miss us."

"Won't the laowon just obliterate them?" said Jon.

"Possibly, but you shouldn't underestimate the Hardscabbies. They will employ many tricks, they will have pops and snaps. If the laowon underestimate them, they may be in for a nasty surprise."

Eblis Bey nodded and committed himself. If he was wrong he would have to move against this Umpuk very quickly. Extra vigilance was required, as if he wasn't tired enough already! The thought brought him an image of the temple schoolroom in L.A., with his students in rapt attention to his historical expositions. It faded into an image of a woman, Aleya, his lovely long-dead wife, the only woman he had ever loved. He tried to blot out the rest of it, the last moments inside the machine. He shivered involuntarily as he recalled her scream. Eblis Bey shook his head to clear the nightmare and headed for the mantids.

The expedition turned and moved off the trail and across the dunes on an angle south and east. Umpuk led them in his dark-green mantid, threading through the machine park toward a distant line of pyramidal structures, which slowly resolved into two-hundred-meter-high circular ziggurats. They might easily have been the tips of gigantic screws thrust from the depths of the landmass.

They cruised onto the ramplike surface and began to climb. The ramp was ten meters wide at the base but narrowed to less than three after two turns and finally came down to two meters, too narrow for the turtle, which had to stop before reaching the flat circular summit.

The mantids reached the top and parked. Jon got out and took binoculars to examine the Oolite trail, which ran past, seven kilometers distant. The fort was out of sight, lost in the dust twenty kilometers north.

Jon scanned the southern part of the trail. The dust obscured everything, however. He was about to give up in disgust when he saw the first black specks charging up the trail.

He called to the Bey, who left the shelter of the mantid and joined him. The wind was fierce at that elevation.

They watched as a pack of forty or more black vehicles rolled up the trail toward Fort Pinshon. Jon noticed that the big balloon tires kicked up relatively little dust; from a distance it would be hard to tell their trail from the normal dust clouds of the belt.

The Hardscabbies went north to punish the normals in the fort and to take fresh meat for the larders. The drum sounds died away with them after a while. Atop the ziggurat they waited, uneasy, with frequent glances northward.

An hour went by and the winds died down. The dust lessened and an ominous hush settled in the north. Midafternoon came and went and abruptly very bright flashes of light sparked from the region of the fort. Soon afterward, appallingly loud explosions cracked across the land.

Angle Umpuk joined them.

More very bright flashes, followed by terrifyingly loud blasts seemed to rock the planet.

"If those are nuclear weapons, do you think we should move?"

"Those are heavy snaps. Must be consuming the entire node with each shot."

"Snaps?" Jon's forehead furrowed.

"Another fragment of the ancient race. Very useful for jewelry, microsurgery. They can cut as finely as our best lasers, but they require no external energy source and, even better, they can cut the interior of something without cutting through it."

"That sounds very useful; they must be very valuable."

"At another setting they explode with considerable force."

More thunder whammed down from the north.

"Will there be anything left of the fort?"

"Oh, yes," Umpuk chuckled. "They'll just toss those big eternite plates around and they'll fall down in another configuration. The old fort will never be the same, that's what they say. This will be the third time in memory that Pinshon's pile of plates was tossed around by the Hardscabbies. Blood Head will definitely be sung of for a long, long time by the tribes of the belt."

"If there's anything left of them when the laowon military are through with them," Jon added a grim note.

"I think it's time we got moving," the Bey said. "While the mutants battle the laowon behind us."

They turned the mantids and followed the turtle, which had to back down part of the way, to the desert surface once more.

Angle Umpuk led them south and east, staying ten or twenty kilometers east of the Oolite trail.

Behind them were a few more flashes of bright light and great cracking blasts echoed through the machines.

Then there was silence but for the moaning of the wind in the latter part of the long afternoon.

When darkness began to fall they were almost two hundred kilometers south and on the fringes of the Inland trail, which curved around the Mock Mountains and down into the first of the Great Boneyards.

Angle Umpuk halted, the other machines slowed and idled. Umpuk came across to their mantid and climbed in.

"We have to choose our course now. Do we head east and go round the mountain and down into the Boneyards or west and take our chances on the Old Oolite?"

"The Oolite ought to be the faster route south," the Bey said.

"Indeed it is."

"But the laowon military will surely be racing down it after us," Jon interjected.

"That is something we must consider." The Bey looked solemn; he pointed westward. "What lies beyond the Oolite and the Hardscabbies?"

"If you head south and west?"

"Exactly."

"A thousand kilometers of dust and then the continental shelf and the ocean bed."

"What if we went that way?"

"The ocean bed is always hard terrain. In the North Ocean there are other hazards."

"Such as?"

"Upwind of the remaining oceans there are frequent hurricanes, sometimes with snow and hail the size of a man's head. Some early expeditions were crushed by the force of what they encountered. Of course, making your way over crevasse country in such weather is even more taxing."

The Bey thought it over. "What of the Boneyards then? That's the way I traveled before."

"You have been south before?" Angle Umpuk's eyes widened.

"Yes."

"And you wish to return there?"

"We must."

"Nobody ever wants to go back. Not even the craziest archeologists." Umpuk rubbed his chin. "I have been as far as the northern fringe of the crustal pit zones. You have seen them?"

The Bey nodded. "Yes, quite astonishing."

Umpuk agreed, "That would describe it." He gulped. "You have gone further?" A note of genuine awe was audible in his voice.

"Yes."

"And that is where you want me to take you?"

"Exactly."

"Good grief!"

"We seek the great equatorial machines."

"The legends—but you must know the risks."

The Bey swallowed. "Yes, I have seen it, I have seen the—"

"The jelly-that-is-flesh, the flesh-that-is-steel," Angle breathed.

"You know the mutants' tales then."

Umpuk nodded. "Among the guides there are many grim tales of old Baraf, but none to match that. They say the equatorial Zun people sacrifice to the horror."

"How ghastly."

"I had a friend once who went south with some archeologists, he was leading them to the equator. He never came back. I often wonder if that was his fate."

"Pray that he met a cleaner death," the Bey said with a strange passion in his voice. They fell silent. Eblis Bey brushed brilliant dust from his trousers.

"Anyway, enough of this. What of the Boneyards? Can we take that trail far enough south to be able to get past the laowon on the Oolite?"

"The trail sweeps two hundred kilometers inland, up the ancient estuaries. Then it passes through the first fossil beds, then through the ancient city sites, and then across the limb of Bolgol's Continent to the southern coast where it meets the Oolite again. It's shorter but it's a rougher ride. The interior is mountainous and volcanic. Which is why most treasure groups go by the Oolite trail around the continental margin to the south coast Boneyards."

"What are the risks in the Boneyards?"

Angle sighed. "Well, there are many bandits' holes to be avoided. Plus there's the outer Hardscabbies and the farther south you go the more Zun people. Attacks by the Zun have inexplicable results and tragic consequences."

Eblis Bey considered the alternatives. His instincts told him the Superior Buro would go down the Oolite trail first. If his party made good time perhaps they could get into the Boneyards before the Buro caught up. Once in that maze they would have a good chance of losing any pursuers. And they could buy relatively safe shelter at one of the numerous holes.

"We go by the Boneyards, all the way to the Guillotine Stone," he announced. They nodded their agreement and returned to the hovercraft. The engines kicked into life and they rode south.

■ CHAPTER TWENTY-FOUR

MELISSA BALTITUDE WAS AMAZED TO BE STILL ALIVE. It felt as if she had gone through enough perils for several deaths by then.

On reflection, her interrogation and programming aboard the battlejumper had been child's play compared to the rest. She gasped again at the pain from her shoulder; she had surely broken some bones. Somehow it hurt far more than she had ever believed it could. To try to push the pain away she reran the memories.

First had come the active battle descent, with the laowon shock troops dumped into insertion orbits at high speed by the military battlejumpers. They had strapped her, her Buro minder, Claath, and a cyborg shock trooper into a descent pod and dropped them with the rest of the shock battalion. Claath had warned her it would be tough, but not even Claath was really ready for it.

The laowon military dropped hard, and of course the cyborg troopers were built to take it, but for ordinary mortals it was an intense experience. The shocks emptied her lungs, her stomach, and finally her bowels.

When they were floating down the last few thousand feet the wind caught their parachutes and tore at the patterns, but the chutes minimized the dispersal and kept them in the drop line to within one hundred meters of Fort Pinshon.

Despite the heavy goggles, the sky had seemed to burn

with the solar fire and the ground sparkled like some monstrous jewel chest, whenever the dust cleared long enough for it to reflect light.

Then she'd been swallowed up in the dust and deposited on the surface by the chute, which of course was programmed to deliver cyborg fighters. Fortunately young human women who keep fit are remarkably flexible creatures. Melissa survived, and even brought off a good roll to minimize the impact.

Nevertheless she lay on the ground afterward like a dead thing, every scrap of strength wrung out of her.

Then Claath had come out of the dust and dragged her to her feet. She'd followed him into a low entranceway beneath what appeared to be a lopsided pile of huge plates, stacked randomly.

Inside she found herself in a big dim space stinking of death. The hall had recently been the scene of a fierce little battle. The "tame" mutants had risen at the entrance of the laowon and their shock troops. They had shaken out weapons, for a half minute they had confronted each other. Then a drunken mutant fired accidentally and the cyborgs had swarmed upon them.

Overawed by the blinding speed of the cyborg attackers, which flitted like flies through the great space and cut the mutants down with dreadful ease, the fort operators surrendered quickly to the laowon.

Burochief Claath and his officers immediately took charge of the fort and began brainwiping everyone, sifting for images of the fugitives. They set the booths up right by the front entrance and hauled the people out, sat them in the brainfield printer, and then tossed the incoherent wretches into a pile where they thrashed helplessly, their brains emptied of all thought patterns. The bodies sometimes lived for days, twitching, thrashing, as long as the heart pumped.

Before the task was half completed there was an alarm. A drumming noise filled the air and from out of the southern dust came a force of vehicles on balloon tires.

Claath ordered the cyborgs to attack, but before the platoon had even reached the gates, the mutants fired several snaps into the fort. Each snap lifted huge plates of eternite and flipped them over in the air. At the first blast Melissa found herself simply hurled a hundred meers across the ground to land with a force that drove all the breath from her body and left a pain in her shoulder. She watched in stunned awe as the enormous, indestructible pieces of the fort, each weighing thousands of tons, rose into the air in a fountain of dust and people and fragments hung for a moment, and then returned to the ground. The desert shook from the impacts.

Beneath the eternite plates were the smashed remains of a battalion of shock troops and two dozen laowon officers of Blue Seygfan, including Burochief Claath.

The mutants fired another round of snaps shortly afterward, turning the whole mess over once more. Melissa had dragged herself another hundred meters away by then, but was almost smashed by an errant disk that grounded not twenty meters from her spaceboots.

The dozen or so remaining cyborgs attacked the mutants, and a horrible carnage ensued from which only a small number of Blood Head's followers escaped, by taking immediate flight.

The cyborgs returned, dripping blood, and lined up in precise parade-ground drill, awaiting fresh orders.

From the sky fresh patterns of troops and laowon officers dropped. Melissa awaited them with a terrible dull ache in her shoulder and nausea in her belly. Tears rose in her eyes. Her mission was aborted, and through no fault of her own. Would they let her live? Would they let her go home?

Through the paling purple twilight the expedition moved down the Boneyards. Around them were piled the fossils of billions of the ancient race. The mantids led, the turtle lumbered behind.

Mounds of forkbones, skulls, and loricae were fused around them in grotesque statuary dozens of meters high. Skulls in rows were propped up in lines on frozen vertebral columns in parade-ground formations hundreds of meters deep. It seemed as if an army of dead beings was marching out of the planet's crust itself.

"The burial sites of an eon of civilization, Mr. Iehard," the Bey said. They stared around them as the hovercraft raced up winding gulleys cut through the enormous graveyards.

"They were a tidy race when it came to burial then."

The Bey smiled. "It may have been an adaptation t the problem of numbers in a successful planet-wide civ ilization. They were marsh cultivators, harnessing th richness of wetlands. Astonishingly frugal—they used n burial ornaments, for instance. Although there is evi dence, if you go deep enough, that in earlier eras ther was horizontal burial and burial ornaments were common When their numbers grew to threaten their own habita they adopted thrifty ways that allowed them to prospe for a very long time."

The hovercraft passed down canyons cut in the orderl stacks of fossils. Around them, where the dead had bee exposed to wind and rain, they had eroded into spine and spires of ribs and vertebrae, but in the long eon whe Baraf had wandered the void, frozen, the processes o erosion had slowed to a crawl. Now the endless wind had carved the huge stacks of dead into endless friezes honeycombs. Drifts of toppled fragments skirted the stee canyon walls.

Jon studied the skulls as they passed. They were mas sive, with projecting, crocodilian jaws. The occipital lobe bulged out behind the faces. The staring eyesocket marched, rank on rank, into infinity. He wondered if an of the ancient creatures—it was hard to think of them a people like humans and laowon—survived.

Beneath them the shining crystal of the machine bel had long since been left behind. Now the dust filled with fragments of fossil. For long stretches they passed ove enormous beds of small bones and skulls.

The shadows of twilight coalesced into a deeper gloom as they navigated the meandering passages of the ancien estuary beds. "This must have been a huge river in its day," Jon commented, awed by the seemingly endless expanse of channels and bone mounds.

"There is much evidence to suggest that it was artifi cially enlarged and that the ancients flooded as much o the low-lying landmass of their world as possible in a effort to maximize their favorite, swampy habitat."

They fled on through the expanses of the Boneyards.

Toward midnight they pulled in at the three red globe lights advertising Bengo's Hole. They parked in the court yard, inside the energy fence, under the guns of the turret set into the mound of bones over Bengo's limestone cavern.

Inside considerable excitement was in the air. At the bar, which cut across Bengo's big room, Bengo himself was buying toasts to commemorate the Hardscabbies' great battle.

"It was on the radio," one merrymaker explained. "The laowon Superior Buro dropped from the skies on Fort Pinshon. Such arrogance, such power! They were in the process of wiping the brains of every poor fool they took when the Hardscabbies came up to avenge the destruction of their larder. The laowon were severely handled by the mutants of Blood Head. Hundreds of laowon casualties, the whole place was turned over."

"The blueskins were almost wiped out. Such a victory as we have never had before," Bengo exclaimed. He was a large rotund man with a jolly red nose and big brown eyes. He caught Jon's sleeve. "Believe me when I tell you there is rejoicing all over Baraf tonight."

Outside in the courtyard the Elchites refueled the hovercraft and purchased water and food.

Jon was moved to buy a round of cold beer for everyone at the news, spending the Mercantile notes of Bompipi with innocent glee. He looked up from his first draught to find the Bey frowning at him.

"Come away from here. This generosity of yours may be remembered by these fellows, and the Superior Buro are likely to follow us here before long."

He finished the beer sadly and joined the Bey. "Shouldn't we warn them? The Buro will brainwipe every one of them!"

"Would they believe us? Or would they simply scoff at us for our fears and continue their drinking, and then turn over their memories of us to the laowon clear and strong?"

Jon looked back. The Bey was correct, unfortunately.

They slipped out. Bengo's was a series of circular rooms of puffcrete. Perimeter shields powered by a Barafi sustainer protected it. In addition, a team of guards manned guns on the tower above the main structure. The central room was Bengo's bar and restaurant, which also served as sleeping space if there were sufficient visitors.

The outer rooms were mostly used for storage and

sleeping quarters. They passed a row of phone booths and saw Finn M'Nee slipping out a door just ahead.

When they opened it moments later, they found themselves back on the courtyard, the wind whistling overhead. Harsh lights studded the dark, and beyond loomed the twisted shapes of bonefriezed hills.

Finn M'Nee was nowhere to be seen.

Jon and Elbis Bey exchanged looks. Jon confessed a feeling that had been growing in him for days.

"M'Nee troubles me. This vendetta of his seems unbalanced—particularly for one who must be dedicated to the mission. I can understand his anger over his wound, but he must know the importance of our mission. Surely he should have put aside such personal considerations."

The Bey nodded in sympathy. "Indeed, I am troubled too. He came to me from the *Churchill* program run by the Elchites of Ornholme. I doubt that I would have chosen him otherwise. He seems an odd one for a temple boy, constantly preoccupied."

As they walked to the mantids in the refueling station, Angle Umpuk came up to them. "I've talked to the other guides here. It seems the eastern trails are the ones to stay on. Zun people have been reported on the western margins of the Boneyards."

The Bey called a meeting. Everyone crowded around him as he squatted against the side of a mantid. "We have been given a reprieve, it seems, by the mutant Hardscabbies. The Buro has suffered a sharp defeat, and so we will take immediate advantage of the opening they have given us. We will go west in the lower Boneyards and head for the Oolite trail again. That will take a day off our travel time at least."

The Bey noted Jon's look of surprise but gave no other reasons for the switch in plan.

Then Braunt spoke up. "Well, I don't fancy the thought of heading any farther south than this. If it's all the same to you I think I'll hole up here at Bengo's and then try and get back to Quism."

"You'll have to get past the laowon. They will most certainly wipe your brain if they capture you."

"Did you not hear? The laowon are discomfited, they are smashed! Who needs fear the laowon?"

"One small force has been destroyed. I would imagine

that others are already landing, probably already have landed, and are getting ready to pursue us. Others are probably slaughtering the Hardscabbies in their holes. They will take Blood Head back to Laogolden itself for the Expiation. What a noise the mutant will make for them! If you go back, you will be taken and we cannot allow that."

Braunt would have protested but Aul stepped in close and showed him the long, shining knife that he held in his right hand. "You will drive under guard. Wauk and Dekter will ride with you, Dekter will spell you at the controls."

Braunt emitted a groan of intense woe. Aul squeezed his shoulder fiercely.

The Bey continued. "We should leave here as soon as possible. Everyone who has yet to buy water or other supplies must do so as quickly as possible. I would like to move out in about fifteen minutes."

Sixteen minutes later, the first mantids roared up and out of the energy screen and headed south again into the dark eerie spaces of the Boneyards at night.

For hours they continued south, then began veering westward, following the trail to the junction at the place called Small Bones.

Here a drift of fragments, ossicles, digits, and fossil shards had piled into great dunes, amid which sat a small fortified dome. To the west beyond it the land humped up swiftly into small rounded mountains, dimly visible in the starlight.

To the south, the braided channels and canyons of the Boneyards went on and on.

Eblis Bey called a halt, then redirected their course south, changing the plan once more.

"Why are we changing course?" M'Nee asked from the turtle.

"Mr. Umpuk has a hunch about weather conditions in the west."

Jon knew Umpuk had said nothing of the sort.

"We cannot allow ourselves to be deflected on the whims of an old trail guide!" M'Nee protested.

"Why ever not, Mr. M'Nee? That's what guides are for."

M'Nee subsided into annoyed silence. The expedition

forsook the west and passed on down the eastern Boneyard trail.

The hours slid by. Jon slept in his seat in the mantid, awoke when the Elchites changed driving shifts.

Dawn found them already enveloped in the fringes of the tropical dust belt. As they plowed on down the trails, the dust grew thicker until by midday they were slowed to less than seventy kilometers an hour, picking their way through sinuous canyons near the margins of the great continent.

Shortly afterward they encountered a mantid limping northward. They stopped. From the damaged machine came three people, one man and two women. One of the women had a bad head wound. All were weak and thirsty.

"Archeologists," they explained. "We were down on the southern coast, about a thousand kloms from here. The Zun people came from nowhere, they surprised us, took our mutants for their own larders. They . . ." The man broke down.

"They took our colleagues away and baked them alive for feast meat," the woman coolly interjected. "They made us watch. They are baldheaded demons."

They gave the archeologists some water and food and set off southward somewhat more cautiously than before.

"What are these Zun people?" Jon asked.

Eblis Bey shrugged. "Another mutation; I know little of them. When I first came here they were talked about but rarely seen. It was said they lived mainly in the southern hemisphere deserts, where outsiders never go."

Aul, who was driving that shift, spoke up. "They have been coming north, even into the Boneyards, in the past decade. A number of atrocities have occurred. They burned out Harib Zar's hole and carried off a hundred normals into the equatorial vastnesses. It is said they worship gods who live in the equatorial machines."

Eblis Bey blanched. "Gods?" he sputtered.

"I've heard it said that the rites are extraordinary. Sometimes the dead come back to life, whereupon they are boiled and ground up to produce an extraordinary substance called n'sool, which the Zun people are able to control with mere thought."

"They are strict communalists," Gesme added. "They share everything, equally, down to the last shreds of flesh.

The most advanced Zun forms lack eyes and noses but still retain ears. They have developed abilities that transcend the need for sight and the sense of smell."

"Let us pray we do not fall into their hands!" the Bey said fervently.

They continued in silence, the channels slipping past them on either side. The bony stares of the billions filling the world. After a while Jon slipped back into an uneasy sleep. The trail stretched ahead, seemingly endless.

His dreams were of little consequence at first. But later strange pictures filled his mind. They were tying them down, whoever they were, and leaving them. But where?

He awoke, felt something stirring uneasily on the fringe of his psi sense. It grew in intensity. After another hour he received a crystal-clear mental picture. Someone with powerful psi ability waited ahead, had already spotted the caravan and signaled the fighters.

Yet he also sensed that the psi ability was unlike his own. The individual ahead was crouching down to aim a crudely built machine gun, scavenged from captured parts.

"Zun people," Jon said. "Up ahead. I can sense them. There's one about a kilometer ahead who's aiming his gun at us right now. But we're not quite in his range, a homemade weapon, I think."

The Bey gave him a swift look. "You're sure?"

"Clear picture. I can feel something else about them, they're all linked, they share a gestalt power. It feels 'big,' a vague description, I know, but that's the feel. As if it stretches back into the desert for thousands of kilometers."

They pulled over, the others took cover. They scanned the mound tops ahead and discovered several other motionless figures dug in behind heavy-caliber machine guns. The faces lacked eyes, the skulls were much larger than those of ordinary humans. It looked almost as if each head had grown two brains, one alongside the other. They wore strips of hide, weapons, and long ochre cloaks.

"Can we get through past those guns?" Eblis Bey asked him.

"Something about their disposition says they possess great confidence that we cannot. I would not risk it if there was a way around them."

"Good enough." The Bey turned to Umpuk. "What lies east of here?"

"We'll double back twelve klicks to the junction with the next channel. There we have a choice of three different courses, each farther east than this."

They turned around and recharted their progress back to the point where the trail branched once again. They sought the farthest course to the east and passed quickly down it. Jon felt the rage and confusion somewhere behind them in the west. He realized that the Zun people had not detected him, despite his clear reading of at least one of their minds. They were linked but they were not "one." Their gestalt was imperfect, perhaps they did not understand it fully yet. But he could sense them clearly, and it seemed they did not sense him.

Eventually, in late afternoon, the Guillotine Stone loomed up ahead. They had crossed the great limb of Bolgol, right down the length of the Boneyard trail. Ahead lay the continental shelf, marked by a few volcanoes, some active, some—like the Guillotine Stone—extinct. Beyond the shelf lay the seabed and the equatorial dust, an endless maelstrom where the superheated atmosphere was rotating frantically about the dying planet.

It seemed to take forever to reach the Guillotine Stone after they sighted it. But finally, they came to the lip of a scarp looking over the volcanic plug and the wind-carved Guillotine blade held high on two side pillars. There was even a semicircular notch cut in the cleft below, although that was said to have been created by an early exploration party as a joke.

They came to a halt as the Bey and Iehard and Umpuk examined the site. No activity was visible. But it was a small, deep-desert post that had few visitors. Only a pair of machines was visible inside the defense shield, which lay above the entrance to the caves.

They were about to send one mantid down for a closer look when a slender figure in a mutant's ochre desert cloak appeared in their midst. A young Elchite, he announced, "I am from the man with half a head. He advises against a visit to the house under the Stone. The Superior Buro came last night and brainwiped everyone there. Fortunately our master had forbidden any contact between us and the fort."

The same intense fires burned in this young Elchite as the others, but an extra quality was there, too: an awareness of desert living on the very extreme of life, a consciousness of death and life and the almost invisible line that separates them at any one moment.

"What is your name?" Jon asked.

"Milon."

Jon found no mental trace, no sign of anxiety.

"Come, follow me, I will lead you to the man with half a head." Milon turned and beckoned them into a cleft in the nearby rocks.

They followed. The lumbering turtle was a tight fit, but eventually they found themselves under great eaves of stone, where an ancient lava flow had cooled over softer rocks that had since eroded. They passed through a maze of passageways between dikes of igneous material until they came into one with lights, where several armed Elchites waited for them.

Eblis Bey stepped out, the mote at his side, and found the figure in the wheelchair, the legendary Doctor Sehngrohn, waiting for him.

"Doctor, we meet again at last."

"Eblis Bey! Welcome back to the dead sands of ancient Baraf. How is Los Angeles?"

"More people live in one building in Los Angeles than live on this world, Doctor. And the diktats are rotten to the core."

"I suspected as much. And thus we were right to take our precaution."

"We were indeed."

"You still remember your half of the position, the latitude?"

"Of course."

"Well, I have the remainder, even if I have but half of my original brain tissue surviving."

"A miracle that *you* survived. We gave praise to Elchis day and night when the news came."

"Well, it was less a miracle than a triumph of Elchite science—the surgeon was the miracle worker."

Jon stared in fascination at the withered figure in the wheelchair. He noticed the medical units to which the man in the chair was welded, including the one that occupied half of his head.

"You know Rhap Dimple, of course."

"I do indeed." He held out a hand and the mote flew to it.

"And this is a young man you should meet. Not one of our original party, he came aboard in the Nocanicus system. His name is Jon Iehard, and a most valuable addition he has proved himself to be."

Jon stood forward and grasped the old man's hand. Ulip Sehngrohn was in the last quarter of his second century. Yet a balefire was alight in his old pale eyes. His hand was hard, his grip strong.

The Bey introduced the young Elchites who had come with him; they were all awed to meet the legendary Doctor Sehngrohn. When it was done, the doctor turned to Eblis Bey.

"Come, let us go somewhere private, we have much to discuss. You know the Buro were on the Oolite trail last night?"

"They came this far south?"

"I hear that they have lost four aircraft thus far. They are trying to survey the trail by flying the aircraft over it. Of course the jets cannot survive the thicker dusts. There was a spectacular crash at Fort Pinshon this morning; a jet with full tanks fell to the ground immediately after takeoff. Seven laowon officers were incinerated."

"They've been having their problems at Fort Pinshon," the Bey commented.

"They certainly have, but I fear that Blood Head has now been taken by the cyborgs. He will go to expiate somewhere far away."

"Such is the Imperial system."

"Not for much longer if we can but succeed."

Sehngrohn and the Bey disappeared into the maze.

■ CHAPTER TWENTY-FIVE

THE WINDS HOWLED OVERHEAD AND MELISSA SWEATED inside her uncomfortable desert suit. Built for a laowon officer, it was much too big for her, and very heavy besides.

The climate of the planet was unrelentingly horrible. In the south a harsh gritty dust constantly flowed. It got into everything, even through the filters into the laowon suits. The darkness at least allowed the lifting of the glare goggles. Then only the polarizers had to be kept over the eyes.

Above them, waiting for the armored car to pick them up from the landing apron, the Guillotine Stone loomed, dimly visible. Beside her stood Officer Bancool, her new minder. Officer Claath's remains had been dispatched to fleet HQ for inspection and delivery to his family. Melissa doubted she would miss Claath, a cynical and sadistic type. On the other hand, Bancool was some kind of advanced religious racist and insisted on being addressed as Klor, the word for "lord" in the general laowon tongue. He had told her of his urge to see the permanent subjugation of the human subrace as part of his own dedication to the glory of the Imperiom. Since those were among his first words to her, they served to stifle any attempts she might have made to initiate conversation.

Her shoulder was comfortable at least, much better now that they were out of that aircraft.

She looked back at the plane with a little shudder. It had started out with four jet engines. One had flamed out and fallen off on takeoff. Another had died before landing.

She recalled watching two earlier jets take off from Fort Pinshon's hastily improvised airstrip only to crash immediately when their engines ingested the corrosive dust.

The smashed planes sent up great plumes of dark smoke into the winds, which promptly scattered them over the heads of the laowon waiting to board the jets as they were assembled out of the landing pod. The morale of the laowon officers on the mission was noticeably poor.

Melissa heard her name called. She turned. It was Magnawl Ahx, Chief Executive Officer of the Superior Buro himself. He who had befriended her, had saved her from the brainwipe when Bancool had found her in the aftermath of the disaster at Fort Pinshon.

"There is no trace of them here, nor did our information last night lead to anything." Immense disappointment was obvious in his voice. "I'm afraid they may have slipped by us. I dread the consequences of our failure. There will be a terrible war. I doubt seriously if the Imperiom, once aroused, will allow any vestige of human independence after the war is completed. Billions will die."

She stared at him bleakly. She could add nothing to what he already knew.

"I'm sorry, Lord Ahx. I knew your fugitive only very briefly. I have told you everything I can remember, down to the tiniest detail. He said he was going to the stars, to find an alien race, that was all."

Ahx nodded, he believed her. In truth, they were facing an appalling situation. Despite the fact that things had begun very well. They had been blessed with a spy inside the Elchite camps from the beginning, yet still they were groping. Now they faced imminent disaster.

The spy had proved of little help in the end. Only computer work had produced the command to search Baraf's main entryport at Quism, which had caught a trace of the Elchite terrorists.

Now the Buro had reacted to what seemed disinformation. Perhaps the spy had turned, in which case they had nothing to fall back on if the fugitives had already slipped past them. The Elchites might already be out there, in that blinding dust storm that went on forever.

"If we have missed them then I may have to order this world burned. Do you realize what that will mean?"

"No."

"It will be carpet-bombed with nuclear devices until nothing survives. The entire surface will be made molten."

"How long will that take?" she asked, staring off into the blinding dust. Her attention distracted by other concerns. Was Jon Iehard out there, alive somewhere, struggling toward attaining the mad dream that had the entire laowon empire writhing?

If he was still alive, what was he doing? An odd mix of emotions brought a lump to her throat.

Magnawl Ahx shrugged. "Before we begin we will have to consolidate the sector fleet. That could take days. After that it will be but a matter of hours."

"What about the people who live here, in the cities?"

"A few of them may be rescued, most will die."

"That always seems to be the way of your Imperiom."

"We are a great power, far greater than any human understands. We must move with the maximum decisiveness, we can never weaken before our enemies. It has fallen to us to unite our Galaxy. Already we become aware of other galaxies that may be united under universal states. Such states must have enormous power, we must be ready within our own Galaxy to withstand any challenge that might cross the great deeps."

The high officers in the Buro always spoke as if they were being recorded for the history tapes. Which, Melissa reflected, they probably were, in a way. The Buro constantly spied on itself as well as everything around it. The obsessions ran deep and strong.

He joined her, staring out through the thick goggles into the whirling dust. The armored car was finally approaching.

Slightly more than a thousand kilometers to the south the expedition crawled forward over the ancient seabed.

In this region near the midocean ridge the terrain was a nightmare of ridges, sharp cliffs, and endless parallel canyons. Their way across the meridian of the ancient ocean bed was marked by endless loops and doubling back. Forward progress was painfully slow.

Time and again they crawled up a long heavy gradient only to find themselves at the head of a scarp too steep for them to descend safely. Then they would backtrack and work north or south to find a way around it.

During the second night on the seabed they passed the first crustal pit, a shockingly abrupt hole several kilometers deep and wide that cut through the landscape without advance warning. Surrounding it there was no evidence of an impact, no piled rubble, no crater walls. And the sides were straight, as if cut with a giant ruler and a knife.

They paused for a moment beside it.

"This cannot be a natural phenomenon," Jon said with a bemused grin to Owlcurl Dahn.

"Certainly unlike any known to science," she agreed.

"The size of it! What purpose might it have served?" He rubbed his chin and wandered along the edge of the cliff. There was erosion, a few gulleys, but for the most part the pit was a perfect cube. The huge walls went straight down.

Angle Umpuk approached. "Astonishing, isn't it?"

"I wonder why it was made."

Umpuk shrugged. "As to that, who knows? The ancients were a strange people with a sad and terrifying end." He surveyed the pit. "This is a young one. Closer to the equator there are many with more advanced erosion characteristics, I'm told. Spectacularly beautiful, if only they weren't so damned dangerous."

"Were they perhaps made to hold water?" Jon mused.

"Unlikely. This was the bottom of the ocean."

They looked into the near distance, as far as the dust would allow.

"Are you nervous about going out there? You seem almost eager." Umpuk scanned him carefully.

"I am eager—our mission must succeed, but we race the laowon, Mr. Umpuk, as I'm sure you have realized. I have killed laowon, Mr. Umpuk, seventeen Superior Buro officers in one system alone. I cannot survive capture in this universe."

"Universe? What do you mean?"

"That we will change the way history has betrayed us, that we will reach out and bring down the laowon tyranny with one crashing blow, if we have to."

Angle Umpuk looked around uneasily. "Then we had

better not linger here too long. By the way, how was it that you sensed the Zun men who were waiting for us?"

"I have slight psi ability, a rating of forty-one in Nocanicus system standards."

"Ah, one of the psi-able. And you worked for the police department there?"

"In a way. I had no choice really, there wasn't a lot else I could do, you see. I grew up on a laowon world, Mr. Umpuk. If you were to look at my forehead carefully you would find the estate brand of Castle Firgize. I have had surgery, but traces remain."

Umpuk felt his jaw drop. "How terrible! I had no idea."

"I go to destroy the laowon, Mr. Umpuk." Jon made a fist of his gauntlet. "I go to expunge them as they expunged my mother and her family. They put them in the Agony Booth. Agony until death—have you ever seen that done, Mr. Umpuk?"

"Uh, no, never." Umpuk stepped back abruptly. "I'm sorry, I meant no offense, I was just curious."

Jon stared off at the amazing walls of the cube and made no reply.

When he returned to his mantid he found Owlcurl Dahn inside. "I asked the Bey to switch places with me for a while, Jon. M'Nee and Chacks whisper together incessantly; they unnerve me. I think I need a change from their company. In truth, I dislike them and they dislike me."

"And they want to kill me."

"I know, they talk of it constantly. They curse someone called 'Bompy' and talk of exacting a terrible toll from him."

"That was the slaver they sold me to in Quism. I was to be blinded and have my tongue put out before being sold off as a slave."

"I never heard about that part."

"Oh, that's the best part, I thought."

She saw his smile and giggled. He was a strange one! He seemed almost as relentless as Eblis Bey. And something in him haunted her, a tantalizing glimpse of a dry humor behind the grim outer face he wore. She wondered if it was connected to psi ability. Before she could decide, the mantids coughed into life and set off once more.

On the third day they finally crossed the midocean

ridge and came down onto a flat basalt floor, scoured of ooze by the endless winds. They made much better speed on this surface, although the lead mantid—crewed by Bergen, Hargen, and Gesme—had to watch carefully for crustal pits. Soon they became more numerous, and the expedition passed a dozen or more within a hundred kilometers. They were clearly of differing ages, some weathered and half filled with scree, others still as sharply defined as the day they were cut from the planet's crust.

It was past noon when they became aware of something hulking out of the dust to the south. They turned to investigate more closely.

As they got closer so the hulking mass grew larger. Soon they saw that it was another machine of the ancients, but this machine was built to a different and much larger scale than the machines of the northern belt.

It was also broken down, great sections had collapsed, shaken perhaps by groundquakes. A cracked dome, or shell, covered the central section, which was at least five kilometers across and three high.

As they pulled up about half a kilometer distant, they gazed up at the behemoth, appalled by the enormity of it.

"Is this what we have been seeking?" Jon asked the Bey.

"No, this machine is broken down. The one we seek is still active. It will be moving, heading west at a rate that takes it around the planet's circumference once every ten terrestrial years or so."

"What fuels it?"

The Bey shrugged. "I do not know. Perhaps some fusion generator inside—it's certainly big enough to carry one. It's not as big as this one though."

They roved the length of the moribund giant, stared at the vast treads sunk into the seabed underneath it. But the Bey refused permission to explore its mysterious interior and eventually they left it behind, continuing south and west. They were approaching the equator, the winds were fiercer than ever and the dust so thick it was hard to see more than twenty meters ahead.

CHAPTER TWENTY-SIX

WHEN NIGHT FELL FOR THE THIRD TIME ON THE SEABED, the expedition paused to take stock and snatch a hurried meal from the supplies in the turtle.

Everyone wore a haggard, desperate air. The men unshaven, the women unkempt, all were tired of riding through the dust-swept desolation in the cramped vehicles.

Eblis Bey brought them together for a last briefing. "My friends, we are about thirty kilometers north of our destination. At least that is what the computer navigator says. We are approaching the end of the mission." He paused and looked around him. They stared back, scarcely daring to hope that the ordeal might soon be over.

"You have kept faith in me throughout enormous peril and hardship, and now I hope to show you that it has all been worth it. Though I hasten to add that the dangers ahead are as great or greater than anything we have faced before."

The old man hunkered down. They followed his example because it was difficult to hear above the wind outside the hovercraft.

"What I hope we shall find up ahead will be a group of machines, several small ones and a single large one. They are still functional, still moving. In fact, they are known in the old charts as the South Tropical Rogues, because of their movements."

"Ah ha!" Angle Umpuk exclaimed. "The famous wanderers. Once they were placed in the south tropics, far below the equator. They have been lost and rediscovered many times. If they are nearby, then they have moved again, for we are still a little to the north of the equator itself."

"Mr. Umpuk is correct, though there are several other mobile machines in the equatorial belt. The one we seek however is different from all the rest. Most are defensive weapons. They produce a barrier field of some kind through which nothing solid can pass. I think it may have been used to keep their terrible enemy from bombing them or invading. However, I only hazard that as a guess. The machine we seek is the other side of the ancient's blade an offensive weapon of a power beyond anything we or the laowon have ever developed. I have seen it, I have seen the records in the main control room. This is an awesome power."

"What does it do?" Officer Bergen asked after a short pause.

"It creates a gravitational flux in the center of a target For a small target, like a spaceship, this is enough to disrupt the engines and explode them. In a large target like a star, it causes a nova, a momentary implosion followed by a huge outpouring of stellar material and heat."

There was a longer pause.

"Oh, my God!" Bergen said.

"No wonder the laowon are expending such energy," Angle Umpuk said in awe.

"The Starhammer," Owlcurl Dahn whispered. "It exists!"

"Yes, it exists and we will use it if we have to, to wrest our freedom back from the laowon."

Jon stared at M'Nee. Was he imagining things or did M'Nee give a little shudder as those words were spoken?

The Bey cleared his throat. "However, it is also guarded. A maze surrounds the central command room. And the Keeper, a powerful robot, rules all the central sections. It is inimical to all outside influences, which I suppose it regards as threats to its purpose, which is to maintain the machine in case the builders ever need it again. Therefore, the Keeper will have to be neutralized. For this purpose I have formulated a plan for communicating with the Keeper with Rhapsodical Stardimple, which we hope will solve the problems we faced the last time we were there. Rhap Dimple will also open the outer door of the machine's airlock. The machine, you see, was originally designed to operate underneath the oceans, a further impediment to attack. The structure is enormously strong. However, Rhap Dimp was grown by an operator of the machine, I cannot pronounce his name, but it appears to translate as 'Stargazer-with-flat-feet-firmly-on-the-ground.' Seems to have been a humorous fellow all right, but he and his fellows in the machine died despite all their defenses."

"How did they die?" asked Jon.

"Their enemy reached them. Too late to save itself from destruction but in time to doom the operators of the machine. They worked feverishly to transport the surviving population of their planet to safety, far far away, and then succumbed to a horror that had penetrated the interior."

The echoes of this ancient struggle to the death seemed to wail around them still in the tormented dust of the dying planet.

The Bey moved on to practicalities. "Once we are close to the machine, a small group will undertake a first reconnaisance. Then, the prime assault group will go inside. This will consist of myself, Gesme, Aul, and Dekter. Should we not return or give a signal within thirty minutes, a second group will enter, consisting of Jon Iehard, Officers Dahn, Wauk, and Bergen."

Jon saw M'Nee and Chacks exchange looks. The Bey had pointedly excluded them.

"On this taper, which I will entrust to Mr. Iehard, I have inscribed the route to take once inside. To the best of my recollection it should guide you through the interior to the control chamber."

The Bey collected himself before continuing. "Inside the machine we will face another danger and thus I must add a final warning. Heed it. If we do not signal within the proper time, you are to think of us as dead men! If you subsequently enter the machine and see us, apparently alive, open fire at once. If you can it would be best if you could destroy our bodies. Use explosive bullets, make the bodies inoperable."

They stared at him.

"And then get away from the scene. On no account whatsoever should you approach such a body, even after you have broken it into pieces."

Owlcurl Dahn voiced the general puzzlement. "Why would this happen? What would have happened?"

"The machine is contaminated by a weapon from the enemy of the ancient race. The enemy that virtually destroyed them, the enemy that they finally annihilated. The enemy that they built these vast machines to defend themselves against."

"What enemy was that?" Dahn said.

"They called it the Vang Oormlikoowl." The syllables rang with an eerie sound. The Bey continued in a hushed voice, "Of course, my pronunciation of the words is incorrect, so Rhap Dimple tells me anyway, but that is approximately the ancient's term. As best as I understand it, it translates as 'High Intelligence Omniparasitic lifeform.'"

"What does that mean?"

"A complex lifeform that sees all other life as nothing but food or an 'environment' of one grade or another. A lifeform that is fundamentally opposed to any like our own. There can be no communication between us and it. To it, we are either food or a hindrance, or worse. To us, it can only be a dire threat."

"What is in that machine, Mr. Bey?" said Officer Bergen in a trembling voice.

"A military form, a deadly peril."

"The jelly-that-is-flesh, the flesh-that-is-steel!" Angle Umpuk said quietly.

"Yes, Mr. Umpuk, exactly."

Haltingly, the Bey described the few characteristics of the mysterious devil inside the machine that he recalled. When it came time to tell of the fate of his beloved Aleya, he forced himself to describe everything, even the weird alien organs that the thing had grown from her, that wobbled like pink ferns in the air behind her as she walked toward him that last time, her eyes conscious, her mouth constricted in a terrible scream of agony but her limbs completely under the control of the other, the slimy thing that winked at him under her skin.

When he had finished they broke up in a somber mood and returned to the hovercraft. They set off again, south and slightly west. Everyone was preoccupied with the tasks ahead.

* * *

Enormous military motion was in train all around them as the components of the Grand Sector Fleet, Admiral Grahsk in command, with poor Booeej locked in his cabin, were assembling in orbit above Baraf.

Aboard the jumpers, battalions of shock troops were readied for deployment. Drones were released into the atmosphere to probe the dusts of the equatorial region.

Superior Buro troops aboard heavy tanks were rumbling across the basalt seabed only a few hundred kilometers behind the Elchites. They were but part of a huge force that was sweeping into the equatorial zone.

Aboard the leading battletank, Melissa Baltitude rode beside Magnawl Ahx. She was right in the cockpit, privy to the activity going on all over the system. The laowon were throwing everything they had into the chase. If they failed, they were preparing to sear the planetary surface with nuclear fire. If they failed, Magnawl Ahx was prepared to sit on the surface and wait for the sterilizing fire rather than the rage of the Heir and certain expiation on Laogolden. That meant Melissa would sit and wait with him.

The tank was a monster, thirty kilometers in length, riding six pairs of heavy treads. It still kept up a steady eighty kilometers an hour over rough terrain. On the flat it did better, edging up to over one hundred.

Arranged in holding pods in rows under their feet were the shock troopers, who would be fired out in ejection harness should they be needed.

Melissa stared out into the murk, and even the massive batteries of lights aboard the laowon battletank couldn't cut the dust for more than fifty meters. The clouds hid everything, and made the going fearsome in among the crustal pits.

Her thoughts roved forward to the fugitives and Jon Iehard. In her heart she prayed they would not catch them. She didn't want to see Jon after the laowon had broken him. She knew he would be broken very small before they allowed him to expiate.

But if they didn't catch him, then there would be the nuclear fire and after that, nothing at all. If she'd had tears left to shed, Melissa would have wept.

CHAPTER TWENTY-SEVEN

FOR AN HOUR THEY PROBED SOUTHWARD THROUGH THE dust. No sight of anything larger than dust grains, or smaller than the seabed presented itself. Throughout, they observed radio silence.

Then they saw a light floating past them to the north. The Bey ordered an immediate halt as he and Jon tried to get an image of the light, but it disappeared too quickly.

"A laowon probe?" said Jon in concern.

"Most certainly, we must accelerate our timetable."

They ran for the hovercraft and returned to the trail of the great machine. And almost immediately they sensed something up ahead, a mass loomed out of the dust.

"The machine!" Jon cried.

But the Bey shook his head. "No this is just the rear marker machine. A rear guard for the Hammer."

"If it guards the Hammer, won't it fire on us?"

"I think it is only programmed to fire at targets up above, in orbit, not on the seabed. In either case it has been dormant for eons. Probably awaiting instructions."

They swung out and around the machine, a hemisphere a half kilometer in diameter. It rested on immense caterpillar treads that were barely visible at its base. The upper surfaces were pitted and marked with lines that seemed to form enormous eyes, a face, something between a toad and a crocodile. The expression was undeniably fierce.

"The face of the ancients," Jon exclaimed, pointing to the markings. The Bey followed his indication and then turned and nodded.

"A strange characteristic for so advanced a species, to decorate a weapon with a ferocious face. Like the peoples of human antiquity in the preindustrial economies. They carried the fetish decoration of weapons a long way. Early body shields wore faces, the prows of ships were carved in the figures of women and fierce beasts, and even during the early industrial era slogans were written on shells and ferocious designs painted on combat aircraft. Of course, we have progressed far beyond that now, our weapons are not decorated anymore, they have become purely utilitarian, surely a signal of the highest civilization."

Eblis Bey's irony was lost on Jon, however, who as yet knew little of ancient history. "Perhaps these were their first high technology weapons. You say they were not warlike. They just hadn't ever done it before."

"And yet, these peaceful beings discovered the most terrible weapon of all."

The still machine—silent, huge, and ominous—vanished behind them in the murk.

"More lights, to the north." Jon pointed out the window of the mantid.

A laowon probe was swinging in their direction, its engines failing, screaming in complaint as the dust ruined them, its lights like probing fingers in the clouds. It passed eastward and disappeared from view.

They came upon tracks, colossal tread marks one hundred meters across, dug a meter deep into the seabed itself.

"We are close Mr. Iehard, very close now." The Bey was consumed with excitement.

They moved directly west, following the north side of the treadmarks. The wind had dropped further as night drew on, the dust was clearing.

Far ahead, Jon saw something huge, round, humping up against the horizon. The dust hid it again, then the veil fell away and he saw a shape in gray-green eternite, like a hen's egg with the pointed end uppermost. It was cradled at its base within huge tubes or folded arms in a rectangular configuration.

The Bey had seen it, so had Gesme, at the wheel. Eblis Bey raised his binoculars to his eyes.

"At last!" he exulted in a quiet voice. "After thirty years I have returned. I will keep my oath to them, who lie entombed within that dreadful hulk." He stared at the distant shape with eyes widened by the proximity to doom.

Jon felt the sweat in his palms. He was trembling slightly, his eyes locked on the distant, smooth shape. It was absolutely colossal, he realized.

And then there were blazing lights, suddenly, almost above them. A laowon probe, a black metallic X-frame swung past at a height of fifty meters. The lights speared them momentarily through the dust. It swung past on its trajectory and stopped, swung back toward them. Jon called Aul to halt the mantid. He sprang out with the grenade launcher and raised it to his shoulder. The probe returned, engines laboring, coming in about thirty meters up. When it was almost overhead Jon fired three grenades. The first two missed, exploding harmlessly behind, but the third blew up in the left side engine and the probe dipped smartly into the ground in a fireball of hydrogen.

"Onward!" the Bey screamed. "We have no time left, we must reach the machine."

Their position was no longer secret. High above them, the battlejumpers would be targeting the drop zone. Cyborg pods were snapping into ejection tubes like cartridges into firing chambers. In seconds dozens of other probes would be swarming toward them.

Their mantid leaped ahead, a gap opened between themselves and the rest. Then the turtle suddenly accelerated. Jon and the Bey exchanged a meaningful glance.

Painfully, slowly, the machine before them grew until it seemed too large to be possible, to be comprehensible, and yet it continued to swell larger and larger ahead, becoming overpowering in scale. It was a bald colossus, the size of a small space habitat. The smooth gray surface bulked into the sky for several hundred meters.

Then the perspective made it seem almost spherical, resting on a base of four monstrous pillow shapes, each of which was supported by a pair of treads more than a kilometer in length.

Jon had been prepared for the thing to be a giant, but the creation was so huge it went beyond understanding.

How anything so vast had been constructed planetside, to run at the bottom of a deep ocean no less, was beyond his conception of engineering possibilities.

They finally drew close to the leviathan and began to pass along its length. The turtle kept up with them.

The Bey pointed up to the flanks of the lower part of the machine, where huge tubes wormed over each other in a braided system.

"Up there is one airlock. To reach it we'd have to get up on the landing surface. There aren't any steps to the seabed."

Of course, Jon realized, everything would have been floated into it through the deep waters of the long vanished ocean.

"The machine is still," Jon said. "I thought it would be moving."

"It will move soon enough. It lives yet."

Streaks crossed the sky, shapes were descending all around the machine, parachutes snapping open only hundreds of feet from the ground.

"Ahead of us!" Gesme said. A human figure, in laowon military uniform, bounded toward them.

Jon had the Taw Taw in his hand, he dropped the window, emptied a clip, the gun roaring, and the trooper shed a lot of flesh and uniform but continued to come straight for them. It left the ground on a forward dive, explosive bullets still hitting it, and caromed across the bowshield of the mantid and smashed a hand through the windscreen.

Jon shot the hand off at the wrist and it flew across the cabin then hit the side window. The cyborg swung the stump, Gesme ducked and the entire windscreen shattered as the trooper slid away, falling behind them while they caromed from one of the giant machine's huge treads.

"Cyborgs!" screamed Gesme. "They're almost impossible to kill."

"Oh great, that's just what we need," Jon said. He looked back, more bipedal figures were landing in the mid distance. The mantids following were barely going to make it.

The Bey pointed through a gap between the treads. "Turn here, Gesme. Take us in between the treads."

The hovercraft curved then sped into the space underneath the giant. Their lights showed a flat, dull upper surface stretching all the way to the next set of treads.

The treads towered over them, and Jon tried to imagine the sound the monster must make when it moved. They were a hundred meters wide and as they turned, the rock beneath was crushed to powder.

"Are the others following us?" the Bey said.

"Only the turtle so far."

Ahead of them a projection jutted down from the belly of the monster. It quickly resolved into a small corkscrew ramp that ended in a cracked and worn flange of eternite hanging only five feet above the plain.

They clambered out, the Bey running ahead with Rhap Stardimple, up the ramp to the heavy circular airlock set in a groove in the belly of the machine.

Jon and the young Elchites took position on the ramp above the hovercraft, assault rifles at the ready.

"We can't hold them off with just rifle fire," Gesme said. "These are Imperial shock troops."

"Accurate fire can still disrupt them. Try for the head and eyes, that must be a weak point."

Jon loosened the Taw Taw in his holster, cast an anxious eye behind him to the airlock door. The mote was pressing itself into a curved depression in the outer airlock surface. Jon banged a clip of explosive shell into his assault rifle.

Lights were coming around the farthest treads, the turtle and the other mantids, in a group, their engines a sudden growl under the machine. Running pursuers were already closing on the last mantid in line. A human figure jumped, landed on the mantid's back. There was a flurry of activity, the mantid lost way, swung sideways and ground to a halt, several more troopers climbed into it.

"Which one is it?" Gesme cried in anguish. Through the binoculars Jon could see three figures in desert costume being dragged out. "Its Bergen, Wauk, and Hargen, they've been taken prisoner."

The surviving mantids, lead by Braunt's and the turtle, roared toward the ramp. Behind them sprang the fleet footed cyborgs. The Elchites fired, a crescendo in the confined, echoing space. Their bullets exploded in a fury of smoke and metal splinters on the distant tread.

The cyborgs did not return fire but continued to sprint

toward them. The Elchites' fire was accurate, they were well trained in the use of firearms, still it was difficult to stop the shock troopers; direct hits had to pierce the armored brain pan to really damage the things.

The great outer door creaked open slowly behind them.

The turtle slammed to a halt, bouncing its rubber apron off the eternite ramp flange. Gelgo Chacks helped Finn M'Nee out. Braunt, carrying a rifle, ran forward. "Did you see those things?" he said in a shocked voice.

"That's part of the reason we are here," said the Elchite Acolyte Aul. "All of this abuse of human beings must stop."

"Those things aren't human."

"Not entirely, the laowon have seen to that."

Braunt added his fire to theirs, still the cyborgs ran forward and many more were coming into view.

The remaining mantids finally sank down by the ramp. The Orners and Angle Umpuk scrambled up to the airlock.

"Hurry now, everyone inside," the Bey said, his voice shaking from nervousness. They turned and ran for the lock.

The cyborgs were closing fast. Jon got off another clip, he hit one trooper, saw puffs rise from the black and blue uniform before the figure staggered. Then it shook off the impacts and resumed running.

The great door was closing. He slipped inside, turned back as three cyborgs hurdled the turtle to land on the ramp flange then leap for the closing lock. One flew straight in, caromed off the wall and landed upside down in the corner. The others were caught in the door, which closed on their waists.

The one in the corner sprang backward, erect, in time to catch the first three bullets from the Taw Taw long-barrel. They staggered it, but its own gun came up and a demiclip began ricocheting around the metal bubble of the airlock interior. Jon fired again and again, the shots knocking the cyborg skull back, slamming it into a wall, until finally something broke and it slumped backward in a heap.

With a slight squeal of effort the huge door was crushing the trapped troopers. To Jon's horror the cyborg upper halves still functioned. An arm shot out, seized Owlcurl Dahn and jerked her to the door.

The mote was activating the inner door of the airlock, and Jon heard it begin to move with a faint hiss.

"Turn your head!" he screamed to Dahn and fired into the cyborg's skull. Three shots were fired before it consented to die.

There had been carnage in the airlock. Two of the young Elchites, Dekter and Aul had been hit hard, as had been Captain Hawkstone, who'd taken a round through the neck. He lay in a lanky tangle of limbs, blood surrounding him in a widening pool.

Jon fought to pry Owlcurl loose from the trooper's closed fist but could barely move the steel-reinforced fingers. He reached down for his monofil blade, snapped it open, and slashed through the cyborg's wrist.

With a tortured sob, Owlcurl Dahn pulled herself away from the thing. She began working the clenched hand down her arm like some obscene bracelet. Jon, meanwhile, had discovered a trickle of blood on his leg, where a bullet had broken the skin, leaving an inch-long gash.

Officer Dahn broke down for a moment at the sight of Hawkstone. She investigated the body, tears streaming down her face.

A strange smell filled the air, salty, corrupt, it made goose flesh on their skins all of a sudden.

They crowded around Eblis Bey who stood inside the darkness, his lamp making a small pool of light against its envelope.

Jon felt a sense of foreboding as he gazed into the blackness. "Where are the risers?"

The Bey aimed his torch along a smooth-walled tubular corridor lined with what seemed to be orange-brown scales. Along the ceiling ran something like an oversized zipper. The tube curved away into darkness.

"They will be about one hundred paces down there." The Bey looked back into the airlock.

"Who is hurt?"

"Acolyte Aul is dead, Mr. Bey," Officer Dahn said. "As is the Captain. Dekter is very badly wounded, I think he will die, too, unless we can get him medical attention very shortly."

"Can he be moved?" the Bey said.

Dahn shook her head. "There's a hole the size of your fist in his back. We left the medical supplies in the mantids; I have nothing to stanch his wounds with. It would probably be best to leave him for the laowon. They might put him into surgery to preserve any information he might have."

Then they heard a faint *screech* of metal on metal on the outside of the lock where a dozen cyborg troopers were attempting to pry the door open.

"The ones caught in the door must have kept it open a fraction, they're trying to exploit it," Jon called.

"We must go on then. We will have to leave Dekter for the moment, Dahn. Come, quickly, to the risers." The Bey turned and motioned in the proper direction with his arm.

The inner lock door began to close.

They pulled their torches and ran down the tube to the risers. The walls, floor, and ceiling all shared the characteristic motif of scales, each plate being about the size of a man's palm.

At irregular intervals along the ceiling were circular protrusions of some rough, fibrous material about a foot in diameter. The scales fitted seamlessly around them, no purpose for the things was apparent.

The risers were simply larger tubes that sank through ceiling and floor. Oval cutaways gave access. There were no doors. The Bey stepped into one, and was immediately carried up on an invisible force. The risers were set in a cluster of four so they rose in groups of four, floating upward on the back of an invisible force through total darkness.

Jon commented on the lack of lights as he floated up beside the Bey and Officer Dahn.

"Yes, it was the same when we first came here, so long ago. Perhaps it is another facet of the ancients' frugality. Perhaps they were accustomed to functioning at dim light levels. Whatever their reasons, the interior of the machine is mostly dark."

By then they had reached a bigger space, they rose no farther and had to step out of the way of those rising beneath them. Once again they stood on a solid floor, their lights the only ones to break the absolute blackness around them.

"Try to find a light switch Rhap Dimp," the Bey said.

Rhap Dimple floated up to the ceiling and connected with a socket. A moment later a few lights set sparsely around the room, came on. The scales were much larger in there and the light made them shine a glossy gold. Structural members in pink and green eternite sectioned the walls.

"Come, we are close now. This way." The Bey lead them around a corner of eternite into another corridor of yellow scales. It split into three, and he took the central passage, small lights gave a dim general illumination.

They spied something on the floor, a litter of bones, a human skeleton, scraps of a desert suit.

They paused beside it. The Bey examined the hand bones. "This is Professor Abeikar I think. He was the first of our party to disappear."

Ahead, a set of doors swung open soundlessly at their approach. Somewhere below a heavy thud sounded, followed by a loud clang.

"Satchel charges," Jon exclaimed. "The cyborgs have opened the outer airlock door."

"That blast will have disturbed more than the door. We must hurry." With those words the Bey increased his pace. The corridor had acquired a slight slope now and they toiled up it as rapidly as possible.

They were panting when they reached the riser to the control floor. Here they had to go in a single file, one at a time. First the Bey, then Owlcurl Dahn, Braunt, Angle Umpuk, Gesme, M'Nee, Chacks, and finally Jon Iehard.

CHAPTER TWENTY-EIGHT

THE DISCOVERY OF THE EXPEDITION AND THE GIANT MAchine had sent convulsions through the laowon military. More than four hundred capital ships swung in orbit above. At the command, a nuclear firestorm could be launched that would annihilate not only the huge alien machine but hundreds of cubic kilometers of the seabed beneath. A force of several thousand cyborg troopers had been dropped to occupy that seabed in the meantime. And pods of laowon officers had accompanied them.

A flier had picked up Magnawl Ahx and Melissa Baltitude and flown them over the intervening two hundred kilometers to the site of the enormous machine.

Ahx then supervised the interrogation of the three captives who had been secured. Officers Bergen, Wauk, and Hargen confessed freely, but in truth, they knew very little about the machine or its operation. Ahx hesitated to wipe their brains, in case they should prove more useful as hostages. He knew it was a remote hope.

Meanwhile, the airlock gates had been successfully breached and the machine lay open, waiting for the command to invade. Two dead fugitives, and one in the process of dying, had been removed from the airlock. Also removed were the remains of three shock troopers. The laowon were amazed that the fugitives had been able to destroy the trooper that had got inside with them.

Small detection robots had been run into the machine

but they reported no signs of life, although the atmosphere was contaminated with high levels of carbon dioxide and some very unusual trace contaminants, complex hydrocarbon fragments for the most part.

All that was in the reports before the commanding officer on the ground, underneath the machine, Battle-general Plezmarxsh. In conjunction with Buro Chief Ahx, the responsibility for making a successful capture rested on him.

It was imperative that they capture the fugitives without further damage to the machine.

The Superior Buro had made an enormous effort to track the case just to take the weapon in working order. The technology was unknown, but it represented a vast power. The Imperiom reached for that power with eager hands.

Plezmarxsh ordered the first squads to investigate and track the humans. Laowon officers, including Superior Buro operatives, went forward into the darkness behind an advance guard of shock troops. A strange odor in the air raised the manes on laowon necks, and in nervous response they flashed their heavy-duty torch lights around them aggressively, hands on pistol butts. The strange, near-circular passageways were oddly claustrophobic and unsettling.

A maze of passages, all lined with what seemed to be scales and zippered shut along the ceilings, confronted them. They explored and soon observed the openings to the riser tubes. They communicated this information back to battlecommand.

The sounds and vibrations of the opening of the airlock had provoked changes within the machine, however. The squad's lights attracted attention. A wild excitation arose in another interconnecting system, which laced the machine interior as tightly as its own energy conduits.

No one in the squad noticed the pale pink stalk, no thicker than a lao little finger, that pushed through the interlocking teeth of the zipper above them. No one saw it grow toward them. A swift change was taking place on its surface. Feathery structures of pink and white tissue a few inches across were sprouting several inches into the air where they soaked up information about the bipedal forms that had entered the machine.

They tasted the exhalation products and passed the information to the higher centers. There was an immediate explosion of activity. Podclusters that had lain dormant for decades, centuries, or far, far longer, snapped open and disgorged "runners." The podshells were reabsorbed by the collaring tissues beneath them.

It happened that a few of the pods had been formed from the flesh of Aleya Bey, thirty years before.

The pink stalk was joined by others; dozens pushed through between the joints of the scales of the walls and ceilings.

The odd-shaped sensory organs began to branch and wobble, becoming things that looked almost like lungs or clumps of seaweed.

The expedition had emerged on the control floor. A hush of eons lay on the place. They played their lights around. A dozen dark ovals lay before them. This was the maze that the Bey had spoken of.

In one doorway, the lights picked out a small, huddled shape upon the floor—another skeleton, a little smaller than the first, still wearing a desert suit. They clustered around it in a circle. Their lights picked out a sparkle of silver among the bones. Eblis Bey dropped down beside them.

"Aleya," they heard him whisper. He reached into the bones and slipped a silver ring from the skeletal hand. They watched him place it on his own ring finger, where it perfectly matched the ring he already wore there. When he stood, tears were visible on his cheeks.

"If your wife died here, does that mean the parasite menace you mentioned will be in this section?" Finn M'Nee thrust forward his question.

The Bey recovered control. "It is possible. To tell the truth I never saw where it came from, or how it attacked. I was saved because I was with Doctor Sehngrohn in the foyer to the control room. The thing cannot get past the barrier set up there by the Keeper."

There were loud noises from far below. The cyborgs were in the ship.

The sounds seemed to decide something for Finn M'Nee. He pulled out his pistol. Gelgo Chacks had raised his weapon as well. "In that case I will take charge now.

Please be so good as to surrender yourselves. I represen the Superior Buro."

Faces were ringed with shock.

"You're the traitor, M'Nee!" exclaimed Officer Dahn

"How is this possible?" the Bey said with a groan "You were in the technical development section. You wer trusted." He broke off with a sob.

They had been betrayed from the start, anticipate from the beginning, guided by the Buro to deliver th Hammer to the Imperiom!

But Jon Iehard had been watching M'Nee and nov acted with characteristic speed. The Taw Taw longbarre boomed deafeningly and the shot hurled M'Nee into th wall, but Jon wasn't quick enough to catch Gelgo Chack before he got off two cartridges from his handgun.

The first chopped down Braunt and Gesme. The sec ond sprayed Owlcurl Dahn, Jon and the Bey before th Taw Taw boomed again and the slug ruptured Chacks chest cavity, tumbling him head over heels.

Jon slumped beside the Bey, who lay ominously still

Owlcurl Dahn was crying through clenched teeth. Sh held her shoulder, blood ran down her arm. "Oh, but i hurts! I never dreamed anything could hurt so bad!"

"Let me see," Jon said, and then he grunted from th sudden pain in his own shoulder; he'd caught a pellet too

There was a movement at the edge of his vision. M'Nee still alive, eyes transfixed with hate, lifting his gun, Jo fired without thinking, the bullets demolishing M'Nee's good hand and forearm, hurling the gun against the wall The pain seared him once again.

The Bey's eyelids fluttered open.

"Where are you hit?" Jon said in a harsh whisper.

"Disaster," the Bey breathed. "We are undone at th last."

Jon shook his head. He parted the Bey's clothes. Ther was a small chest wound, low down on the right side There was also blood from the thigh and the calf of th right leg. He would have to carry the old man the last le of the journey. Officer Dahn wouldn't be much help. A quick look around showed nobody else left alive, and the he saw Angle Umpuk grinning down at him from the dark ness.

"Where did they get you from?" the guide said with a

strange smile. "They warned me about you, but I had to see it to believe it." Jon's heart sank. "You were just a piece of greased murder back there in the airlock. Really wonderful shooting. But this was amazing. Damned good thing I stepped around the corner eh?"

Umpuk brought up a small handgun. Laowon military issue, it fired small pellets that released a powerful tranquilizer. "I had a feeling you'd get M'Nee. I thought it would be best if I waited until that was over with. Now if you'll just hold still a second I'll paralyze you and you won't have to suffer another thing until they get you into hospital. I imagine your expiation will be one of the most prolonged in the history of cruelty. Of course, you won't know much about it since they're likely to wipe your brain pretty thoroughly first."

"No," Jon said, tonelessly.

"Yes," grinned Umpuk.

And Rhapsodical Stardimple swung out of the shadow and knocked the gun from Umpuk's hand. With an oath he dived for it, but the Taw Taw longbarrel beat him to it. The reverberations died away.

Owlcurl Dahn forced herself to get on her feet. There were more distant sounds from below. Jon turned to the prone figure of the Bey.

"We are finished, the cyborgs are coming," Eblis Bey said.

Jon shook his head in stubborn disagreement.

"I cannot move," the Bey said. "You will have to go on without me." He grabbed Jon's forearm and his face contorted from the effort. "When you get to the control chamber let Rhap Dimp do all the talking when the Keeper comes. I have primed the mote with the coordinates of our likely targets. Be careful not to make sudden movements when you face the Keeper." He coughed, then renewed his grip. "Now go, leave me."

Jon looked at Rhap Dimp. The glossy little optics stared back. He wondered what was going on in that bizarre little mind. An awful lot would be riding on it—the entire expedition, the fate of the human race, everything.

He turned back to the Bey. "We can't give up now, let me get you on your feet. It's not that far away." Ignoring the old man's objections, Jon braced himself, lifted the Bey, and placed him over his good shoulder.

He set off into the maze, Rhap Dimple floating just ahead. Officer Dahn, clutching her arm, leaving a trail of blood, staggering behind.

The troopers waited by the first set of risers. The officers came up behind them. They were put through directly to General Plezmarxsh.

One of them shone his handlight up at the ceiling. He observed the odd lunglike things on pink stalks, and the white cone-shaped objects that were extruding from cracks between the scales of the ceiling. Abruptly the cones exploded with puffs of dust and fired threads tipped with needles into most of the officers and troopers.

The threads thickened visibly, into wires, then to strings that inspired immediate screams of agony from the officers.

The cyborg guns came up. A staccato drumbeat of fire echoed in the narrow space. The lung-shaped things were destroyed. The threads were cut in some places. But in others they had become ropes that drew their victims into the air.

The screams were horrible, as the vang military form went into action. Once piercers had broken into the flesh of the food, a network of controlling nerves began to grow from the site of infection, working through the existing nervous system, drilling straight through it, linking with terrible rapidity the various organs that would be required for primary control.

To the victims it was as if hot needles were being passed through their flesh in many different directions at once. At the same time, they were losing control of their bodies, their own nerve tissues no longer responding to the higher centers of the brain.

Helpless, in agony, they were hoisted toward the ceiling while the vascular connections thickened into hawsers, rich, sucking, devouring pipes of fresh military-form tissue.

The cyborgs were affected too, but they could ignore the pain. Their nervous systems were a blend of organic circuits and phototronic controllers. The Vang system of nervous invasion was simpler with organic systems, but at a pinch the military form could harden a section of nervous system and switch it from weak chemical-ion transmission to more robust techniques. Piercers and controllers would have to be toughened considerably. This realization set off further explosive changes. Materials that had lain piled in drifts around a storage chamber for hundreds of millions years, looking like nothing so much as flakes of breakfast cereal, abruptly swelled, changed, began manufacturing complex chemicals. The storage chamber, which had contained much of the residues from the conversion of the original crew of the Hammer, filled with a strange stench.

In the passageway leading to the risers, the cyborgs reached up and snapped the connectors or tore them out of their flesh. Their guns continued to stutter as they received orders to destroy all laowon that had been infected.

The profusion of stalks and other organs withdrew suddenly into the ceiling. The cyborgs stood grouped beside the risers, ankle deep in fragments of their officers, and awaited new orders.

When Plezmarxsh reported to Magnawl Ahx, the latter's face paled when he heard of the alien lifeform. "Lashtri Three," he said in a hushed whisper.

Plezmarxsh's forehead furrowed. "Where have I heard that name?"

"It was the world that was burned by Red Seygfan in the interregnum."

Plezmarxsh gasped. "Of course, and this horror must be the same lifeform. But in such widely separated star systems? It doesn't seem possible."

"Baraf did not originate in this part of the galaxy. Who can say where it wandered before it joined this system."

Plezmarxsh looked up at the airlock entrance uneasily. On Lashtri Three, the thing had spread with a terrible rapidity. "What will we do?"

"I will report to the high admiral at once. Send the troopers in, try to track the fugitives, we must know where they've gone to ground."

"The humans are doomed then. They will be attacked and converted."

"They are doomed anyway. We have two spies among them. Superior Buro has followed this case from the beginning. But I still want to know where the humans are.

The machine is huge, they could hide in there for days. We may not have so much time."

Jon lurched down each passageway as the mote led him. The walls of yellow brown scales were monotonous, endless. Each time they came to a new opening, the mote considered the passageway carefully and then directed Jon forwards.

The Bey had grown very heavy. Jon's shoulders ached from carrying the old man, who had been silent for some minutes. They reached another junction of passages.

Suddenly, there was a tremendous noise down below. Distantly, they heard screams and gunfire. The eruption made Owlcurl Dahn gasp in fright. Jon stopped and turned, the effort cost him considerable pain in his wounded shoulder. The sounds of firing were clear, but still distant, far below them, somewhere in the bowels of the machine.

He paused, carefully set the Bey down, and listened intently. Eblis Bey came awake as long ripping sounds wafted up from the small arms fire of the cyborg troopers. Eblis Bey knew only too well what it was they were firing at. "The devil is awake now."

They looked around them with distinct unease.

"Which way now, Rhap Dimp?" Jon asked the mote.

"Left. Close now. Emergency, lack energy."

Jon put out a hand to keep the mote warm. It had the coordinates of their primary targets. He passed the mote to Officer Dahn, who cradled it carefully.

Then he lifted the Bey across his shoulders once again. They turned left into another passage and proceeded to its end. The maze seemed endless, as if they were just tracking back and forth in it forever, and Jon was close to despair. The cyborgs would soon climb the risers and find them, wandering about stupidly, within twenty meters of their goal.

And then the mote led them through a doorway that opened onto a large circular space. Ribs of pink eternite rose from the perimeter and curved together in a mesh to form the roof.

Immediately, the space above their heads filled with man-sized flashing holograms. Lines of some alien code, ideograms, images. Jon set the Bey on his feet and propped him up. He stared at the codes in awe.

"At last, at last!" The Bey was overcome with wild emotion.

An onion-shaped chamber was swelling out of the floor with a sound like a huge balloon inflating. A door opened in it like an enormous iris. From within came a deep orange glow. The chamber was looming over them like a giant head. The iris widened.

"Rhap Dimple, come to me. Now you must give the Keeper all the codes it will need." The Bey's voice quavered slightly.

The mote rose from Dahn's hand and floated across to the Bey, who held the mote up to the door. Rhapsodical Stardimple warbled a stream of notes.

There was silence. Then a light shone directly onto the mote. Rhap Dimple uttered another stream of tones.

The iris glowed a fiery pink and slowly opened. In it stood a batrachianoid robot, three meters high, like a surreal mechanical toad. It glowed where its eternite segments met. In what looked like a huge toad's head, enormous eyes suddenly lit up. It extended a vast palm, into which the mote delivered itself. Blue and green sparks flew between them. The globular optics turned and focused on Eblis Bey, Jon, and Owlcurl Dahn.

■ CHAPTER TWENTY-NINE

AT THE ENTRANCE TO THE MAZE, ANGLE UMPUK LAY dying. To move was to expose himself to agony. He lay back against the wall and tried not to think of the blood he was shedding. He prayed the medics would get through in time to save him.

Thoughts of failure pounded gloomily through his mind. That accursed mote! He had never expected a robot to interfere like that. Even if the damned Superior Buro people reached him in time, it was unlikely he'd get paid for this job. The Buro didn't believe in rewarding failure. The whole thing was an awful mess.

He heard something, a small slithering sound. It was coming closer with great rapidity. He lifted his handlight.

Along the wall, a pink worm was approaching with uncanny speed. He watched it ripple down to the floor and zip across it with a sinuous wriggle that took it to Gelgo Chacks' body. Umpuk estimated it was about a foot long and as thick as a man's finger. With horrible vigor, it shoved under the body and disappeared.

Bizarre things began to happen to Chacks' corpse. There were sounds like the tearing of meat. With astonishing speed, humps rose up and broke through Chacks' clothing. The limbs of the corpse began to jerk in an uncanny imitation of life. The uniform broke open completely to reveal weird growths, like a clump of pink ferns, that sprouted out of the dead man's back.

Another worm was approaching, it reached Umpuk's foot, and he began to scream.

More runners arrived. Umpuk's writhing body was already jerking and twisting violently. Suddenly, it rose up, tearing an awful scream from the doomed man's throat. It stood next to that of Chacks, itself imbued with a strange, leaden vigor. M'Nee's corpse was now twitching its limbs. Coral-shaped growths were exploding between the shoulder blades. Braunt and Gesme were also jerking about on the floor, fronds pushing from their necks.

Soon, the entire group was shambling down the passageway, toward the command module, following the trail of blood left by Officer Dahn. To his horror Angle Umpuk found himself still alive, but completely helpless inside his own body. His wounds had ceased to bleed, but his tormented nervous system continued to present him with an overflowing ocean of pain. But he could no longer even scream as he lead the zombies of the former Orner crew down the passageway. The thing that now controlled them seemed to know the way perfectly.

The Keeper was puzzled. The mote claimed that there were urgent new targets. It passed a stream of coordinates.

New targets! After such an eternity of waiting, the machine was finally to be used once more. The Keeper almost succumbed to a fit of electronic excitement.

But the beings accompanying the mote were not the comrades of the battery command. They were not even of the wisdom seeker race.

There were no precedents, no commands, no programming to go to for a solution. The first code level demanded that the Keeper exterminate the beings. They might be enemy cells. The presence of the mote however produced an option. The Keeper read through the secondary code then scanned the beings as instructed, and immediately felt a prick on the scanning field.

One of them carried a Trace with Honors from a hallowed master. It indicated the being thus Traced had mental powers of the same order of magnitude as the masters themselves. Automatically, the Keeper shifted to third-level code. It consulted the Trace and read its arguments.

In Jon's pocket, the tiny silver cube he'd carried so

far grew a few degrees warmer for a moment as it surrendered a tiny amount of its mass to the Keeper. The Keeper appeared to ruminate over the new data. They waited breathlessly on its decision.

A sudden shriek turned their heads. Owlcurl Dahn was pointing to the doorway. Angle Umpuk, Gelgo Chacks, Finn M'Nee, stood there weaving slightly on their feet.

"It's impossible, they're dead!" she screamed.

Indeed, there were huge, gaping holes in M'Nee's torso that still leaked blood. But it was the other things, the odd pink growths that trailed in the air behind the men, that set Jon's trained reflexes to work. The Taw Taw came up and he fired half the clip. The bodies were chopped down, M'Nee cut almost in two, blood sprayed back onto the walls. The dead were thoroughly dead once more.

And yet, there was furious activity in that ruined flesh. They stared, horrorstruck, as Chacks' torso sat up. As ruined hands began pushing at the floor, raising the body to its dead feet.

Then the top half of Finn M'Nee, eyes vacant, rose up on the arms and began hopping toward them.

Dahn's scream was matched by the thunder of the Taw Taw.

The bodies tumbled again.

"Rhap Dimple, tell the Keeper to save us!" implored Eblis Bey.

But the Keeper had already taken note of the arrival of enemy cells.

With ponderous grace, it stepped around the humans and opened its mouth. An incinerating blue flame scorched the ruined tissues of the damned to smoke and char.

Incredibly there was still something living, struggling inside Angle Umpuk's smoking remains. It glistened, it pulled free, they glimpsed a wet, pink flash, and it was gone, escaping a final blast of the fire by a fraction of a second.

"We must get inside. It will never give up!" the Bey said in a tormented voice.

Jon watched the Keeper turn to face them, its mouth still open. They could be dead within seconds. The Taw Taw felt quite puny in his hands, he doubted he could do more than scratch the Keeper before that flame thrower crisped them.

But instead of flame, a pale orange light came on in the Keeper's eyes and the barrier faded and the iris door was open to them. They entered the command shell, the Keeper followed, and the great machine's main battery went on targeting alert.

Inside the command shell, Jon set Eblis Bey down on the closest equivalent to a couch, a mushroom-shaped structure that looked like it might be great for big toads to squat on.

Screens of hexagonal design and unusual color coding had lit up. On one was a reproduction of Baraf in black and harsh green, with a cloud of red dots in orbit above.

He tried to revive the Bey, succeeded at last. At the sight of the control panel, Eblis Bey made a great effort. With Jon's aid, he leaned over it and tried to puzzle out the six arrays of small levers. An inset panel contained a single, massive lever.

The Keeper glided into the room. Jon looked at it apprehensively, the mote floated beside it. Between them flowed more sparks.

Jon experimented, pushing a black lever. On the left hand screen the viewpoint switched to a star pattern.

"What are the coordinates for Laogolden?" He asked the Bey.

"Rhap Dimp has all that information. The Keeper has it now. It is up to the Keeper."

Eblis Bey tried other levers in that array. All the screens showed star fields. Then the final lever, and a spray of ideograms filled one screen.

Eblis Bey spoke to the mote. "Rhap Dimp. Ask the Keeper to open a radio channel, we need to talk to the laowon."

The mote flew to hover before the huge Keeper. Once more it warbled. The Keeper's eyes glowed momentarily.

Levers in the other panels moved by themselves. The view on screen narrowed to a far distant sector of the Orion galactic arm. Stars, dust, more stars, grew rapidly in size under a purple targeting overlay. One star finally lay centered in the middle of the viewscreen.

"Laogolden's primary, the Kbark itself!" whispered Eblis Bey. "Now we must try and set up a way of working directly with the machine. The mote can translate most of what we need, I think."

Somewhere above them a speaker crackled into life. Radio hiss filled the space.

"How can we tune it? We need a laowon military channel."

But the hiss was suddenly broken by harsh laowon voices. The Keeper had assumed that the ships orbiting above were a part of this new emergency and had automatically scanned for the fleet's communication channels.

Jon spoke, demanding to speak to the commanding officer of the laowon forces. There was consternation for a few moments, then Magnawl Ahx was switched through.

"By the authority invested in me by the Heir and the Imperial Command Council, I call upon you to surrender immediately." He said. "You are offered a complete pardon in return for your cooperation. Please help us to prevent any further bloodshed."

To Jon's concern, Eblis Bey had slumped back into unconsciousness. Owlcurl Dahn stared back at him helplessly. When she tried to speak, she was incoherent. Jon realized with a tremor that he had just become the Earth's chief negotiator. On his shoulders lay the responsibility for the human race in the coming confrontation with the most powerful of all laowon.

His voice quavered a little at first, but then it hardened, rather to his own surprise.

"Our surrender is out of the question. Instead, I demand that you call off your troops. We have taken command of the Starhammer. The primary target is Laogolden itself. If we have to, we will fire the Hammer and Laoprimary will become a nova. The Hammer operates by creating a gravitational disturbance. It works instantaneously across great distances. We have targeted Laoprimary and we will fire if we have to."

As he finished, he felt a burst of pride. He liked the sound of that little speech. He rubbed his brow, he was sweating heavily although it was far from warm in the control chamber.

He wondered how the cyborgs would try to get at them. Possibly they would just plant explosives inside the machine. Of course, he was sure that they would much prefer to seize control of the machine itself. But that would require a successful breakthrough into the fire-control chamber, and from what Jon had seen of the mechanism that seemed to grow it out of the floor, that would take some doing. The technology of the ancient batrachians was radically different from human and laowon norms.

And if cyborgs did get in, they would have to contend with the Keeper. Jon doubted that he had seen more than a fraction of the Keeper's combative abilities.

But in the battlepit of Plezmarxsh's lead tank, Ahx smote his forehead in consternation.

"Who am I speaking to?" the Superior Buro chief said.

"This is Jon Iehard, speaking on behalf of Eblis Bey, and for the human race."

"Where is Officer M'Nee?"

"Officer M'Nee is dead." Jon stopped himself from saying more. It would be better to keep them dangling in the dark concerning Umpuk.

Magnawl Ahx gave a great groan. It was clear that both spies had failed. They held no further leverage and the damn weapon had already been targeted on Laogolden. He looked to the others in the pit, including Melissa Baltitude. It was too late, too late even to use her. She stared back at him with wide, wild eyes. Animals, all animals, these humans, but treacherous and surprisingly tenacious. Too late!

"We have failed," he said in a voice of flinty despair, and he signaled the high admiral to begin the nuclear hailstorm that would destroy the threat to the Imperiom forever. Ahx tried to steel himself against the swift death that he knew was coming. He prayed the Heir would not demand an expiation from his family.

Jon spoke, breaking into these thoughts. "These are my demands. You will immediately open a line of communication to the High Council of the Imperiom. I will need to speak to the Heir himself. There is vital business to discuss. The ways of the worlds are to be changed from this day. No longer will the Imperiom weigh down the human race."

Jon was already feeling a little intoxicated with the negotiations.

Ahx smiled bitterly. "I'm afraid I cannot do that. There will not be time."

The battlejumpers unlimbered their missiles, swept in for the kill, unleashed a broadside toward the great machine hidden in the dust-laden atmosphere below.

Several things happened at once.

The outer screens of the defense machines detected the incoming missiles as they were launched, then shifted to full alert. The great machine's automatic defense systems came onto full power. The Keeper awoke to the call.

Enormous beams of ionizing energy flashed to the defensive machines. Their fields swelled, arched into the sky and interlocked above the primary machine.

The Keeper's eyes glowed brightly. A battle hologram appeared in the center of the control chamber.

One hundred and eighty kilometers to the north and east a cube four kilometers to a side began to vibrate insanely in its socket in the planetary crust. Then with a great flash it was gone, taking with it a small tribe of Zun People and their meat larders.

Laowon missiles struck the screen and exploded harmlessly, before the targeted nuclear detonation points. The sky high above the machine filled with the debris of smashed rocketry, which slid off the screens and tumbled toward the seabed, burning furiously as it fell.

From the great machine came a pattern of defensive fire, which created gravity voids in any nearby centers of high temperature. The fusion engines of the battlejumpers in close orbit detonated in a sparkling array of fireworks, covering the northern limb of the planet.

Ahx waited, stared dumbfounded at the screens of the battletank. No nuclear fires erupted. Instead the bulk of the battlefleet had disintegrated violently in orbit.

Magnawl Ahx turned to Plezmarxsh. He swallowed heavily.

"It appears that the security of the Imperiom itself has now fallen to us alone. You must break into the control chamber and destroy the humans."

Plezmarxsh bit his lips.

"If we fail, they say they can destroy Laogolden. Don't you think you had better open a line to the Heir? The Grand Council should be summoned. This weapon just disposed of an entire battlefleet. It appears to be immune to nuclear attack. What if their claims are correct?"

The Superior Buro would be forever shamed.

"Do you think you will survive this debacle if I do that? You will expiate, alongside myself. The Heir himself will operate the hot tongs that extract your liver, piece by piece."

Magnawl Ahx turned to the commanders of the cyborg troops. "Break into the control chamber and kill or incapacitate these humans."

They hesitated barely a second, glancing to Plezmarxsh. "Blue Seygfan flies alone," Plezmarxsh said unhappily.

"Of course not, the Buro is with you."

Plezmarxsh pursed his lips.

Inside the machine, the troopers ascended in the risers, and as they ascended, the first waves were met by freshly hatched runners that burrowed into their flesh and made directly for the brainpans inside the armored skulls. Once there, they produced a powerful acid that let them through the metal casings in seconds.

The cyborgs rose to the higher floors with dead circuits. They collapsed and their flesh was quickly absorbed by suckers that sprang from the walls. The vang military form fed with a frantic frenzy. Within minutes, all that was left were the cyborgs' metal components and bone structures.

The news of the failure of the cyborgs sent Plezmarxsh into action. He whipped out a stilleto and sank it to the hilt in Magnawl Ahx's back. The Superior Buro Chief slumped over the side of the command pit. Aides ran forward and pulled him away. Melissa Baltitude watched in stunned amazement.

Two Superior Buro spies, planted in Plezmarxsh's private guard sprang into action. A short gunfight ended with both dead, along with one of the remaining guards.

The interior of the big battletank stank of smoke and blood. Two screens had been blown out along with a big hole in one of the command chairs. Melissa's ears were ringing from the incredibly loud gunfire.

Plezmarxsh reopened the channel to Jon Iehard inside the great machine. "Jon Iehard, this is Commander Plezmarxsh of the space group shock division. The Superior Buro are no longer in command here. I am initiating contact with the Grand Council on Laogolden. The Heir himself will stand by to speak with you, please be patient."

Inside the firing chamber, Jon Iehard let out a whoop of victory that momentarily awoke Eblis Bey.

"They're putting me through to the Heir." Jon exclaimed. The Bey struggled to a half-sitting position.

"We have them worried. They know the machine's power. They've had an ample demonstration. Now they calculate and scheme and will pretend to negotiate."

"But they're trapped," Jon exclaimed, "we just destroyed half of the fleet up there!"

Inside the tank, Melissa pushed forward to the microphone.

"Jon, is that you?"

He jumped at the sound of that voice. "Melissa! Where are you? How?"

"I'm out here with the laowon, underneath this machine. They caught me, soon after I left you. But they weren't able to use me the way they wanted to. There's been quite a little gun battle in here and I can vouch for the commander. He's telling the truth. The Superior Buro Chief is dead. They're calling Laogolden now. You've won Jon, you've done it!"

General Plezmarxsh switched off her microphone.

Jon let out a whoop. "Battlegeneral, are you listening?"

Plezmarxsh grunted reluctantly.

"Put Miss Baltitude back on the line. I want her to join my negotiating group. She can monitor such things as the evacuation of the machine. I want all your troops out and I want that main airlock door closed or I will destroy Laogolden and as many other laowon homeworlds as I can target and fire at."

Plezmarxsh could find no way out of the box. He turned Melissa's microphone back on.

Inside the Hammer control chamber, Jon smiled grimly. Eblis Bey laughed lightly, despite the pain it caused him.

"Bring on the Heir," Jon shouted. "We have some proposals to make, proposals that he cannot refuse."

He reexamined the control panels.

"We need a video link."

But Jon had been anticipated by the laowon military communications people and now on one of the screens there appeared the image of the Heir Apparent, surrounded by several members of the high council of court.

Jon heard them arguing in laowon, the radio link was amazingly strong. He could even hear the rustle of their robes of seygfan.

For a moment he stared in awe at the fountainhead of authority in the known Galaxy.

The Heir hushed the council with his raised hand. Jon concentrated on him, a laowon in his middle years, firm of flesh, with fiery eyes. Reportedly a person of ferocious tastes and instincts. He had unseated his senile parent at the age of thirty and ruled alone ever since. But now fear was reflected in the Heir's eyes, a fear unlike anything Jon had ever seen in a laowon before. It brought a strange little smile to his lips, and just for a moment he recalled Hut 416 on North West Alley, far, far away.

"What do you want?" the Heir said in laowon, the inflections one used for servants.

"Many things," Jon replied quietly, "A great many things. Beginning, I think, with a general removal of laowon power from the human hegemony."

"I am not inclined to negotiate with feral bandits."

"I don't think you have much choice."

"I have ordered the High Fleet to prepare to depart to Earth. They will firebomb the planet at my command."

Earth! Jon's heart jumped at that name for some reason he could not explain.

"Then I will destroy Laogolden, and you."

The Heir stared at him flatly. Behind him, the Seygfan leaders boggled in bloodshot rage.

"You will have to prove that you can do as you say."

Jon swallowed. There was a throb in his shoulder, blood matted inside his shirt. Eblis Bey stirred slightly and groaned. Owlcurl Dahn had lost consciousness.

"You would have me send a star nova? That's what this weapon does, you know."

The proud eyes flashed back in fury. Like a wild beast caught in a trap. "Prove it! Only then will all Seygfan of the Imperiom believe."

Jon looked to Rhap Dimple.

"Rhap Dimp, I need a secondary target, one with no habitable worlds, near the primary target."

The mote exchanged flickers of light with the Keeper. On the screen the purple targeting feature around Laogolden became mobile. One of the control levers moved the target overlay.

A bare seven light-years from Laogolden blazed Mayark, a hot white star with no planets. Jon targeted the hammer on Mayark. "The white star that marks the center of your constellation 'Justice,' the balance of law over disorder?"

"Mayark!" the Heir exclaimed.

"What have you there?"

"A few robot probes, maybe some asteroid miners, the Second Orbital Fort."

"The forts are tough, aren't they? Well, this one's going to get a pretty thorough workout. As for your miners, I just hope they're working the outer parts of the system. I want you to set up a deep link with Mayark. Then I want you to watch."

A few moments later the Heir said, "It is done."

Jon ordered Rhap Dimp to activate the Hammer.

"This one's for Meg. For all the gigahabs, all the breathers," he whispered to himself.

Another cube of Baraf was consumed in a fiery flash and instantaneously a gravity void appeared in the heart of mighty Mayark. For a fraction of a second the massive star lacked gravity. An enormous puff of material rose off the surface and then as gravity returned and Mayark fell together again there came a flash, a bubbling on the star's surface, indeed seconds later there was no surface and Mayark increased in magnitude by several degrees and blew a sizable fraction of its own mass into surrounding space.

It was impossible to see anything on that screen except the blazing whiteness. It threw stark shadows, Jon, the mote, the looming mass of the Keeper, against the wall.

"Are you satisfied?" Jon said grimly.

The Heir had paled. Around him the Grand Council were bathed in the death light of the nova. All rushed to speak.

"We shall have to confer. We will reopen communications in ten minutes."

"Don't be a second late, remember I have already targeted Kbark." He switched back to Melissa for a progress report on the closing of the outer airlock hatch. The cyborg shock troops had withdrawn beyond the treads.

Jon ordered Melissa to keep a sharp eye for anything that might mark an attempted attack with an atomic weapon. Not even the great machine could be immune to a nuclear device at close quarters.

The screen blanked. Jon looked around, Eblis Bey was unconscious. Owlcurl Dahn was curled up in a fetal ball. Only Rhap Dimple remained, resting on the console beside the screen. "Just you and me now Rhap Dimp." Suddenly Jon was afraid of relaxing, terrified of falling asleep by mistake, he was aware of his acute exhaustion.

"Incorrect, we are three who are 'on.' You forget the Keeper."

And Jon looked up at the immense batrachianoid robot that squatted silently behind them.

"Yes I'd forgotten about him. Well then, there are three of us to man the Starhammer."

"Incorrect," warbled Rhap Dimp, "you are manning the Hammer. We are part of the Hammer."

And, he realized, without him they would just sit there and do nothing. They were machines, they had no self will. The mote's enthusiasm for their cause was the result of the bond between Rhap Dimp and the Bey.

Jon took a deep breath, pulled himself erect. Ignored the stab of pain in his shoulder. The ten minutes ticked by.

Precisely on time, the screen came back to life. The Heir had a weird expression on his face. His eyes seemed to waver in his head.

"Well, what is your decision?" Jon said.

"We shall have to negotiate," stammered the Heir.

"Call off the High Fleet first then."

There was a long tense moment. Finally, the Heir bowed his head with a little sob. "I will do so." He turned and issued a stream of orders to an aide.

Before he had finished there was a commotion, the sound of gunfire.

On screen, figures in the red robes of the lao cult had appeared. They shot and stabbed the Grand Council with every evidence of joy in their hearts.

"I am the new High Minker!" shrieked a voice in a heavy Laogolden accent. A narrow-faced fanatic had taken over the screen. It bayed at Jon in harsh laowon syllables, demanding surrender and blood.

Jon stared into those eyes, they lacked the slightest glimmer of reason.

The figures in red were actually garroting the Heir on

screen, a warning to all members of the Royal Family th
treachery to the racial mission of the laowon would b
punished by the cult with death.

"All of these treacherous Aristocrats will be slain fo
their appalling weakness. As High Minker I will imme
diately order the High Fleet to attack the planets of th
under-race. Not a grain of sand will be left unfused!"

Jon checked the targeting patch. "One last chance,
he said to the mad eyes in that blue face.

"Surrender!" it screamed in a rage close to insanity.

He ordered Rhap Dimple to fire.

Jon assumed Laogolden would be a few minutes fro
the primary and so it proved. The High Minker howle
and roared threats and prayers until the connectio
abruptly cut off in a blaze of furious light.

There was silence for a long minute or more. Then
bewildered-looking Battlegeneral Plezmarxsh appeared o
the screen. It had been an unexpected turn of events
"The deep link is gone. We cannot raise anyone on Lao
golden."

"I am sorry," Jon said, appalled by the enormity o
what he had just done. He had killed an entire world
indeed an entire system. Billions upon billions of peopl
were dying in the catastrophic effects of the nova flas
of the primary. Laogolden's rotation carried the remainin
population on into the incinerating fire, minute by minute
The Imperiom had been beheaded.

"What will you do?" Jon said. "Who can negotiate no
for the laowon?"

"I will have to enquire. There is considerable confu
sion."

"Better hurry it up. Also, I want a deep link opene
to Earth at once. If the High Fleet attacks Earth, I wi
continued to fire the Hammer at your homeworlds. W
now target the Feress system and planet Ratan. The pop
ulation is, I believe, three billion. In addition, I want you
troopers moved further away at once. And I'm only goin
to give you a couple of minutes. You'd better think abou
what that could mean. So, make haste; we are about t
change the ways of the galaxy."

Plezmarxsh went away. Minutes dragged by with in
finite anxiety levels until he reappeared on screen. H
looked perfectly flustered.

"There is a search now being undertaken for repre-
entatives of the Royal Family. The only agreement we
ave been able to reach is agreement to abide by the social
ontract with the Monarchy. Only the Crown can hold
ogether the Imperiom in this crisis." There was consid-
rable irritation in the Battlegeneral's voice. He had been
truggling with a chaotic situation and the ugly turmoil
hat had broken out in the remaining Seygfan.

"What about the link to Earth? Where is the High
'leet?"

"Coming, it is being made now. You forget that we
ave suffered heavy losses to the fleet here. But we are
pening a line to the assembled Diktats of Earth. The
ligh Fleet has been recalled."

"To where?"

Plezmarxsh was in agony.

"Where?" Jon repeated, "I may have to target it before
hings are done."

After a long moment the Battlegeneral broke down.
'Fatuz, the fourth orbital fort."

"The coordinates in human digital code, please. Do not
ttempt to deceive or dissemble if you value your home-
vorlds."

Tonelessly, Plezmarxsh obeyed.

"By the way, what happened to the Second Orbital
'ort?"

There was a long moment of silence.

"We are still trying to regain contact."

"Not tough enough, then. I'm sorry, Battlegeneral, be-
ieve me. But I won't hesitate now. What made them do
hat, do you think?"

Plezmarxsh looked acutely uncomfortable.

"Ah, you don't want to comment on that, eh? I suppose
'ou're afraid of them, too. I must admit they frighten me.
Now they've made me history's greatest killer."

Plezmarxsh stared into the screen for a long moment.
Then he turned away.

Minutes dragged by. Jon pondered the tactical prob-
ems surrounding him. He had no food, no medical sup-
lies, and two wounded colleagues. He could not hope
o negotiate for very long, he needed a swift set of de-
:isions. In addition, there was the problem of the vang
hat was aroused and watchful now in the machine inte-

rior. How would a rescue party get in? And how woul he and the others get out? He swallowed, his throat wa dry from thirst.

"Rhap Dimple, is there any way of getting some water?"

"You lack vital fluids? There is medical emergency!" Rhap Dimp turned to the Keeper who opened a sma cabinet set into a wall. Inside were some modular boxe and a spherical water container.

Jon held the sphere up to his face. Water spurted out straight into his face. He opened his mouth and took drink. When he lowered the sphere the flow stopped.

In turn, he held the sphere to Owlcurl Dahn and Ebli Bey and bathed their faces in a little water.

The Keeper reached the end of a long interior dialogu between levels of programming. It decided to turn ove command to the control chamber to the mote and the stil functional comrade biped. The Keeper had a naggin housekeeping problem that might at last be attended to

Light flashed from its eyes to Rhap Dimple, bathin the mote in code.

"The Keeper is turning over control of the Hammer to this unit. The Keeper is going out to deal with enem cells."

"Enemy cells?"

"The machine is infested with them."

"Like the things that were inside M'Nee and Chack and the rest?"

"Enemy cells!"

The iris door opened and the Keeper, protected in ar mor of flexible eternite, went out to end forever the energ drain in the engineering section.

Another screen brightened. A collection of wide-eye humans in the ceremonial robes of the Congress of Dik tats. At their center was a sturdy fellow with a red fac and massive jowls. "I, Borgis Belan, speak on behalf o the Diktats of Earth. Who are you and what is all thi about?"

Jon explained.

Belan's eyes grew wider still. "You have turned th Kbark nova? There is no life left on Laogolden?"

"The cult gave me no choice, they garroted the Hei to the Imperiom right in front of us."

"But, what are we to do? How will we keep order?"

Another Diktat, a slender, brownskinned man wearing narrow hat with no brim, spoke up in a sing song voice. Diktat Belan does not relish the idea of a world without e laowon to back him up, you see."

The voice caused Eblis Bey to stir uneasily, but not nough to bring him round.

"I am the Diktat of Sumatra, I believe I know one of e members of your expedition. Is the man called Eblis ey among you?"

"He is indeed, although he's resting for the moment. Ve have been traveling for many days."

"Incredible," the Sumatran Diktat said.

On another screen Battlegeneral Plezmarxsh reapeared. He announced that the new Heir to the Imperiom ad been proclaimed and that he would be in communiation in just a few seconds.

Jon waited breathlessly. Finally, the screen brightened ith Innoo of Firgize's face. He stared at Jon Iehard's eciprocal image in obvious shock. Jon guffawed.

"Lord Innoo? Can it be you? The new Heir?"

"How?" Innoo was dumbfounded. "How has this hapened? How have you perpetrated this terrible tragedy?"

"There are a number of things you will have to learn, nnoo of Firgize. Firstly, you will have to accept a radical eordering of the balance of powers between our peoles."

"They tell me you have destroyed Laogolden. That I ave no choice but to negotiate with you, a feral slave! What have you done?" Innoo was distraught. Jon thought ne young laowon lordling was doing rather well considring the circumstances.

"First Innoo, you must learn to call me Lord, I'm tired f being called a feral slave. Then you can begin with a roclamation of immediate freedom for all humans now eld in bondage in laowon systems. Do you understand ne, Innoo of Firgize? The days of laowon rule of humans re over!"

ABOUT THE AUTHOR

CHRISTOPHER ROWLEY was born in Massachusetts in 1948 to an American mother and an English father. Soon afterward he began traversing the Atlantic Ocean, a practice that has continued relentlessly ever since. Educated in the U.S., Canada, and for the most part at Brentwood School, Essex, England, he became a London-based journalist in the 1970s. In 1977 he moved to New York and began work on *The War For Eternity*, his first science-fiction novel. Published by Del Rey Books in 1983, it won him the Compton Crook/Stephen Tall Memorial Award for best first novel. A sequel, *The Black Ship*, followed. *Starhammer* is Rowley's third novel.